Pursuit into Darkness

Also by Daniel Pollock

Lair of the Fox
Duel of Assassins

Pursuit into Darkness

Daniel Pollock

POCKET BOOKS

New York   London   Toronto   Sydney   Tokyo   Singapore

This book is a work of fiction. Names, characters, places, and incidents are either products of the author's imagination or are used fictitiously. Any resemblance to actual events or locales or persons, living or dead, is entirely coincidental.

POCKET BOOKS, a division of Simon & Schuster Inc.
1230 Avenue of the Americas, New York, NY 10020

Pollock, Daniel, 1944–
   Pursuit into Darkness / Daniel Pollock.
     p. cm.
   ISBN 0-671-70575-X
   I. Title.
PS3566.0534607 1994
813'.54—dc20   93-10330
                                                           CIP

First Pocket Books hardcover printing September 1994

10 9 8 7 6 5 4 3 2 1

POCKET and colophon are registered trademarks of
Simon & Schuster Inc.

Printed in the U.S.A.

To David, my big brother,
who led the way

Acknowledgments

Many people helped me gather information for this novel: Scott Swanson of Lost World Adventures in Marietta, Georgia; in Caracas, Argimiro Araujo, Jesús Iván Blanco and Francisco Da Costa; in Ciudad Bolívar, Guillermo Rodriguez of Aereotuy Airlines. For additional assistance I wish to thank Arlene Worwa, Lee Barr, Ramira and Robert Commagere, Dudley Frasier, Dan O'Toole, Russ Parsons, and Larry Spears.

My deepest bow goes, as ever, to my wife, Connie, who shared the entire adventure, from walking through waterfalls to proofing galleys.

Cerro Bolívar, Venezuela's famed mountain of iron, is a principal landmark of the savanna south of the Orinoco River. Cerro Calvario exists only in the following pages.

Thus does the great Orinoco divide Venezuela . . .

—W. H. Hudson, *Green Mansions*

Pursuit into Darkness

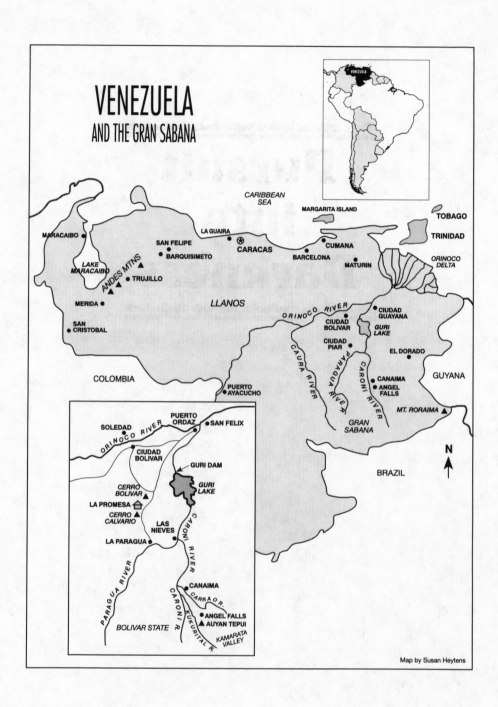

VENEZUELA
AND THE GRAN SABANA

VENEZUELA

CARIBBEAN SEA

MARGARITA ISLAND

TOBAGO

TRINIDAD

MARACAIBO

LA GUAIRA

SAN FELIPE

CARACAS

CUMANA

BARQUISIMETO

BARCELONA

ORINOCO DELTA

LAKE MARACAIBO

ANDES MTNS

TRUJILLO

MATURIN

MERIDA

LLANOS

ORINOCO RIVER

CIUDAD GUAYANA

SAN CRISTOBAL

CIUDAD BOLIVAR

GURI LAKE

CIUDAD PIAR

EL DORADO

CAURA RIVER

PARAGUA RIVER

CARONI RIVER

CANAIMA

ANGEL FALLS

COLOMBIA

GUYANA

PUERTO AYACUCHO

MT. RORAIMA

GRAN SABANA

N

BRAZIL

SOLEDAD

PUERTO ORDAZ

SAN FELIX

ORINOCO RIVER

CIUDAD BOLIVAR

GURI DAM

CERRO BOLIVAR

GURI LAKE

LA PROMESA

CERRO CALVARIO

LAS NIEVES

CARONI RIVER

LA PARAGUA

PARAGUA RIVER

CANAIMA

CARRAO R.

ANGEL FALLS

AUYAN TEPUI

CARONI R.

YUKURITAL R.

KAMARATA VALLEY

BOLIVAR STATE

Map by Susan Heytens

1

The ranch hat and hand-tooled boots were pretty much standard, but Sam Warrender didn't usually show up at corporate headquarters in faded blue jeans and a dusty chamois shirt. He had come to New Orleans on a hurry-up because of an emergency call he'd taken on horseback that morning on his Oklahoma ranch. The company had a new problem in Venezuela, a major one.

Before holstering his cellular phone, Sam had called a neighbor and canceled afternoon plans to fly over and check out some breeding stock. Then, without bothering to change clothes, he'd packed his black satchel for South America and hustled his twin-prop Cessna off the end of his ranch strip and out across the Panhandle haze toward the Crescent City. He'd parked the plane about eight hundred miles away and four hours later at the municipal airport beside Lake Ponchartrain, arranging to have oversize tail numbers affixed for Caribbean customs, a life raft and vest stowed aboard, and the long-range fuel tanks topped off. Then he grabbed a taxi for the central business district and the Proteus Industries building on Lafayette.

Inside, the security guard greeted him warmly and ushered him into the private elevator serving the skyscraper's three top floors. Sam's fifty-nine years showed far more in close-up, under the bright elevator gridlights, than they had in his ambling stride across the vaulted lobby. Considerable history was stamped in the rough-hewn features, in the hollowed, stubbled cheeks and hooded, wolf-gray eyes, and on the weathered brown hide and prominent veins of his large hands. The thinning, silvery hair, however, was deceptive. Sam's hair had actually darkened a bit over the decades from the dazzling snowcap of childhood. It had been a comfortable stretch of years, thank God, since anyone had invoked his schoolyard name of "Whitey."

A chime bonged, and the mirror-polished brass doors opened on the thirty-first floor. Evangeline Birdette, corporate receptionist, stood welcome with her benign, schoolmistress smile. Behind her, under the atrium skylight, water trickled discreetly from a welded-sculpture waterfall.

"Good afternoon, Mr. Sam. Another short retirement?"

"What the hell, Birdy. You know I hate golf."

"They're all waiting for you inside, Mr. Sam. LuEllen just sent out to Copeland's for your favorite red beans and rice." She made a grab for the ranch hat, but he whisked it behind him.

"I hope she got it to go, Birdy. I'm not staying long."

A full-fledged war council was assembled around the oval slab of black marble, a panoply of top corporate management and divisional vice presidents. Among the missing was the company's new president, D. W. Lee, who was off vacationing on his private yacht somewhere in the Caribbean. And several faces along the window wall were blotted out by the afternoon panorama of the great river basking in the Delta sun. On the wall opposite, Proteus's global operations had been rendered as chromium tentacles embracing a Mercator spread of hammered-copper continents, from Alaska to Antarctica, and from South America to Siberia.

Sam made a quick social circuit of the room—it had been several weeks since his last flying visit—then turned to Hardesty Eason, a big red-faced man with a square-cut jacket, who had just cleared his throat. As Proteus's chief financial officer and a company director, Hardesty ranked second only to Sam among those present.

"If you're ready now, Sam, we can start."

"Hold your fire, Hardy. Let's keep this real simple. Ray, why don't you just show me the situation on one of those maps you got there?"

Ray Arrillaga, head of South American mining operations, came around the table. He was a small bronze man with steel spectacles and doctorates in engineering and geology. He had been executive vice president of one of Proteus's major competitors when Sam had hired him away. Arrillaga unfolded a large geological survey map of Venezuela's Bolívar State and placed a manicured finger on the site of the company's recent iron-ore find, Cerro Calvario, a hundred miles south of the Orinoco River and Ciudad Bolívar.

Sam grimaced. "That bad, Ray? Right on top of us?"

"I'm afraid so."

"So some academics stumble on a bunch of broken pottery on *our* land, and now we got a cultural minister threatening to shut down our entire operation?"

"Not threatening, Samuel," Hardesty cut in. "We're dead in the water as of this morning."

"*Temporarily* dead," Arrillaga suggested. "Our friends at the Ministry of Energy and Mines are on the case."

"Well, shit! Did anyone think about just roping off this archaeological site and working around it?"

"Their site survey shows artifacts scattered all over the mountain, in a pattern roughly coextensive with the high-grade ore."

"Goddammit, Ray, sounds like someone's seeding the dig, just to stop us. Who are these guys, and what the hell are they doing on Cerro Calvario?"

Arrillaga hesitated.

Hardesty Eason spoke up: "*You* okayed their presence, Samuel. In fact, you arranged it."

"I don't remember doing a damn-fool thing like that!"

"It was when we were down in Caracas last spring, after we agreed to help fix up their Natural Sciences Museum in that run-down park beside the Hilton. You gave your big hemispheric speech, Sam, then threw money at a couple of scientific groups. One of them, as I've been reminded this morning, was an outfit doing archaeological research along the Orinoco. Apparently you also gave them access to our sites."

"Jesus Christ, Hardy! You mean we've been *paying* these assholes to shut us down?"

"That is exactly what we've been doing, Sam. In fact, we still are."

"Well, stop the damn checks!"

Sam glared at the assembly, as if daring anyone even to smile. When the room tension reached an uncomfortable level, he gave a low chuckle—a cue for general laughter.

"Now, Sam, nobody's blaming you. Exactly." Parry Joyce was old and harmless enough to get away with this bit of *lèse-majesté*, having recently been eased out as CEO of a Proteus subsidiary and given the meaningless post of chairman of the executive committee.

"Maybe not, Parry. But next time any of you high-paid wazirs hears me shooting off my mouth for a bunch of Third Worlders, shut me up quick, okay?"

"Want me to cut a memo on that, Sam?" deadpanned Rowland McCall, vice president of public relations.

"Good idea, Rollo. And while you're at it, put something in there on how you probably just got fired, okay?" Sam flashed a predatory grin, then nodded to Ray Arrillaga. "Ray, I'd like to take along copies of your relevant maps."

"They're in your office, packed to go."

"That's fine."

"Hold on now, Sam," Hardesty interrupted. "You don't need to go rushing off to South America like an old fire horse."

"The hell I don't. I'm sure not solving anything up here, staring out this wonderful big picture window, waiting for the sunset."

"Sam, you're forgetting about D.W."

"*You're* forgetting, Hardy. The man's on vacation."

"A working vacation."

Sam squinted across the table at the speaker, visible only as a broad-shouldered silhouette against the afternoon glare. Ex-Marine Dave Twyman was general manager of the company's South American petroleum and LNG (liquid natural gas) operations. "I was on the phone with D.W. this morning, Sam. He was a little north of Tobago, en route to Venezuelan waters to check on our LNG platforms in the Gulf of Paria. When I gave him the news, he changed course for the mouth of the Orinoco. I think he gets around fifteen, sixteen knots."

"D.W. wants to handle this mess all by himself?"

"With our help, Samuel," Hardesty said. "He *is* president, after all, and like Dave says, he's already down there. And look at the job he did for us in Indonesia."

"Hardy, I'm not saying anything against D.W. Hell, I picked him for the job. But Indonesia—that's more D.W.'s neck of the woods." A naturalized American citizen, D.W. had been born in South Korea; the initials stood for Duk-Won. "He doesn't exactly speak the lingo down south."

"He's going to need our help, Sam. That's why we're having this meeting. While you were flying down from the Lazy S, the rest of us have been drafting our strategy ideas."

"That's fine, Hardy. Let D.W. run the show, you folks back his play every way you know how, and I'll do the same. You might just tell him I'm on my way down—and bringing my old machete, just in case the red tape gets kinda thick."

"Dammit, Sam!" Hardesty exclaimed.

"Hardy, relax. Gentlemen, if you'll excuse me. I've got a plane to fly."

Sam wheeled and strode out of the conference room. After the heavy door latched behind him, the executives traded uneasy glances. All were aware that though the meeting would now continue, it had just been rendered, along with their carefully drafted memos, utterly irrelevant.

2
≋

By the time Sam had his Cessna aloft and banking sharply over Lake Ponchartrain, the Gulfstream IV that had preceded him down the runway was only a smudge of vapor and a wink of gunmetal on the eastern horizon. Sam chuckled. He'd recognized the fancy logo when the sleek bizjet had swung around on the taxiway. It belonged to an Atlanta industrial-contracting firm Proteus had almost gobbled up the year before, kind of a throw-in of a larger deal Sam had eventually walked away from. He pictured an executive team hurtling home in the G4's plush cabin, strapped into their big-butt lounge chairs, clinking highballs or fiddling with their laptops, while the hired help did the driving—just like that old Greyhound bus motto.

Sam preferred it his way, logging his solitary stick time. He seemed to think more creatively up here, whether occupied with visual or instrument navigation, or just sitting back and letting the plane fly itself while the globe unrolled below. By the time the Big Muddy fanned out into the blue Gulf, he had reached a cruising altitude of five thousand feet, leaned out his engines, and plugged in the first set of coordinates on his loran.

The afternoon ahead promised plenty of contemplative time —a thousand nautical miles over water, south by southeast through the Yucatán Channel, then a short dogleg left past Cuba to Grand Cayman Island where he'd refuel and spend the night.

Pursuit into Darkness

The late October weather was achingly clear, with a ten-knot tailwind. He figured to pick up the VOR-DME beacon at Owen Roberts Airport on Grand Cayman in about three hours and be on the ground in a little over four. Jamaica was only a short hop beyond, but some recent pilot warnings had prejudiced Sam against parking his plane overnight at either of that island's airports.

Off to his right, a few cloud shreds drifted over the sun-lacquered surface, casting paltry shadows. Sam scanned the horizon, checked the gauges, watched the loran tick off ground speed and distance remaining to the first coordinate—and thought back to his first trip to Venezuela.

It had been in 1958, the first year of his marriage and his third at the University of Oklahoma. Sam had taken a reduced load that spring in order to work for Standard Oil, replenishing his bank account at the cost of delaying his petroleum engineering degree. The company wanted to loan him south for two weeks to their Venezuelan subsidiary, Creole, as part of a team preparing bids for exploration concessions on Lake Maracaibo. Sam had talked Caroline into joining him in Caracas for the first week as a sort of delayed honeymoon.

It had been a complete disaster. Caroline had gotten airsick on the flight down from Miami and endured with mute protest the careening taxi ride from the seaside airport up the new *autopista* to the three-thousand-foot-high capital city. She had hated Caracas on sight, considering it noisy, filthy, and squalid. Sam would have understood her being appalled by the sprawling shantytowns on the encircling mountains or even the teeming streets below. But Caroline's reaction seemed to go no deeper than simple disgust. The kaleidoscopic sensory barrage, the sheer vitality of Latin culture, had no appeal for his offended bride. Sam found himself constantly apologizing for everything, and trying to cope with her increasing rigidity and brittleness, caricatures of her familiar poise and delicacy.

Once installed in the Àvila, a rambling, Spanish-style hotel with a spectacular city overlook built during World War II by Nelson Rockefeller, Caroline all but refused to venture beyond its parklike perimeter. In the event, it had taken a state occasion to pry her loose. On the third day of their trip, Vice President and Mrs. Nixon had swung into Caracas on an extensive South

American goodwill tour. Sam and Caroline had taxied down from the hotel to the nearby Panteón Nacional to watch the Nixons lay an honorary wreath on the tomb of Simón Bolívar. At least that had been the plan.

While several blocks away, their cab was caught in sudden gridlock. Over a bedlam of honking and shouting from angry motorists, they began to hear rhythmic chanting, followed by a many-voiced roar. These crowd sounds were definitely of the street, not any *plaza de toros*. And they grew swiftly louder— and thus nearer.

Sam used his crude, oil-field Spanish to quiz their driver, a villainous-looking *caraqueño* with bad teeth and a magnetized Blessed Virgin on the dashboard. The man was clearly apprehensive. There had been much anti-American talk, he said, apologizing that he was unable to turn around and drive them to safety, and that the locks on his doors did not work too well. He advised them to get out and find another cab; or better, to return on foot to their hotel—and quickly. They took his advice.

Later, at the Àvila, they learned that Nixon's motorcade had been stormed by hundreds of protesters wielding sticks and throwing stones and excrement. The mob had shattered windows in Nixon's limousine, defying Secret Service men with drawn guns, in an attempt to drag the vice president and his wife out. Fortunately the motorcade had escaped back to the U.S. embassy compound in eastern Caracas. President Eisenhower was said to be dispatching emergency airborne and Marine units to Guantánamo, ready to deploy farther south if needed. The next morning, considerably ahead of schedule, the vice presidential party slipped out of Caracas on streets closed to traffic.

Sam had put Caroline on a plane home two days later, also ahead of schedule. She had spent most of the intervening time in their room, alternately sulking or blaming him for—well, for everything. She certainly could not understand why he insisted on staying another week in the godforsaken country. Sam could only argue that there was still a job to be done and that he had given his word to do it. But even while apologizing and sympathizing, Sam could not quite conceal from Caroline the fact that he was fascinated by Venezuela, that he had found the whole experience exciting, even their pell-mell flight through the streets. He had said his airport farewells with a mingling of

8

despair and relief—and a dreadful sense that their young marriage was doomed.

In fact, it had lasted five more years and produced a son, before Caroline had demanded and gotten her divorce. And yet, thinking back, Sam had been right. The breach that had opened between them in Venezuela had never really been bridged. His son, Tony, had grown up on the other side of that gulf and, even now, in his midthirties, remained a remote and critical figure.

And here Sam was heading back to Venezuela again, as eager as ever. The latest operational crisis supplied the obvious rationale for his energizing; but frankly, the unexpected shutdown of Cerro Calvario was only a handy excuse to saddle up and ride south. He felt the familiar pull of the land itself, of the frontier, something Venezuela embodied for him more than anywhere else on earth. Its cities were jumping-off places for outrigger islands and Andean peaks, rain forests and rolling grasslands, jungle rivers and breathtaking waterfalls, and a vast highlands studded with giant sandstone mesas. Its cornucopia of resources included one of the world's largest deposits of oil, plus diamonds, gold, silver, iron, bauxite, manganese, coal, and hydroelectric power—the modern fulfillment of the El Dorado dream that had once lured Sir Walter Raleigh to the region. And now, thanks to Proteus's geologists, there had been another big iron-ore strike in the Orinoco Valley, the third in the last fifty years.

Sam had been too long away, both from Venezuela and hands-on company operations. In his concern not to cramp D.W.'s managerial style, he had been spending most of his time lately up at the Lazy S, either getting in the way of his ranch foreman, Chick Hooper, or trying and abandoning one damned-fool hobby after another. No wonder, as Hardy Eason had put it, he was ready to charge off like an old fire horse hearing an alarm bell. His greatest fear was not the crisis itself, but that D.W. might contrive to solve it before Sam could hit the ground running.

The second leg of the flight the following day, twelve hundred miles from Grand Cayman to Caracas, was almost a repeat of the first. Again the route forecast was ideal, and Sam lifted off shortly after dawn from George Town's Owen Roberts Airport. His flight path took him over Jamaica, then six hundred blue-water miles past Aruba and Curaçao. Except for a few white puffs hovering over those idyllic islands, the oceanic mirror reflected hour after hour of cloudless skies.

By ten-thirty Sam caught his first glimpse of the Venezuelan *cordillera* on the southern horizon—a steep wall of mountains along the South American littoral. Fifteen minutes later he made out the creaming shoreline at the base of those mountains, then watched it resolve into a scalloped line of breakwater-enclosed beaches. He remembered the resort names—Macuto, the favorite beach of *caraqueños*; then La Guaira, which served as the port of Caracas; finally Maiquetía, whose sands bordered the east-west runways of Simón Bolívar International Airport. Getting his final clearance from the tower, Sam came in from the west behind an Aeropostal DC-9, got the Cessna's wheels down without major point deductions, and taxied to the general aviation area at the airport's east end.

As he climbed out into the tropical heat, a delegation of local Proteans scurried forward to escort him through customs and immigration. As per Sam's radioed instructions, they had booked his favorite suite at the Àvila, arranged for refueling and a guard to watch his plane—and to mark access panels, doors, and fuel tanks with security tape. Within minutes Sam was in the back of a stretch Mercedes on the twisting four-lane highway up to Caracas—and afternoon meetings with the top bananas of the Ministerio de Energía y Minas, Ferrominera Orinoco, and the Corporación Venezolano de Guayana.

Sam fully expected those meetings to be successful; but whatever their result, he intended to take off again in the morning —three hundred fifty miles southeast to Ciudad Bolívar on the Río Orinoco.

3

Dr. Arquimedeo Laya López stood on the summit of Cerro Calvario in Venezuela's Bolívar State, looking out across the savanna. Along the northern horizon, an afternoon parade of brassy thunderheads marked the unseen Orinoco River. Nearer, a dozen miles to the northeast, the flatland scrub was interrupted by the red-rock bulges of the San Isidro Group. Preeminent among these was Cerro Bolívar, Venezuela's most famous iron mountain.

Or what had once been a mountain.

Since the discovery—by U.S. Steel geologists in 1947—that the 1,800-foot-high outcrop contained high-grade iron ore, hundreds of millions of tons of it, Cerro Bolívar's ridges and flanks had been drilled and dynamited and devoured until only a well-carved carcass remained. If he possessed sufficiently powerful optics, Arquimedeo knew, he could witness the relentless process from here. Even now, dinosaur-sized shovels would be scooping newly blasted ferruginous rock into hundred-ton trucks, which trundled along wide-terraced roads toward an endless line of empty rail cars. Once filled, these would wind down seven miles of track to the plains, be assembled into hundred-car trains, and be hauled ninety miles north to Puerto Ordaz, the industrial district of Ciudad Guayana on the Orinoco. Some of the rail cars, each with a capacity of ninety metric tons, would

11

off-load at Fior, Venezuela's iron-ore reduction plant, others at steel-making Sidor, to feed its electric-arc furnaces. The rest would be destined for giant ore ships waiting dockside to make the downriver journey to the Atlantic and steel plants around the world.

Arquimedeo dropped his gaze to the red rock under his feet. A similar dismantling had seemed certain for this smaller peak, Cerro Calvario. Several weeks earlier geologists from Proteus Industries had discovered extensive iron deposits here. This in itself was hardly surprising. Two hundred fifty years ago Capuchin monks had set up forges beside iron deposits south of the Orinoco; the bricklike soil of the entire region was known to be ferrous. But no one had expected the element in such concentration—nearly 60 percent, richer even than Cerro Bolívar. Previous surveys had obviously failed to probe deeply enough below Calvario's upper slopes to reach the main ore body. Increasing the value of the strike was its proximity to the existing rail terminus—only twelve miles away across the savanna.

After the mineral analysis was confirmed by the government mining company, Ferrominera Orinoco, events had moved with an administrative swiftness Arquimedeo had rarely witnessed in his native land. A joint mining venture between Proteus and Ferrominera was drawn up and signed in Caracas. The right-of-way for a connecting rail link had been cleared, legally and physically, of all encumbrances, and grading had begun. Ballast for the rail bed was on order, along with ties, track, rolling stock, and several two-thousand-horsepower diesel engines. A mile to the east, surveyors had started laying out a workers' camp on the model of Ciudad Piar, the huge mining company town of Cerro Bolívar, and construction firms were already advertising for skilled laborers.

But Arquimedeo and his assistant, Félix Rosales, had managed to bring this entire juggernaut to a screeching halt. Incredibly, for the moment, *he* was the king of this mountain, a slight, bespectacled figure who resembled a bank clerk—or would, if one disregarded his khaki shorts, hiking boots, baseball cap, and José Canseco T-shirt. Arquimedeo and his younger colleague had accomplished this unlikely miracle by virtue of their own recent discoveries on Cerro Calvario—a scattering of potsherds, some quartz flake-scrapers, bone fragments, and only that morning, a splendid fossil fragment of an ancient bone flute. The earlier finds were bagged and tagged and en route to Caracas.

To be sure, it had also taken some strategic telephoning to stop the mighty engines of industry. Arquimedeo had made a dozen radiotelephone calls to the capital—to colleagues at Simón Bolívar University and the Natural Sciences Museum, allies at Bioma, Venezuela's largest conservation organization, and at the Foundation for Anthropological Research. They, in turn, had taken the battle to the relevant ministries—of Environment, Culture, Natural Resources, and Energy and Mines.

The governmental turf war was still raging, Arquimedeo knew, its ultimate outcome still in doubt. But for the moment he had prevailed. Farther down the mountain, the geologists' core-sampling equipment stood idle, as did the bulldozers and earth-movers on the nearby railroad grading project. The only crew currently active on the mountain had arrived in a cloud of dust just twenty minutes before, in a Jeep Wrangler with the logo of Noticolor, Ciudad Bolívar TV news. They were now downslope, interviewing Félix. A Venevisión crew from Ciudad Guayana was due the following day. Arquimedeo had been advised to move swiftly on the PR front. The faster and farther he could disseminate news of his archaeological finds, he had been told, the harder it would be for anyone to sweep them aside.

"Arqui!"

The hail was from Félix Rosales, striding up the ridge ahead of a blond newswoman and a stringy-haired cameraman. As they had watched the woman dismount the Jeep in skintight safari suit and Aussie bush hat, Félix had begged Arquimedeo for the privilege of escorting her around and fielding her on-camera questions, at least the noncontroversial ones. Reluctantly, Arquimedeo had deferred to his younger, overly muscled colleague. What else could he do? Félix was almost salivating, and Arquimedeo had been cursed from childhood with an obliging nature. He strolled down to meet them now.

Félix flashed his muscular smile. "Arqui, Señorita Estévez keeps asking me about politics. I told her you were the man to talk to."

"Oh, did you?" Arquimedeo showed mock disapproval. He noticed again that, close up, the blonde aged at least ten years, with a tight mouth and turquoise eyeliner that gave her a hard,

Egyptaic look. "Félix and I are merely scientists, *señorita*. Just because we like to dig in the dirt doesn't make us politicians."

"Very amusing, Dr. Laya," Señorita Estévez said with no trace of smile. "But we both know this story is about politics. You've got to give me something I can use."

Arquimedeo pursed his lips. There was no reason he couldn't score a few political points while sticking to his archaeological catechism. "Very well, *señorita*, since you insist. But I'm afraid I'm not very presentable."

"You're perfect, Doctor. Exactly the way most people would picture an archaeologist. It's Indiana Jones here"—she tipped her bush hat toward Félix—"who looks phony. Of course, with all those muscles, I'm sure he can dig."

"Please, *señorita*," Félix protested.

"I'm sorry, Félix," Arquimedeo said dryly, "but apparently it's me she wishes to photograph." He quickly tucked in his Canseco T-shirt and gave a hitch to his tool belt.

Señorita Estévez's preparations were more extensive. She pivoted, putting the afternoon sun over her shoulder, while her cameraman positioned a tripod reflector to fill in shadows. Then she checked a compact mirror, poking stray golden tendrils back under her bush hat. Finally she snatched a microphone, pulled Arquimedeo close beside her, licked her lips—and nodded to the cameraman.

"Dr. Laya," she began, "according to your colleague, Félix Rosales, you have uncovered only a few small artifacts here on Cerro Calvario. It isn't like you've stumbled on a buried city. Why, then, in a time of acute national need, do you feel justified in halting a major industrial project that could pump billions of *bolívars* into our economy?"

Arquimedeo hesitated. Judging by her lead-off question, he was in for a thorough grilling. The best tactic, then, would seem to be to keep his responses as long-winded as possible. He commenced in this vein:

"*Señorita*, I assure you neither I nor my colleague opposes development. And we are certainly aware of the need for economic expansion. Ecologists may debate to what extent another vast industrial project here in Bolívar State will deplete unrenewable resources or damage the ecosystems of the Orinoco and

14

the Gran Sabana. That is their concern. As archaeologists, our interest is simply to uncover and preserve sites of earlier societies—both prehistoric and historic—and advance our knowledge of how our distant ancestors lived their daily lives. We are, in this sense, guardians of Venezuela's history—"

"Doctor, how much history can there be in a few stones and broken pots?"

"What we have found on Cerro Calvario—thanks to the co-operation, by the way, of the mining engineers—is evidence of several layers of ancient habitation. The pottery shards are undoubtedly pre-Columbian, fashioned by Arawak Indians—the original Venezuelans. And the preceramic artifacts—the lithics and bone fragments—were found at a much deeper stratum and might easily date back eight or nine thousand years before the present, indicating an early Holocene adaptation to a savanna environment—"

Dr. Laya broke off, noticing that Señorita Estévez's eyes had glazed over.

"I apologize, *señorita*, for being obscure. What I mean to say is, agreed, we didn't find a buried city, but even that is still possible. We've only made a preliminary physical survey, and yet already we've found some wonderful things—enough to tell us that a great deal more awaits us. We must now begin some real excavations at several promising sites. All we are asking, *señorita*, is that mining operations be suspended until we have completed those investigations. The iron has been here for many millennia. It won't go away. But once this site has been destroyed and its historical treasure lost, it can never be recovered."

Félix signaled a thumbs-up, but Señorita Estévez motioned her cameraman to switch off, then shook her head pityingly. "Doctor, this isn't a classroom full of captive students. If viewers can't understand what the hell you're saying, they just change channels."

"I'm sorry. I only—"

"Forget it. We'll edit it down to a sentence or two. Okay, I've got one more question here. Think you can keep it simple?"

"Certainly, if—" He broke off; the camera's red eye had winked on.

"Dr. Laya," Señorita Estévez began again, "do you have any

comment on the visit to Caracas of the chairman of Proteus Industries, Señor Warrender? Is it true he is here to persuade government officials to resume full-scale mining here?"

"I'm not aware of such things. Politics and international business are both outside my area of expertise—and interest. I can only repeat that the Proteus engineers and mineralogists we've dealt with have been extremely cooperative, and I gather this has been at the company's directive. And I'm sure that once Proteus executives are made aware of the situation here on Cerro Calvario, they will endorse our government's enlightened decision to suspend all mining operations."

Despite this strong statement, Arquimedeo found himself very much troubled by Señorita Estévez's final question. Later, accompanying the TV people down to their vehicle, he asked if she knew any more about Warrender and his visit. As it happened, thanks to a zealous researcher at the station, she had a clipping file on the executive in her Jeep. She let Arquimedeo glance through it. What he gleaned only added to his misgivings.

It seemed Samuel Warrender had been friends with several presidents of Venezuela, including the current one. His links to the country dated back to the late fifties, when, as a young Standard Oil employee, he had negotiated favorable oil concessions on Lake Maracaibo. And in the mid-seventies, when the petroleum and mining industries were being taken over by the Venezuelan government, Warrender had come south on behalf of Proteus and obtained extremely generous compensation for its nationalized assets. He was considered a very tough customer.

The blonde bid him "Ciao!"—Venezuelans had long adopted the Italian expression—and waved airily as the Jeep drove away. Arquimedeo remained in its dusty wake with a sinking feeling. The implications were clear. This Señor Warrender was coming down to change Venezuelan policy with a satchel of corporate cash and would have little trouble finding palms to grease. *La mordida*—the bite, the bribe—was a time-honored institution in Venezuela, as in many other countries. High-level corruption scandals were commonplace. According to some cynics, half of all funds moving through government channels vanished into someone's pocket. Arquimedeo could not help visualizing a balance scale, with a stack of gold bars on one side and his pitiful artifacts on the other. It was awfully hard to see the outcome tilting in favor of science and truth.

And, of course, as Arquimedeo well knew, Samuel Warrender was not only Proteus's chairman, but a principal benefactor of the Natural Sciences Museum in Caracas—the place where Arquimedeo's artifacts would ultimately be displayed. And not only had Warrender cooperated with Arquimedeo's archaeological survey, his company had actually helped underwrite it. Should such a distinguished patron of progress now wish to halt that survey in its tracks . . . well, it was difficult to imagine him failing.

As he contemplated these matters, Arquimedeo felt the long shadow of the multinational Goliath stealing forth across the plains to engulf him and render him, in his own estimation, a most insignificant and impotent David.

But Arquimedeo knew something else. Like David, he would not give up without a battle. For Cerro Calvario was certainly the archaeological opportunity of a lifetime—*his* lifetime. There would never come another, any more than Schliemann had found another Troy, Carter another tomb of Tutankhamen, Arthur Evans another Knossos.

The slight man squared his narrow shoulders, turned from watching the Jeep's dust trail, and began to climb back up his iron mountain, prepared, if need be, to defend it against the world.

4

It so happened that Venezuela's president and foreign and finance ministers were all off in Jakarta attending a three-day conference of something called the Group of Fifteen—but referred to by one commentator as little more than a Third World pep rally. The resulting power vacuum in Caracas had played perfectly into the hands of the environmental and cultural ministers, as well as those opposed to what they saw as a flood tide of foreign-controlled industrial schemes. It was a hasty alliance of these several factions that had shut down the Cerro Calvario mining operation.

Sam learned this vital information from Proteus staffers while en route to his afternoon meetings and realized at once that those meetings would be pointless.

"Screw the schedule," he told the keen young man crouched in the facing jumpseat. "Let's cut through the bullshit, Eric." He gestured at the car phone. "Call Jakarta and get me *el jefe*. I don't care what time it is."

There was a slight problem with that idea, Sam was told. It seemed D.W. had already tried it—had in fact been patched through from his yacht now on the Orinoco. The Venezuelan president had informed D.W. that he was keeping abreast of all developments regarding Cerro Calvario, but categorically refused to make any decision or even offer a comment until his return.

"You mean we're supposed to wait three days?"

"No, Sam, at least a week." On the way back from Indonesia, he was told, the Venezuelan delegation was stopping off first in Egypt, then in Senegal.

"What the hell for?"

"Reciprocal photo ops. They're all members of the Group of Fifteen."

His staffers pleaded with Sam to keep his afternoon appointments. Canceling at the last minute, they said, would be taken as a major insult. Besides, they said, he might learn something.

So Sam went along, shook hands, slapped shoulders, dusted off his Spanish—and learned little he didn't already know. Over the years he had attended many such meetings with Venezuelan officialdom, under the obligatory Napoleonic portrait of El Libertador, Simón Bolívar. In the course of the long afternoon he found himself frequently gazing out the nearest window, for the view from Caracas high rises, while familiar, was invariably spectacular.

Ever-present clouds wreathed the surrounding peaks, trailing purple shadows over green-clad slopes. Lower down, but inching higher and higher every year, were the mountain-clinging *ranchitos*, the shantytowns of adobe brick in the *cinturón de miseria*, the misery belt. And finally, winding through the long, narrow cityscape of concrete and steel, was *el pulpo*, "the octopus," the network of arterial expressways, clogged at all hours with traffic, much of it composed of low-end muscle cars from Detroit's past, all enjoying flatulent Latin American afterlives. Whatever else was endemically wrong with the Venezuelan economy, gas was still cheaper here than anywhere else on the planet.

Sam exited his last meeting at five-thirty, after pumping hands and declining dinner invitations. A government car took him back through a steeply twisting maze of streets and crumbling neighborhoods to the Ávila, where he did thirty laps in the pool beside a cocktail crowd of twittering academics. He dined on room service, watched CNN, read a chapter of Xenophon's *Anabasis*, and nodded off around eight.

An hour before dawn he was back in a Proteus Mercedes, heading down the *autopista*, past hillsides spiderwebbed with flickering *ranchito* lights, to Maiquetía and the airport. His

19

Cessna was refueled and ready, its security tape undisturbed (it would have changed color had it been tampered with). The world was still gray when Sam completed his checklist, got his final clearance, and hurtled down the runway. Then, as he climbed into the eastern sky, the sun flared over a ridge dead ahead, showering him with light. Sam pulled on Serengeti sunglasses and plowed into the fireball, following the shoreline and gaining height on the wall of mountains to his right.

His flight plan took him eastward beside the mountains another half hour to Puerto Píritu, where the coast range dropped away. Then he turned right, south by southeast, along a corridor served with radio direction aids, two hundred miles down to Ciudad Bolívar. In the pastel early light Sam found himself flying over blue jungle toward a pink-streaked horizon. But as the sun lifted and the cockpit warmed, variegated greens and earth tones began to show below.

Sitting back and letting the avionics do their intricate work, Sam found himself for some reason replaying his son's twelfth birthday party—more than twenty years before. Sam had arranged to fly Tony and his entire Little League team up to the Lazy S from Dallas, where the boy was living with his mother. Caroline and her new husband, thank God, had declined to come along. There was swimming, horseback riding, a barbecue—and a couple innings played against a local Little League squad on a regulation diamond Sam had laid out.

Standing behind the backstop, Sam had watched his son play a scrappy second base, but fail to connect in his only time at bat. After the last out, Sam turned and noticed his Mexican housekeeper, María Elisa, watching from the pool terrace with her two-year-old daughter, Teresa. Sam felt an odd twinge—both pride and queasiness—suddenly seeing his two children in such proximity. For the Indian-dark toddler was also Sam's, a fact at that point confided only to his lawyers, and Chick Hooper, the Lazy S's foreman. María Elisa had sworn to tell no one—until she and Sam decided Teresa was old enough to know the truth.

But the incident stirring in memory all these years later didn't concern the children. It was what Sam himself had done that day. After the game, a skinny redhead kid from Dallas had taken the mound and challenged the Oklahomans. He threw impressive heat for a twelve-year-old and struck out several boys in a row. Then Sam had grabbed the biggest bat he could find and come around the backstop, asking if he could take a cut. His son, Tony, had shouted a protest from second base, but the redhead kid on the mound only grinned and waved Sam to the plate.

Sam had been thirty-seven then, in fair shape, though he hadn't played baseball since high school, where he'd been an all-state shortstop. And he'd never handled a bat like this tapering aluminum pipe, cold and spindly in his big hands. But as the first pitch sailed in, he realized the kid wasn't really that fast. What he ought to do, Sam told himself, was swing wild at the next one and walk away, making a joke about a bad back. Instead, old instincts keyed in. Thigh and arm muscles bunched, wrists cocked, the chin nestled atop the left shoulder. As the ball spun toward him, Sam waited confidently, then shifted his hips as he whipped the bat-head around. The ball rocketed off the metal bat, still climbing as it passed over the motionless left fielder to land far out in the pastureland. Sam remembered the stunned look on the redhead's young face.

Sam yelled out an apology: "Honest, I just shut my eyes and swung. I never figured on hitting the dang thing." He made another apologetic gesture to the boys still waiting to take their cuts, then made a hasty escape. But up on the terrace, he walked into one of María Elisa's hard glares.

"Now come on, Ellie, it wasn't that bad," he said. "I was just fooling around with the kids."

"*Qué vergüenza, Samuel!*"—Shame on you!

Her use of his given name instead of her pet name for him, Blanco, underlined her seriousness. And, of course, she was right. He'd made a competitive fool out of himself. Like an old zoo ape he'd once seen pushing the females and younguns out of his way to get first grab at some tossed peanuts. Sam had not only shown off, but stolen the game from the kids. And if María Elisa had seen it so clearly and was disgusted by it, what must Tony and his friends be thinking?

Okay, so he was ashamed.

Should he apologize to Tony and all the rest of the boys or just pretend the damn thing never happened? Sam had opted for the latter—and the rest of the party went off fine. Except here the incident was again, surfacing all these years later, an insoluble turd in the punch bowl of memory.

Why now?

Well, Sam knew the answer to that. It was pretty obvious that he was doing the same thing again—flying down here, in defiance of Hardy Eason and the whole Proteus team, to take the play away from D.W. It had been no sweat to let his president run the show in Indonesia, Alaska, off the Siberian coast, a lot of other places. None of those projects had posed a territorial threat. But Sam regarded Venezuela as his backyard, his personal fiefdom.

And what was so wrong about that?

Sooner or later, of course, it would drive D.W. away, just as it had the last two handpicked successors. But no matter what he said for corporate consumption, Sam didn't want a successor, never had. He liked scaling back, and he was willing to delegate as it pleased him. But he still reserved the right to play head ape, ready at the drop of a peanut to abandon his comfy, swinging tire and run the cage.

Okay, maybe he was ashamed—a little. And maybe he was even a little afraid D.W. could handle things down here without him. Whatever it was, from that first phone call he'd gotten at the ranch, Sam had been unable to rein himself in. Whether he should or shouldn't stay out of it was for sure debatable, but dammit, he just couldn't. Here he was, for better or worse, strapped in and speeding over jungle greenery at nearly two hundred knots per hour toward the Orinoco. There was just no way in the world he could think of to stop himself. Once the bat was in his hands, Sam was by God going to get his swings.

On approach to Ciudad Bolívar he passed over the red-orange gas flare of an Anaco oil field. Moments later, under a low cloud fleet ahead, he sighted the long silver sweep of the Orinoco. Here, two hundred seventy miles from the Atlantic, the river was only two-thirds of a mile wide, tending to its business calmly and quietly. But its sinuous, sixteen hundred-mile journey to the interior and its vast tributary system made it second on the continent only to the Amazon.

Still north of the Orinoco, as the tin roofs of Soledad flashed sunlight beneath him, Sam got his landing clearance and lowered his airspeed to a hundred knots, dropping flaps and gear. Then he was banking sharply left over the river and the twin white towers of the Angostura Bridge and, as the city wheeled below, lining up for a straight-in approach at ninety knots to Aeropuerto Ciudad Bolívar. Once down on the concrete, he taxied over to the beige-block terminal and was guided to a parking spot near an Aereotuy De Havilland Twin Otter revving its turboprops.

As Sam climbed down the Cessna's retractable steps, a stocky man in slacks and sport shirt hurried out of the terminal, shielding his ears from the Twin Otter's engine shriek. Sam recognized Owen Meade, the bright young man in charge of local mining operations. A half dozen strides off, Owen extended his hand and came on with a big smile creasing his soft, heavily freckled face.

"*Bienvenido*, Sam. A real pleasure."

"*Bienvenido*, Owen. Ray's always telling me good stuff about you." Owen Meade reported directly to Ray Arrillaga in New Orleans.

"Not lately, I bet."

"Hey, none of this crap is your fault, Owen. Just standard South American politics. Anyway, we're gonna fix it."

"I sure hope so, Sam. Hell, with you and D.W. both on the scene, how can we lose?"

Sam halted in midstride. "D.W.'s already here?"

"Last I heard he was still on the river, around Ciudad Guayana. Nice flight, Sam?"

"No complaints."

"I took care of your landing fee and arranged for tie-down. Here, let me throw your stuff in the Land Cruiser, then we'll grab a bite at the hotel across the street and head south."

Owen reached for the black satchel, but Sam pulled it away, preceding the younger man inside the terminal. "Thanks, I'll keep it with me. And no need for a tie-down, Owen, just a quick refuel. I'll be taking off again right after lunch."

Owen frowned. "I thought you came down to see Cerro Calvario."

"That's where I'm going."

"Sam, there's no landing strip down there—unless you're thinking of the one in the artist's rendering of our future workers' city." Owen allowed himself a little chuckle at the boss's mistake. "I guess you'll have to settle for a bumpy ride with me."

23

"Actually, Owen, there's a twenty-five-hundred-foot dirt strip down there, maybe ten, twelve miles southwest of Cerro Calvario."

"You must mean that cattle ranch—Hato la Promesa? I know it, sure. But no one told me Proteus was connected with it."

"It isn't, but *I* own a little chunk of it. We're going to be selling a lot of beef to the mine workers once we get this show on the road. I'd invite you along, Owen, but I'd rather you go separate. I want to show up at the mountain and poke around some without calling attention to myself."

The two men had come to a halt amid the airport's drab, bus-station-like waiting room. "How you going to do that, Sam? You can fly down to your ranch, but you're still going to have to drive in from the main road."

Under his tilted ranch hat, Sam grinned his widest. "You want to make a small wager on that?"

5

Arquimedeo Laya López found himself not only at the center of political controversy, but suddenly in command of a large-scale logistical operation. Over his portable transceiver from the slopes of Cerro Calvario, he was now routinely being patched through to top-level bureaucrats in Caracas, as well as to leaders of several scientific and cultural organizations. In the course of these conversations he found himself making decisions so rapidly he had trouble recording them all in his field notebook.

In one early aftershock of the mining shutdown, Arquimedeo learned he had lost his funding from Proteus Industries. This was a blow, if hardly a surprise. What Arquimedeo had not expected was the swiftness with which others rallied to his defense. Universities and scientific foundations came forward with pledges of support, financial and otherwise. Within twenty-four hours he was accepting offers of camp trailers, tents, generators, refrigerators, freeze-dried food, computers, microscopes, plus much-needed electronic surveying equipment—metal detectors, soil-resistivity meters, and photon magnetometers.

As far as staffing, Arquimedeo's office fax machine at Simón Bolívar University had turned overnight into a full-time résumé printer. In fact, job requests were coming in from all over the globe as a result of CNN's rebroadcasting a Venevisión interview from Cerro Calvario. Many applicants were trained field archaeologists, but most were amateur enthusiasts, students or volunteers from archaeological societies. Arquimedeo arranged for a departmental colleague to screen candidates, then began drawing up an organization chart for his excavation team. He put himself as director, Félix Rosales as field supervisor, then drew little tributary boxes labeled diggers, assistant diggers, recorder, photographer-artist, and volunteer labor. He stopped at fifteen boxes. As results justified it, he could easily expand.

He also decided to lower his media profile—as rapidly as possible. The initial dose of publicity had obviously been a benefit; beyond that, he felt, it would quickly become counterproductive. What they needed to be doing here was archaeology, an arduous and exacting process, not wasting time handling drop-ins from reporters or tourists.

In fact, Arquimedeo was already paying a nuisance price for his unaccustomed visibility. His mother in Caracas had been contacted by a half dozen relatives asking to be hired on the project as unskilled laborers. Arquimedeo would have liked to oblige, especially in light of the country's horrendous unemployment—as high as 40 percent in some estimates—but he simply could not. That level of funding was definitely not available. Of course, archaeological excavations involved large amounts of backbreaking manual work, but that was what volunteers were for.

In one case, however, Arquimedeo had yielded to family pressure. It had happened just that afternoon, while the two archaeologists were laying out a grid for more trial trenches. Félix, holding the surveyor's rod, had suddenly pointed downslope. "Arqui, better check this guy out. Tell me if I should get my shotgun."

Arquimedeo glanced up from his transit and squinted down into glaring sunlight. There was a shadow-black figure on the dusty access road. Arquimedeo swiveled the twenty-five-power surveyor's scope on the visitor. The first focus was on the elaborately soiled crotch of once-gray work pants. Next he tracked over a venerable polo shirt, sun-bleached pink with crimson sweat stains. Finally he arrived at a long, hangdog face behind a grizzled beard and mustache, surmounted by a red headband. The general effect was of an old pirate down to his last doubloon.

"*Mierda!*" Arqui exhaled.

"What's he look like?"

"Like my Uncle Oscar."

Félix nudged him aside, sliding behind the eyepiece. "That old bandit's your uncle?"

"It's not my fault. My mother's sister is the one who married him. Don't worry, Félix. He may look villainous, but he hasn't killed anybody in years."

"That's a joke, right?"

"Of course it's a joke. Uncle Oscar *was* a revolutionary, though. Back in the early seventies. My mother told me he knew Carlos."

"Carlos who?"

"Carlos the Jackal. The famous Venezuelan terrorist."

"You forget, Arqui, if it happened much after the Bronze Age, I probably don't know about it. So what's he want, your uncle?"

"Have a beer, Félix, while I go down and find out."

Despite his disreputable appearance, Oscar Azarias Rivilla carried himself with great dignity, befitting one who had lived many hard years in many hard places and had come through them all, where many others had not. This dignity was very much on display as he sat on a camp stool in the bluish shade of Arquimedeo's tent fly, a leathery hand wrapped around a cold can of Cerveza Polar. The angular old man was plainly waiting for his nephew to begin the conversation.

"Tell me, Uncle Oscar, how did you get in? Wasn't there a guard at the gate?"

"I told him I was your uncle, and they waved me through. You are a famous man now, Arqui. I saw you on television in a tavern in Maturín."

"It won't last, believe me, Uncle. I'll be obscure again any day now. So, why didn't I hear your truck?"

"I left it on the road about a kilometer from here."

"Out of gas?"

"No, water. The radiator needed a drink, just like me. But I prefer Polar." Oscar took a swig of the Venezuelan beer, working his lips in a simian way that occasionally exposed his teeth and gums. The old man needed major dental work.

"No problem. We've got plenty of both here. You can take a case of Polar with you, if you like."

At this point Arquimedeo hesitated, sensing delicate ground ahead. The reason for Oscar's visit was obvious. Just as obviously, the proud old man expected his nephew to broach the matter. Having made a clumsy start at this, Arquimedeo proceeded delicately: "But, Uncle, I'm afraid that's really all I have to offer you. I mean, if you're looking for a job—"

"A job?" The forehead furrowed down over tufted brows, but the gray eyes harbored slyness. "That is what you think, Arqui, that I came here to ask you for a job?"

Arquimedeo could only shrug.

Oscar regarded the dust, then glanced up, shaking his head sadly. "Arqui, I am thinking that you have heard too many stories about me—from your mother, eh?"

"I'm sorry, Uncle. I didn't mean to—"

"Arqui, don't apologize. I don't blame you. In fact, now that the matter has been raised between us, it is true I could do many things here. If you need a cook, or a mechanic, I can do both. I can haul rock in my truck. I can dig. In the Caribbean I operated bulldozers, you know, also skip-loaders and backhoes." He cocked his head thoughtfully. "Of course, digging with shovels is a different matter at my age. I am nearly fifty, Arqui, did you know that?"

Arquimedeo shook his head. In fact, he knew his uncle to be at least five years beyond fifty.

"Mind you, Arqui, I wouldn't make an issue of salary. I leave it to you to be fair. To put all blood ties aside." His palms spread, conveying his total trust in his nephew's sense of justice. "Of course, it is true I have no degree from the university. The opportunity was never there for me. From the earliest age, I was forced to work in the streets, to help my family. But experience—as is well known, Arqui—experience is the greatest teacher of all. How can you put a price on this?"

"Uncle Oscar—"

"Yes?"

Instead of voicing his exasperation, Arquimedeo stood up and fetched two more beers from the cooler. He needed a moment to collect his thoughts. No matter how unassailable his arguments, as long as he continued in a diplomatic fashion, he was positive the old man would just keep advancing his request. Eventually, Arquimedeo must either give in or abandon politeness and flatly reject his uncle. Oscar, naturally, would be betting on the former outcome, convinced Arquimedeo would not risk insulting the husband of his mother's only sister. And, of course, if this was his strategy, it was diabolically good. To counter it, Arquimedeo would have to strike a tone respectful but very firm. He sat down again, sipped his beer, finally resumed:

"Uncle, I'd love to have you here. It would make me very proud. Wait, wait, please let me finish. The problem is that I cannot hire you. And not because of your lack of a university degree, believe me. We simply have no budget here. All the workers here, except for myself and my colleague Félix and a few other poorly paid archaeologists, will be volunteers. We've already had many applicants. They'll work all day in the trenches for a little bit of food and enough tent space to roll out their sleeping bags. And believe me, Uncle, this is not the kind of labor you would wish to do, nor I to ask you."

The old man absorbed this, then nodded slowly. "I understand, Arqui."

"You do?"

"Certainly. Let us forget the digging. I have a better idea. You have enemies, Arqui. Yes, this was mentioned on the television. Big and powerful capitalist enemies. Proteus and their paid lackeys in our government. These people would like to crush you." As if to demonstrate, Oscar crumpled the empty blue-and-white beer can in his horny fist.

"And *you* can protect me from such enemies, Uncle Oscar?"

"I could help, Arqui. I could be your bodyguard. I could also be a night watchman and protect your excavations from sabotage and looting. I also would require very little beyond food and a tent. Perhaps only a few thousand *bolívars* a week."

Arquimedeo hesitated—far too long to say no. He was thinking—as the old man obviously intended him to—that for little more than the national minimum wage, he could purchase family tranquillity and, perhaps, once Proteus withdrew its perimeter security, actually protect the premises. It was still extortion, of course, but the price was surprisingly reasonable.

"Oscar, I really don't think we're in that kind of danger here. Proteus Industries is certainly trying to stop us, but they're doing their dirty work in Caracas, not here. And I doubt if we will be digging up gold or anything else looters would want. Wait, I'm not finished. I'm not saying no. Perhaps we could use a night watchman. Some of the university volunteers might sleep better knowing you were guarding our perimeter." The old man was smiling now. "But, Oscar, I can pay no more than eight thousand *bolívars* a month."

It was apparently enough. Oscar arose from the camp stool to bestow the traditional Venezuelan *abrazo*, throwing both arms around his nephew and thumping him on the back. Sweat-soaked and malodorous as he himself was, Arquimedeo was still not prepared for his uncle's rank embrace. The old man would need to be quartered as far as possible from the digging crew, he decided, perhaps in one of Proteus's engineering shacks.

Over a final round of beers they settled a few details. Oscar would begin in two days, but would require a week's wages in the interim to procure a few supplies. Arquimedeo, anxious to have done with the interview and get back to work, agreed to everything.

And it was with considerable relief that he watched his uncle's scrapyard pickup, with its radiator refilled, shudder and bounce down the dusty road. If the old man drank up the advance wages and was never heard from again, fine. If, on the other hand, he appeared as pledged, he could indeed go to work as night watchman. After all, what mischief could Oscar make that would equal the wrath of Arquimedeo's mother, had the old man been turned away?

When the truck was lost to sight, Arquimedeo scrambled back into his own GMC pickup and fired it up. As he nosed it around toward camp, he was astonished to see two men on horseback emerge from the brush up the road and start walking their mounts directly toward him. Both faces were deeply shaded by broad straw brims. Then the man on the right lifted his hat in greeting, revealing a shock of white hair.

6

The riders had to be from La Promesa cattle ranch, which, Arquimedeo knew from the survey maps, bordered two sides of the Cerro Calvario federal property. The obvious deduction was borne out by their outfits—boots, chaps, and rolled-straw ranch hats—typical of *llaneros*, the cowboys of the *llanos*, the Venezuelan plains.

Arquimedeo idled the truck as the horsemen drew abreast, then poked his head out. *"Buenas tardes, caballeros*. Looking for strays?"

"Buenas tardes, amigo," the white-haired rider replied, replacing his straw hat and resting both hands on the saddle horn. Astride a big chestnut horse, with his rugged features and cowboy trappings, the rider reminded Arquimedeo of the Marlboro Man. The man's Spanish greeting, too, while delivered rapidly with the *r* rolled, had sounded foreign accented. The horseman tilted his head toward his wiry, leathery-skinned colleague. "Since we seem to be neighbors, Enrico and I just wandered by to say hello. I hope we're not trespassing."

"You must ask the owners, Ferrominera Orinoco, to determine this, or perhaps their partners, the engineers from Proteus Industries. As it happens, I am only—"

"Professor Laya López, I know. I saw you on the news last night, Professor."

"Indeed?"

Both men, Arquimedeo noted, looked to be in their fifties, roughly his uncle's vintage, though in far better shape.

"*Caballeros*, you must please excuse me. I don't mean to be rude, but I must get back to work."

The white-haired rider spread his palms. "I'm sorry, Professor, I certainly didn't mean to offend you."

"You saw me on the television, so you are aware of the controversy. We both know that my scientific activities here will prevent your ranch from selling beef to nonexistent mine workers in a nonexistent mining camp over there. All this is obvious. But none of it is my concern. I am here, and intend to remain, so long as the government supports me."

"Hold on there, my friend," Enrico said. "You assume many things. For me, more beef on the hoof means a lot more *llaneros* and much more work."

"And also more money," Arquimedeo replied, "unless you're just hired *llaneros* yourselves, which I somehow doubt."

"Yes, a little more money, perhaps," Enrico admitted.

"Enrico's the foreman of La Promesa," the white-haired man volunteered. "He was actually born in Brescia. That's in Italy—"

"I know where it is. I did graduate work in the Dolomites. And you, where are you from? Texas?"

"Good guess. Very close. Folks mostly call me Blanco, by the way. I'm down here studying local methods of range management. But I've always been curious about relics and fossils and such." The man glanced up at the red-rock shoulder of Cerro Calvario. "Would it be all right for us to see what you're doing up there?"

"No, I regret that is not possible. Another day, perhaps . . . Señor Texas."

The white-haired man nodded. "Well, Enrico, we better let our neighbor go back to his business, and do likewise. Until then, Doctor."

The two riders waved and swung their mounts. Arquimedeo sat watching as the horsetails swished and the hindquarters sashayed massively down the dirt road, then cursed himself—not for what he'd just done, but for what he was about to do. It was his mother's fault, this irrational fear of offending others. She must have stamped it into his infant psyche, saddling him with a lifelong curse while imagining she was inculcating a virtue. He slid the pickup into first gear and moved slowly ahead. The horsemen glanced around as Arquimedeo eased alongside. He couched his concession in brusque terms:

"Please, *caballeros*, you must understand. Suppose you were branding calves. Would you want me, a total stranger, riding along and asking questions? Wouldn't this interfere in your business?"

"You make your point well, Professor." The man sidestepped his horse, leaning down. "We don't want to bother you further."

Arquimedeo rolled past, then stopped, waiting for them to catch up. "If you can leave your horses here, I'll take you up for a quick look around. But I won't have time to answer questions, and you'll have to hike back down."

There, he'd done it, retreated once more from a prior resolve. Wasn't that exactly what he'd done in hiring Uncle Oscar? The maternal curse was again fulfilled.

"Very obliging of you," the white-haired man observed—quite unnecessarily, from Arquimedeo's point of view.

"You go, Blanco," Enrico offered. "I'll watch the horses."

"Thanks, *compadre*. I'll make it quick." Señor Blanco handed his reins to his companion and dismounted.

"Mount Calvary?" the white-haired American said as they jounced up the spiral track in Cerro Calvario's steep sides.

"The summit is vaguely cruciform," Arquimedeo explained —then added, "shaped like a cross."

"Got you."

"You can see it better from the air."

They left the pickup at the end of the road and hiked up to the rocky shoulder where Félix Rosales, shirtless, with sweat and dust caking his muscled torso, was laying out a baseline for the excavation grid. He looked up, smiling under his sun-squint.

"Arqui, where are you finding all these folks?"

"Señor Blanco is a visitor from Hato la Promesa."

"Glad to meet you, *señor*. Know anything about surveying?"

"A little. And I've dug a few ditches in my time."

Arquimedeo, meanwhile, took the tape Félix handed him and stretched it out from the steel-pipe corner marker along a north-south compass marking. Señor Blanco watched a moment, then pitched in. As Arquimedeo measured off two-meter intervals along the baseline, the American handed him wooden stakes, then, as they were positioned, drove them into the ground with the blunt side of a hand ax.

In a relatively short time the three men had laid out a grid of stakes and string lines. They called a brief halt while Félix went to fetch beer. Only then did the American ask his first question:

"Tell me, Professor. How do things get buried?"

"This is no mystery. Time buries everything."

"I realize that. But how, specifically? The soil here looks the same as La Promesa's." He clawed up a handful of brick-colored sand, letting it crumble through his fingers. "It's no damn good for agriculture, only for grazing—and mining. Full of iron."

"Correct. That's because heavy rainfall has washed out most of the minerals, except certain silicas and iron and bauxite. And high heat has baked these compacted mineral particles into what is called laterite—a bricklike clay of extremely low fertility."

Señor Blanco nodded. "That's what I thought. It's basically the same stuff then, up here and down there? Only this is considerably harder?"

"Something like that. Cerro Calvario is composed of ancient ferruginous sandstone, like the great table mountains of the Guayana Shield. The iron-oxide deposits are extensive, but the richest ore concentrations here are buried under what the mining geologists refer to as *canga*, a conglomerate of other silicas—quartz, manganese, and other minerals. This is why this ore wasn't discovered decades ago, when U.S. Steel found Cerro Bolívar."

Señor Blanco scuffed the rocky surface. "Canga, sandstone, whatever you call it, it's still pretty tough stuff, right? So wouldn't artifacts, even thousands of years old, be pretty close to the surface, or maybe washed down gulleys to the plains? I still don't see how they get themselves buried."

Arquimedeo examined the white-haired *norteamericano*. "What are you suggesting? That we are lying about our discoveries, or where they were made?"

"No, I didn't mean anything like that. Like I said, I'm just curious."

"Then I will tell you we *do* expect to find objects washed

34

down the talus slopes. And we *have* found artifacts near the surface. But the most promising finds thus far have been at a depth of several meters, in areas initially exposed by the mining engineers' core drilling." Arquimedeo paused. "Would you care to see an example? Something we discovered, in fact, only this morning?"

"I'd love to."

"It's in my tent—this way." Arquimedeo led off on a winding track around a knob of eroded red rock, which artfully resembled the crumbling ruin of a castle turret. Once beyond this they encountered Félix coming back, swinging a plastic bucket loaded with cans of cold beer.

"Going to show him our latest treasure, Arqui?"

"Yes. Do you think Señor Blanco will be more impressed than the skeptical Señorita Estévez?"

"Good question. Have a Polar first, *caballero*." Félix handed out the chilled cans. "And what about your friend?"

"Enrico will survive a while longer. He's got water."

Farther on, the path slalomed through a rockfall, then ended at two patched and faded work tents in the shadow of monumental boulders. Beside some fifty-gallon gasoline drums, a portable generator hammered away, with power cords snaking into the nearest tent. Outside the tent fly was a plastic garbage pail covered with a round screen, which was threaded by a plastic hose. Arquimedeo slapped it as they passed. "That's for wet-sieving our soil samples. It helps us recover small particles of organic matter."

Arquimedeo walked upright into the tent, while the other two had to stoop. Most of the interior was taken up by a long plywood table. Arquimedeo fumbled with a clamp-on lamp, illuminating the surface clutter: an unfolded survey map scribbled on in colored inks; a Toshiba laptop; plastic trays full of potsherds, mineral fragments, and organic remains; an *El Nacional* sports page, presumably of recent vintage; mapping pens and bottles of waterproof ink; a sidelighted microscope and micrometer calipers. One tent wall was lined with plastic storage crates and rock-filled buckets, while plank shelves opposite sagged under a burden of books, magazines, ring-binders, and yellowing newspapers. In a far corner a small refrigerator hummed, fed by the generator; in the other, behind a tripod-mounted Polaroid camera, two wood-and-canvas folding chairs faced a TV and VCR.

Arquimedeo ducked below the worktable, rolled aside a canister vacuum, dragged out a rusty, padlocked ammunition case. He opened this and took out a sealed plastic bag, then stood and held it to the light.

Inside the clear pouch, embedded in rock, was a bone fragment shaped like a human finger and only slightly longer. One end was jaggedly broken off. But the other had been carved into the unmistakable semblance of a mouthpiece—something to blow into—while the tubular shaft had four evenly spaced, neatly drilled holes.

It was a tiny flute.

7

Sam Warrender, alias Blanco, moved closer to study the ancient artifact. Here before him was history, or prehistory, not in the form of a droning lecture or a textbook time line, or even an illustrator's fanciful rendering, but in the handiwork of some early artisan. Someone had played this ingenious instrument, perhaps generations of musicians had done so, before it had been consigned to its millennia of silence. What would it have sounded like? But why theorize? Why couldn't it be freed from its fossilized prison, repaired, and actually played again? Sam turned to Arquimedeo. The archaeologist met his glance with undisguised pride.

"Dr. Laya, could it be played somehow?"

Arquimedeo shook his head. "We will of course attempt to dissolve away the limestone around the artifact, but we must be extremely careful, or the acid will damage the bone itself. Félix and I think it is probably made from the femur or tibia of a large bird. We will also attempt to reconstruct the missing fragment, but not to regraft it.

"But you must not think us without imagination. Here is what we shall do, Señor Blanco. I have already discussed this idea with a university colleague, in the department of ethnomusicology, and he is most enthusiastic. With his help, Félix and I will attempt to carve an exact reproduction of this flute, including the missing fragment. And then, perhaps, we shall have our prehistoric recital. Would you like to attend?"

"Absolutely, if I'm still around. How old do you think it is?"

"There's no need to speculate. Since this is the remains of a once-living organism, it can be carbon-dated. We will send it to Caracas for testing as soon as possible."

Arquimedeo turned the plastic bag slowly in the light, much as a wine connoisseur revolves his glass. In the process, an affixed label eclipsed Sam's view of the relic inside.

"What's all that writing?"

"Each artifact is assigned a number. We also record a brief description, along with the grid coordinates and information about the stratigraphy where it was located. Here, you see, this is from a site very near the summit of Cerro Calvario, at a depth of nearly four meters."

Arquimedeo bent and locked the artifact lovingly away.

Outside, the three cooled off in the narrow shade of a rocky overhang, and Arquimedeo returned to Sam's earlier question—on how things could have gotten buried. He explained that the mountain might have been used extensively for burials, in which case they might be tapping into ancient pits. Artifacts—such as the flute—might also have been deeply deposited by natural disturbances, such as cave-ins, flooding, or landslides, all possible despite the rocky surface. The geologists' core samples showed considerable interruption in strata.

He spoke matter-of-factly, but Sam remained under the spell of the primitive woodwind he had been shown. Indeed, he seemed to hear its faint and far-off note. And now, as the archaeologist went on to discuss methods of excavation, Sam was able to envision the electric instant of discovery—Dr. Laya's first tantalizing glimpse of the flute, for instance—something buried for centuries, emerging suddenly, or painstakingly, millimeter by millimeter, into the light of another era.

He interrupted the scientist: "It's a pretty immense job you guys have ahead of you, isn't it? A hell of a lot harder than just getting iron out of the ground."

Félix laughed. "I guess so! The mining company uses dynamite and hydraulic shovels. Arqui and I do it with trowels and paintbrushes, and sometimes dental picks."

"How long will the job take, do you think?"

Arquimedeo shook his head. "The Minister of Mines has asked the same question. But how can we answer? Everything depends on what we find here. There's a Japanese man, Señor Blanco, who has spent the past fifteen years exploring and documenting just one pre-Incan site in Peru. On the other hand, there's what we call salvage archaeology—digging in panic before the road graders arrive or concrete is poured or floodwaters back up from some new hydroelectric dam. Take, for instance, our wonderful and colossal Guri Dam. How big is that lake, Félix?"

"Guri Lake? I'd say around five thousand square kilometers."

"Now how many archaeological treasures do you think were lost beneath all that water, Señor Blanco?"

"Impossible to know, right?"

"Exactly. And such things are typical."

"But a huge project like Guri Dam? That's awfully rare."

"My friend, there is always something. That is why we are here on Cerro Calvario at this moment, attempting to stop the world. Most archaeological excavations these days are on sites exactly like this—under threat of imminent destruction, with no time for proper procedures or systematic documentation. If you are lucky, you may have a month. But maybe only a week —or a few days! How much time will we have here? What do you think, Félix?"

Félix shrugged eloquently.

"You see," Arquimedeo went on, "again we have absolutely no idea. All we know is that our ministers are fighting each other over this, and so far we are barely winning. But now we hear the chairman of Proteus Industries has arrived in Caracas with a big briefcase of money. It is absolutely true! Believe me, this man is no fool. He knows Venezuela very well, and how decisions are made. I am extremely pessimistic."

As they finished their beers, the afternoon clouds had thickened and darkened over the savanna, and the clammy heat grew steadily more oppressive. The rain was coming, Arquimedeo knew, and would bring cooling relief, but only for an hour or so, while he and Félix huddled in their tents, catching up with paperwork.

Arquimedeo shook his head. "You know, Félix, I was thinking,

perhaps this foreign devil will offer us some of his dollars—
enough to leave this godforsaken rock. Enough, perhaps, for us
to retire to a walled estate in the Country Club district."

"Without a doubt," Félix said.

"If he did," Sam asked, "what would you tell him?"

"To go fuck himself," said Félix.

Sam laughed. "You're men of courage, then—and high principle."

"Also of stupidity and stubbornness," Arquimedeo suggested,
"the virtues for which mules are justly famous. Why else would
Félix and I dig ditches in the hot sun with tiny tools, sifting
every spoonful for ancient debris? Yet that is what we will do,
we and our crew of equally foolish people, most of whom are
coming down here to work for nothing. And while we do our
drudgery, we will say our prayers that the bastards in Caracas
don't sell us out."

"*Bravo*, Arqui!" Félix applauded, then upended his beer can
and gulped it dry.

"And *buena suerte*," Sam added—good luck.

"Now, Félix, perhaps we should put the tarp back over the
control pit on the East Hill," Arquimedeo said, "before the rains.
And you, Señor Blanco, must return to your friend. And I insist
you take him a can of Polar."

The *norteamericano* shook their hands and thanked them
again for their time and hospitality.

"And you also, for your assistance," Arquimedeo said. "If you
will continue to work for nothing, perhaps we would hire you."

As the trio drifted out of the shade, they heard an approaching
drone on the access road. The note sustained, intensified, then
shifted into a full-throated growl. A vehicle was laboring up the
grade. They went to the nearest overlook.

The sound echoed now off the rock walls, but there was still
nothing to see. Then a Toyota Land Cruiser hove into view, its
cherry-red coat powdered with dust. A rear door panel was em-
blazoned with the Mercator-global logo of Proteus Industries.

Arquimedeo spoke first: "Félix, you know who I think this
is?"

"The devil himself?"

"Exactly. We know he was in Caracas yesterday." Arquimedeo
turned to Sam. "You know, the man I spoke about?"

40

"The foreign devil with the briefcase full of money?"

"Yes."

"Maybe he's not such a devil," Sam said. "Maybe if he could come up here and actually see what you're doing—see the flute, for instance—he might change his mind. Hell, he might even support you."

"And maybe the industrialists and oil barons will wake up tomorrow and give all their profits to the poor," Arquimedeo added blandly. "Yes, I think these things are very possible."

The Toyota had stopped in the turnaround. As they looked down, three doors swung open. The driver was first out, a stocky young man in sport shirt and slacks, wearing a Proteus golf cap.

"Señor Owen Meade," Arquimedeo explained. "He's their chief engineer down here."

From the rear door stepped a compact, dark-haired man in a stylish khaki bush outfit reminiscent of the one worn by the newswoman from Ciudad Bolívar. This man assumed a wide stance, surveying the scene all around, before spotting the trio on the ledge above. Arquimedeo detected what looked like Asian features behind mirrored sunglasses, but the face was unknown to him. From the other side, meanwhile, a long-limbed girl in a yellow jersey and baggy denim shorts had emerged. As she hurried around the Land Cruiser's hood, her dark hair swung and flashed in the light—a spectacular, sun-burnished cascade down to her waist.

"Félix," Arquimedeo said, "this seems to be our day for visitors. Shall we go down and meet them?"

"Especially her."

"Behave yourself, Félix. Señor Blanco, you see what can happen when a young man is too many days in the field?"

Arquimedeo started toward the downward path, chuckling at his own witticism.

Below, the archaeologist was met by Owen Meade, who began introductions in English:

"I'd like you to meet Señor Duk-Won Lee, president of Proteus Industries. Mr. Lee, this is Dr. Arquimedeo Laya López, professor of archaeology at Simón Bolívar University."

Arquimedeo found himself staring at double reflections of himself in the executive's mirrored lenses. Lee's handshake was

41

firm, his smile crooked and oddly pleasing. Arquimedeo returned the smile, and Lee's grin widened, exposing the gleam of a gold tooth. The features were blunt, the jaw squared off, the black hair cropped close on the sides, thinning above.

"I am very pleased to meet you, Doctor. Very pleased. *Mucho gusto*, huh?" He spoke with guttural force, yet managed to convey congeniality along with toughness. In spite of himself, Arquimedeo found himself susceptible.

"*Mucho gusto*, Mr. Lee. Welcome to Cerro Calvario."

"And this is my daughter, Jacqueline."

The girl stepped forward. She was taller than her father and, like him, wore sunglasses—hers had Day-Glo orange frames—and her smile was even more infectious. Her features, while exotic, did not seem clearly Asian.

"Dr. Laya." Jacqueline Lee stuck out her hand and widened her smile a notch, dimpling one cheek. Arquimedeo detected dark brows arching above the lurid sunglasses. "And who is your friend, Doctor?"

Arquimedeo turned. Only Félix was in evidence, shaking hands with Lee while surveying the daughter. At least, thank God, Félix had his shirt on.

"That is my colleague, Félix Rosales—" But the girl had already moved past him toward Félix.

Arquimedeo returned to her father. "Excuse me, Mr. Lee, but I was told that your chairman, Mr. Samuel Warrender, might be arriving here as well."

The mirrored lenses stared back, the crooked smile tightened. "But, Dr. Laya, you've already met Sam."

"I have?"

"Yes." The executive pointed a stubby finger over Arquimedeo's shoulder.

Thoroughly confused, Arquimedeo swiveled. Lee was pointing directly at Señor Blanco, who was slowly descending the path and planting his boots carefully. Lazily the *norteamericano* lifted his ranch hat and waved to the newcomers.

"Afternoon, D.W.," he called out. "Looks like I barely beat you here."

8

As he strolled by, the *norteamericano* gave Arquimedeo a rueful glance. But the archaeologist, uncertain what sort of game was being played on him, did not react. He simply watched the tall man approach the smaller Duk-Won Lee.

"I'd offer you a beer, D.W.," the white-haired man said to his apparent corporate colleague, "but it's promised to my foreman." The can of Polar was lobbed over all their heads—and grabbed out of the air by Enrico, who had just ridden into view, trailing his companion's chestnut horse. The *llanero* saluted and popped the can, which promptly geysered in his grinning face.

Arquimedeo finally spoke up: "*You* are Samuel Warrender?"

"Yes, Professor, I am. Some folks do call me Blanco, though. I apologize for the, uh, little subterfuge."

Still puzzled, Arquimedeo accepted Warrender's handshake, but retracted quickly. Little by little, anger was percolating within as he recalled all that had transpired between himself and "Señor Blanco"—including the American's remark that, if only Proteus's chairman could see the dig for himself, he might be willing to support Arquimedeo's work. The arrogant Northerner had clearly played him and Félix for a pair of fools and was offering now only the most insolent apology. Or had that disingenuous promise of support been intended as an enticement?

Was Arquimedeo supposed to grovel in the dust now and beg financial favors of these corporate conquerors?

Mierda!

The scientist surveyed his adversaries, all etched starkly against the ever-darkening sky: the lanky, insouciant Warrender; the sturdy, mirror-eyed Mr. Lee; the *llanero* Enrico standing beside Meade, the henchmen; and the young lady so thoroughly distracting Félix from the urgent business at hand. Twice already this day Arquimedeo had gone out of his way to accommodate others. Let others now reckon with him. He drew himself to his full height—perhaps a centimeter above Mr. Lee—and assumed his most ironical lecture-hall manner:

"Mr. Warrender, I suppose you found it amusing—"

"Call me Sam, please, Dr. Laya."

"—spying on Félix and me? Pretending to be a Texas cowboy, asking your innocent little questions while secretly planning to throw us off Cerro Calvario?"

D.W. interrupted, "Sam, what is this? You did not tell Dr. Laya who you were?"

"You know me, D.W. I've been known to indulge in a little tomfoolery now and then, and I guess that about describes my visit here this morning." He turned back to the archaeologist. "I'm sorry, Dr. Laya. But I was afraid you wouldn't give me the same tour if you knew who I was. And I admit I was frankly suspicious."

"And what exactly did you discover through your spying?"

"I was impressed. Hell, you saw that. Obviously I discovered you're both dedicated scientists—"

"How flattering to have one's integrity validated by such an exemplar, such an arbiter as yourself, Mr. Warrender."

"I didn't intend it as an insult, Doctor, I really didn't."

D.W. inserted himself between them, breaking into his most cordial growl. "Perhaps you will let me add my apology to Samuel's, Doctor. We are not here to spy on your work, believe me, or to influence you in any way."

"What about intimidation? Do you consider that exerting influence?"

D.W. shook his head emphatically. "Absolutely not, Doctor. You must not think this."

"I'm glad to hear that, Mr. Lee, because I, for one, am not

easily intimidated." Arquimedeo folded his small arms across his José Canseco T-shirt, just below the square-jawed cartoon. "Then why, if I may ask, *are* you here?"

"I cannot speak for Samuel," D.W. said. "Believe me, nobody can do that. My daughter and I were on holiday in the Caribbean when my company asked me to have a look down here, then return to Caracas. Once there, Doctor, I intend to make all necessary arrangements for Proteus to comply with whatever is ultimately decided by your government."

"But perhaps you and Mr. Warrender also brought your checkbooks along, to help our ministers render the correct decision?"

"Are you accusing my father of bribery?" Jacqueline Lee spoke out.

"Jacqueline, please!" D.W. motioned her to silence.

Félix Rosales was making similar gestures in Arquimedeo's direction, apparently seeking to de-escalate the conflict. But while D.W.'s daughter immediately subsided, Arquimedeo continued what, in any case, he considered a well-justified counteroffensive. He turned to answer the girl:

"Miss Lee, I know nothing about your father. But I do know that Proteus Industries lavishes money on its allies and withholds it from its enemies. You ask, how do I know this? It is simple. The instant Félix and I announced discoveries of sufficient magnitude to halt mining operations, our own Proteus funding mysteriously disappeared."

Jacqueline appealed to her father: "Daddy, is this true?"

But Sam supplied the answer: "That was my decision, Jacqueline, not D.W.'s. And it was a dumb decision, I'm willing to admit. Believe me, I've made a few of those in my time. Professor Laya, I'll get your money turned back on as soon as I can."

"Let me add a promise of my own, Doctor," Lee said. "Even if mining resumes on Cerro Calvario, provisions can still be made for you to continue working in the general vicinity—perhaps even on a section of the property here."

"Did you hear, Félix? These gentlemen may permit us to keep digging in the vicinity. Where exactly might that be, Mr. Lee? Perhaps you and Mr. Warrender and Mr. Meade could draw us a map?"

"There is no need for this sarcasm," D.W. said grimly.

"Mr. Lee," Félix spoke up, "in all due respect, you can't expect us to be digging around here while you guys are blasting the mountain with dynamite! That's loco."

"He's got a point, D.W.," Sam said.

"Perhaps I phrased my offer incorrectly."

"No, I'd say you made yourself very clear," Arquimedeo said. "Fortunately, you are *not* in control of the mountain at the moment, we are. And as I told Señor Warrender when he rode up in his clever disguise, Félix and I are extremely busy just now. We have a digging crew arriving tomorrow afternoon, along with many supplies. There is a great deal of organizing to do. If you wish to contact me again, gentlemen, please arrange an appointment through my office at Simón Bolívar University."

He about-faced toward the path, gesturing for Félix to accompany him. D.W., meanwhile, moved beside Sam, pitching his growl low. "Sam, what the hell did you do? The whole idea was to keep the situation down here as quiet as possible."

Sam whispered back, since the archaeologists were not yet out of earshot. "I maybe screwed up a little, D.W. But to tell you the truth, I've had a change of mind. I'm thinking about doing a one-eighty down here, letting the professor go ahead with his dig—in fact, sponsoring it full blast, and using it to boost our corporate image."

"Sam, don't make jokes! This is a serious matter."

"I'm dead serious. Dr. Laya's found some incredible stuff up there—"

Lightning flashed through the dark clouds, severing Sam's speech. An instant later the sky crackled with thunder and the deluge began. Owen Meade broke for the Land Cruiser, but Félix Rosales wheeled around on the path and bellowed above the sudden roar of falling water for everyone to make for the shelter of a nearby equipment tent.

No further persuasion was needed to start a small stampede in that direction. Félix, first inside, held the tent flap open as the others rushed in, soaked to the skin and gasping. The final pair, mud-spattered and streaming water, were Owen Meade, who had abandoned the Land Cruiser, and Enrico, who had rapidly tethered the horses under a rocky overhang.

As it happened, the equipment tent was already occupied—by wooden stakes, stacked lumber and rolled mesh-wire for making sieving screens, folded tarps, garbage bags, nested buckets and trays, picks and shovels, trowels and dustpans. With seven people now crowded into the narrow center aisle, there was scant space left. Félix Rosales, who began shifting cartons of plaster of paris to make more room, was reminded of the Caracas metro at rush hour and in the rainy season—bodies sardined together in a collective pungency of perspiration and wet clothing. To Sam Warrender, surveying faces faintly jaundiced under the yellow tent-skin, which was being furiously hammered and lashed by the rainstorm, it was like standing inside a giant kettledrum. His neighbors in the Panhandle, he figured, would more colorfully liken the sound to a giant cow pissing on a flat rock.

"How long?" Lee shouted, pointing skyward.

Arquimedeo, who had set about boiling water on a propane stove, called back, "One hour, maybe less!"

Lee felt a pluck at his shoulder. He turned to see Enrico tapping his watch. "Rain maybe twenty, thirty minutes," the *llanero* suggested. "All finish by three!"

Félix, meanwhile, had cleared enough space to break out some camp stools. With a flourish he offered the first to Miss Lee, then gestured expansively. D.W. and Owen Meade took seats, but Sam and Enrico remained standing, looking out through the tent flap at the silver barrage. There was an ozone freshness in the air as the rain sounds crescendoed—drumming the Gore-Tex fabric overhead and pummeling the hard clay all around, sluicing and gurgling in the drainage ditches, banging away at the basin of a nearby wheelbarrow.

Funny, Sam thought, how quickly nature—announced by one offstage thunderclap—had swept aside their quarrel. Here they were, moments after preparing to go their separate, indignant ways, huddling together for shelter—exactly like those primitives whose artifacts Dr. Laya was unearthing. They, too, would have fled to caves or crevices on this ancient mountain while the sky gods warred. Perhaps even members of enemy tribes had on occasion sought common shelter from the elemental fury and shared a similar brief comradery.

"Sam?"

He pivoted directly into the gaze of Jacqueline Lee. She was offering him a chipped enamel cup brimming with some hot beverage.

"Coffee?" She mouthed the syllables.

"Thanks."

As she moved past to hand the next cup to Enrico, Sam inhaled the heady essence of her rain-drenched mane, along with something more subtle—some Parisian decoction, he supposed, favored by young women of cultivated tastes and unlimited allowances. Jacqueline was actually enjoying this, he thought. Was it the simple adventure of being caught in a tent in an equatorial downpour? Or perhaps the added element of finding herself confined with six men, five of whom were not her father?

If it were really primitive times, Sam wondered idly, which of them would prevail with her? The obvious front-runner would be Félix, given the brawny young archaeologist's good looks and sideswept wave of black hair, and the girl's subtle reactions thus far. As for the rest, well . . . Owen Meade was too bland and soft, Enrico too old and leathery, and Sam older yet, the obvious patriarch of the tribe. Or perhaps he and D.W. would bash it out with thighbones for that coveted title. And what about Arquimedeo, with his birdlike brightness of eye and coiled, nervous energy? What was *his* sexual orientation? A repressed sensualist, perhaps, a dedicated autoerotic of unusual persuasions?

Sam chuckled to himself, the guttural sound drowned out by the continuing onslaught. Out of the corner of his eye Sam noticed Enrico grinning over the brim of his steaming cup. The *llanero* tilted his head toward the girl and said something Sam couldn't lip-read. He bent closer to hear.

"Che bella ragazza!"

Sam nodded. Enrico enjoyed an occasional reversion to his boyhood Italian, but the observation was apt enough. If not quite a beautiful girl, Sam thought, Jacqueline Lee was a very near thing, a happy confluence of East and West. Without D.W.'s bluntness, the young woman's oval face and doll-like features seemed appealingly Korean, yet with subtle contouring likely traceable to her French and Italian maternal ancestry. Her personality, meanwhile, seemed emphatically Western.

Sam's previous glimpses of D.W.'s daughter had been most often at corporate shindigs, the last one almost a year earlier in New York City. He recalled her in an eye-stopping black dress, off-the-shoulder and above-the-knee, with some preppy fellow on her arm. She hadn't looked at all like an NYU film student, which, according to D.W., had been her latest collegiate pursuit.

Sam turned from the sheeting rain. Between the squatting figures of D.W. and Owen Meade, he glimpsed her yellow jersey, a hooded spill of black hair, a vivid gesture for the benefit of an unseen Félix Rosales. Sam checked his watch, then put his face again close to Enrico's.

"*Caballero*, what do you think? Another ten minutes?"

Enrico rocked his hand, palm down, an Italian gesture of equivocation.

As it turned out, fifteen minutes brought patches of blue through scattering nimbostratus, twenty an abrupt end to the rain. Sam yanked back the tent flap and stepped out into steaming warmth. The others followed and bid their good-byes quickly, and without noticeable rancor. Sam was even able to shake Arquimedeo's hand and thank him for his hospitality without getting a caustic reply. While Enrico picked his way through the mud to fetch the horses, Sam turned to the waiting D.W.

"Guess we ought to have a meeting," he suggested.

D.W. shot back a steely glance. "This is an excellent idea."

"The trouble is, I'm still thinking this through. How about tomorrow? Nothing cataclysmic is going to happen until the president and his top cronies get back to Caracas."

They settled on the following afternoon on D.W.'s motor yacht docked in Ciudad Guayana. With this decided, D.W. began to make his way down toward the Land Cruiser, and Sam turned to find Enrico and mount up for the ride back to La Promesa. As he caught sight of the *llanero*, Jacqueline called Sam's name and came quickly toward him through the mud, careless of her once-white Reeboks.

"Sam, can I ask you a favor?"

"Sure can."

"It's kind of, well, presumptuous."

"Jacqueline, why don't you just tell me what you want?"

"Well, Owen was telling me your plane is parked not far from here—at your cattle ranch. And I was wondering if—well, if you would possibly have any time to fly me over Angel Falls before we have to go back downriver?" She made a face of comic trepidation—as if expecting a bomb to go off the next instant. "If it isn't convenient, just say no, okay?"

How many men tell you no? was Sam's immediate thought. But he answered more judiciously, "That'll be fine. In fact, since your dad and I just arranged a shipboard powwow for tomorrow afternoon, it's perfect. I can fly you back to Ciudad Guayana. Heck, why don't you ask D.W. to go with us? It might help him get the big picture."

"Daddy *hates* small planes, Sam. He doesn't even like big ones."

Behind him, Sam heard the rhythmic slop of hoofs in the sucking clay—Enrico bringing the horses. "Ask him anyway. And while you're at it, better get his permission to fly with me."

"Sam, I'm twenty-two years old!"

"And you're D.W.'s little girl. If he says yes, you got yourself a pilot."

"Okay, thanks! Really, it's not inconvenient?"

"I said no. Now go on with you."

"Okay." She ran a few squishing steps, then whirled. "Would it be all right if Félix came along?"

Sam quickly focused past her, where young Rosales stood nicely profiled in the tent opening, staring out across the savanna. So, one of the principal attractions of the flight was to be yonder prime specimen of Latin manhood. Sam suppressed a smile, then nodded his assent.

9

Muchas gracias, Samuel, but as *el jefe* around here, I have many other things to do this beautiful morning besides look down at Salto Angel." Enrico and Sam were having an early breakfast on the tiled veranda of Hato la Promesa's main house or *casa grande*. Sam had just invited his foreman along on the flight over Angel Falls. The *llanero* added, "And what about you? Have you nothing better to do than be tour guide for Señor Lee's daughter?"

"Maybe more chaperon than tour guide. As far as I can tell, the point of today's outing is so Señorita Lee can spend time with that muscle-bound, glorified ditchdigger, Félix."

"And this is all right with you?"

Sam shrugged. "It's no hardship. Have plane, will travel."

"*Caballero*, if you're going to escort a young lady, what about Anacleta?"

"Which sister-in-law is she again? I kind of lose track."

"You danced many dances with her at my cousin Silvia's wedding two years ago. You liked her, Samuel. You spoke of her laughter, remember? And Anacleta speaks of you often."

"She's still not married, eh? How old is she now?"

"Thirty-two."

"Too young for me, *hombre*."

51

"A perfect age, I think. Exactly what you need, *caballero*, for those cold winter nights up in the Panhandle."

Sam dropped the newspaper on his empty plate. "Why don't you go geld some bulls or whatever you do around here, Rico, and leave me in peace."

"Ciao!" Enrico stood and tugged on his ranch hat, then chuckled as he turned away, fishing a cigarette pack from his shirt pocket. Sam watched his lean, slow-moving foreman exit the veranda and angle off toward the stables. Enrico Tosto had been happily hitched—forever, it seemed—to a Venezuelan woman now twice his size. Romalda also happened to be a woman with a great many younger sisters. And over the years—ever since learning that María Elisa was no longer sharing Sam's bed—Enrico had tried to match him with one or another of those girls and get him to retire down here. And who knew? One of these days before the supply of nubile sisters was exhausted, Sam just might give in. But not yet. He picked up the newspaper.

It was *El Guayanes* from Ciudad Guayana. Sam had already discarded *USA Today* and a Caracas daily, *El Diario*. All three were a day old; today's editions wouldn't arrive till afternoon, trucked down from the airport at Puerto Ordaz. Which was fine; Sam had already caught the CNN headlines on the ranch TV. Enrico subscribed to the papers mainly for baseball standings and box scores, Sam knew, along with livestock prices. The *llanero* was a certified expert on baseball, major leagues as well as Venezuela's winter season, which would get under way in a couple weeks, right after the World Series. Enrico could practically recite all the U.S. rosters, especially teams with Venezuelan players. Sam had lost track of such ephemera years before. What was the point in an age of team-switching mercenaries?

He flipped quickly through the paper, absorbing and ignoring information. Bad news, good news. Student riots in Caracas and Barquisimeto, a transport workers' strike, two Falcón State judges accused of running an auto-theft ring. On the credit side of the ledger, as far as business was concerned, another state bank had been sold to private interests, the inflation rate had eased a percent, a national coordinating council was trying to attract more foreign investment, and the World Bank was expected to approve a major agricultural loan.

The pendulum had swung violently since the midseventies,

when Venezuela kicked out foreign companies and nationalized its petroleum, mining, and other strategic industries. Now, after more than a decade of decline and crippling debt, the move was back toward privatization and industrialization—and with a vengeance. Companies once branded as imperialist exploiters were being invited back in on an unprecedented scale, through joint ventures, investments, or outright sales. Throughout Latin America, in fact, governments had been busily auctioning off everything in sight—unprofitable airlines, banks, energy resources, metals, telecommunications, even public works such as roads and docks and zoos.

In this counterrevolutionary capitalist climate, Sam doubted the government would hold off much longer on Cerro Calvario, simply to appease a few vociferous history buffs and anti-industrial activists. The Venezuelan economy needed jobs and every foreign nickel it could get. When the real showdown came over mining, Sam was willing to bet, Dr. Laya and his idealistic friends would have to fold their cards and abandon the table to the big boys.

But this left Sam with an awkward question: Which side of the table was *he* on now? He'd come charging down here to crush a rebellion. Was he now, after one day on the ground, ready to switch allegiances—over a scrap of petrified bird bone? The idea was ludicrous. And yet, wasn't that how he felt?

The damn flute aside, Sam respected the testy little scientist. He reminded Sam of an Oklahoma wildcatter, off by his lonesome on that godforsaken mountain, drilling dry hole after dry hole, then spudding a well and coming up with some promising ooze, only to be chased off before it could gusher.

It wasn't fair, and it shouldn't happen. But there were other questions to be weighed. The ultimate decision on Cerro Calvario could go either way. But what if even Samuel Warrender, exerting all his corporate leverage, was unable to save Arquimedeo's project, or even to postpone mining operations for a few precious months? That was not inconceivable. And if Sam pulled Proteus out of the deal now, the government might simply buy back its leases and sell them to another energy consortium, which would go full-speed ahead. Dare Sam risk his personal and corporate reputation in such a quixotic attempt?

Obviously he shouldn't. And yet, Sam couldn't make up his

mind. He was looking forward to the time aloft, over some of the most spectacular scenery on the planet, to help him reach his decision.

At seven forty-five, Sam was out on the strip, checking the Cessna's fuel levels as part of his preflight inspection, when he heard honking. He hustled around the two-story brick hacienda to the graveled courtyard, where another Proteus-logoed Land Cruiser—this one midnight blue—had just rolled to a stop beneath the big araguanay tree. Sam headed for the passenger side, from which Jacqueline Lee was already emerging. She'd dressed for the day in snug blue jeans and a baggy denim work shirt with rolled sleeves. She waved as she hurried to meet him, a canvas carryall slung over a shoulder and her ebony mane flailing.

"*Buenos días, señorita.* Right on time."

"Hi, big Sam!" She gave him a peck on the cheek, then took possession of his arm.

"Who's your chauffeur, Jacqueline?"

They turned as a short, brown-skinned boy climbed out from behind the wheel. He looked scarcely old enough to drive, but walked with a comical cockiness. He had a spiky black crew cut, wore a Chicago Bulls T-shirt, jeans, basketball high-tops, aviator sunglasses, and an infectious smile.

"That's Bernardo. He works for Owen. Owen didn't trust me to drive by myself in Venezuela."

"He is so right."

Jacqueline wrinkled her nose at Sam, then turned to the approaching youth. "Nardo, this is Señor Warrender."

"Please call me Sam."

They shook hands. Bernardo spoke rapid English. He wanted to know who was the biggest boss at Proteus Industries, Sam or Jacqueline's dad.

"Let's just say we have different assignments, Bernardo."

"Sam's the big boss," Jacqueline said. "He's chairman and CEO. My dad's only president."

"Yeah?" Bernardo looked impressed. "Nice ranch. Does it always smell like this?"

Sam laughed. "Only when the wind is wrong. There's a big feedlot over there in the north pasture. Put a few hundred cattle in there, standing around in their own dung, it can be pretty strong. Clears the sinuses though. Are you coming with us this morning, Nardo? There's room."

The youth shook his head. "I've seen Angel Falls. I thought maybe I could just hang out." He was eyeing the big satellite dish beside the *casa grande*. "You got ESPN?"

"ESPN, CNN, MTV, HBO—you name it, I bet we got it. Come on in and we'll get you set up."

Skirting the tiled fountain on the way to the front door, Sam turned to Jacqueline. "I didn't have a chance to call D.W. this morning. What's he up to?"

"He and Owen are touring the steel and iron-ore plants in Puerto Ordaz. Then a late-afternoon meeting with you, right?" She rolled her eyes. *"Boring!"*

"Reckon grass don't grow under your pa. Truth is, I should be up there with him this morning."

"I forbid it! You're all I've got, Sam."

"Not quite. I think I see your boyfriend coming." He halted their progress to point back at a dust plume along the dirt access road.

"Félix is not my boyfriend, Sam. *If* I had a boyfriend, it would definitely be—Nardo." She brushed her palm over his spiky hairdo.

"Yeah, cool." The boy winked at Sam.

"My mistake," Sam said.

Presently a primer-spotted Mazda pickup rolled under the crossbeam gateway and crunched to a stop on the gravel beside the Land Rover, and Félix Rosales climbed out. The young archaeologist wore khaki walking shorts and a tank top affording maximum exposure to swollen deltoids, biceps, and triceps. This was one scientist, Sam figured, who'd logged more hours in the gym than the lab.

Sam gave them a quick tour of the *casa grande*, depositing Bernardo in a leather recliner in the den. The youth quickly fathomed all the remote buttons, zapping a Venezuelan *telenovela*—undoubtedly one of the favorites of Enrico's wife and daughters and sisters-in-law—in favor of tag-team, superhero wrestling.

In the kitchen, they picked up a thermos of coffee, a cooler packed with beer, soda, and sandwiches, and headed out the back door to the airstrip where the gleaming Cessna waited.

10

As they approached the airstrip, Jacqueline unzipped her shoulder bag, took out a small Sony camcorder, and began filming—first Sam and Félix, then the ranch buildings and the purple-streaked morning landscape. She certainly *looked* professional, Sam thought. She even photographed his little twin-engine, sparkling white with maroon-and-gold trim.

"What kind of plane is it, Sam? It's really cute."

"A Cessna 310."

"It looks brand-new."

"Vintage 1979, with a wash-and-wax. I prefer to call it a classic." Sam smiled. "Cessna stopped making small planes back in '86. Hardly anybody makes 'em now in the U.S. Sharp lawyers took care of that. Damn near wiped out the whole industry with product-liability lawsuits. But I wouldn't trade this one in, even if I could." He slapped a wingtip tank as he walked by. "The 310 suits me fine. It can take me and five full-grown folks just about anywhere I want to go, just about as fast as I want to get there. And up where I live in Oklahoma, it's perfect for getting down to the main road to check the mailbox."

"Hmm, did I warn you about Sam?" Jacqueline called over her shoulder to Félix as they went up the retractable double step into the forward cabin. "Don't take everything he says literally."

She moved nimbly into the right-hand seat, and Félix slid behind her. Sam stowed the cooler aft, then paused beside the young archaeologist. "So, how was Dr. Laya this morning?"

"Angry with me for coming. I must be back by one."

"Ordinarily that wouldn't be a problem. But now that Jacqueline has cast doubt on my veracity, I better not promise anything. Still want to go?"

Félix nodded. "Oh, yeah. Actually I've never seen Salto Angel in person."

"The tallest waterfall in the world, right in your own backyard, and you never went to see it?" Jacqueline asked.

"Most Venezuelans can't afford to fly, Jake," Félix said, invoking a nickname Sam had never been invited to use. "Even the lucky ones with jobs. And flights over Angel Falls cost thousands of *bolívars*."

"Oops!" Jacqueline turned to face Félix, looking slightly chagrined. "There I go, exposing my cultural insensitivity. I suppose you think I'm terribly spoiled?"

"I would never say such a thing!"

"Spoken like a real South American gentleman."

"No. I think you are fantastic, Jake—you and Sam both, for taking me along."

"Happy to do it, Félix," Sam said. "I'd even take Arquimedeo, if he asks."

"Actually Arqui has flown over quite a bit of the Gran Sabana doing aerial photo surveys for archaeological sites. That's really what got him interested in Cerro Calvario."

And then the clever little bastard snookered me into bankrolling him to explore it, Sam thought, taking the left-hand seat. He turned to his passengers. "Okay, folks, time to buckle up— seat belts and shoulder harnesses. And put on your headsets. It's about to get real noisy in here."

Sam had completed his preflight before their arrival and had gotten a benign forecast from the airport at Puerto Ordaz—scattered morning cumulus, building to thunderclouds by late afternoon. Now he went through the prestart checklist, peripherally aware of Jacqueline watching his movements. After turning on the master switch and surveying the comm radios and navaid frequencies, he adjusted the controls for fuel mixture, propeller, and carburetor. A few strokes primed the motors. Next he made a visual sweep down the runway and around both props, before keying the ignition.

The propellers spun and, one after another, the 260-horse engines caught, melding into a full-throated roar. Sam nudged the throttle, and the Cessna began to trundle along the rough taxiway onto the only slightly smoother runway. He took it down to the end, where the hardpan gave way to rutted earth and clumps of grass. Then he spun and halted for the final run-up.

After testing the controls and rechecking instruments, Sam planted his feet on the brakes and throttled up. As the revs climbed and the engines reached full scream, the Cessna began to shudder, like a two-and-a-half-ton sheet-metal cat waiting to pounce. As Sam held it there, he turned and read the childish excitement in Jacqueline's eyes.

After a last skyward scan, he trimmed for takeoff, released the brakes, and let the plane fling itself forward. He fed it more throttle, till the savanna went streaking along the side windows. Sam had used up nearly half the twenty-five-hundred-foot strip, watching his airspeed indicator, before he eased back on the yoke and felt the Cessna lift off the deck.

Once gear and flaps were up and rpms and fuel mix were adjusted, he spoke into his headset: "I'm going to take you over Cerro Bolívar first. That's the only iron mountain on which— so far—no ancient artifacts have been uncovered. Then we'll head back south."

The mountain appeared a moment later, a reddish hogback rising 1,800 feet above the grasslands and stretching west to east nearly four miles. As it loomed larger, they began to see the huge scars that had transformed the massif into a vertical open-pit mine. Cerro Bolívar's sides had been blasted and bulldozed into a spiraling series of fifty-foot-wide benches, which, viewed from above, resembled the hachures on a contour map. Yet there was a raw beauty in the scarifying. The exposed ferrous rock was streaked and veined with a lurid variety of mineral hues—ochers and vermilions, rusts and golds, even pinks and maroons—and dotted, here and there, by the green of shrubbery.

As they passed directly overhead, Jacqueline pointed her palmcorder down. "I can see tiny yellow trucks down there."

"They're around a hundred tons each," Sam said.

"Félix, look." Since the archaeologist was behind the wing's leading edge with an impaired downward view, she urged him to lean forward. "Is that what will happen to Cerro Calvario?"

"If our government feeder permits it," Félix said, peering over her shoulder. "Of course, you might try to talk Sam and your father out of their plans."

She glanced over at Sam. "You don't really think it's justified, do you, Sam?"

"This is going to sound real evasive, but why don't you ask your father first?"

"I already did. In fact, I told him last night I thought it was unthinkable to go ahead with mining—I mean, considering what Félix and Dr. Laya have already discovered."

"And what did he say?"

"He doesn't like to discuss business with me. Or politics. He doesn't mind lecturing me, though—as long as I sit in silent worship."

"Somehow I can't picture your doing that."

"It doesn't happen a whole lot. Not that I don't respect his opinion—on a lot of things really. But—I mean, you don't exactly have to be a radical Green, or a neo-Marxist or whatever, to know we don't have the right to bulldoze everything in sight, just to max out earnings for a bunch of stockholders." She took a breath. "That's heretical, I know. But I'm on Félix's side on this."

"I was beginning to suspect that. Speaking of lectures . . ."

"Sorry, Sam."

Sam laughed heartily. "You can speak your mind all you want around me, Jacqueline. I might learn a few things. By the way, that's Cerro Calvario coming up on the right. Anybody want me to waggle the wings?"

Fifteen minutes later they crossed over a sweeping curve of the Río Paragua, its surface shimmering in the morning light. Ten minutes after came another river, the iron-tinted Caroní, a major tributary of the Orinoco. Stretches of the Paragua, the Caroní, and their feeder streams, Sam explained, were still being dredged for diamonds and gold.

59

"And other treasures," Félix added. "For instance, the alluvial terraces also contain pre-Columbian relics, which some people consider even more valuable than gold."

Sam ignored the editorial comment, busy banking left to follow the Caroní between its jungled banks south to another affluent, the smaller Carrao. As the Cessna leveled out, Sam resumed over the headset:

"From here on we're in Canaima National Park. It runs all the way to the Brazilian border, but we'll only see a tiny corner of it today. Now, if you look ahead there on the right bank of the river—that little clearing and lagoon? That's Canaima Camp. We'll be stopping back there for lunch."

At their cruise altitude of 7,500 feet, the resort camp constituted only a small scar in the luxuriant, riverine greenery—a slash of asphalt and raw earth, a scatter of palm thatch, a molten gleam of quiet water below a white froth of cataracts. Then the jungle closed back in and they were into the Gran Sabana, the Great Savanna of southeastern Venezuela.

As Canaima slid behind to starboard, the first of the great sandstone plateaus, or *tepuis*, were already visible out the portside windows. Sam reached into a map case and handed Jacqueline a well-thumbed *National Geographic* with an artist's rendering of the region. This showed a cartographic panorama of these majestically eroded tablelands interlaced with canyons and rivers. Jacqueline found Canaima on the map, then called out the names of the formations appearing on their left—Kurún Tepui, "Kurun Mountain," Cerro Venado, "Deer Hill," and several more. "Next stop Angel Falls," she announced, passing the illustration back to Félix. "How much farther now, Sam?"

"About thirty miles—ten, fifteen minutes. If the falls are veiled in mist, don't worry. We can try it again later. Anyway, you'll have plenty to look at. I've flown over some spectacular stuff in the U.S.—Yosemite, Zion, the Grand Canyon, Monument Valley. Believe me, what's coming up is as good as it gets."

"Perhaps we should hire you for our tourist bureau," Félix suggested.

"Hell, no! I don't want this corner of paradise stomped flat. Let the hordes keep going to Club Med or Rio or Disney World—all the places they've already gunked up. But let's keep 'em out of here."

"Now *you* sound like an environmentalist, Sam," Jacqueline observed.

"Guess I do," he admitted with a grin.

"Also an opponent of progress and industry," Félix put in. "After all, a tourist invasion would help Venezuela's struggling economy, more perhaps than another iron-ore mine."

"All right, you've both drawn the old man's blood. Now let's all sit back and enjoy the ride, okay? We're gonna start climbing here—another fifteen hundred feet, if we want to get sufficient clearance over Auyán Tepui, which, in case you didn't notice, is that big son-of-a-bitch mountain dead ahead."

11

It was not a mountain so much as a vast, flat-topped island rearing out of the rain forest. Its sheer sides—which, as they neared, became striated ramparts of red and ocher rock—soared more than three thousand feet. And its wedge-shaped, northernmost apex cleaved the green waves of vegetation like the prow of some gigantic, monolithic ship.

Another *tepui*, called Roraima, which Sir Arthur Conan Doyle had selected for his fanciful tale *The Lost World*, was larger, Sam explained. But this approaching colossus, with its deep, waterfall gorges and crenellated rock towers, Sam considered the most dramatic of Venezuela's great table mountains. Its brooding size, and the fact that it was often hidden in clouds and thunderstorms, had inspired its Indian name, Auyán Tepui, Devil Mountain.

The drone from the Cessna's engines changed pitch as Sam worked to find the steepest angle over the huge obstacle. With three aboard and a conservative 140-knot cruise climb, he could only manage around fifteen hundred feet per minute, but this was enough to lift them above the mountain rim and to reveal a forbidding summitscape of barren black rock.

The pockmarked surface passed slowly beneath them, veiled in ragged streamers of mist, in places vanishing into crevasses and elsewhere fissured into a labyrinth of storm-sculpted pillars. Tangled among these eerie formations were darkish clumps of vegetation, tenacious shrubs and dwarf trees. Higher, flat-topped against the encircling skyline, were other "lost worlds," members of a geologically ancient chain of *tepuis* marching south to the borders of Brazil and Guyana.

Suddenly the summit dropped away and they were looking down into a green-bottomed gorge. The enclosed forest floor was threaded by a silver stream, the runoff of several waterfalls they spied along the ragged parapets. One of these cascades, Sam pointed out, burst from an opening halfway up a sheer cliff.

"It's fantastic!" Jacqueline switched on her camcorder. "But where's Angel Falls?"

"Wrong canyon. Although this one did show up a few years back in a scary movie about spiders."

The gorge passed beneath them and was succeeded by another expanse of summit. Félix, meanwhile, had moved forward between the front seats.

"Jake, look down there," he said. "What do you see?"

"Not much. It's awfully bleak."

"No, it's actually full of life. Isn't that right, Sam?"

Sam nodded, but deferred to the archaeologist, who obviously had a point to make. Félix went on:

"Señor Doyle was not completely wrong about his 'lost world' of dinosaurs. This is the first time I have seen a *tepui* so close. But like most Venezuelans, I studied them in school. They are perhaps the oldest rock formations in the world—pre-Cambrian. This is nearly two billions of years old."

"Where are the big lizards, then, Professor Rosales?" Jacqueline asked. "And don't tell me they're all napping in their pre-Cambrian caves."

"There may be some unusual saurians up here, I cannot recall. But many plants and animals have evolved on these isolated summits that are existing nowhere else—species of orchids and bromeliads and many strange amphibia and insects. Even giant carnivorous plants."

Jacqueline began to stare keenly at the *tepui*'s rock-strewn surface.

"I'm afraid you'll have to take Félix's word for all that," Sam said. "Or hire some daredevil chopper pilot to land you up here."

"This is quite close enough, thanks. Besides, I happen to like the pilot I've got."

"Glad to hear it. Okay, get ready for the main event. We're about to enter the valley of the Churún River, also known as Devil's Canyon. Angel Falls will be on the right in a couple minutes—if we're going to be able to see it this morning." Again the plateau slid away, and a great rift valley tilted below as Sam banked right to fly down its center.

"Oh, my God!" Jacqueline gasped, raising her camcorder. "There are waterfalls everywhere!"

Sam had noticed the same thing. Thanks to heavy recent rains, there was more than the usual runoff along the canyon escarpments.

Beside him, Jacqueline was tracking and zooming from one breathtaking cascade to the next. The valley yawned before them like a verdant Grand Canyon, with sheer rock walls plunging thousands of feet to green-clad talus slopes and a forest floor vagrantly cloud-shadowed and center-laced by a burnished watercourse, the Río Churún. The sun was now high enough to slant across the rosy sandstone cliffs and cast deep cathedral shadows behind the ridges, leaving untouched the many side canyons and defiles, like the recessed chapels of some winding, primeval nave. Through this vast, magnificent hush the little plane droned, a high-tech pterodactyl, self-aware and insignificant.

As spectacular as the view ahead was, Sam couldn't help but notice the girl's excited reactions, and the occasional delighted glances she threw him and Félix. She also treated them to a scenic commentary, which made up in sheer enthusiasm what it lacked in descriptive variety.

Then, abruptly, she cursed and lowered her Handycam to her lap.

"Out of tape?" Sam asked.

"No—out of my mind! Sam, it's just too awesome. Unless you happen to have an IMAX movie camera lying around."

"I don't seem to remember one on the manifest."

But an instant later, as Sam took them around a sharply projecting cliff, she snatched up her video camera with renewed zeal. Below on their right Angel Falls was suddenly unveiled in its full-length plunge down the mineral-streaked, exfoliated face of the canyon's west wall.

Nobody spoke. The only sound was the insistent engine vibrato through the earseals on their headsets. Below them the rain-swollen, mesa-top river simply exploded from the cliff in two majestic horsetail plumes, free-falling in solemn parallel through sunlight and shadow, nearly a thousand meters to the canyon floor and a caldron of seething vapor.

"There's a rainbow down there!" Jacqueline cried.

And there was. At the base of the falls, hovering above the swirling mist, was a delicate, prismatic arch. Beneath this, several cataracts interlaced into a silvery stream that went coursing down a rocky channel before vanishing into the jungle en route to the Churún.

Gradually, then, the spectacular view was intruded upon by the starboard engine nacelle, then eclipsed altogether behind wing and windows.

"Hang on," Sam said. "Preparing to come about. You'll get it back on your left. And I'll take us down a bit, too."

They did a gradual one-eighty, losing both airspeed and elevation on the cliff face. But in the cockpit it seemed as though they hung motionless, while the rough-faceted canyon walls swung round them in a grand cyclorama. Finally the falls wheeled into view, above and below them now. Glancing up, they could see water gouting out of notches beneath the summit, while straight down was the boiling spillway.

At Sam's suggestion, Jacqueline scrambled across to the left-hand window behind him, her long, denimed legs extending into the tiny aisle. Then, at an urgent summons from her, Félix squeezed in beside her to share the view.

Sam, meanwhile, kept an eye out for possible air traffic in the confined area and continued to monitor the pilot frequency. As an added precaution, he had arrived a half hour ahead of the usual morning tours from Puerto Ordaz and Ciudad Bolívar.

He made another pass before climbing back out of the canyon and continuing south. The final glimpse—of the falls subsiding again into the great valley of the Churún—left him as always with a residue of sadness, and wondering if he would ever see them again.

For sheer solitary magnificence, in Sam's opinion, this waterfall surpassed all its rivals. Yosemite, the world's second highest, spilled its thunder only a short stroll from a tour-bus parking lot, while Niagara, Iguassú, and even Victoria were all subjected to streams of onlookers arriving steadily by vehicle or boat. For the most part, however, Salto Angel made its endless, breathtaking drop into this isolated canyon unwitnessed, like the philosopher's tree toppling soundlessly in the forest. Except for a few daily tourist flybys, Devil's Canyon was empty of humankind. The only surface access was via river, a journey of several days by motorized dugout from Canaima to the north or the Kamarata Valley to the south.

"Well, what do you think?" Sam inquired of his passengers.

Jacqueline threw up her hands at the question. "I don't know what to say! At the moment I feel sort of verbally inadequate."

Sam grinned. "But you liked it?"

She nodded vehemently. "Yeah, I'd say that. I don't know where you're taking us next, Captain Sam, but after that, believe me, it's got to be anticlimactic."

"Let's call it a change of pace then. We're going to take a peek at the Kamarata Valley, just the other side of Auyán Tepui, then head back to Canaima. You'll see a lot more waterfalls there, though nothing like Angel. That's the mother of 'em all."

As they continued south over the plateau, Sam told Jacqueline about Jimmy Angel, the American bush pilot who, while searching for gold in 1937, crash-landed his monoplane on top of the falls. Angel, his wife, and two companions had not only survived the accident, but eventually hiked their way out. The pilot's name, however, had remained behind, felicitously linked to the falls ever after.

"But only for non-Indians," corrected Félix. "The Pemón still call the place simply Churún *merú*, the falls of the river Churún."

"Excuse me, Félix," Jacqueline said, "but at the risk of sounding politically incorrect, I prefer Angel Falls. Of course, if the guy's name had been Smith or Jones or Jimmy McGillicuddy, I might agree with you."

"I admit it *is* a pretty name," Félix relented. "And it sounds even prettier in Spanish with the soft g—Salto Anhel. You can see his original plane, by the way. It's parked on the grass right in front of the Ciudad Bolívar Airport."

A moment later Sam took them past the southern rim of Auyán Tepui and out over the broad Kamarata Valley, which instantly reminded Jacqueline of the African veld. Sam agreed; the resemblance *was* striking. Both were tree-dotted, rolling grasslands with distance-purpled table mountains on the horizon. This was the real look of Venezuela's Gran Sabana, he explained. And one of these years he intended to drive through it, taking the road from El Dorado all the way south to Santa Elena on the Brazilian frontier.

"Actually, Sam, you don't have to drive," Félix said. "You can rollerblade. I had a student who worked as a guide out of Puerto Ordaz, and he told me about it. It is especially popular with young German and Italian tourists now. They get out of their four-wheel-drive vehicles, strap on their 'blades, and take off."

"You're serious?" Jacqueline asked.

"Absolutely. The road is paved all the way now, and there is little traffic, so they can go extremely fast. Fifty kilometers per hour, I am told, right through the Grand Savanna."

"That sounds real interesting, Félix," Sam said. By his rough estimate now, the young archaeologist had contradicted just about every other damn thing Sam had said or else tried to top it. Was there some sort of adolescent male rivalry afoot? "I'll have to try that sometime."

Twenty minutes later Sam deposited them on the jungle-hedged landing strip of Camp Canaima. Several commercial planes were already on the tarmac—a Metro-Merlin from Cave, an Aereotuy Twin Otter, and the morning jet from Caracas via Ciudad Bolívar, a big Avensa 727.

Sam taxied over to the edge of the strip and parked alongside another private craft, a twin-engine Beech. As the three climbed out into a forenoon steam bath, Sam handed the cooler chest to Félix, motioning toward a palm-thatched shelter at the end of the runway.

"You can catch a tram over there to the beach. Why don't you both go ahead while I button up here?"

Félix started off with the cooler, but Jacqueline held back, looking concerned. "Sam, you're not angry with Félix, are you? I know he's been showing off. But he can't help being jealous of you."

"Is that it? I guess I should be flattered. Anyway, why don't you go ahead with him? I do want to lock up and arrange for some avgas. I'll catch up in a minute."

"You're sure?"

He chuckled. "Jacqueline, stop me if I'm out of line here, okay? But we've just arrived at one hell of a romantic little spot. Wait till you see the lagoon. Pink sand, palm trees, waterfalls. Probably the most photographed place in Venezuela."

"So?"

"So—I thought maybe you and Félix might like to have a few minutes to enjoy it by yourselves."

She looked at him searchingly. "Sam, I'm quite capable of making those decisions for myself. Is that okay with you?"

"Absolutely. I just thought—"

"And another thing, while we're at it."

"What might that be?"

"Call me Jake."

12

Sam Warrender was definitely goofing off.

The evidence was pretty conclusive.

He wasn't rounding up rambunctious local politicos and herding them back into the company corral. Neither was he silencing pressure groups by all available means, or jump-starting stalled mining operations on Cerro Calvario, then ramrodding them into high gear. He was, in fact, doing none of the masterful things he had promised Hardesty Eason and the other Proteus vice honchos he would do.

Instead, he had his butt solidly planted on a pinky-beige sand beach, his back against the bole of a moriche palm, a chilled can of Cerveza Polar in his fist, and scarcely a thought in his head. His mind was at present thoroughly occupied in marveling at the snowy thunder of Hacha Falls across Canaima Lagoon. He was in your basic postprandial, sun-dazed limbo, seriously inclining toward a nap.

The urgency that had flamed up three days ago and sent him skedaddling down here in his Cessna was not forgotten. But he hadn't yet resolved on a course of action, or even what he would tell D.W. later that afternoon.

In the meantime, with key decision-makers out of Caracas for another day or two, there seemed no harm in having D.W. doing what he was doing—glad-handing the industrial elite of Puerto Ordaz and inviting them aboard his big motor yacht, which was apparently serving as a dockside hospitality suite. The company might as well get some use out of that floating pleasure palace, Sam thought, having contributed handsomely to its upkeep.

For his part, Sam much preferred kicking back down here and enjoying Canaima, one of his favorite spots on earth—the Almighty's version of Adventureland. You had to admit the landscaping here was first rate. Against a theatrical backdrop of redrock mesas, the Río Carrao, tinted the color of fine sherry by minerals and tannin from leaves and tree roots, flowed past a palm-fringed, emerald greensward that bore an uncanny resemblance to a country club fairway. Then, after flashing briefly into rapids, the river fanned out across seven mighty cataracts, exploding down into a tranquil lagoon, which just now mirrored the noon-blue sky. And the entire panorama was ingeniously arranged for viewing from anywhere along a scalloped crescent of palm-shaded beach.

D.W.'s daughter suited the setting, from her velvety laughter to the way the equatorial sun sheened the apricot skin of her forearm and kindled fiery highlights in her dark mane. A lavender orchid, for instance, would not be out of place tucked behind that ear. And, as Sam recalled, the delicate *Cattleya mossiae*, Venezuela's national flower, grew wild hereabouts for the plucking.

If Jacqueline Lee guessed at his mute, avuncular admiration, she certainly wasn't showing it. She was sitting beside him now, hugging her denimed knees and digging her bare toes in the pink sand, with her face turned away from him—and toward the barechested Félix Rosales.

Sam had caught snatches of their intensely *simpatico* conversation before tuning out. It had to do with the latter-day revisionist gospel of how Columbus had laid waste to the New World. Sam had heard and read enough of that historical slaughter of innocents all around the Caribbean basin not to argue the point. Still, predictable orthodoxy of any sort bored him. So, as digestion proceeded and the sun poured down its stupefying balm, he let his thoughts stray elsewhere, appropriately enough to images highly erotic.

These were not fantasies, but vivid recollections of another young woman, María Elisa Cárdenas. Not the formidable matron she was today, to be sure, but the combustible creature she had been twenty-five years earlier, when first she came into Sam's ranch house as a domestic. María Elisa then would have been about the same age as Jacqueline Lee now, though in most respects it would be difficult to imagine two young women more unlike. And yet, Sam suspected, it was proximity to D.W.'s self-assured and sophisticated daughter over the course of the morning that had summoned up these memories of the earthy young Latina who had once bewitched him.

It had not occurred at first glance, he remembered. No, it was the second glance that had inflicted the real damage.

She had been standing at his sink, scrubbing a large cast-iron pot, when he cut through the kitchen en route to the garages and a meeting in town. The thick black braid and mahogany skin tones were those of his regular housekeeper, Adela, but these ample curves, unlike Adela's butterball bulge, cinched snugly at the waist. Sam halted.

His initial inquiry was drowned out by salvos of spray drilling the metal pot, and his shouted follow-up caused the girl to whirl with the fearful eyes of a doe transfixed by headlights. Then, as Sam apologized in Spanish and introduced himself, she melted into her smile—and her common prettiness was transformed into radiant sensuality. It was a trick weapon, this high-voltage smile of hers, against which Sam was to discover no effective defense.

María Elisa had come that morning to fill in for her older sister, she explained, because poor Adela was having her terrible allergies again. María Elisa hoped Señor Warrender would not object; it would only be for a few days. Sam was far from objecting to the substitution, but the girl offered further reassurances. Adela had instructed her as to where everything was kept, she told him, and exactly what needed to be done and in what order, on all of which María Elisa had taken careful notes. Wiping her hands on her apron, she produced a sheet of notebook paper. Sam came closer and saw that it was covered in plump purple handwriting.

When their eyes met over that childish scrawl, Sam felt his

face lapse into an idiot grin. *Something* had passed between them. Whatever it was—basic lust, recognition of a strong mutual attraction, dangerous susceptibility—María's eyes blazed back with it, and Sam damn well felt it, too. He had escaped then, and quickly.

Accelerating away down the ranch road, he had resolved to avoid the house as much as possible until this incendiary creature was safely out of it and the fat sister returned. There was, after all, no local shortage of beddable, weddable females. Several such had advertised their availability in the four years since his divorce from Caroline. There could be not the slightest justification for Sam's allowing any foolishness between himself and this apparently willing spitfire. Whatever pleasures afforded them en route, he couldn't envision any affair ending happily or fairly for her. The solution was to steer entirely clear.

During the next three days he saw her only twice in passing. On both occasions, however, that primal awareness had been present. On the third evening Sam had sat in a Tulsa restaurant across a candlelit table from a woman of considerable charm and cultivation—and found himself repeatedly conjuring María Elisa. When he returned to the ranch late that night, long after María had left, he discovered some of her little touches. There seemed to be more every day. Now his dresser-top clutter of keys, comb, and pocket change had been arranged artfully, his bedside books stairstepped in an impressive pyramid, and a pair of rarely used silk pajamas exhumed from a bottom drawer and laid out on the coverlet.

On the fourth day Sam had flown early to Amarillo and back, reserving the afternoon to inspect a few head of longhorns he'd recently acquired from a Texas A&M breeding program. Instead, on his return he found himself wandering, with no apparent purpose, from room to room.

He found María in the serving pantry off the dining room. She was poised on a stool, at full stretch, putting away china on a high cupboard shelf. The starched cotton of her uniform was also at full stretch over hips and bosom. At the squeal of the door's spring hinge, she turned, targeting Sam with her point-blank smile. He absorbed the impact and backed out of the room.

Pursuit into Darkness

Once out in the corridor and fighting a dizzying rush of desire, he gave himself the best advice he could think of: *Keep going, you damn fool!*

Then he heard María Elisa call his name inside, making of it three plaintive syllables—"Sam-u-el?"

As if in sleepwalk, he had gone back in to her. She said not a word, but her child eyes implored him. He was still a step away when she launched herself at him. Suddenly Sam had all her humid abundance clinging fiercely to his neck, mouthing Spanish endearments that he hastened to smother with their first kiss. In a daze, with her in his arms, he had headed off toward the master bedroom, knocking into a hall table and caring not a damn.

A door slams in memory, the massive, carved Spanish oak door of his old bedroom in the years before the south wing was built. His conqueror's strides lead across a cushioned oatmeal carpet. On the other side of the big room, casement windows admit a warm afternoon breeze, which stirs gauzy, sky-blued curtains. Sam looks down into eyes signaling simultaneous surrender and victory.

He deposits the exquisite burden onto his big bed, atop the copper quilted coverlet that she herself has spread this morning and tucked tight. Now, when it is all too wonderfully late, she begins giggling and twisting, as if to evade her erotic fate. But when he plays her game and hesitates at arm's length above her, pretending last-minute reservations, she explodes off the mattress, grapples him downward, crushes herself beneath him.

They had succeeded somehow in undressing each other without letting each other go. They had behaved, in fact, like rabid teenagers, although María had been twenty-three then, and Sam nearing thirty-five, if feeling suddenly seventeen. But why not? Never had he beheld such a cornucopia of delights in his bed. He could still see María's pillowy breasts with their blindly staring areolas; the amphorical hips enfolding the dark, nested triangle; the dark, brimming eyes and rose-petal lips, inviting endless intimacy.

And on that long-ago, golden afternoon, Sam had set about plundering all those proffered treasures of hers, not once but again and again, like a bovine blundering into overrich pasture, eager to graze itself to death. . . .

Cold water splashed his face, shocking him out of reverie. Shrill laughter opened his eyes. Jacqueline Lee stood above him, tall and dark against a magenta flare of sun. He squinted up and saw her leaning over him and twisting a rope of her long hair, releasing another shower down on his face.

13

Coughing and laughing, Sam levered himself to his elbows, focusing on this very palpable, very contemporary young thing demanding his attention. She wore a look of little-girl mischief and a black cutaway tank suit that displayed a sleek, big-girl body. Where María of wanton memory had been compact and curvaceous, Jacqueline Lee was long-waisted and willowy. But in native coquettishness, Sam decided, the two were equally endowed. Jacqueline's mud-splattered Reeboks, jeans, and work shirt lay discarded on her bright beach towel; Félix's shorts, shoes, and tank top were strewn beside them.

"Come on, Sam!" she insisted. "The lagoon's fantastic. It's like swimming in champagne."

"Thanks, Jacqueline, but I'll sit this one out."

"Oh, *merde!* Don't give me any of that 'You kids run along and play' stuff."

"Down here they say *mierda*—but it's not ladylike."

"Hmm, I've got an answer to that, but I better not say it." She flashed a sly smile. "But I'm warning you, Big Sam, if you're just sitting up here thinking, 'Ah, youth,' and being a damned martyr, I'll—I'll—"

"You'll what?"

She swung a shapely leg and sent sand flying in his face.

Sam exploded off the towel.

Jacqueline shrieked and dodged away, sprinting down the beach ahead of him—long legs scissoring, wet hair whipping across her bared back. Close inshore, Félix Rosales stood hugging his muscled torso and watching.

Jacqueline was still squealing as she high-stepped into the water and arced forward in a graceful dive. Sam, several strides behind, stopped just short. It took him half a minute to return to the towel, strip down to his trunks, and join them, belly-slapping the surface and pinwheeling into his old trudgen crawl. The embracing lagoon was every bit as fantastic as Jacqueline had said, and as Sam remembered it. He came up blinking, the sun-glossed water rippling before him all the way across to the foaming splendor of Hacha Falls.

Sam turned around. Jacqueline was stalking him from behind, her eyes triumphant. She yelped and began skimming water into his face, drenching him with spray. Sam let himself be drawn into the water fight, which quickly turned into a triangular, point-blank duel that whipped the surface into a froth. Then Jacqueline was caught in a crossfire between the two men—and screamed for a cease-fire.

On their way back to the airstrip, at Jacqueline's request they stopped off at one of the jungle camp's whitewashed souvenir bungalows. This one boasted an adjoining cage full of fretful-looking howler monkeys, while, perched just under the eaves, a somnolent pair of red and blue macaws eyed each entering and departing customer. The shop's murky interior was heaped and festooned with the usual jungle knickknackery. In fact, Sam found it difficult to move without knocking his head against bamboo toucans suspended from the log rafters or toppling nested towers of native basketry. After several such encounters, he retreated to the open doorway, not far from the stuffed-looking macaws, where he was soon joined by an equally disinterested Félix Rosales. Jacqueline, meanwhile, vindicating the shopkeeper's faith in the buying habits of *Homo peregrinus*, conscientiously browsed all the aisles of tropical schlock, picking out postcards, a coconut-shell monkey mask, a palm-woven bag and floppy hat, and several "I ♥ Canaima" T-shirts.

Outside Sam remarked, "What, no blowgun?"

Jacqueline looked upset. "Where were they? I didn't see them."

"Try over there," Félix suggested.

Across the road, a tour group was watching an Indian, naked except for leather breechcloth and feathered headband, demonstrate his prowess with a much abridged version of the native blowgun, or *cerbatana*. Several darts flew from his two-foot wooden tube dead center into a styrofoam target hung on a tree trunk. Next, the Indian grinned and handed the weapon to a big potbellied man in bright plaid shorts. This brought raucous protests from the man's companions, all of whom scattered hastily from the line of fire.

"Hmmm," Jacqueline commented. "That has definite possibilities."

Moments later, as the three continued along the camp road, a miniature *cerbatana* was protruding from her woven souvenir bag along with four palmwood darts.

"At least they didn't sell her the deadly curare to go with it," Félix said.

"Thank God," Sam agreed. "But I think we better get Jungle Girl here back to her father before she goes completely native."

Afternoon plans got altered drastically when they landed back at the cattle ranch. While Jacqueline phoned her father, Sam and Félix went in search of Bernardo. They found him right where they'd left him—in the den, camped in front of the television. He begged to stay for one final event—an imminent showdown between rival monster trucks.

Sam thought of all the majestic scenery the young Venezuelan had gladly bypassed in favor of this dark room of flickering images. "Five minutes max," Sam said. "Then I pull the plug."

Bernardo instantly riveted his attention back on the TV. He didn't bother to glance up when Jacqueline walked in and handed Sam the cordless phone.

"It's Daddy," she said. "He's pretty upset."

"What for? Was there a decision by the government?"

"No. He got upset with me—when I told him I won't be flying back with you to Puerto Ordaz this afternoon. I didn't have a chance to tell you, Sam. Félix has offered to take me back up to the dig."

"When did all this happen?"

"Sam, don't you be upset, too! I was counting on you to calm

Daddy down." She pointed meaningfully at the phone, which was still in Sam's hand, percolating D.W.'s voice into his palm. Sam placed the phone against his ear.

"Sam, are you there?" D.W. was shouting. "Sam? Jacqueline? Dammit, will somebody please—"

"It's Sam, D.W. What seems to be the problem?"

"Didn't you hear? Sam, stop her! I forbid Jacqueline's going into the jungle by herself! She's acting crazy!"

"Hold your fire a minute, D.W. She just sprung this on me, too." He put down the phone and looked pointedly at Jacqueline. "You want to explain this in a bit more detail?"

"It's not a big deal, Sam, really."

"Well, your father seems to think so. And—excuse me." Bernardo had turned the sound down, but Sam was distracted by the pulsing TV screen. Two jacked-up pickups went racing up a ramp, sailed briefly through the air, then crashed down together, flattening junk cars into scrap metal beneath gargantuan tires. In two steps Sam switched off the set. Bernardo started to protest, saw the look in Sam's eye, and wisely shut up.

Sam resumed, "Jake, your father's a lot more than upset. And he has every right to be." He saw her face tighten. "Now wait. Try and see it from his viewpoint, okay?"

"But, Sam," Félix interjected, "I assure you—"

"Please stay out of this, Félix. This is between Jake and her dad—and me. That's right, Jake. I have a stake in this, too. As long as you're down here, D.W. expects me to look after your safety, and I damn well intend to do it."

"Who says I'm at risk?"

"You're in Venezuela. In my book, that's defined as being at risk. This happens to be one hell of a fantastic country, Jake, but it's not the safest by a long shot. I'm not just talking about student riots and barroom stabbings and coup attempts. Venezuelans are famous for their hospitality, but there are plenty of desperate people out there with guns and knives, and not much future and not a whole lot of food on the table. Ask Félix, if you don't believe me. Or read the papers. Hell, read our State Department advisories. All I'm asking is this. Stick to the itinerary. Don't go wandering off into the bush. This is nothing against Félix. But he's not responsible for you."

"And you are?"

"For the moment, yes. Look, if you want to visit the dig again, I'll be glad to take you."

"Are you through, Sam?"

"Pretty much."

"Then it's my turn." Sam watched her chest heave, her nostrils flare. She was very angry, he thought, but fighting for control. "I'm not a child, Sam. I'm a twenty-two-year-old woman. That makes me an adult, just like you. I am, ergo, responsible for myself. *You're* not responsible for me, *I* am. And this may be Venezuela, but it's not Saudi Arabia. Women have rights."

"Come on, Jake, aren't you kind of overreacting—"

"It's my turn, remember? Now, as for danger." She took a deep breath. "I happen to be a brown belt in tae kwon do, but that's not the point, is it? Okay. Maybe this is. At NYU I was sound assistant on a student film shot in the South Bronx. Our director had worked for ITN news crews in places like Belfast and Beirut. He said our shoot was scarier. And guess what? I didn't ask Daddy's permission. It never occurred to me, actually. And I certainly didn't ask you. Wait. I'm not through yet, Sam.

"Know what I want to do at the dig? I've decided to take my video camera and start documenting what they're doing up there—before you and Daddy bulldoze it into the ground. Now, do you think I'm going to let you stop me from doing that?" She shook her head. "Absolutely not.

"I'm not some spoiled socialite, Sam. Maybe I kid around, but I've got a serious streak, too. And okay, a couple of years ago I did have this bad rep as Miss Campus Dilettante who kept switching colleges and majors. But I outgrew that. Right now I've got the credentials and the know-how to make a film of what's going on up there. Maybe not an important film, but some kind of film. Maybe I can even get a grant to finish it—in case somebody decides to cut off my allowance. So, the only person whose permission I'm really seeking now is Dr. Laya.

"But if you're still worried about my safety, Sam, Félix tells me at least four women are arriving on Cerro Calvario today— all graduate archaeology students from Simón Bolívar University. And they'll have their own tent, and an extra sleeping bag for me. I tried about six times to tell Daddy that, but he couldn't seem to stop shouting."

She exhaled slowly, then resumed, "Look, I didn't mean to

dump on you like this, Sam. You've been wonderful, and I just
had one of the most fantastic days of my life. But I don't appreciate being treated like a child, not by you or anybody."

"Forget about me, Jacqueline. But your dad now, that's pretty
hard for him to stop doing—treating you like his little girl, I
mean. And down deep, I bet you really wouldn't want him to."

"Now you're twisting the words around, Sam. You know what
I mean."

"Okay, maybe I do. Let's call a truce—just like in the water
fight. But promise me one thing."

"What is it?"

"I gather Dr. Laya's got a radiophone up there. Give your dad
a call, tonight or tomorrow. In the meantime I'll see what I can
do for his blood pressure. Deal?"

She smiled, softening further. "I'll call you both. I was kind
of hoping to go for a horseback ride here."

"Anytime."

She stepped forward, squeezed his hand. Then, nodding for
Félix to follow, she exited the room. On the way out, the archaeologist gave Sam a brief, backward nod. Sam chose to interpret this as meaning, "Don't worry, she'll be perfectly safe
with me." If it meant otherwise, Sam thought, he'd personally
flay the skin off all those bulging muscles.

He lifted the phone. "Still there, D.W.?"

"Dammit, Sam, stop her! You heard what she said!"

"Now hold on, D.W. Maybe it's not so bad. I'll have Bernardo
follow her down there and look around, make sure everything's
like she said. If there's the slightest problem, believe me, Enrico
and I will yank her out fast. Meanwhile, I'll have our guard
station call me the instant she enters or leaves. Now, as to our
afternoon meeting—"

The line seemed to detonate in his ear. Sam figured this for
blasphemy, Korean-style.

"My sentiments exactly, D.W. Look, why don't we talk early
tomorrow?"

But D.W. had switched back to English. "Dammit, Sam, she
is just like her mother! Always pulling this shit on me! I knew
something like this would happen!"

"Then why the hell did you bring her down here?"

"I tried to get her to fly home from Trinidad! But you don't know how Jacqueline is, Sam! She argues and argues and argues—till you have no damn fucking choice!"

Sam gave a horselaugh. "Sorry, D.W. But maybe we should put her on the payroll. The company could use a hard-nosed negotiator."

14

Swallowing a final expletive, Duk-Won Lee cradled the phone with deliberate control, then glanced at the other two men in his mahogany-paneled shipboard office. As it happened, neither Owen Meade nor Ray Arrillaga was looking in his direction. Owen, across the steel and glass desk, was absorbed in the latest issue of *Chemical Week*, while Ray stood by the starboard windows inspecting the afternoon sundance on the Orinoco.

D.W. cleared his throat. Owen put down his magazine and looked up expectantly, but D.W. swiveled toward Arrillaga, head of Proteus's South American mining operations, who had flown down overnight from New Orleans. "How old are your girls now, Ray?"

"Eleven and thirteen."

"And how do they treat you?"

"You know how it is, D.W. Every year old Dad seems to know a little less, gets more out of touch. They try to be understanding about it."

D.W. nodded. Since Jacqueline's call had come in on the speakerphone, Owen and Ray had heard the embarrassing family flare-up. At least until D.W. switched to the handset.

"I didn't realize she'd need a baby-sitter down here. And I guess Sam can't handle that job either. So what do I do now, Ray? Go down there myself?"

Owen spoke up. "I can put extra security on at Cerro Calvario while she's there."

"So I shouldn't worry—about my only child?"

"No, I didn't mean that exactly, just—"

"Yeah, why don't you go on down there and give her a good spanking?" Ray suggested. "Owen and I can handle the meeting with Machado and de Villegas. I can say something like, you know, 'Thanks for flying back two days early from Dakar, gentlemen, so we can finalize matters. Unfortunately, Señors Warrender and Lee couldn't make it this afternoon. Could you guys come back tomorrow?' "

Machado and de Villegas, high-ranking government officials, were due on board in less than two hours, bringing documents authorizing full resumption of mining operations, documents already bearing the presidential signature—provided all other terms proved mutually agreeable. Getting these men to come here directly—and in advance of the presidential delegation's return to Caracas—was a considerable coup. D.W. and Ray Arrillaga had pulled it off through sheer persistence; while Sam, with his vaunted Venezuelan connections, had accomplished basically nothing. In fact, Proteus's legendary chairman and CEO had reportedly attended only a couple of skyscraper meetings—at the Ministerio de Energía y Minas and with Ferrominera Orinoco and Corporación Venezolano de Guayana—before flying south to his Promesa ranch.

Five years ago, perhaps even two or three, Samuel Warrender would have been on top of this situation, D.W. knew. But Sam was not the man he had been. His preposterous aside at the mining site yesterday—that he was "thinking about doing a one-eighty down here, letting the professor go ahead with his dig"—was an eloquent testimonial to that. It wasn't so much the about-face that shocked D.W., as the ease with which Sam had announced it. Did he really imagine he could reverse major corporate policy at his own whim, as he had in the old days, consulting neither Proteus's directors nor its president?

It was unfortunate, considering all D.W. owed the man, to so thoroughly show him up now before the Proteus board. But Sam had had ample opportunity to slip gracefully into semiretirement on his ranch. Months ago he had relinquished control of day-to-day operations, hinting to D.W. that the CEO title would soon be his, and eventually even the board chairmanship. Yet these glittering promises remained far from fulfillment. Obviously, despite his stated intentions to abdicate, King Sam would have to be deposed.

And the time was propitious. A clear demonstration of D.W.'s ascendancy would have a major impact on the Proteus board.

A glint of gold inlay betrayed D.W.'s smile. "Jacqueline will have to wait for her spanking, Ray. I do not intend to miss our afternoon meeting."

"Glad to hear it. What about your appointment with Sam?"

"He just canceled. If he hadn't, I would have. If all goes well, I'll invite him to our victory party—the night after tomorrow."

"How will he take it, do you think?" Ray asked.

"Are you afraid of him, Raymond? Feeling pangs of disloyalty?"

"Maybe a little. Then I suddenly remember he's ready to scrub all mining operations—without consulting either of us."

D.W. merely grunted.

"It's a hell of a thing to happen, isn't it?" Owen Meade remarked. "I really like the guy."

"Everybody likes Sam," Ray said.

"So how'd he turn into such a—such a loose cannon all of a sudden? Flying down here without checking strategy with you guys, then riding up to the mountain like that, acting like a cowboy—"

"Sam *is* a cowboy," D.W. said. "And there was a time when Proteus needed a cowboy, and Sam made a great chairman. But now, I'm afraid, decisions must be more . . . what is the word I'm looking for, Raymond?"

"Collegial."

"Exactly. Well"—D.W. shrugged—"let's just say that Sam will make a better chairman *emeritus*. He can ride his horse in all the parades."

Owen Meade chuckled. At the window, Ray Arrillaga nodded approval. But hearing himself attempting to pass summary judgment on the life and character of Sam Warrender, D.W. felt certain misgivings. He found himself, in fact, unexpectedly experiencing those little pangs of disloyalty he had moments ago attributed to Ray Arrillaga.

Pursuit into Darkness

What *would* Sam think? Ultimately he would have to understand and approve D.W.'s effective actions, just as he had done the first time they'd met, a decade before, as industrial rivals. Sam had not only lost that first head-to-head contest, but congratulated D.W. for having bested him. It had been the founding of their friendship—and their subsequent business relationship.

Back then, of course, the white-haired, eagle-eyed Oklahoman had been a man very much at the top of his game. . . .

It was the spring of 1983, but in the Sultanate of Oman on the southeastern tip of the Arabian Peninsula, it already felt like midsummer. At least it did outside. Inside any of the air-conditioned caravansaries of the modernized seaside capital of Muscat, weather was an irrelevance. Duk-Won Lee had browsed the corridors and lobbies of several of these hotels—the Inter-Continental, the Sheraton, the al-Bustan Palace, the al-Falaj. And among the business-suited foreigners and paisley-turbaned Omanis, he had noted emissaries from all the Seven Sisters—Exxon, Mobil, Chevron, Texaco, Gulf, Royal Dutch Shell, British Petroleum. There were also delegates from lesser titans—Occidental, Getty, Unocal, Sun, and Proteus. Then, of course, there were even smaller fry, such as D.W. himself, newly appointed managing director of Soderholm Petroleum, a little-known crude producer out of Houston.

It wasn't a convention. They had all assembled to submit bids (and discreet bribes) to the Omani government for oil and gas drilling rights in the Rub' al-Khali or Empty Quarter, along with offshore tracts in the Gulf of Oman. For, despite a swoon in world oil prices, the big companies realized their futures still depended on foreign reserves. In fact, as a result of recent nationalizations in Kuwait, Libya, and Nigeria, and ongoing convulsions in Iran, the Sisterhood had lost a good deal of its supply. The Omanis, counting their own diminishing petrodollars, were ready and willing to help rectify those losses.

British Petroleum was considered to have the inside track. They had been partners in the Omani fields since 1964, and England had backed the bloodless 1970 coup in which Sandhurst-educated Qaboos bin Said had toppled his father, the old sultan. But Louisiana-based Proteus was rumored to be closing fast. Sam

Warrender had been early and active on the scene. And lately he had been spotted riding with the forty-year-old sultan on a pair of prize Arabians apparently flown in from Sam's Oklahoma ranch.

Such deal-sweetening had to be done judiciously, D.W. learned, for Qaboos was known to scrutinize all cabinet-level officials for mysterious enrichments. But D.W. took this as a positive. Such constraints would fall heaviest on the Seven Sisters, he reasoned, with their massive slush funds and their willingness to move those funds into numbered offshore bank accounts. The premium would be instead on the best proposal, put forward with the greatest initiative, persuasion, and personal charm. Of course, Sam Warrender was already making the most of these altered rules, forging a bond with the sultan as a fellow horseman.

How was D.W. to compete? Undercapitalized Soderholm was in no position to procure such royal inducements. Even if it were, D.W. had not even been invited to Qaboos's gleaming new Al-Alam palace overlooking Muscat harbor. D.W.'s highest government connection was a Korean martial artist who taught tae kwon do to the teenage sons of the Minister of Petroleum and Minerals. Still, with nothing to lose, D.W. conceived and executed his modest plan of influence and submitted his bids. Then, like everyone else, he waited.

A week later, to general astonishment, the Sultanate announced that the concessions would be divided among British Petroleum, Proteus—and obscure Soderholm. The lion's share would, as expected, go to BP, but a potentially lucrative smaller area was assigned to D.W.'s company. Proteus, meanwhile, was only awarded drilling rights for some offshore wildcat wells.

Suddenly the little Texas company with the Scandinavian name and the Asian-sounding managing director was on everybody's lips. Who the hell was this Duk-Won Lee character? And how had he and little Soderholm pulled off their giant-killing coup?

Sam Warrender was the first to catch up to D.W., literally, and pose these questions. It was shortly after dawn, several hours before the official sultanic announcement of drilling awards. D.W. had been jogging along the corniche road, logging his miles in advance of the day's heat and the day's business. As he watched a container ship furrow the glassy surface of Muscat harbor en route to the Arabian Sea, he was overtaken by a tall, loping figure in a hooded blue sweat suit. The man slowed to jog alongside and threw off his hood, exposing sweat-soaked white hair and a barracuda grin. D.W. immediately recognized the Proteus chairman. They introduced themselves and shook hands.

"So," Sam managed between lungfuls of air, "you're the little son of a bitch . . . who whipped my ass . . . and everybody else in town."

"Ah, then it is official?"

"Yes, it's official. . . . So how the hell did you do it?"

"The Force was with me, Sam."

"Force? What force you talking about?"

"The Force that binds the universe."

"What is that? Zen?"

"No. Obi-Wan Kenobi. Didn't you see *Star Wars?*"

"I don't go to movies much . . . not since John Wayne died."

"Ah, Sam, that was your mistake."

"Okay, D.W. Now suppose you tell me . . . what in the name of Allah . . . a goddamn movie has to do . . . with getting the sultan by the short hairs."

D.W. obliged.

By "chance"—D.W. skipped over the tae kwon do connection—he had discovered that the Omani Minister of Petroleum and Minerals had teenage sons who were fanatic followers of the *Star Wars* films, especially the martial arts stuff. All D.W. knew about such things was by way of his thirteen-year-old daughter, Jacqueline, who was similarly infected. Telephoning her in San Francisco, he had learned that fans all over the world were anxiously awaiting the final film of the trilogy, *Revenge of the Jedi,* due out later that year. But Jacqueline boasted that she already had secret information about the movie's plot, from a schoolfriend whose uncle was an accountant at Lucasfilm, where the movie was being made.

Sam cut in, "Okay. So Farid's kids are *Star Wars* junkies. I got that much. So what does that buy you?"

D.W. smiled ruefully. "I agree it is not much. But it was all I had, you see?"

Through his daughter's schoolfriend, he managed to get his

hands on storyboard material on the new film, now retitled *Return of the Jedi*, along with an invitation to an advance screening in a small-town theater near Skywalker Ranch, Lucasfilm's Marin County, California, headquarters. D.W. had added first-class air tickets and Nob Hill hotel accommodations in San Francisco.

The oil minister had received the gratuities politely. It was only later, after his hard-to-please sons reportedly went into ecstatic shock, that his gratitude had taken more tangible form.

"I just hope they like the movie," D.W. concluded his account to Sam.

"I bet you do, you crafty little son of a bitch!"

D.W. caught the gleam in Sam's eye and replied in kind, "Ha! Eat my dust, you horse-thieving bastard!"

That night in Sam's suite the two men got drunk together. They talked of their separate careers and were amazed at a number of peculiar parallels. Both had been in Pusan at the same time during the Korean War in 1952, Sam briefly as an eighteen-year-old PFC with the U.S. Second Infantry Division, Duk-Won as a six-year-old orphan in a Methodist missionary school. During high school and college, both had worked an assortment of odd jobs—Sam as a barbed-wire stringer and roughneck for drilling contractors, and D.W. doing everything from boxing urinals to shucking oysters in a Baltimore cannery. Both got married in college, to the wrong girl, and neither had remarried.

These congruities continued into their professional careers. Both men had served short stints for corporate leviathans—Sam with Standard of New Jersey, D.W. as a field geologist for Royal Dutch Shell—before declaring for entrepreneurial independence. After his divorce at the age of thirty, Sam had gone wildcatting in the Oklahoma and Kansas oil patch, chasing leases and investors, living out of his pickup, washing up in cattle tanks—and running through a half million in drilling money before bringing in his first producing well. D.W. had jumped ship from Shell in Indonesia in order to prospect for natural gas. After a few hard years, each had abandoned his brave solo attempt for salaried security, this time with lesser but more venturesome outfits— Proteus and Soderholm respectively.

Before they'd called it a night, each had dealt wallet snapshots onto the coffee table. Sam led with Tony, then a twenty-four-year-old Harvard MBA student, whose blue-blazered pose and languid smile showed a careful adaptation to his Ivy League habitat and a cultivated disdain for all things Oklahoman, which happened to include his father. Sam was far more proud of the plump and lovely Teresa in her pigtails and full Girl Scout regalia. The girl was then fourteen and living with María Elisa in Albuquerque. Sam's Teresa, it turned out, was only two years older than D.W.'s Jacqueline, who attended an exclusive San Francisco girl's school and was depicted on horseback, with a blinding smile and a big blue ribbon. In another intriguing parallel, both girls were lovely hybrids—Mexican-American and Korean-American.

Sam and D.W.'s chat had resumed two days later on a nine-hour flight to London. A month after that, D.W. accepted Sam's invitation and had flown to the Lazy S for a weekend of skeet and trapshooting.

"There's got to be something I'm better at than you," Sam had observed after D.W. narrowly defeated him on both ranges. "But I'm kind of leery of trying you at poker."

"A wise decision. Of all my college jobs, playing poker paid the best."

At least D.W. wasn't much of a horseman, but gritted his teeth and hung on gamely as they rode out on a Sunday morning to look over some of the Lazy S's twenty-two thousand acres of rangeland. On the way back, Sam had casually asked the younger man if he'd like a job.

"Only yours," D.W. had replied.

"That may not be out of the question. They keep after me to find a successor."

"Be careful, Sam," D.W. had said. "I might say yes."

And he had. Ten years ago that had been. D.W. had started as general manager of Far Eastern operations, putting together joint ventures with Korean companies in steel-making, aluminum smelting, even shipbuilding. Five years later Sam brought him back to New Orleans as a divisional vice president. Three years after that D.W. became Sam's designated understudy as corporate president. As long as two years ago, it became apparent—to everybody but Sam and some of his old friends on the board

—that Duk-Won Lee was running Proteus Industries. It was now past time for Sam to saddle up and ride into the sunset. . . .

D.W. stood behind his desk at the rosewood sideboard and splashed Suntory into three shot glasses. He handed one to Owen Meade and one to Ray Arrillaga. Then he held his drink aloft and drew their glances to him.

"To Samuel," he said, and gulped.

15

For the past three days Félix Rosales had felt himself caught up in a real-life *telenovela*—just like *Lágrimas de Amor*, "Tears of Love," or perhaps *Mujer Prohibida*, "Forbidden Woman." He was the handsome young guy who comes to Caracas from the farm or the *ranchito*, lucks into a job as, say, a limo driver, then glances into his rearview mirror at a dazzling, high-fashion blonde. Instantly, her eyes are drawn to his in the mirror. Their pupils dilate, their eyebrows tremble. Her star-lashed gaze moves down, taking in the thick, curly hair under his little cap, his powerful jaw, his broad, uniformed shoulders. Their colliding passions are underscored by a guitar, or maybe an *arpa llanero*, the harp of the Venezuelan plains. It is only a matter of episodes before the two wind up on satin sheets in a high-rise penthouse, or maybe in one of those walled estates in Altamira or the Country Club district—or better yet, in some Margarita Island beach hotel with palm trees waving outside the window.

Jacqueline Lee wasn't a blonde, of course, but she was rich and beautiful, and their first glance had been *muy tórrido*. Félix saw it impact on Jacqueline the same way. He was definitely not imagining this. He had experienced many such combustible events.

As far back as he could remember, he had been fussed over by the ladies of the family and the barrio. Then, as boyish charm grew into machismo, he took serious stock of his powers, making a study of what things worked best so he could be most devastatingly himself.

But women were the best teachers of all. And Félix had never experienced a shortage of willing tutors or practice partners. The street girls of the Propatria barrio in the Caracas hills had not waited for his puberty to initiate him in the arts and mechanics of love. The tutelage continued during his adolescent years, especially at the hands of a plump, *norteamericana* housewife to whom Félix had bicycled groceries. Each new teenage job brought forth a fresh cadre of instructors, more than the young man could possibly satisfy—though he had tried his best. In retrospect, their faces and names and bodies blurred; they were collectively the sweating, giggling *chicas* of the factories and shops and restaurants. And during his nonworking hours, the cafés of the Sabana Grande and the discos of El Rosal and La Mercedes seemed always filled with lovely *caraqueñas*.

By the time he found himself—quite unexpectedly—at the university, Félix had learned to be somewhat selective. True, he could not now recall all the coeds and lady professors and faculty wives on whom he had honed his amorous skills. Yet there had been many he had passed over. And the older he got, the pickier he had become.

On the same day he'd met Jacqueline, for instance, there had been the overripe blonde from Ciudad Bolívar TV, Señorita Estévez, who looked *estupenda*—at a distance. She had gone so far as to rub her big *chichis* against Félix's biceps while pressing her business card into his palm. The card was now somewhere in his backpack—if he ever got truly desperate. Two of the female grad students who'd arrived at the dig yesterday had also clearly signaled their availability (and the two who had not were obviously *lesbias*). But in Félix's immediate habitat, only one female interested him now.

Jacqueline Lee.

She could have stepped out of a *telenovela*, like the girl in the limo mirror. She was smart and sassy, one of those leggy creatures with flawless smiles who are either born to money or marry it deliciously young and exist therefore in an essentially different world from the rest of humanity. They travel in yachts and limos and behind first-class curtains. They sleep late and dance all night. At least, Jacqueline Lee represented all these unattainable things to Félix. And yet here she was, suddenly in his world, hiking through the mud on Cerro Calvario, diving into Canaima Lagoon, eager for adventure. Almost her first words to him—spoken thrillingly into his ear in the equipment tent while they waited out the deluge—were: "Call me Jake."

And there had been that unforgettable moment yesterday in the plane when she'd squeezed beside him to see Angel Falls out his window. As she pushed closer to the Plexiglas, her long hair brushed his cheek—then completely curtained his view of the great waterfall. But Félix hadn't minded. Her proximity intoxicated, and mingled fragrances hinted at erotic intimacies. He had quickly grown excited. Then, as the plane circled and Jake twisted to return to her seat, hadn't her elbow brushed his lap? And her eyes, hadn't they flashed private mischief?

The rest of the day Félix had had only filtered appreciation of the unfolding grandeur of the Sabana, so galvanized was he by Jacqueline Lee. At Canaima, while Sam napped on the beach, they splashed together in the lagoon, and Félix had lifted her out of the water, a dripping prize. And she *was* an armful, though Félix pretended she was all but weightless. She fought back, squealing, slapping at his chest, flailing her long legs. But even in play, their eyes had exchanged a serious awareness of each other—exactly like the dueling glances in the limousine mirror.

Though there had been no more provocative incidents that afternoon, the subtle awareness continued between them. Then had come her announcement that she was going back to Cerro Calvario to start a documentary film—in defiance of her father and Sam Warrender. Félix, too, had been stunned at first, though he quickly suspected himself of being a factor in her decision. Then, while driving her back to the mountain, he had felt like a returning conqueror.

He had imagined how it would be, with Jacqueline Lee in camp. She would film him working the pits, bare-chested, sweating on behalf of science. And he would keep his eye on her, ready to intercede in her behalf. And here, in the belly of Venezuela, he would have no rivals—only Arqui and his usual flock of nerdy volunteers. Félix could reel her in at his own sweet pace.

Their initial consummation might occur inside his tent, or perhaps under a star-smeared savanna sky. But ultimately, whether Jacqueline completed her documentary or simply wearied of camp squalor, he saw them making love in luxury, surrounded by all the glamorous *telenovela* trappings. He saw himself climbing out of a Ferrari Testarossa and lounging about in baggy Italian silk suits like those *Miami Vice* dudes. In such reveries, Jacqueline was the perfect ornamental adjunct.

But once at the excavation, nothing had gone according to his plan. Last evening, and again most of this day, Arquimedeo had kept Félix on the run, straw-bossing the volunteers in countless tasks, from unloading supplies to pitching tents and digging drainage ditches. Whenever Félix had glimpsed Jacqueline, she seemed to be in convoy—often attended by Arquimedeo himself, who was embarrassingly flattered by her documentary intentions and eager to facilitate the filming. Félix had managed only an occasional wave in Jacqueline's direction.

And worse was to come.

A few minutes earlier, after digging half a latrine himself, and with his pecs pumped and his lats spread, he had gone stalking the camp for her, determined to rekindle the spark between them. From an overlook, he'd spotted her down by the car park, hurrying toward the access road. Mercifully she was alone. Félix had yelled, "Jake!" But when she had spotted him, she merely waved, shouted something unintelligible—and continued on.

Félix moved laterally along the ridge, straining to follow her receding figure. Where the hell was she going in such a hurry? Then, beyond her, he saw a man approaching on horseback, trailing a spare mount. The horseman lifted his hat and made a flourish. Even from a distance, Félix recognized the gesture—and Sam Warrender's shock of white hair. Moments later, with what seemed practiced ease, Jacqueline swung herself into the empty saddle and wheeled her horse in tandem with Sam's, heading back down the trail. Félix watched them vanish behind an edge of rock.

He stood there, unable to move away—until someone pinched the bulge of his left triceps muscle. Then he swung around so swiftly that his elbow nearly clubbed the young woman who had stolen up behind him.

It was Marta Mendes, a short and not very pretty girl of Portuguese parents from Cumaná in Sucre State. She had already proved herself a tireless worker and persistent nuisance, dogging

Félix's footsteps and doting on him with spaniel eyes. They were brimming up at him even now, enormous in her narrow face with its unfortunate, acne-pitted cheeks. The rest of her was impressive, Félix thought, had Marta only been a man—broad shoulders, a hard, flat chest, knotty arms, small hips, and muscle-grooved legs. She'd bragged to Félix that she'd outworked her brothers hauling nets on the family's fishing boats in the Gulf of Cariaco. Not exactly what Félix was looking for in a female. But he, apparently, was quite close to her ideal of manhood.

"Hey, I didn't mean to scare you, Félix," she apologized. "You were going to show me some of your workout routines, remember?"

"Marta, believe me, with all the shitwork up here, the last thing you're going to need is extra exercise."

"*You* pump iron, you said so."

"Yeah, but I'm a freak."

"That's what I like about you." She paused. "So, were you watching Jacquie just now?"

"I wondered where she was going is all."

"Why?"

"*Madre de Dios!* All I know is, she's supposed to be filming us up here. Now, all of a sudden, she's riding into the sunset with some cowboy."

"Don't worry about it, okay? She'll be back for dinner. That 'cowboy,' he's an old friend—her father's boss, she said."

"When did she tell you all this?"

"At lunch. They had a big fight, and Jacquie felt bad about it. So she telephoned him from camp about an hour ago. He has a big ranch over there." Marta paused, then added significantly, "If you ask me, the way she talked about him, she kinda likes him."

Félix *hadn't* asked her. What the hell could Marta know about it? She was probably just making it up, trying to remove Jacqueline Lee as a possible rival. Anyway, Jake couldn't possibly be interested in an older guy like Sam Warrender. Riding with him had to be . . . sort of a diplomatic gesture on her part. Didn't it?

But Félix couldn't undo the damage. For nearly three days he had dreamed his private *telenovela*. Now, in a matter of seconds, with what he had just seen and Marta had speculated, that dream was rapidly unraveling.

He gripped Marta's strong shoulders. "Look, I'm supposed to be helping Arquimedeo schedule evening lectures for the crew. Tell you what. Catch me tomorrow about the workout. Okay?" To forestall her disappointment, he spun her around and swatted her tight fanny. "Now get out of here, *muchacha!*"

Marta yelped, but scampered up the path, looking back several times. Félix waited till she was out of sight, then followed slowly, mired now in familiar self-pity. He was back where he'd been too many times before—full of improbable dreams, waiting for a big break that never came.

The same euphoric cycle had played out years earlier at a Caracas bodybuilding gym, Los Gigantes in Chacaito. When he wasn't wet-nursing new members, swabbing the locker room, or reracking dumbbells, Félix managed to squeeze in some of his own training—and made solid gains. One morning a visiting IFBB bodybuilder dropped in before a local posing exhibition. The ageless Jamaican with dreadlocks, twenty-inch arms, and a booming baritone announced that Félix had "damn good genetics," "damn good potential," and ought to train for the pro circuit. The rewards described were mouth-watering—international appearances, endorsement fees, freaky women, even movie contracts, like Arnold and Ferrigno got. Before leaving Caracas, the Jamaican jotted down a crash bulk-up program. Félix lasted exactly one gung-ho week before giving it up. The workouts weren't the problem. There was just no way he could afford the protein, enzyme, and vitamin supplementation, let alone the expensive injections. In fact, Félix couldn't even afford a fucking *dentista* to fix his rotten teeth.

But, in a last-ditch attempt to follow the Jamaican's blueprint, he'd approached several club members with the idea of their sponsoring him for a few months in exchange for a percentage of later earnings. When one of them complained to the club's owner about being harassed, Félix promptly found himself out on the pavement beside his gym bag.

Even then, Félix hadn't completely abandoned his dreams. So maybe he couldn't get huge on liquid protein and Dianabol. He could still work on his "cuts"—increase his definition and vascularity. And he found a job that let him do exactly that. He got

himself hired by a distant relative—Arquimedeo Laya López—
at an archaeological site deep in the Territorio Federal Amazonas
near the confluence of the Orinoco and the Cataniapo rivers. For
the next several months, Félix had labored beside bare-assed
Makiritare Indians, digging mud and sifting silt, looking for ancient flake-scrapers. The wages were a joke, but the spadework
thickened his delts and lats, the endless twisting and spilling of
shovelfuls ripped his intercostals and obliques, and the equatorial sun baked his hide nearly as dark as the Jamaican's. Even
the Spartan rations did their part, helping to burn off body fat.
In three agonizing months, Félix turned himself into a bronzed
anatomy lesson. Then he quit the dig and hitched a mail plane
back to civilization just in time for the Mr. Caracas contest—
where he got blown out in the prejudging by a stageful of steroid
monsters.

That was the end of Félix Rosales' bodybuilding career.

Somehow he'd picked himself up. Tried some odd jobs, and
some downright bizarre. He even auditioned as a porno actor,
but quit when his debut required him to be suspended from
ceiling hooks and flogged by a flabby Brazilian dominatrix in
Nazi garb.

Totally out of funds but rich in self-contempt, he'd finally
hitchhiked back to the jungle—where he caught the only solid
break in his life. Arquimedeo not only rehired him, but took
him along on subsequent digs, encouraging him, meanwhile, to
begin some basic coursework in archaeology, anthropology, and
paleontology.

Now, several years, maybe a dozen courses and a half dozen
expeditions later, a degree was nowhere in view; but under Arqui's patronage, Félix had advanced steadily from assistant digger
to digger to field supervisor. He was confident of his skills in
the camp environment, and he liked showing the ropes to the
amateur and student volunteers—especially the girls. As a class,
these were far from attractive; many tended to look like Marta
Mendes, and many worse. But there were always a few acceptable
ones. And even after squatting and troweling all day in the
trenches, one or two always seemed willing to volunteer for
hammock or sleeping-bag duty.

Félix still had no real passion for archaeology. But this was far
from the worst job he'd ever had, and he had considered himself

reasonably content. Until two days ago, that is, when Jacqueline Lee had stepped out of her father's Land Cruiser and reawakened all his adolescent fantasies.

Félix had now reached the main tent area beyond the rockfall. Through a gap between the larger work tents, he glimpsed Marta Mendes in a huddle with the two *lesbias.* Was Marta gossiping about *him,* telling those two man-haters how she'd found him staring after the departing rich girl? But what did it matter? Let those *putas* think what they liked.

Okay, so maybe he should have made a decisive move on Jacqueline yesterday in his truck, when Sam wasn't around. But he hadn't, dammit, so now it was time for him to make a move for himself—or spend the rest of his life as chief flunky to Arquimedeo the Great. And, as usual, Félix had a half-assed plan in mind.

He'd actually thought it up yesterday, on the droning flight back from Canaima. But he'd set it aside as being too risky. Besides, even if he pulled it off, it would definitely screw his chances with Jacqueline. Now, with the millionaire's daughter apparently galloping out of his life, what did he really have to lose? His fucking scientific career?

He pushed into the largest tent and closed the flap behind him. It was empty, as expected. Arquimedeo would be on the East Hill another hour or two, showing some of the newcomers how to sink pairs of electrical probes into the ground and measure the resistance between them. Félix ducked under the long worktable and pulled out the single sideband radio that was stowed right beside Arqui's ammo case. The SSB radio was wired to an antenna mast lashed to the tentpole, and its hundred twenty-five watts fed off the Honda generator just outside. Félix powered up, keyed the microphone, and pressed the presets for the standby frequency of a twenty-four-hour operator at Simón Bolívar University in Caracas.

When the woman came on, Félix gave her a Ciudad Guayana telephone exchange, the one Jacqueline had used last night when Félix had helped patch her through to her father's yacht. Then he waited, feeling his thigh muscles bunch and knot, the sweat trickle down his sides and between his pecs. There was still time to abort. Even if someone walked in on him—even if it was

Arqui—Félix could say he was just ordering supplies. But the number was ringing now. Once . . . twice . . .

A man answered: "Hello?" A *norteamericano*.

"Mr. Duk-Won Lee, please." Félix's voice sounded a little shaky. But he was committed now.

"Who is this?"

"An archaeologist on Cerro Calvario. Tell Mr. Lee it's urgent."

"I'm afraid Mr. Lee is in an important meeting."

"What I tell him will change his plans. It is about the mining of Cerro Calvario."

"You can tell me, and I'll tell him."

"Please—I must talk to Mr. Lee. No one else."

"Okay. Wait a minute."

Félix's palm was wet now, coating the microphone he was clenching. His heartbeat felt jerky. There was a vertiginous feeling in his stomach, like the way he'd felt in Sam's plane, watching Angel Falls plummet down the cliffside of Auyán Tepui into the yawning depths of Devil's Canyon. He could still back out of this. He could still—

The radio's speaker crackled into life, and a voice growled at him:

"Hello? Is this Dr. Laya? This is D. W. Lee. What do you want?"

Félix hesitated an instant, then words tumbled out:

"No, Mr. Lee. This is not Dr. Laya. This is his assistant, Félix Rosales. We met two days ago, on Cerro Calvario. I have something urgent to tell you."

16

"How do I look?" Jacqueline Lee asked Sam Warrender as they walked their horses down the winding flank of Cerro Calvario.

"Terrific. Of course, you're the first female *llanero* I've seen." He'd just presented her a ranch hat tufted with red feathers from a *gavilán*, or sparrow hawk. After some tugging on her part, the brim now haloed her grinning face. "Your hat size is a wee bit larger than I figured."

"It's my massive brain," she said with a mock sigh. "I try to minimize it, but there you are."

The quip probably conveyed more than a little truth, Sam thought. He knew, from her father's occasional boasts, of Jacqueline's academic prowess, though D.W. lamented her frequent switching—not only of majors, but universities. And assuming Félix Rosales somewhat indicative of her taste in men, Sam could picture her being drawn to collegiate jock types and having consequently to blunt her natural wit and edit her showy vocabulary. Sam had observed her doing precisely this with Félix. But then maybe she did the same thing with Sam himself. The embarrassing thought caused him to chuckle softly.

"What was that Mephistophelian rumble?"

"Just speculating. Actually, I think you just cleared up my quandary. You obviously assume a weather-beaten Okie like me knows who Mephistopheles was. Or maybe you just figure I've made a few Faustian bargains in my time."

"Actually, Sam, the girl didn't give it that much thought. Her mouth opens, and—lo!—words fly out."

"Well, I choose to be flattered. By the way, Jacqueline, if I forgot to mention it on the phone, I'm delighted you came along, especially after our little set-to at the ranch. And before we go any farther here, I want you to know I'm not doing this to keep an eye on daddy's little girl."

"Clarification accepted. And appreciated."

"Okay. Now, where'd you learn to sit a horse? Miss Hepplewhite's Equestrienne Academy, was it?"

"Something like that. How'd you know? Am I sitting funny?"

"You're doing just fine. The night I met your dad—that would be in Oman, back in '83—he showed me a picture of you on horseback, beaming and holding a big blue ribbon. You were in one of those short-stirrup, English saddles, with your knees up."

"That's the way we gentlefolk were taught to ride, I'll have you know."

"Absolutely. Wouldn't want our future debutantes posting and cantering and doing dressage, or whatever it is, in one of these big stock saddles. Those leather postage stamps work fine for that horse-show stuff. But if you're going to be bouncing around all day across cattle country, now that's another matter."

"Oh, fooh! Is that all we're going to be doing—cowpoking along? I was hoping to have a chance to shift this little pinto into high gear."

"I'm afraid Esmeralda there doesn't have that many gaits. She's an Appaloosa, by the way, not a pinto. The way you tell is by all those little brown spots on her rump."

"Got it. And now maybe you'll explain why you've got plain old stirrups, and I have these fancy leather whatchamacallems?"

"*Tapaderos*. Taps for short. They're just stirrup hoods to keep your feet from slipping through—though Enrico has *llaneros* who ride barefoot. Anyway, I didn't have time to order you a pair of high-heel boots."

"You seem to think of everything."

"I try."

The spiral track leveled out, leading to the Proteus gatehouse and the paved north-south road. But Sam swung his big chestnut gelding in the opposite direction, walking west alongside a tall steel-mesh fence topped by concertina wire.

"Where are we going, Sam?"

"There's a sort of postern gate along here, which opens onto the rangeland." After a moment, Sam dismounted, walked to a padlocked hasp, and fished out a key. Then he froze while his eyes swept a brow of rock a hundred yards to their left.

"*Quién anda allí?*" Sam yelled out. "Show yourself!"

A man rose up slowly from the rocks. Sam made out a faded red shirt, a darker red headband, gray beard and mustache, and dangling binoculars. It must have been the lenses flashing back the westering sun that Sam had seen. But what caught his eye now was a holster-sized hip bulge. The man waved—and ducked down again.

Sam turned to Jacqueline, who had waved in response. "You know that guy?"

"I forget his name, but he's Arquimedeo's uncle or something. He got himself hired as a security guard. Looters and treasure hunters are apparently a legitimate concern around digs."

"Maybe so." Sam indicated the high, barbed-wire barrier. "But the company already strung this perimeter fence and put on a couple armed guards around the clock. Dr. Laya doesn't need to be hiring old guys with guns."

"I think he's pretty harmless, Sam. What happened, I gather, is that Arquimedeo caved in to family pressures to hire him. It turns out even Félix is some kind of relative."

"Well, I better let our guards know there's a harmless old fart roaming around up there with a sidearm. I don't want them running into any nasty surprises on their patrols."

Oscar Azarias Rivilla watched the white-haired man latch the swinging gate, then mount up again beside the black-haired girl. So, there was a back door to the property, a way to bypass the Proteus guardhouse. To use it, of course, one would need a key to that padlock—or good bolt-cutters. And with a pair of those, one could open the barbed-wire anywhere one chose. All in all, Oscar decided, the scrap of information was of minimal value. He filed it in memory among other vagrant, possibly useful items.

He lifted the binoculars and watched the two ride into the rolling savanna. The *anglo* was unknown to him, but he had made it his business to find out about the girl. She was the daughter of a very wealthy man, Señor Lee, the president of Proteus Industries. This information, too, Oscar had filed away, with a higher priority.

Not that he was planning anything. Not at all. With Oscar it was simply a process of selective observation that never really got switched off. One went to the store to purchase beer and cigarettes, nothing more. All the same, one could not help noticing where the cash was kept, and what quantity was likely to be there at any one time, and who looked after it, and with what caliber of weapon, and how many exits were available.

For now, of course, the prudent plan was to content himself with the measly wage Arquimedeo was offering. Oscar needed a place to stay and a little something in his pockets. But was it not incredible, after less than a full day on this godforsaken job, to discover a capitalist princess almost under one's nose—here in the Guayana bush, more or less on her own? What might such a prize fetch at auction, especially if her father was to open the bidding? The prospect was alluring, considering the pittance Oscar was being paid.

Amazingly, the presence of this girl had now all but convinced Oscar to split that pittance with two Kamarakota Indian brothers he had met in a *cantina* the previous night in San Félix. After all, with his bedroll and meals already provided, four thousand *bolívars* a month wasn't that much less than eight. Oscar could give the brothers two thousand each, perhaps less, and thereby free himself from the daily necessity of guarding the camp, or even appearing to do so. At the same time he would be securing two very capable helpers, should a profitable course of action suggest itself.

These issues swirled in his mind as he refocused the binoculars. They were exceptionally good—rubber-coated Nikons, liberated from a Nissan Stanza in the big company lot of Venalum, the Venezuelan-Japanese aluminum consortium in Puerto Ordaz. The seven-power optics showed the mounted figures side by side, seemingly motionless against the afternoon horizon. The man was nothing to watch, a *norteamericano* as old, perhaps, as Oscar himself. But the girl was a circus for the eyes. Her shiny mane tossed in syncopation with the horsetails, while her pear-shaped, tight-jeaned *nalgas* moved up and down, up and down, just skimming the saddle. And now her arm fluttered in the air. Was she pointing out something, or merely being theatrical?

Oscar smiled. She reminded him of one of the girls Carlos Lehder had kept on his island in the Exumas. Not Chocolata or Liliana, but the oriental one, with the flower-petal features. Of course, all those *putas* had been kept constantly coked, and their spirits had been broken. Not this bright creature. She had never been broken, not all the way. Oscar watched her out of sight.

"So now we're on the Warrender Ranch. Just how big is it, Sam?"

"Hato la Promesa isn't all mine, by any means. I've got several partners. And Enrico's got a stake in it, too. It's about, oh, twenty-four hundred hectares."

"Help me out. I'm not that good with metrics."

"Just testing. That's roughly six thousand acres, or what we'd call back in Oklahoma ten sections of land. Say fifty miles of barbed wire. We run about two thousand head. Originally it was part of a much larger cattle ranch, Hato la Vergareña, which begins south of here off Route Sixteen by La Paragua. Back in the early fifties, an American industrialist got the ruling junta to sell him almost a half million acres, and he cleared several thousand for livestock."

"Who was he, the American?"

"Daniel Ludwig. The world's richest man—at the time."

"Isn't he the same man who started raping the Amazon rain forest?"

Sam chuckled. "You heard about that, eh? Must have been one of those PBS documentaries."

"It's not a joke, Sam."

"No, it was a pretty thorough debacle, all right. Not only ecologically—for the planet, I guess you'd say—but financially for Ludwig. Cost him a good chunk of his fortune by the time he bailed out. He burned millions of acres of Brazilian jungle just to plant some exotic African trees, basically for pulpwood, only they never grew a goddamn.

"But his La Vergareña ranch worked pretty well. Venezuela's cattle ranches are mostly up in the *llanos*. Those are the grasslands north and west of the Orinoco. But when U.S. Steel found iron ore on Cerro Bolívar, Ludwig decided to try and grow cattle down here, so he could supply the construction crews and miners. And Big Steel sweetened the deal as I recall, giving him concessions to haul a lot of the ore down the Orinoco in his ships. But the risk paid off nicely down here. Once the land was cleared and his access problems got solved, it turned out the savanna made even better cattle country than the *llanos*. And we don't get the droughts and floods like they do up north. From June to September, those *llaneros* up there use little flat-bottomed boats to round up their strays."

"Then you're actually going Ludwig one better with Cerro Calvario, aren't you? I mean, you'll *produce* the iron, plus sell your workers beef from your ranch?"

"Guess maybe I should have brought my lawyer along, to defend myself."

"I'm not saying it's wrong, Sam. I only meant—"

"The fact is, Jake, Proteus only found ore on Cerro Calvario because I was already down here and told our geologists to look for it there, and look deep. And believe me, I wasn't thinking about ways to broaden my cattle business. But forget all that. There's actually something else about this whole deal I want to talk to you about."

Jacqueline gave him a dismal look. "Maybe you shouldn't. All I want is to have a really good time with you today, okay? Let's not argue. Because, believe me, Sam, there's no way you're changing my mind."

"What about *my* mind?"

"What about it?"

"Can't I change it?"

She eyed him sharply. "I don't know. Can you?"

"Guess I already have." He slowed his horse to an amble, and she dropped back alongside. "I flew down here intending to kick Dr. Laya's butt off the mountain, along with his broken pottery. Same reason your dad sailed up the Orinoco. Only I made the mistake of taking a look at what he's doing up there first, what he's found so far. And what I saw changed my mind." He shrugged. "Simple as that."

"You're saying you actually want Arquimedeo to continue his work, and you'll stop the mining in the meantime?"

"Right. Until he's satisfied there's nothing more to find. Like he says, the ore's still gonna be there when he's finished. But suppose he discovers something—oh, I don't know, like petroglyphs, or cave paintings, something that can't be moved. Then we try and work around it, or we write off the iron altogether. That clear enough?"

"Sam, when did you decide all this?"

"When I was snooping around up there. Ask your dad. I told him at the time. I know he thinks I've gone wacko or senile, or both. You may have noticed we're sort of estranged at the moment."

"But why didn't you say anything yesterday, instead of letting Félix and me make all those nasty little remarks about bulldozing everything in sight?"

"I almost did. I guess I wanted to get you alone—before I bared my soul."

Sam grinned at her, then glanced away self-consciously, focusing on the horizon. A moment later he felt his gelding jostled by her mare, heard the creak of saddle leather, then felt her arm snake around his middle. He turned slowly.

Jacqueline was leaning far over toward him, her young face inches away. He had a split second to read her intentions and react. He turned his cheek, presenting it to be pecked. But Jacqueline had other ideas. The brim of her hat slid under his, while her lips pursued, then pressed fiercely against his. There was nothing friendly about it, and it hit Sam like a mule kick.

17

Sam started to lean into the kiss. Then, by an access of will, he extricated himself and caught his breath. As they jogged along together, he regarded the young woman warily—and wondrously.

And Jacqueline stared right back. *Unrepentant* was the word to describe that look, Sam thought. Various reactions flashed to mind. They ranged from avuncular indulgence to stodgy reproof—all embarrassingly inappropriate. And while he was debating his response, she spoke:

"Sam, I don't want you to get the wrong idea, okay? I mean, I hope you don't think I kissed you to influence corporate policy or anything, okay? Because I didn't. I kissed you because—"

"Whoa!" Sam held up a palm. "There's no need for you to be telling me—you know, whatever it is. And less need for me to hear it. And Hector here would appreciate it if you'd keep Esmeralda from crowding in on him. He doesn't see too good out that eye, and he gets kinda jittery when he gets blindsided. Now, as far as you and I are concerned, the best thing all around, I think, is to go back to what we were talking about before whatever happened, happened."

"You mean pretend 'whatever happened' *didn't* happen? That's called denial, Sam."

"Now you got it," he said with a grin. "Trust me on this, Jake. Now, what the hell were we talking about?"

She sighed theatrically. "Politics? Changing your mind? My dad thinking you're wacko?"

"Much obliged. Now, I was getting ready to say, if D.W. wants to go to the mat on this—and I think that's the way to bet—we could have a hell of a fight on our hands. Time was when the board pretty much did whatever I told 'em to do. But like it or not, those days are gone. I still oughta be able to swing enough votes to win a showdown on this. But I wouldn't bet the ranch on it. There's too much involved here, for us and the Venezuelans. You follow?"

"Don't worry, I'm listening. And I'm more optimistic than I was five minutes ago. I mean, I thought it was strictly Arquimedeo against the world, including Sam Warrender. But speaking of the Venezuelans, what about them? I mean, they did vote to suspend mining."

"True. But, by my guesstimate, only three members of the Council of Ministers are still solidly behind suspension—Culture, Information, and Environment. The rest are either for resumption or are up for grabs, and the president's chief of staff used to be Energy Minister, so we know which way he's voting. I figure D.W. doesn't have too many arms to twist—or palms to grease."

"Arquimedeo says the way things usually get done down here, they could combine all those ministries into one big one and call it the Ministry of Corruption."

"There is, unfortunately, more than a grain of truth in that."

"So, the situation is basically hopeless?"

"No, but let's say the odds aren't good, and things could get nasty. My point is, there's no sense in your getting caught in the crossfire, especially between me and your dad. So far D.W. has been doing exactly the job I hired him to do. *I'm* the guy who's got to take him on, not you, savvy?"

"Don't worry about me and Daddy. We've butted heads on stuff like this for years, Sam. Eventually he calms down and everything is fine between us. Of course, he's still wrong."

"But you forgive him?"

"Eventually." She smiled. "For instance, you're not going to believe this, but guess who's going to hostess D.W.'s shipboard party tomorrow night."

"Not you?"

"I promised him days ago, before I learned the real situation on Cerro Calvario. And I'm going through with it. We'll call a ludicrous truce for one night. You're going to be there, I take it?"

"I wouldn't miss it for anything now. So far I've mostly seen you in blue jeans."

"Well, tomorrow you'll see me in my Dior black strapless, smiling till my dimples ache, at all those ministers you were just talking about, plus their wives and mistresses or whatever. Daddy's planning a real blowout. But God, Sam, wouldn't it be delicious to smuggle one of those lipstick-sized videocameras in my purse—the kind FBI guys use on sting operations—and get it all for my documentary—you know, like in *Roger and Me*? Oh, don't make ugly faces, Sam. I'm only kidding. But I will take careful mental notes. And what will you be doing?"

"At some point, I expect I'll be trying to talk sense to D.W."

"Well, as someone once said, it should be a bumpy night."

"Bette Davis, right?"

"Very good, Sam! I seem to remember Daddy telling me you only liked cowboy movies."

"Well, if you want to update your file, put in there that I sometimes watch the old black-and-whites, like at three in the morning. Beats staring at the ceiling, fighting insomnia and, you know, the usual middle-aged angst."

"My, my! Sam, are you trying to dazzle me with your vocabulary?"

"Maybe just a tad. Truth is, I am kind of partial to John Wayne movies."

Throughout this diversionary dialogue, Sam had been thinking more or less nonstop about the topic he had ruled out of bounds. He wondered, for instance, what had or had not happened between Jake and Félix, and if today's outing and its little amorous surprise had been engineered with an eye toward exciting Félix's jealousy.

In any case, Sam remained on guard as they slow-walked their mounts onto a rounded bulge of exfoliated rock. The outcrop,

Sam explained, was one of many in the savanna known as *lajas*—Cerro Calvario being a rather larger example—rust-colored crowns carved and contoured over millennia by rain and wind.

From the modest summit, Sam showed her part of the herd grazing in the distance, and a lone horseman working the fringes. Then he dug in a saddlebag and tossed her a plastic bottle of Andean mineral water, opening one for himself.

"So tell me, Sam," Jacqueline asked, gesturing at the landscape, "with no mine workers next door, who're you going to sell your beef to?"

"That's Enrico's problem, and he doesn't seem to be particularly worried. Lately, though, he's been talking about turning the place into one of those fancy dude ranches. Hato Doña Bárbara over in the *llanos* is already doing it, he says. And there are ranches in the Argentine *pampas* that cater to polo players. What we'd do, I gather, is add a wing to the *casa grande*, use the airstrip for flyovers of Angel Falls and day trips to Canaima. If things work out, we could throw in archaeological tours of Cerro Calvario. What do you think?"

"I think you're putting me on."

"Maybe a little. I really don't want to come down here and find he's rented my bedroom to three guys from Düsseldorf on holiday. But tell me something about your filming. Can you really make a documentary with only a camcorder? Don't you need professional equipment?"

"That depends. Without a crew, the eight-millimeter Handycam is really the best way to go. If I had my sixteen-millimeter Arri, I'd also need a sound tech with a Nagra—or one of those DAT recorders synched to the camera with a time code. But actually a lot of terrific Gulf War footage was shot in Sony Hi8. You can detect scan lines if you transfer it to sixteen-millimeter or thirty-five film, but it's done all the time."

"Okay. But if you change your mind and need something, give me a list. I can scrounge stuff in Caracas and get it flown down overnight."

"Thanks, Sam. I appreciate the offer."

It dawned on Sam that she was smiling at him too long—and he at her. He broke the spell with vintage flatland twang: "Reckon we oughta be gettin' you back, missy, afore the sun gets any lower." With this, he laid the right rein against his horse's neck, and the big gelding swung obediently left, planting its shod hoofs gingerly as it descended the sloping rock.

Jake followed, calling out from behind, "Coward."

There was no further dialogue for several minutes as they pursued their elongated shadows over the brushy ground. Then, entering a dry arroyo, they came upon a dozen light-colored, humpbacked cattle—strays—with several calves strung out behind.

Jacqueline remarked that they looked like rodeo bulls. Sam explained they were indeed Brahmas, or zebus—a breed that old man Ludwig had imported from India, figuring, correctly, that they'd handle the tropical climate better than other breeds. It was about this point that he glanced over and saw that he'd lost her.

"Sorry about that," he said. "Sometimes I forget cattle breeding isn't the most fascinating subject in the world, except to other breeders."

"No, *I'm* sorry, Sam. I guess my mind was wandering."

"Where to—or should I ask?"

"I was thinking about you, if you must know."

"That's what I was afraid of."

"Daddy told me you have a daughter my age."

"Couple years older, actually."

"What's her name?"

"Teresa. A lovely girl—or woman, I should say. She'll be twenty-five in December."

"Do you see her often?"

"Often as I can. What else did D.W. tell you about her?"

"Only that you and her mother never married."

He shrugged.

"I'm just curious, Sam. You don't have to talk about it."

"I don't mind. I was going to propose once. María Elisa stopped me—that's Teresa's mother. She knew I was just trying to do the right thing. Showed a lot more sense than I did. It wouldn't have worked."

"And Teresa, what's she like?"

"In some ways like you—proud and independent. Which is also like her mother. But she's much more creative than either María or me. Teresa's good at all kinds of things. She got her fine-arts degree in painting and ceramics. She's a teaching assistant at UNM in Albuquerque, working on her MFA and studying with some Indian potters at local pueblos. And dating the assistant basketball coach, last I heard. Nice guy." Sam grinned. "Thinks I'm a small-time rancher over Oklahoma way. Teresa's still not ready for her friends to know too much about her disreputable old dad. Says it'll screw up her social life."

"It can, believe me. I mean, D.W.'s been a great dad, and I've had so many advantages in life thanks to him, and he knows I'm grateful, and proud of all he's achieved—I mean, after coming here as a war orphan and all. But honestly, Sam, it can be a royal pain sometimes."

"What can I say? Change your name and move to Albuquerque."

"Do you have a picture of her?"

"Just might." He sidled Hector over, took out his wallet, handed her a snapshot.

She studied it intently. "She's lovely, like you said."

"Like her mom." He showed her one of María Elisa at twenty-five, one reduced from a studio portrait.

"She looks like a saint."

Sam chuckled. "Santa María. She has a few livelier moods, believe me. I'd guess that was taken around the year you were born."

"Where is she now?"

"In Albuquerque, too. She has a New Mex-Mex restaurant over there—María's Cocina. Sopaipillas, posole, green-chili stew, blue-corn tortillas. I get hungry just thinking about it."

Jacqueline handed back the photos, but held her Appaloosa alongside. "All those years since María. Why didn't you ever remarry?"

"Funny, Enrico is always asking the same question. He's still got a couple candidates in mind."

"Seriously, Sam."

"Seriously? There've been a couple—well, close calls, I'd guess you'd say."

"What happened?"

"What *didn't* happen, you mean? Probably the same as with your dad. Why hasn't he remarried?"

"I'm asking *you*."

Sam shifted in his saddle. "Well, without going into lurid detail, the first one was *real* close—actually one of the reasons María took off with Teresa and moved to New Mexico. For a while there the lady and I even made the Tulsa society pages. And she would have been the perfect wife, in the corporate sense. Maybe in a lot of other ways. Number two was pretty much the same deal. But both would have tamed me some, I could see that coming. I wouldn't have been able to do a lot of the damn-fool stuff I seem to like to do. Fly down here at a moment's notice. Hang out with Enrico. Go on an afternoon ride like this, at the drop of a hat. In short, my secret adolescence would have been"—he drew a finger across his throat—"cut short."

"A strategic mistake," Jacqueline said emphatically. "They shouldn't have tried to change that in you. You're obviously not ready to let go of the little-boy side of you. Know how I know?"

"Let's see. Could it be because I went snooping around the dig, pretending to be a ranchhand? I mean, some folks might say that's not the way CEOs of Fortune 500 companies are supposed to act."

"I was thinking more about your almost chasing me into Canaima Lagoon in your jeans—just because I kicked sand in your face. And what about the water fight, and grabbing my legs and pulling me under? That wasn't what you'd call real mature behavior, now was it, Big Sam? Hmm?"

Their horses were suddenly close enough to rub flanks and nuzzle each other. And Jake was even closer.

"No," Sam answered after a blank moment. "You have a point there."

They met halfway this time, with a dizzy-making impact. Sam had almost forgotten it could be like that. It took him back to that first falling-into-his-arms kiss with María Elisa—then all the way back to high school and octopus clinches with Suzie O'Malley in his toy-sized '49 Nash, pre-orgasmic kisses that somehow lasted all night. Ironically, never once had Sam experienced this implosive ferocity with the woman he'd married, Caroline Lindquist—she of the breathtaking profile, cool passions, and muted climaxes. What a terrible waste!

Slowly their lips disengaged, and Sam opened his eyes. Jacqueline Lee filled his vision, studying him with a kind of fierce tenderness. Her ranch hat had departed. Sam saw it out of the

Daniel Pollock

corner of his eye, skimming the brush twenty feet behind her. Jacqueline frowned at his wandering gaze and promptly refocused it on herself—taking his face in her hands, then smoothing her palms down his stubbled cheeks, drawing their lips slowly back together . . .

Until Hector stamped his hooves, snorted, and sidestepped. And suddenly they were grabbing their saddle horns to keep from tumbling into the widening breach between them.

Which triggered much laughter and blew off accumulated tension. Which also gave Sam a chance to catch his breath—and Jake to retrieve her cartwheeling hat. But she accomplished this swiftly and wheeled around with a purposeful look in her eye. Sam knew he damn well wasn't ready for what was going to happen next and ought to do something decisive and take advantage of Hector's fitful interruption. Instead, he chose cowardice—and spurred his gelding into an abrupt canter.

But Jacqueline's horse had a running start and in no time at all was loping alongside, while her rider posted easily in the saddle and threw Sam a look of complete nonchalance. She really was a skillful horsewoman—grasping the reins lightly as she pinched the Appaloosa's sides with her legs and braced her feet in the stirrups. But Sam decided to test her further. He urged Hector into a gallop and was surprised to see the usually sluggish Esmeralda move right with him, while Jacqueline bent forward over her neck. For maybe half a minute they went hell for leather, pounding across the savanna, dodging and flashing between the scrubby trees. Gradually, then, they shifted down to an easy trot, letting themselves and their mounts get their wind back.

"Looks like you can't escape me," Jacqueline said, leaning back against the cantle and grinning over at him.

"That presupposes I was trying to escape."

"Sam, aren't you being a little childish?"

"I'm trying my damnedest *not* to be childish. What you're being, on the other hand, is naughty. And you'd better be careful. If you'll look ahead, you'll see Cerro Calvario is just ahead. Félix could be up there somewhere, watching us at this very moment."

"I don't care *who* sees us. Anyway, it's none of his damn business."

"Hmm. Do I detect a little anger at Félix? That wouldn't have anything to do with what happened today, would it?"

114

"That's a really rotten thing to say, Sam!"

"I have this rotten streak."

"If you ask me, it sounds like you're jealous of Félix."

"Oh, for God's sake, Jake."

"And I really should make you pay for it—by teasing you unmercifully about him. But I won't. Félix is a hunk, okay? Conan the Archaeologist. And from what I hear, he's a real stud, too. But alas, like a lot of beautiful boys, he's been going steady with himself for too long. And it's not exactly a secret love affair. Am I making you feel any better? Let's see, what have I forgotten? Shall we discuss his *mind?* His cultural literacy—outside of archaeology and geology and bench pressing? Believe me, Sam, I've had several boyfriends just like him. Want to hear about them?"

"No, thanks. I didn't really want to hear about Félix."

"Liar."

"Now, Jacqueline, you go easy on me."

"Only if you promise not to bring up Félix again. And I'm just teasing about all the boyfriends. There haven't been that many. I'm not really a wild child, Sam. I just talk big."

"It's not your talk that worries me, Jake, believe me."

On the other side of the border fence, they walked their horses back toward the access road, sharing another long silence. An unresolved question hovered between them, looming larger—exactly as though they were two teenagers driving home after a first date. How would they say good-bye? Sam was disgusted to catch himself seriously pondering such a juvenile issue. When the time came, he would damn well handle it and stop all the foolishness. The trouble was, the tactile memory of their previous kisses kept replaying itself, undermining his resolve.

Luckily, the problem was solved for him. Halfway to the road, a *bandido* figure stepped out from behind a small tree. It was the old bearded man with the holstered sidearm—Arquimedeo's uncle. He was grinning.

"*Buenas tardes!* Señorita Lee, here is the truck to take you back to the camp, and your supper." He gestured farther on, and in the shadows beside the barbed-wire fence they saw the rusted hood of Félix's old pickup, with a head and wide shoulders silhouetted behind the wheel.

Jacqueline glanced at Sam, and they dismounted together. She handed him the Appaloosa's reins. They stood in silence a moment, while the horses nibbled saw grass and swished flies with their tails. Then Jacqueline smiled.

"Don't worry, I'll let you off this time." Then: "So long, Sam. I had a wonderful afternoon."

"So did I." And he thought, *a little too wonderful.*

"See you tomorrow night, Sam."

"Right. *Hasta mañana.*"

And between now and then, Sam intended to do some hard thinking about what had happened between them. Think about it, savor it, then kill it dead.

Jacqueline set off toward the waiting truck, then swung around on the path and flashed her best little-girl smile:

"And thanks for the hat!"

18

Nearing noon of the following day, Oscar Azarias drove his dilapidated pickup south on Route 16 through watery chaos. He had hoped to complete his early-morning business at Guri Lake and be back at Cerro Calvario before the rain clouds opened their dark bellies. Instead, he now wrestled his scrapyard 1950 Dodge half-ton through a swirling maelstrom, fighting to keep the slick tires from skidding off the flooded two-lane blacktop into the swampy shoulder.

To intensify his ordeal, the midday deluge not only hammered the cab's tinny roof, but trickled steadily down through rust holes, soaking the back of Oscar's neck, both pantlegs, and the decomposing upholstery of the old bench seat. And this wasn't the worst of it. The wiper motor had shorted out, so the pitted, two-section windshield was now a streaming silver curtain. Oscar was forced to supplement his dangerously impaired vision by cranking down the window and sticking out his grizzled head, drenching himself in the process.

Despite all this, he'd managed to catch up to a laboring Alcasa flatbed stacked high with aluminum ingots. CARGA LARGA warned the big bumper sign—WIDE LOAD. Oscar figured he'd tag along in its wake till the torrent abated. But the damn truck was crawling up easy grades, belching black diesel clouds, and throwing spray from its rear duals.

Oscar waited till they'd crested a small hill, then popped his head out. The wide load completely blocked his vision of on-coming traffic. So he eased out little by little, peeking around, but the obscurity was impenetrable. Finally, in frustration, he yanked the wheel over, committing himself to pass. But the instant he was exposed, he thought he saw *something* out there in the murk ahead.

Hija de la chingada!

Oscar stomped the pedal flat to the fire wall, squeezing every-thing he could from the old flathead six to overtake the long flatbed, while his fate rushed to overtake him. A breath-holding eternity later, he swerved and skidded the Dodge back into the right lane, just as a Lagoven petroleum tanker thundered past, its wind-rip nearly buffeting him off the road.

Oscar sagged back against the exposed springs. Just then, out the window, a roadside shrine flashed by—a doghouse-sized *ca-pilla*, chapel, topped by a cross. Venezuela's highways were dot-ted with these macabre reminders, erected by family members to mark the spot where a loved one had been killed, and to provide temporary shelter for the departed soul. If that tanker had been a split second earlier, Oscar thought, somebody could plant three more crosses out there.

He glanced to his right. The Kamarakotas were both grinning and sipping their beers. They thought it was funny!

Chucho, the elder, was a squat-bodied elf, with a scraggly haircut and perennial grin to match. He wore a traditional Ven-ezuelan *liki-liki* shirt over untraditional pink Day-Glo baggy shorts, and his bare, horny feet straddled the Dodge's three-speed column shift. His younger half brother, Angel, a massive head taller, was slumped against the opposite door in camouflage pants, flip-flops, and a Ninja Turtle T-shirt. Thick black bangs hung to his eyebrows, and a smile split his usually gloomy Mayan face as he compacted a beer can in his fist, tossed it behind the seat, and reached for another. Oscar began to worry the sup-ply of cold Polars he'd bought at the Guri Lake market wouldn't last the day.

It had taken him an extra half hour to track the Indian brothers down. They weren't waiting on the Hotel Guri terrace where they said they'd be. They were snoring under some oleander bushes across the road. It seemed they'd had a big night. They'd spent half of it turning over rocks with a flashlight and trapping inch-long toads, and the other half out on the lake, one of the world's finest bass-fishing habitats, in an aluminum boat "borrowed" from Guri Bass Camp. No artificial lures and such for the crafty Kamarakotas. They preferred live bait, hooking the toads through the lips, then trolling and drift-fishing the shallows. Their odorous catch was currently wedged in the tool storage area under the bench seat, five plump peacock bass, all in the six-kilo range, iced and wrapped in newspaper.

Oscar was beginning to suspect he'd blundered in recruiting them. When the time came for desperate action, could he rely on these guys? Or would he find them flaked out under a tree or wrapped in a hammock, dead drunk or zonked on native hallucinogens?

In the San Félix *cantina* the other night, under the influence of a great many *cervezas* and a form of raw cocaine called *basuco*, the brothers had seemed formidable. They had boasted of extensive criminal pasts and an eagerness to undertake dangerous things. Little Chucho claimed they had worked briefly for the Ochoa brothers of the Medellín cartel in Mérida State, where Chucho had been a courier and Angel an enforcer. With seeming modesty, Angel pantomimed how he had once cut the throat of a Guardia Nacional soldier. Their prison tattoos tended to authenticate their boasts. Chucho explained he had done five years in Sabaneta penitentiary in Maracaibo for minor trafficking (arrested after having swallowed cocaine-filled condoms), while Angel spent three years in Tocuyito in Valencia (for beating up riot police after a particularly exciting soccer match).

But alcohol-fueled boasts and jailhouse credentials were not enough to remove Oscar's doubts. Could the Kamarakotas follow instructions? Could they even remember instructions? Could they, if the situation called for it, act on their own, without specific orders? These were the qualities of a good soldier—whether in the cartel or the Guardia or the revolutionary cadres of Oscar's youth. And one had only to glance at the brothers now, giggling together and stamping their feet on the truck's broken floorboards, to be deeply concerned.

The old joke Venezuelans told on themselves was that God had endowed their country with every conceivable form of natural wealth—gold, silver, diamonds, pearls, oil, iron, bauxite . . .

the list was truly staggering. Then, as a final and delicious irony, He had created inhabitants too indolent to exploit those riches. This complacency was typical of most Venezuelans, in Oscar's opinion, including himself, but Indians most of all. For them, idleness seemed always the natural state, and work a temporary aberration. They might labor terribly hard on a specific task— making a boat or a blowgun, hunting monkeys or clearing land so their women could plant manioc—but they never let it become habit-forming.

On the other hand, the brothers came cheaply and knew the Sabana. They told Oscar that they had grown up in the Kamarata Valley, east of Auyán Tepui and inaccessible except by small plane or dugout canoe. There, besides their native Indian language, Pemón, they had learned Spanish from the Capuchin friars at the mission school and picked up bits and pieces of a half dozen other languages from adventure tourists who sought out their spectacular valley. A tribal dispute caused the brothers, while still teenagers, to leave their village—forty families dwelling in thatch-and-adobe *churuata* huts near the Kamarata Mission—and paddle a canoe down the Río Caroní to Canaima Camp. There they joined the Indian community, making and hawking souvenirs, driving trams, and barbecuing chickens for tourists. Most of their native brethren seemed quite content with this existence, but Chucho and Angel, for whatever reasons, were not. It was at this point that their future career path suddenly opened. They left Canaima hurriedly one afternoon, vanishing into the bordering jungle with a plastic bag full of watches and wallets entrusted to them by a planeload of Italian tourists who had been about to walk under a waterfall.

Oscar had been intrigued by their history, and particularly by the idea of simply vanishing into the jungle. He had peppered the brothers with questions about the Gran Sabana—how long they thought one might remain undiscovered there; how far and fast one might travel undetected over the network of rivers, depending on the season, rainy or dry; how many people and supplies could be carried in a large *curiara*, or dugout canoe; and so forth.

The practical applications were obvious enough. Of the various plans currently revolving in Oscar's mind, all required a method of escape and a place of retreat. And the Kamarakotas, whatever their shortcomings, obviously possessed considerable skills in both these areas. With them as accomplices, Oscar could start out with his getaway, then tailor the crime to fit.

But all that would have to wait. At the moment, he was fully engaged in keeping the ancient pickup on the road with its battered nose plowing ahead through the downpour. The Indian brothers, meanwhile, had started to chant in Pemón, gradually drowning out the storm with their roaring, plaintive choruses.

Oddly enough, Oscar found the primitive noise comforting. After a few moments, he began to bellow along.

19

A hundred kilometers north in Ciudad Bolívar, Sam Warrender was also watching the downpour, watching it churn the sliding surface of the Orinoco into slate gray froth. The rain was almost heavy enough to qualify as a real Oklahoma frog-strangler, he decided, easing the stifling heat with a brown-bottled *cerveza*.

He was momentarily alone at a table under the large circular shelter of the Mirador Angostura lookout along the Paseo Orinoco, the old city's riverside promenade and arcaded shopping street. Despite the deluge, postnuptial festivities were in full swing around him—the dozens of tables filled, the dance floor congested. Loudspeakers pumped out Eydie Gorme and the Trio Los Panchos' *"Sabor a Mi,"* accompanied by what sounded like a continuous ovation as rain sheeted across the roof. Sam gave the midday monsoon another fifteen minutes. Brassy light was already starting to leak through the gray.

Through the crush, he caught a glimpse of a wiry man in the throes of a cha-cha. It was Enrico, dancing with one of his sisters-in-law. Sam marveled at his friend's all-night stamina. Then, estimating the extent of Enrico's imminent dehydration, he signaled a passing waiter for another round.

The partying had started the evening before at the Hotel Río Orinoco a mile and a half west, after a steam bath of an afternoon wedding in Ciudad Bolívar's colonial hilltop cathedral. The

122

groom was one of Enrico's countless local cousins, and Sam had decided to attend only at the last minute, in hopes of blotting out persistent, cloying thoughts of Miss Jacqueline Lee.

So far the plan had worked. It wasn't easy, after all, to slip into romantic reverie with a percussive hangover and less than three hours sleep. Not that Sam had worked at stupefying himself the night before. It had come about quite naturally. He had made the slight mistake of dancing with one of Enrico's female relatives. The next he knew he was being dragooned onto the floor by one after another, gyrating and perspiring before the amplified shriek like a tormented soul, then staggering back to Enrico's table and more rum punches.

And now, while this fiesta was finally winding down, it was already time to begin girding himself for the next one—D.W.'s shipboard bash a hundred kilometers downriver in Ciudad Guayana this evening. Sam hung out for another half hour with Enrico's family, watching the rain dry up and the afternoon sun come steaming out. Then he lifted a last toast to the bride and groom, danced a final rumba with Enrico's hefty but nimble wife, Romalda, and negotiated a tipsy gauntlet of Venezuelan good-byes—smooches and squeezes and man-to-man *abrazos*.

Enrico had tossed him a set of keys to some poor fool's black Alfa-Romeo Spyder convertible. Sam found it and fired it up, was momentarily intimidated by its pantherine growl, then decided it was just the animal to chew up all those boring kilometers between Ciudad Bolívar and Ciudad Guayana—and maybe clear his throbbing head in the process. He put the top down, let out the clutch, and rocketed back to the hotel. After a cold shower—a good idea made compulsory by a hot-water shortage—he dressed in slacks and sport shirt, grabbed his leather satchel and rented tux, and buckled himself back into the black Alfa.

Once safely beyond the city's impoverished outskirts, where the Avenida Perímetral merged into the four-lane Route 19 highway, he let the Alfa have its head. Suddenly it was like barreling through the American West, across rolling, scrub-dotted rangeland under high-wide blue—except over his left shoulder, where the usual afternoon cloud drift traced the Orinoco. Seeing a cassette protruding from the tape deck, Sam chunked it in, and the Gipsy Kings washed over him with their Spanish guitars, rhythmic hand claps, and flamenco passion. Sam yammered along and slapped the wheel. He felt, for the moment, unassailable.

But forty-five minutes later, as the shining river reappeared on his left and the highway descended into Puerto Ordaz, numbing fatigue had overtaken him again. It would be a hell of a long day, and night, Sam knew. He slowed the Alfa to a sedate snarl through the city's industrial parkland, past turnoffs and distant pluming smokestacks marking the various giant metallurgical enterprises.

Ciudad Guayana was one of the world's fastest-growing industrial centers. It was also, like Brasília, a planned metropolis. And the site had compelling advantages. Within a hundred-kilometer radius were the mines of Cerro Bolívar and El Pao to supply iron ore, and Guri Dam upstream on the Caroní supplying cheap hydroelectric power. Easy access and egress were provided by the Orinoco; with steady dredging, the river was navigable by large ore ships from here to the Atlantic. The laying out had begun in the early sixties, with new commercial districts marching westward from the old port of San Félix at the confluence of the Caroní and Orinoco.

The city planners had deliberately placed the smoke-belching industrial zone at the extreme end, buffering it with a spacious green belt. Beyond this began the high-rise suburb of Alta Vista, a sterile grid of office and apartment towers and tree-lined avenues.

Once through these geometric precincts and the adjacent airport, Sam drove down a long avenue sloping toward the Intercontinental Hotel, then spanning the Río Caroní, a half mile wide here. On the other side was San Félix, the old section where most of the industrial work force lived. Here was familiar South American suburban sprawl—pavement uprooted and overgrown by lush vegetation; asphalt lanes leaving off at graveled or earthen driveways; derelict vehicles; spiderwebbed power lines; banana leaves screening roofs of red pantile or corrugated tin; houses of adobe brick or bright-splashed stucco; and political graffiti everywhere.

From San Félix's main drag, Avenida Guayana, Sam turned left, following the rail line from El Pao, the iron mine fifty kilometers south, state-owned now, but developed in the forties and fifties by Bethlehem Steel. The tracks led toward the river and the ore-loading port of Palúa. Presently Sam saw the familiar harbor skyline of cranes and gantries. He followed the twin rails almost to the waterside, where they vanished into a vast steel-beamed structure.

This was the ore-handling terminal of the Orinoco Mining Company. Here, as Sam had witnessed many times, the long trains were uncoupled, shoved into an automatic dumper where individual cars were turned upside down like toys, and their tonnage spilled into a primary crusher. The ore was crushed several more times, sorted and weighed, then transported over miles of link-belt conveyors to stockpiles or sent cascading into the holds of ore ships. And this was just the El Pao terminus. An even larger operation across the river in Puerto Ordaz processed ore from Cerro Bolívar—and would also process ore from Cerro Calvario, should there ever be any.

But at the moment, Sam was far too weary to concern himself with his industrial impasse. He guided the Alfa between the Ferrominera terminal and a transit shed, nosing out onto the Orinoco quayside. Three ships were strung out along the wharf. To his left, portside snug against the ore-loading dock, was a rust-hulled, Swedish-flagged ore-oil carrier, the *Franz Berwald* out of Göteborg. Judging from the distance between the Plimsoll mark and the waterline, she was waiting to take on cargo.

Straight before him, with gangway lowered to the passenger landing stage used by Orinoco cruise ships, was something fatuously called the *Dreamstar*, a snow white loveboat of Liberian registry and shallow draft, maybe two hundred feet long. Holiday pennants fluttered along the stays, the company ensign flew from the masthead, and next to it the Blue Peter, indicating the *Dreamstar* was getting ready to sail—probably as soon as her passengers got back from their overflight of Angel Falls and a quick splash in Canaima Lagoon.

But the ship Sam was looking for was a couple hundred yards to his right, warped to the old wooden San Félix docks. She was smaller than the other two, but not by that much. The *Kallisto* was a sleek hundred fifty feet and $1.9 million worth of ocean-going pleasurecraft, with a cruising speed of fifteen knots. A hell of a toy, though D.W. did contrive to give the company considerable use of her—in exchange for a generous subsidy.

Sam eased out the Alfa's clutch and rolled along the docks, bumping over embedded crane tracks, toward the Korean-built, steel-hulled motor yacht. He parked alongside, between a party caterers' panel truck and a Japanese pickup, from the back of which a ponytailed, goateed youth was off-loading guitar amps and speakers. Next to it was a blue Proteus Land Cruiser, the one that had brought Jacqueline to Sam's ranch two days before.

Sam glanced from the Proteus truck up to the upper-deck taff-rail, where a kid in sunglasses and Chicago Bulls shirt was tying a string of party lights to the ensign pole. Sam recognized Bernardo, the boy who'd driven Jacqueline around that day. He shouted and waved, and the spiky-haired kid looked down and saluted back. Then Sam hefted his gear and boarded the gangway amidships.

On deck a caterer pushed a trolley past him, and Sam followed him aft to the enclosed afterdeck, where a crew was setting up serving tables and chafing dishes. Across the polished teak, the ponytailed guy now arrived to help another longhair plug in the sound system. D.W. was planning a real blowout, Jacqueline had said. And there would be plenty of room for it once the doors were opened to the main salon adjoining. When the *Kallisto* was quartered in New Orleans, D.W. regularly hosted cocktail parties for fifty or more out on the Mississippi.

Sam drifted forward next into the salon, an art deco effusion of etched glass, mauve carpeting, walnut paneling, and uphol-stery of chocolate leather and suede. At the wet bar a sleepy-eyed bartender was uncrating glassware. Sam glanced at him, then looked forward into the dining salon. Still no D.W. or daughter.

Another wave of dizzy fatigue washed over him as he spun down and around the brass-railed stairway to the lower deck. D.W. had his office down here, off the master stateroom just forward of the four guest staterooms. Sam had started in that direction when D.W.'s office door opened suddenly and Owen Meade shouldered out, effectively blocking the narrow alleyway. Owen turned, saw Sam—and was a split second slow finding his smile.

"Sam, hey, I've been trying to reach you."

"*Buenas tardes*, Owen. What for?"

"To see if you needed a ride. I called the ranch this morning,

126

talked to some woman. She said you'd gone off to a wedding in Ciudad Bolívar. Leastways, I *think* that's what she said. Sometimes my Spanish gets me in trouble."

"No, you got it right this time, Owen. I decided to come early. Sometime before the party, I'll be needing a cabin to change and spruce up in. Right now, though, I'd like a word with D.W. Is he inside?"

"He and Jacqueline are off seeing Llovizna Falls with some folks from Sidor. Since you've got a couple hours, Sam, maybe you'd like to relax? If you don't mind my saying so, you look kinda beat."

Sam's belly laugh echoed off the paneling. "You could say that. Anyway, I'd love to sack out for an hour. Any vacancies?"

"Sure. Take the room all the way back on the left."

"You're forgetting we're aboard ship, Owen. Don't you mean the starboard cabin aft?"

"Right, that's what I meant to say. The door's unlocked—or is it hatch?"

"Door's fine. Thanks. Oh, and I'd like somebody to wake me when D.W. gets back. I need to talk to him before things get crazy topside."

The "cabin" was really a double stateroom, with TV, VCR, burled cabinetry, tiled bath. But Sam had eyes only for the double bed. He closed the door, hung up his tux, dropped his bag. Then, too exhausted even to kick off his shoes, he belly flopped onto the big mattress—and sank right down through its hollow center into a black and bottomless pit.

20

He woke to a cattle stampede—the pounding sound of a large herd on the move. Sam fought his way up out of stupor. His head felt leaden, his heart hollowed-out. But the pounding didn't go away—became, in fact, louder than ever. His brain fumbled with the sound barrage, unable to decode it. Then his eyes focused, and the pieces tumbled suddenly together—the wedding, the drive to D.W.'s ship, sacking out in this stateroom. So, those iron-shod bovines running amok up there were probably party-goers, tattooing a dance floor, which must be directly overhead. In support of this theory, Sam's ear now caught the steady thud of a bass guitar resonating through the ceiling bulkhead.

But if the party was already in full swing, what the hell time was it? And why the hell hadn't Owen Meade awakened him? Sam lurched off the bed, tripped over his leather bag, bounced off the wall, but located the light switch. Several art deco fixtures cast an indirect radiance, yet enough to set Sam's head throbbing. It was dark outside the cabin window. He scanned the room groggily for his watch, found it strapped to his wrist. It was a quarter to nine. He'd slept almost four hours!

He needed a quick jump-start—the old late-for-school routine. He stripped, splashed his face in cold water, brushed his teeth and gargled, electric-shaved, slapped his underarms with deodorant, his cheeks with Royall Lyme, his snowy thatch with military brushes. Then he threw on his studded shirt, monkey suit, cummerbund, and black tie, towel-buffed his patent leathers. Finally he checked the mirror. All things considered, he didn't look too damn bad. He turned out the lights and stepped into the alleyway.

The corridor was congested and noisy, and foul with cigarette smoke. As he eased by a conversing couple, the voguishly emaciated woman looked away from her pomaded male companion and flared her nostrils at Sam. He nodded and kept moving.

He slalomed through more couples on the curving staircase. And the main salon looked to be at or near capacity, a burnished, buzzing pool of humanity that was thrown into immediate ripples by Sam's mere surfacing from below. Heads turned and people began eddying unmistakably in his direction. Though most faces were unfamiliar, he recognized several from previous Venezuelan sojourns. Immediately in front of him, a bald, bull-necked dome revolved to reveal a deputy minister of agriculture, a man Sam had often entertained at La Promesa. Beyond was a vice president of the Central Bank, sidestroking nearer with a showy new wife in tow. Sam quickly found himself besieged and began pivoting from one to another, volleying back greetings while his hand was pumped, his cheeks were bussed, and his back repeatedly slapped.

As often as this sort of thing had happened to him, Sam had never really gotten used to it, even when he judged it useful—as at stockholder meetings, for instance, with a plan to present or a slate of directors to install. Mostly, his minor celebrity status was just a damn nuisance. Early in his career, the rolled ranch hat and faded jeans had served as a city disguise. But once the media had trademarked these into a "corporate cowboy" persona, they only made him more conspicuous. Which was one of the prime reasons he had lately chosen to spend more and more time at the Lazy S and let D.W. get *his* face glossed on the cover of *Business Week.*

But Sam worked this cocktail crowd like a good politician, scanning hopefully for D.W. or Jacqueline. After several minutes, when neither appeared to rescue him, he simply disengaged and began moving, like an amiable zombie, toward the afterdeck. His head was once more mildly athrob, and despite the *Kallisto*'s air-conditioning, he felt the imminent need for oxygen.

Outside the salon, the air was considerably better, with wrap-around windows wide open to the Orinoco breeze. There was a younger crowd out there as well, and the teak decking was indeed taking a beating, as a dozen couples jerked and stomped to what sounded like a bossa-nova version of "I Heard It Through the Grapevine." Sam couldn't help noticing one pneumatic and brassy blonde, who seemed to be trying to shimmy her way out of her metallic gift-wrap.

But still no sign of host or hostess.

Of course D.W. could be quite near, Sam realized, and simply eclipsed by taller folk. He began listening for D.W.'s basso growl. Instead, from deep in the salon a moment later, came a distinctive girlish glissando.

Sam retreated inside—and spotted Jacqueline at the far end of the room, encircled by men. She was in profile, nodding and listening, while absently stroking a wing of her sideswept hair. The artless gesture belied her sophisticated look. She was a stunner in off-the-shoulder black chiffon—obviously the "Dior black strapless" she'd mentioned on their ride. Sam felt his emotional fortifications crumbling.

Then he recognized two of the men around her—Nelson Machado and Luís de Villegas. Machado was deputy planning minister, and de Villegas carried the turgid title of presidential secretariat minister—roughly equivalent to chief of staff. During his Caracas meetings Sam had been told that both influential figures were on the presidential junket to Jakarta, and thus not due back for at least two more days. And here they were, not just back in Venezuela ahead of schedule, but attending D.W.'s floating soiree. The sight gave Sam's heart a secondary fibrillation, almost equal to the revelation of Jacqueline Lee in chiffon décolleté. What strings had D.W. pulled to get them down here, and to what purpose?

As he pondered this, Jacqueline laughed again, tossed her head, and suddenly locked on Sam through the crowd. Everything else in the room instantly diminished. It was only an incandescent moment before she swung back to her companions, but the damage done to his defenses was profound.

He started toward her, but collided with a large man.

It was Owen Meade, and Sam's anger flared.

"Goddammit, Owen, why the hell didn't you wake me?"

"Sorry, Sam. D.W. and I just got back a few minutes ago. I was on my way to your room."

"Got back from where?"

"Puerto Ordaz. We had to go for a quick meeting."

"Where's D.W. now?"

"In his suite. Dressing."

D.W. was standing behind his desk, fiddling with a red bow tie. Ray Arrillaga, also in evening clothes, got up quickly from a leather sofa to shake Sam's hand. Sam had not known Ray was down here, but let it pass. Larger matters were at hand. He turned to D.W.

"So, what are Machado and de Villegas doing here?"

"Ah, you noticed that, Samuel?"

"I noticed."

"Please, have a seat. I am happy to report that we have made considerable progress in our discussions on Cerro Calvario."

"Apparently. Let's have it."

D.W.'s eyes squeezed tightly above a wide smile. He was unusually pleased with himself, Sam thought. D.W. went to his rosewood sideboard, opened a drawer, and withdrew a flat, black-leather folder, brandishing it like a sommelier would a pricey wine list.

"What's that?"

"Authorization to resume mining, to extend the rail line from Cerro Bolívar, and to construct a workers settlement." D.W. flipped open the leather case to a typeset page bearing a gold seal under a florid signature. "It is signed by *el jefe* himself, you see? And Señors de Villegas and Machado assure us that the Council of Ministers will meet within the week to, shall we say, rubber-stamp their approval?"

Still smiling, D.W. handed Sam the leather-clad document. Sam glanced through it quickly.

"How much is all this going to cost us?"

"Sam, you sound just like Raymond here. He's convinced the entire postponement was only a government tactic to extract a bigger bite from Proteus. But surely we are speaking of mutual interests here."

"How much, D.W.?"

"A few million—discreetly deposited in Caribbean banks. Hardly worth mentioning."

"How many is a 'few'?"

"A final figure is still under negotiation. But I'm not concerned, and neither should you be."

"So why didn't you tell me what was going on?" Sam handed back the document, and D.W. slid it back into its drawer.

"Things moved too swiftly, Sam. I finally reached Señor de Villegas in Dakar. He was with the president, as you know. Suddenly our discussion reached a critical phase. I was forced to make a commitment over the phone. Without consultation, you understand. In any case, you were out showing Jacqueline the local sights in your little plane. Fortunately Raymond had come down, so I at least had his input." D.W.'s smile returned, broader than before. "But what does this matter, Sam? We've won! And I decided to make a surprise of it." He gestured at a silver tray with blue crystal decanter and glasses on the sideboard. "Shall we celebrate?"

"What's in there, Suntory?"

"I've got some Wild Turkey in the cabinet. A double, Sam?"

"Sure. Why the hell not? Only there's one slight problem, Duke. Remember me saying something about changing my mind? Back when we met on the hill—before the rain?"

"Of course. You said you were thinking about doing a 'one-eighty,' I believe." D.W. chuckled as he handed Sam a double shot of bourbon. "Very droll. *Salud!*"

Ray Arrillaga seconded the Hispanic toast, with considerably better pronunciation.

"And now, I propose we all rejoin the party upstairs, before my daughter is convinced I've totally abandoned her."

"The way she looks, D.W.," Ray said, "I seriously doubt if anybody's missed us."

"Yes, Jacqueline's a princess," D.W. agreed. "Sometimes a good princess and sometimes a naughty one. Tonight she is being very good."

Sam stood up, blocking their passage to the door.

"Hold on a minute, D.W. You, too, Ray. What I said about changing my mind, that wasn't a joke."

They froze, and Sam continued, "I assume you talked to Hardy

132

Eason about all this. But did you happen to call either Rollo or John?" Rowland McCall was Proteus's vice president for public relations, John Godell its general counsel and a company director. "Or maybe you should have checked with the flak-catchers over at Exxon—because you're getting ready to walk into exactly the kind of PR debacle down here that Exxon had in Prince William Sound. And, criminal and civil penalties aside, that could wind up costing us lucrative deals all over the globe."

D.W. remained frozen.

"Sam, aren't you maybe exaggerating a bit?" Ray Arrillaga suggested.

"If anything, Ray, I might be underestimating. When the media get word we're blasting away archaeological treasures down there, they'll crucify us."

"Sam," D.W. said emphatically, "there *are* no treasures down there."

"I'm telling you what I saw with my own eyes, D.W. That's why I went snooping around. We're not talking about a bunch of broken pottery, goddammit. Dr. Laya has uncovered some incredible stuff—museum pieces—and believe me, he's not going to be shy about showing 'em to CNN, *Nightline, 60 Minutes,* or anybody else he can corral."

D.W. swung around and opened another drawer.

"Perhaps this is what you mean, Samuel?"

D.W. held a clear plastic bag under the desk lamp. Sam moved closer—and was stunned. The pouch contained the elegant bone-flute fragment Dr. Laya had shown him, a treasure Sam remembered the archaeologist had kept carefully locked away in an ammunition case.

"D.W., where in the hell did you get this? And please, for chrissake, don't tell me you and your new friends in Caracas got some Guardia Nacional thugs to run Dr. Laya off the mountain and confiscate his finds. Because if you did, you are in some very deep shit here, my friend, and you could take the whole fucking company down with you."

"Calm yourself, Samuel. This is being turned over to the Natural Sciences Museum in Caracas tomorrow. I'm showing it to you now only to reassure you. You see, there is absolutely no need to shut down archaeological exploration in the area of Cerro Calvario. It happens that this valuable artifact was found at considerable distance from the ore concentrations. Excavations can and will continue at this site, without any effect on our mining operations."

"Who the fuck told you this, D.W.?"

"The man who brought this to me."

D.W. rapped his knuckles on the door connecting to his stateroom. Seconds later this door opened, and Félix Rosales walked into the room.

21

The young archaeologist looked like a goddamned male model, Sam thought, with his droopy forelock and his gap-toothed smile. His thick-muscled frame was stuffed into a leather bomber jacket, white shirt, cotton pants, and moccasins.

"Félix," Sam said, "just what in hell is going on here?"

"Didn't Mr. Lee explain?"

"I'm asking you. But on second thought, maybe I just figured it out." Sam swept his hand back toward the artifact now on D.W.'s desk. "Dr. Laya told you to deliver this to Caracas for carbon-dating, right? Only it looks like you came up with a better idea. You decided to stop off and visit my esteemed colleagues here with a little story that happened to fit right in with their mining plans. You figured there just might be something in it for you. How am I doing so far?"

Félix wrinkled his lips into a bland smile. "I know you don't like me, Sam. That's why I came to Mr. Lee instead of you—not with a 'little story,' but the truth."

Sam swung to D.W. "What did he get from you?"

"Samuel, you're wrong. Professor Rosales merely—"

" 'Professor'? Did Félix tell you he was a professor?"

"No, I never claimed that," Félix said. "I have been a teaching assistant, however."

"Somehow I got the idea you were just head ditchdigger."

135

"Sam, there's no need for insulting Señor Rosales. I may have assumed he was a professor, but that's not the issue. He came to us with important information."

"I know what he came to you with—a load of horseshit. I just can't believe you guys lost your sense of smell."

"Sam," Ray Arrillaga spoke up, "will you calm down a minute?"

"Sure, Ray. After I tell you both something. Our friend Félix knows goddamn good and well where that prehistoric flute was dug up—on the summit of Cerro Calvario, buried in high-grade ore. Hell, it's all right there on that label—grid coordinates, soil composition, everything. Unless Félix changed it."

"Sam, goddammit, will you please just sit down and listen a minute?"

Sam glared a moment at Arrillaga's hard, bronze face behind the steel spectacles, then sank beside him into the leather sofa. "Go ahead, Ray. Speak your piece."

"Thank you. Mr. Rosales here is alleging that Dr. Laya had falsified the feature description you saw, relocating the find several hundred meters from the actual discovery site and claiming it was found in the midst of an ore concentration, in order to prevent mining anywhere on the mountain. Which, basically, is just what you said back in New Orleans, remember, Sam? You said someone was probably seeding the dig with artifacts to stop us. Mr. Rosales says he has now corrected the tag, to show the correct placement." Carefully, Ray lifted the plastic pouch from the desk and handed it to Félix, who began to read the attached label:

"This artifact is item SH seventy-five—"

"Skip that stuff," Ray suggested.

"I was just explaining that I had to change the artifact designator back to an SH sequence, because it was actually found in a control pit at the foot of what is called the South Hill, in horizon IIAb. A horizon is basically a level or stratum in an excavation. It was buried at a depth of three meters, in a mixture of clay and granodiorite." Félix looked back at Ray.

"Mr. Rosales pinpointed the actual location on our mining maps," Ray added. "It's nowhere near any significant main ore bodies, Sam. And the surrounding soil, we know from our own surveys, is nonferruginous conglomerate. There's some bauxite there, but not in sufficient concentrations to be of interest."

Sam folded his arms. "Ray, I know how much this whole operation down here means to you. Hell, I was as gung ho as anybody, you know that, charging off with my machete to cut red tape. So I understand why you'd want very much to buy the version this guy is selling. But I'm warning you, Ray. And you, too, D.W. Better listen to the old man on this. And the old man is telling you to be real, real careful here. Understand?"

"That's exactly what we're doing," Ray said.

"And, Sam," D.W. said, "let's not be making threats."

"That was a warning, not a threat. But I got a few more things to say here, D.W., if you don't mind." Sam leaned forward from the sofa, bringing Félix into his line of sight. "Now these are what you might call real serious charges, Félix. And I'm sure wondering why you went along with Dr. Laya's story when he was showing this artifact to me—and even after, when you knew who I was."

"He ordered me not to tell anyone, Sam. It's like Mr. Arrillaga just said. Dr. Laya wanted to make sure there was no mining anywhere on Cerro Calvario. And, I admit, I felt the same way. For a lot of reasons—mainly archaeological, but also ecological and political—what he was doing seemed justified to me. So I agreed. But inside, it still bothered me. And when it came time to deliver this artifact to the Natural Sciences Museum with a false site profile, I just couldn't do it. Don't you see? That defeats all the principles of our science, and the whole purpose of archaeology."

"Then why didn't you report all this to the museum, or other scientific authorities? Why come here?"

"The director of the museum is a longtime friend of Dr. Laya. So is almost everyone else in the natural sciences in Venezuela. Who would believe me? Then I remembered Mr. Lee. His daughter told me his ship was docked here in San Félix. So I came here, hoping Mr. Lee would listen and perhaps help me contact authorities willing to investigate my story. And that is what Mr. Lee and Mr. Arrillaga have done."

"Satisfied?" D.W. asked, coming around the desk to freshen their drinks.

"Not exactly, D.W. Guess I've just been around too damned long to start being naive. I mean, when Félix says no one would believe him, guess why that is. It's because he has no credibility in the world of science, and he knows it. There's just no way you or I or anybody can take his word over an accredited Ph.D., the chairman of a university department, for God's sake. It's not Félix's story we need to check out, as much as his motives for stabbing his employer in the back."

"Unfortunately, Sam, there are other allegations which cast doubt on Dr. Laya's own motives."

"Whose allegations?"

"I admit, they're from Mr. Rosales also. But, unfortunately, they have been corroborated."

"What the hell are they?"

D.W. returned to his executive chair, leaned back, and laced his fingers behind his head. "Why don't you tell him, Ray? Samuel hasn't been receptive to anything I've said so far."

"It's called arguing, D.W. Hardly a new concept."

Ignoring this, D.W. gestured again to Ray, who addressed Sam:

"D.W. and I just got back from a meeting on this whole Cerro Calvario situation in Puerto Ordaz, along with Owen, Mr. Rosales, and several deputy ministers. The bottom line, Sam, is that it looks like there's a great deal to be investigated here, and the relevant ministries—Interior and Justice—are now doing just that. Pending the results of those investigations, Dr. Laya has been suspended as director of the excavation."

"Oh, for God's sake! What the hell for?"

D.W. pushed a sheet of paper across the desk toward Ray Arrillaga, who took it up and consulted it during the ensuing:

"Mr. Rosales told us he suspected that Dr. Laya had hired as a security guard on Cerro Calvario a man with a criminal history. Those suspicions were confirmed during our meeting by Ministry of Justice computer records. In fact, the man in question has a much more extensive criminal record than Mr. Rosales was aware of. He was identified as a Marxist revolutionary as far back as 1969, when he attended a Cuban training camp with the notorious Venezuelan terrorist known as Carlos the Jackal. In the decades since, he was arrested and imprisoned several times, for robbing a bank in Mexico City and twice in Venezuela on drug-trafficking charges." Ray glanced from the paper over at Sam. "Those are just highlights, you understand."

"The guy's called Oscar something, right?"

Ray glanced down at the paper. "Oscar Azarias Rivilla. You knew all this?"

"I didn't know his past. Jacqueline told me he was Dr. Laya's relative, just like Félix is. Oscar's an uncle or something. Isn't that right, Félix?"

"Yes, I mentioned that to the officials," Félix replied, "and that Dr. Laya is a distant cousin of mine. But I am not a criminal or an ex-convict or a former terrorist."

"Okay," Sam said. "It looks like Dr. Laya may be guilty of bad judgment, or at least excessive loyalty, in regard to a family member. That doesn't exactly make him a fraud, or a perpetrator of a scientific hoax."

D.W. again signaled Ray Arrillaga, who cleared his throat before resuming:

"Unfortunately, Sam, he seems to be guilty of a bit more than bad judgment. According to the Ministry of Justice, Dr. Laya also has a criminal record."

"Dr. Laya? I don't believe it."

"It's true. He was arrested in February 1992, right after the abortive military coup, passing out pamphlets at Simón Bolívar University on behalf of the coup's ringleader, Lieutenant Colonel Hugo Chávez."

"Christ Almighty, Ray! You know how that played down here. Half the fucking country was out banging pots and pans or demonstrating in the street against Pérez and in support of Chávez. But shit, how did this even come up? Or did Félix happen to tip the police to this as well?"

"I only mentioned Dr. Laya's political activism," Félix said. "I didn't know he'd been arrested. They discovered that."

"Did they now?" Sam turned to D.W. "So, besides defending the principles of science and law and order, what does our friend over here get out of all this? I mean, if Dr. Laya is being sacked, isn't Félix out of a job, too?"

D.W. looked slightly uncomfortable at the question. "Not immediately. Since Mr. Rosales has been second-in-command to Dr. Laya, and therefore the only other qualified person on-site, the government is putting him temporarily in charge of the excavation. Pending the results of an investigation."

"What kind of investigation? Is the government sending archaeologists out to check the two sites, to see who's telling the truth?"

"Ray?" D.W. prompted.

Ray shook his head. "We didn't get into those kinds of details."

Sam drained his glass, got to his feet, paced across the handwoven Chinese carpet to a photo blowup showing the New Orleans skyline, with the *Kallisto* steaming past the Proteus skyscraper.

"Look," he said, turning suddenly, "does Arquimedeo know about all this?"

"Not yet," D.W. said. "A delegation is driving down in the morning."

"What about Jacqueline? Did you tell her?"

"I haven't had a chance. We just got back."

Sam shook his head. "Duke, I've backed every play you've made for Proteus, and most of 'em paid off handsomely. You've been a hell of an executive—that's no secret—and probably I should have turned the whole damn thing over to you before now. So maybe that's what's made you a little itchy on this deal. Whatever it is, you're getting ready to blow your damn foot off down here, my friend, and maybe a lot worse than that. And it looks like I'm gonna have to pull rank to keep it from happening."

D.W. remained serene. "Sam, you're missing the point. I'm not doing anything. Proteus isn't doing anything. The Venezuelan government is taking all these steps, assuming all the responsibility. We are simply proceeding on the basis of their authorization to resume mining."

"D.W., if somebody shows me conclusive proof that Dr. Laya is a charlatan, that's one thing. Until then, I don't give a shit what Caracas does or authorizes. Proteus is not going to be a part of it—and that includes those offshore payments. Now, do you understand *me?* You're not going to use Proteus drill bits to start tearing up that goddamn mountain."

"Sam, I'm afraid I've already taken that decision. And I've done so with the full knowledge and backing of the board." He brought his chair to vertical and fixed his gaze on Sam. "I might add that several officers and directors have expressed their concerns to me about your, how shall I say, apparent lack of interest and involvement during the last several days."

Sam shook his head slowly. "Well, well, D.W., it looks like you've finally gone and done it. Pulling a real Félix Rosales on the old guy, eh? Ray, I'd be interested to hear your opinion on all this."

"Sam, the fact is you've been basically out of the loop here. Several times we tried to reach you and couldn't. So I have to say that, yes, I think D.W. is steering the correct course, and I think a majority of the directors and the stockholders will agree with that."

"You do, eh?" Sam seemed to consider the question himself, with cocked head. "Well, I guess we'll soon see about that. You both understand, my appeal is not to anybody's altruism here. It's purely on the basis of self-interest. Until all these questions are resolved, my view is that a continued moratorium on mining makes sense politically, economically, PR-wise—any way you want to slice it." Arms folded, Sam swiveled to face D.W. "Are you sure you really want to fight me on this, *amigo?*"

"I stand by my decision, Samuel. I wish you would endorse it."

"No, you don't. You want a goddamn shootout. But you picked the wrong time and place. I would have given you my job, D.W., I really would have. Now I'm afraid I'm going to have to take yours."

"Samuel, I'm not going to respond to that. You're reacting emotionally and saying things you will regret later. It's late, and Ray and I must rejoin the party. Why don't you come along with us? Or if you'd like, since you look a little tired, maybe you'd like to spend the night here. There's an empty stateroom."

"I'm feeling fine, D.W. By all means, let's all go up arm in arm and practice our corporate smiles."

But Sam *wasn't* feeling fine. The cabin floor seemed increasingly unsteady, more than was attributable to the Orinoco current. He glanced over at his empty glass. Had it been one double shot of Wild Turkey, or two? And he hadn't eaten since when? Christ, just when he needed his head. He was in no condition, really, to work the crowd upstairs, and what would be the point of it? His next real showdown wasn't here, or even in Caracas, but back in New Orleans. He needed to have the board solidly in his corner before he came out swinging. Which meant he needed to fly out tomorrow—commercial. There was no time for the Cessna. Anyway, he was too damn preoccupied to be solo-hopping the Caribbean.

He turned back to Félix. "You make damn sure that thing goes into the Natural Science Museum tomorrow, okay?"

Félix's only response was a smile that bore strong resemblance to a sneer.

"Sam," D.W. said, "before we leave, there's one thing I forgot to mention."

"Shoot."

"Mr. Rosales informs me you've been spending a great deal of time these last few days with Jacqueline. I appreciate your hospitality to her, and I know she thinks highly of you. But maybe it's not a good idea right now, do you understand?"

Sam stopped short, letting D.W.'s words have their full impact. Then slowly he nodded and walked out, leaving the door ajar.

22

Lights glimmered along the San Félix waterfront, making a carnival tracery of the transit sheds and port offices, the traveling bridge cranes and the vertical-pivot booms of the ore-crushing plant. At the adjoining passenger wharf, the *Dreamstar* was long gone, but the Swedish ore ship still waited at the berth beyond, with bulbs burning at funnel and bridge and along the mast stays, casting skittery reflections over the oil-skinned water. Outside the twinkling harborscape, the residential and commercial barrios of San Félix flickered faintly, like *luminarias* scattered across the Orinoco night.

Impinging on this nocturnal tranquillity were party sounds percolating up from the *Kallisto*'s fantail and echoing off the wharves and warehouses. But Sam could retreat no farther than his present pinnacle, a tiny, sheltered sun deck wrapped forward of the radar mast above the pilothouse. He had made his way up several companionways to this isolated spot in search of a clear head. Wild Turkey on an empty stomach on top of a hangover was sufficient formula for dysfunction. Add to that his head-on collision with D.W., and it was little wonder Sam needed a recuperative time-out.

To put it another way, he was hammered.

He braced his arms above the rail and stared out at the broad, black river. He was trying to steady himself, but the world kept shifting on him, tilting out there on the edge of vision. People and events also seemed to be more and more skewed, and at multiplying cross-purposes—he and D.W. and Jake, Arquimedeo and Félix, while the future of Cerro Calvario was now apparently to be decided by internecine warfare within the Proteus corporate hierarchy and the Venezuelan ministries. It made for one hell of a Gordian snarl-up. And he had no idea where to start hacking at it.

"Sam? What are you doing up there?"

He glanced down. Jacqueline Lee stood on the starboard bridge wing immediately below. Her upturned face shone ivory between pearl-drop earrings, as a breeze fanned her black mane into the night sky. A downwash of light from the pilothouse further polished her alabaster shoulders and the pale swell of bosom above a black chiffon bodice.

"Howdy, Jake."

"Howdy, yourself. Is there somebody up there with you?"

"Doesn't seem to be."

"Sam, are you drunk?"

"I'd say that was a pretty fair assessment."

"I'm coming up."

"I don't think that's such a good—"

But she'd already pivoted, heading for the nearest companionway. Sam followed the sound of her high heels drumming along the planking, and then, a moment later, ringing up the metal treads. There was no escaping her, except by an undignified scramble down the portside companionway, which he was in no condition to undertake. Anyway, this was undoubtedly as good a place as any to end things between them. No final clutches, no emotive speeches. Just straight talk. Bulldoze her with the bad news about Cerro Calvario and his smash-up with her father. That one-two punch ought to obliterate any amorous fantasies, unilateral or otherwise.

"Sam?"

He turned as Jacqueline stepped upward out of shadows and into a spill of light from the masthead. In addition to the strapless gown, she wore a very purposeful look, Sam thought, as he experienced another bout of the wobbles. A plump champagne bottle dangled from her right hand, while her left palm cradled two crystal flutes. This was obviously not going to be easy.

"A lovely gesture, Jacqueline," he said, offering a small salute. "But as you see, I'm already half-smashed, and I'm afraid there's nothing to celebrate."

"I know all about it, Sam. I just heard."

"Heard what?"

"All about Daddy's big power grab—at the expense of Dr. Laya, and you." She moved closer, with a rustle of fabric and a clink of stemware. "When you never came to see me, I went hunting for you—as soon as I could break away. And guess who I found outside Daddy's office?"

"Uh, let's see. Could that be Conan the Archaeologist?"

"Very good! Actually I saw Félix's back, scuttling away down the corridor. I mean, he didn't exactly look like he belonged at the party, not in a leather jacket. Inside Daddy and Ray Arrillaga had their heads together. Sort of like the Coneheads on the old *Saturday Night Live*, you know? So I basically started screaming, demanding to know what he'd been up to while I was playing dutiful hostess for a solid hour."

"And he told you?"

"In his own infuriating, patronizing fashion. When I figured out what he was really saying, I called him a vile name and came looking for you."

Sam nodded sagaciously, covering his intermittent stupor. "So you know the worst. Then why the champagne?"

"Isn't it obvious? To drink a toast—a before-the-battle toast. Looks like we're in this together now, Sam."

"Together? I'm afraid not. Maybe D.W. didn't get around to this part, but he asked me to, uh, well, pretty much stay the hell away from you."

"Félix!" She plunked the champagne bottle and glasses down on the deck. "That fucking slimeball! I wonder what lies he told Daddy about us! What did you say? You didn't agree?"

"Of course I did."

"Sam! In case you didn't notice, Daddy is busy being a shit-heel, and he is not *my* CEO, or lord and master. So, as far as your silly, chivalrous pledge to stay the hell away from his girl-child, namely me"—she reached and straightened his bow tie—"I hereby absolve you from it, Sir Samuel. Is that clear?"

"Unfortunately, I happen to think your father's right. For all kinds of reasons."

"Oh, you do? Well, name one."

"Jacqueline, you could make this a whole lot easier, you know?"

"No way I'm making this easy."

"You want a reason? Okay. D.W. and I are about to go *mano a mano* to see who's running this goddamned company."

"So I gathered. One guess as to whose side I'm on."

"Goddamn it, Jake, that's the point. You can't be involved. Hell, I told you that before—if it comes down to a fight between us, I don't want you anywhere around. And now the battle lines are drawn."

But his show of anger only incited her own: "You're telling me I can't take a stand?"

"No, I don't mean that exactly. I mean—oh, goddammit to hell!"

"You mean you're afraid to be seen with me, isn't that it? You think maybe Daddy's going to spread nasty little rumors about you, claiming you're trying to seduce his precious daughter?"

"No, I don't think D.W. would do that. But let's just say the timing here is not exactly, uh . . ."

"Propitious?"

Sam laughed. "Yeah, that's the word. Even if I'd remembered it, believe me, in my present state, I'd never have pronounced it."

Jacqueline closed in, till her face was just inches away. "Okay, Sam. I understand the corporate politics, and I'll accept them—for now. But I'm not letting you off the hook that easy. I want to hear it straight from you, not from my father's ultimatum. Do *you* want me around or not? I mean, aside from the obvious fact that I belong in a playpen."

"I never said that. I only said—"

"That I'm too young. Okay, what else? Am I too whimsical for you? Too tall, perhaps? Too collegiate—or postcollegiate? Or maybe too incredibly Eurasian?" With her forefingers, Jacqueline tugged her eyelids, narrowing their almond shape. "Or maybe I'm just not your type? After all, we know you favor hot-blooded Hispanics."

Sam merely chuckled at her antics, but Jacqueline frowned back at him, then folded her arms in no-nonsense fashion below the notch of décolletage.

"Well? I'm awaiting your answer."

"Jacqueline, I think you already know the answer to all that."

"I want to hear you say it."

Sam turned away from her gaze. "This isn't exactly going the way I planned. But I guess that shouldn't surprise me, since everything else has been out of control lately."

When he glanced back, she was right there, her face shadowed, but her eyes large and luminous. "Sam, you're fighting everybody. I can see that. But don't fight me anymore, okay? I want to be with you on this."

She ducked down, gurgled out champagne, rose up again with an overflowing glass in each hand.

"Jake, hey, I'm barely coherent as it is."

"Just have one sip with me. It's Veuve Clicquot."

"Well, hell, why didn't you say so?" Outside of Dom Pérignon, Sam didn't know one brand from another, but he accepted the fizzing glass. She was right in his face now, twining her forearm and glass around his.

"Here's looking at you, kid," he offered with a grin.

"Right back at you, old-timer," she murmured, then gulped, never taking her eyes off him.

Sam knocked it back, felt the bubbles explode in his mouth. The world skipped another beat then, creating a sensory blur of fantail salsa with swimming river lights, and Jacqueline's floral perfume with a sweet trace of citrus blossoms borne on the Orinoco breeze. When he refocused, Jacqueline was leaning against him—on tiptoe, bringing them eye to eye.

And then they were kissing.

This time there were no horses and saddles to get in the way. Steering his hand with one eye, Sam managed to abandon his champagne glass safely on the teak rail, before surrendering his full attention to the moment. Below the passionate kiss, they maneuvered jointly into the tightest possible embrace. Sam spread his palms across the warm, satin planes of her bare back, while Jacqueline kept squirming forward, face and torso, hips and thighs, till Sam nearly lost his balance. He caught himself against the railing, while somehow maintaining the sealed kiss, just as she released a warmed spurt of champagne deep into his throat.

The surprise of it nearly buckled his knees. He came up gasping. "Why, you little vixen!" he said when he caught his breath.

"What are you going to do about it, cowboy?" she said defiantly, from only an inch away.

But Sam was already snaking a hand down for the neck of the Veuve Clicquot, while keeping Jacqueline tightly corraled in his other arm. "I guess you'll just have to wait and see," he said, then swigged straight from the bottle, storing the effervescent ammunition as he lowered his face to hers and stifled a delighted giggle with his lips.

There were several more point-blank, liquid salvos before a mutual surrender was proclaimed and they slid down behind the sheltering windscreen to occupy themselves with more serious intimacies. Jacqueline kicked off her pumps and deposited herself more or less in Sam's lap; while he, with stripe-trousered legs splayed out upon the deck, explored alternately her delicious face and the jungly precincts of her hair. He could savor now to the fullest those commingled scents he had encountered first during the rainstorm on Cerro Calvario, when Jacqueline had brushed past him in the tent.

Sam's alcohol-induced disorientation had by no means lifted. It had, in fact, been augmented by Jacqueline's intoxicating presence, as well as by the recent infusions of Veuve Clicquot. But if Jacqueline was in part the cause of his vertigo, she was also its nearest remedy, an adorable anchor to be clutched, while all of Ciudad Guayana pinwheeled past, trailing a skyful of equatorial constellations in its wake.

And while nothing very much resembling thinking was going on amid this sensate whirl, there were some erratic conjectures. Sam wondered, for instance, just how it was that a girl—almost, but not quite, a woman—could appear so suddenly on his personal horizon and proceed to convince herself and him of the preposterous notion that she was exactly what was needed to make his life complete.

The damn thing had started, Sam was sure, in the front seats of his Cessna, when he had taken rather furtive and frequent delight in Jacqueline's girlish exuberance. Again and again that glorious morning he had glanced away from Angel Falls or some other cinemascopic marvel to scrutinize the detailing of his lovely seatmate—the exquisite ear; the baroque curve of her smile, cunningly echoed in a recurrent dimple; her tapered

golden fingers working the palmcorder; the dark brown firelights
in her satin black hair. Once begun, the infatuation had obviously been both insidious and cumulative, building into the
fever that had now burst upon them. The only hope for sanity,
of course, was that the fever would quickly pass—leaving them
both in depleted puzzlement.

But for the moment, it was irresistible. Jacqueline's face was
everywhere he looked, and her kisses voracious. No longer able
to endure anything between her flesh and Sam's caressing hands,
she tugged impatiently at her bodice, spilling her breasts into
his grasp. She moaned as he palmed them, then slid her fingers
beneath his cummerbund, probing the extent of his desire.

Well, now, Sam thought, she certainly wasn't going to be disappointed. Nor was she. Her eyes widened as she encountered
the battle-ready hardness that had been there, lying in wait and
addling his brains, almost since she'd tweaked his bow tie.

But this, finally, triggered an alarm too strident for Sam to
ignore, despite his condition. With great reluctance he backed
off, then took her firmly by both wrists, restraining her from
further erotic mischief.

"Sam, what's wrong?"

"I'm calling time-out here, okay?"

"Okay, okay. You're absolutely right." She leaned back from
him as he released her hands, and they faced off, still seated and
breathing like two boxers pried loose from a late-round clinch.
"We can use my stateroom. It's on the starboard side—"

"No, Jake, we can't."

"Okay, what about the Inter-Continental? We'll take your car,
but I drive, okay?"

"No, dammit."

"Why not?"

"Because I said so."

"Sam. I don't believe this. You're still afraid, aren't you?"

"Yeah, could be. I mean, D.W. does have one hell of a gun
collection."

"I'm not talking about Daddy. You're afraid of me. Of us."

Sam let that one penetrate his benumbed skull. "Maybe I am,
Jake. Whatever it is, I'm just not ready for whatever comes next.
So we stop right here."

"With your virtue intact?"

"I know, it sounds weird to me, too."

"Well, the part about not being ready certainly does." She giggled. "I mean, there's some awfully hard evidence to the contrary."

"Jake, just hush a moment, okay? And stay over there." She had begun to lean toward him. "Look, I don't know what all this adds up to. But yes, dammit, it scares me. All of it—you, me, D.W. And for sure I'm too snockered to know what the hell I'm doing. All I'm proposing is that we pull the plug—until this whole mess is resolved, between me and your father, and you and your father. I mean, who knows what kind of dynamics are operating here? Maybe this is all part of your rebelling against him—"

"Come on, Sam! You don't really think that's what this is about?"

"I honestly don't know, Jake. I admit the thought certainly occurred when I watched you corral that prime hunk of Latin beefcake."

"I was not trying to corral Félix. I just flirted with him!"

"Well, that's what I figured you were doing with me, just flirting. I mean, why would you want to do anything more with a sun-wrinkled coot older than your dad, for God's sake?"

"Sam, this is stupid. What am I supposed to do now, sit here and try and convince you that I'm really serious, and not trifling with your manly feelings? Well, I could. I could write you a whole gooey Hallmark card about how I love your sun wrinkles and your stubbly jaw and overgrown eyebrows . . . and the shape of your big hands and the sound of your laugh . . . and the way I know just how to get under your skin and tease you—and elicit one hell of a rise, if I do say so myself. But I refuse. So there." She folded her arms and glared at him. And when he didn't immediately respond, she prodded him angrily with her bare foot. "Damn you!"

"I'm sorry. I'm a complete and thorough bastard."

"No, you're not. You're just a damn, sun-wrinkled, snockered old party pooper. The party *is* pooped, right?"

"I'd say that's a safe bet." Somewhat shakily, he levered himself upright, then extended his hand and helped her to her feet. Jacqueline treated him to a long-suffering look as she stepped into her pumps and adjusted her little chiffon dress. Then, as

Sam began fiddling ineffectually with his own dishevelment, she slapped his hands.

"Oh, for heaven's sake, let me." Sam obeyed, looking somewhat sheepish as she tucked in his dress shirt and straightened his cummerbund and jacket. "Voilà," she said with a final and unnecessary upward tug on his zipper, "you could pass anywhere for a respectable captain of industry. No one would guess what unspeakable things you've been up to."

"Thanks."

"Don't mention it."

"Jacqueline"—he tilted her chin up to look into her eyes—"I've got to go up to New Orleans tomorrow and fight for my position, and incidentally for Dr. Laya and a bunch of old buried bones. But it's going to be very hard for me to get my mind off you, for a long while, you know that. But, dammit, I'm going to try. And I expect you'll do the same. And if this was my only chance here, and I blew it, well, I'm sorry. It'll have to rank right up there with some of my other damn-fool blunders."

An ensuing interval of silence was marred by the sudden sounds of a drunken argument below, apparently lurching in their direction—and imparting an unwanted urgency to their leave-taking.

"That's a nice speech, Sam. And I guess it lets you off the hook. Temporarily. But we will be allies. Because you know where I'll be, don't you? Back on Cerro Calvario, shooting a film. I hope it's about archaeology, but maybe it'll be about bulldozing history and other nasty things. Who knows? But whatever happens, you haven't seen the last of me, Big Sam." She paused. "And you *better* be thinking about me—a lot."

"Believe me, Jake, I will."

She went on tiptoe to give him a butterfly-light kiss on the lips. *"Buenas noches*—darling."

Then she was gone, clattering down the companionway.

23

Sam's plan was straightforward. His leather satchel and the car keys for the Alfa Spyder were in the guest cabin below. He would retrieve them and get the hell out of here. He had enough residual judgment to realize that, in his present condition, there was no plausible way he could drive the hundred kilometers back to Ciudad Bolívar. But with any luck, given the Venezuelan police's laissez-faire policy toward vehicular behavior, he should be able to steer a safe course two or three kilometers to the Inter-Continental Hotel in Puerto Ordaz.

Sam could sleep off his stupor there for a few hours, then get a wake-up call in time to gun the Alfa back to Ciudad Bolívar for the morning Avensa or Aeropostal jet to Caracas and connecting flights to Miami and New Orleans.

Now, to implement his plan. He oxygenated his lungs, oriented himself with the constellations and harbor lights, then began descending the companionway to the upper deck.

Halfway down he realized it wasn't going to work. The moment he had set himself in motion, the world around him had launched into a reciprocal movement—and on several axes simultaneously, very much like a rotating and tilting carnival wheel. As a result, Sam found himself grabbing the railing to avoid being hurled centrifugally into space. Had he been behind the wheel of the Italian sports car during such a planetary per-

152

turbation, he could easily have killed himself—and possibly taken an innocent victim or two with him.

Of course, he'd brought it all on himself. The chain of bad decisions went back several days at least, perhaps further. And he'd surely forged the last link climbing up to the sun deck in search of a clear head, then, at the first opportunity, making a drunken ass out of himself. Oh, yes, the images featuring himself and Jacqueline Lee remained indelible and erotic—mouth-to-mouth intoxication, for God's sake! But analyzed in hindsight, his behavior was irresponsible, if not downright juvenile—especially all the subsequent fondlings and gropings. The girl was, after all, his associate's daughter, and younger than his own Teresa. Thank God he'd finally found the gumption to call a halt. Unfortunately, restraint had come too late to salvage sobriety.

But plastered though he was, Sam negotiated a careful descent to the upper deck, where, with both feet well planted, he stiff-armed the nearest bulkhead. This helped to keep the luxury yacht from listing any more than it already was. Which, of course, had to be a subjective perception, since the Orinoco was hardly known for storm waves, and the *Kallisto* was obviously still tethered to the dock.

But what next? He couldn't drive to the nearest hotel. All right. What was the alternate plan? Call Enrico to come and fetch him? That would be a hell of a sadistic trick to play on a friend who was probably just getting to sleep after two days of nonstop partying.

But Sam had to do something if he didn't want to finish flat on his face for D.W. or Jacqueline to trip over in the morning. So he squinted at the glossy swarm of limousines under the dock lights. Why not hitch a ride in one of those? But staggering up to the nearest politico in his present disarray wasn't exactly going to enhance his prestige—and he was going to need all his prestige intact in the days to come. Which left what? Hitchhiking through some of San Félix's more colorful districts? Trying to flag down a *por puesto* minibus on the waterfront and getting rolled for his Rolex?

Samuel, he exhorted himself, for God's sake, do something!

Gradually, then, he became aware of a masculine murmur from farther down the deck. The words were indistinct, but Sam

153

recognized Spanish cadences and a tone vacillating between charm and menace. Sam surveyed aft, expecting to find a wavy-haired lothario putting the make on some toothsome señorita. For a dreadful instant, he even envisioned Félix Rosales with Jacqueline Lee in the role of enthralled listener.

He was relieved—and amazed—instead to see Bernardo, Owen Meade's youthful factotum, posed nonchalantly forty or fifty feet away, readily identifiable by his spiky hair and basketball high-tops. In apparent deference to the occasion, however, Bernardo *was* wearing a suit, or a hip facsimile thereof. It was altogether the baggiest jacket-and-trouser ensemble Sam had seen outside of a clown act.

The young man was definitely on the make, but all that could be seen of his feminine target was a forward-thrusting knee, nicely linked to a swell of naked thigh above and calf below. The rest of her was hidden behind the fiberglass curve of one of the *Kallisto*'s two speedboat tenders; but gauging by the upward tilt of Bernardo's face, she had to be considerably taller than he. This was confirmed an instant later as a bangled arm extended into view and brushed slowly over Bernardo's spiky crown. It was almost a maternal gesture, and the young man rose to it like a cat to a caress. Despite his grogginess, Sam found the vignette arousing.

But, what the hell, the kid was a Proteus employee. So he could damn well stop hustling the guests and drive Sam to the Inter-Continental. Sam pushed away from the bulkhead and began navigating in the general direction of the cradled speedboat. He traversed the distance in a series of surprising tacks, the last of which fetched him hard against the *Kallisto*'s starboard rail, before he spun off and teetered directly in front of Bernardo. It took a moment before the young man's puzzlement yielded to a grin of recognition.

"Señor Sam, you got bombed, eh?"

"Very observant," Sam said, weaving ever so slightly as he stood. "I am indeed bombed, Nardo. And I am, therefore, in need of your assistance."

"Oh, yeah?" Bernardo's enthusiasm dimmed noticeably as his eyes wandered back toward his erstwhile quarry, who had just leaned into view. She was indeed taller than Bernardo, considerably heavier, and, Sam reckoned, easily a couple decades older.

·A mass of brassy curls overhung a hard, glamorously preserved face. The woman's carmine-caked lips and plucked-and-penciled eyebrows reminded Sam of Hollywood sweater girls of the forties and fifties. Bernardo had picked a rather formidable target, he thought, as those improbable eyebrows arched and turquoise-shadowed eyes appraised him, while the bombshell lips crinkled into a sensuous smile.

Sam smiled back. *"Buenas noches, señorita."*

"Buenas noches, Señor Warrender. This is a really fantastic yacht."

"It's not mine. But if you like it, I understand it charters for around twenty thousand a day."

The blonde laughed artfully, while Sam wondered how she knew his name. But he couldn't waste his remaining coherence finding out. He got back to business: "Nardo, I need a ride to the Inter-Continental."

"You don't mean now, Señor Sam?"

"Yes, I do mean now. But first I want you to go down to the lower deck." Sam struggled to recall the layout. "There's a cabin all the way back on this side. It should be unlocked. If not, get the key from Owen or D.W. Inside, on the floor, you'll see a big black satchel, clothes on the bed, car keys on the desk. They have an Alfa-Romeo logo. Just grab all that stuff and meet me on the dock in five minutes, okay? I'll be right by the Alfa. It's a black convertible. Got all that?"

Bernardo nodded his spiky head. "Sure. But I could get you a limo, you know? Those drivers, they're just hanging out down there, getting bombed on José Cuervo."

"Bernardo, just do what I asked."

"Hey, no problem!" He gave Sam a cocky salute, turned, and tossed the same salute to the woman. *"Espérame*—wait right here for me, babe." Then he swaggered off toward the companionway.

"Señor Warrender, what is the matter?"

Sam turned to find the big blonde right in his face, and wearing a look of deep-etched concern. It took Sam a second to figure out why. He must be tottering again. In fact, she apparently thought he was going to hit the deck, as she seized his arm.

"I'm okay," he said. "But maybe I could sit down a second."

"Hold on to me." Bracing her hip against him and using her

forearm as a crutch, the woman marched him several steps to a nearby bench, then eased him down.

"Look, I'm sorry," Sam said. "I think I just need to catch my breath."

"I'm in no hurry," she said. "Anyway, my boyfriend told me to wait."

"Bernardo? He's your boyfriend?"

"That's a joke, honey."

"You never know, right?"

"Frankly, Señor Warrender, you're more my type."

"How do you know my name?"

"You are a very famous man, Señor Warrender, especially in Venezuela. I know of your exploits. So tell me, this ship, it truly costs twenty thousand *bolívars* each day?"

"Dollars, not *bolívars*. Plus tips for the crew."

She threw her head back and laughed. "To have such money, I think one must be in the coca export business."

Sam, meanwhile, took in the brassy tangle and the assiduous war paint, then slid down to cavernous cleavage above her gold-beaded and sequined cocktail dress. He got momentarily lost in these scenic regions, before working his way back up to her face.

"You naughty boy," she said when he reached her elaborately mascaraed eyes, which nevertheless seemed to be tracking him shrewdly.

"I remember you now, *señorita*. Weren't you doing some kind of cha-cha or bossa nova earlier?"

"It is possible. I love to shake it up, you know? And you, Señor Warrender, do you dance?" Her hip nudged him massively.

He shook his head. "Call me Sam, okay? It saves syllables."

"And I am Marina. Marina Estévez. Perhaps you have also seen me on television?"

"Shaking it up in that little gold dress?"

She launched another histrionic laugh. "Oh, please, you are making fun of me. No, I am not a professional dancer. I am a reporter. I work for Noticolor—Ciudad Bolívar TV. And sometimes I anchor the weekend news."

Sam struggled with the implications of this unlikely revelation. "A TV reporter? Here to cover D.W.'s party?"

"Don't worry, Sam. I am only here to amuse myself." She leaned close enough to prod him with her nearside knocker. Her scent also invaded his space, enveloping him in a potent musk cloud. "But perhaps I should warn you, Sam, there is a video crew on board from Venevisión. And Bernardo saw some paparazzi guys hanging around the limos." She waggled a lacquer-clawed finger under his nose. "So, if you wish to leave the ship discreetly, you will have to be very careful."

"Oh, Christ! I'm probably already late. Nardo will be waiting."

"We could leave together, Sam, and you can hide your face right here." She patted her deeply cleft bosom. "No one will see you. They will see only me, and the back of your head. If you like, I can even accompany you to the hotel."

"Uh, no, I don't think so, but thanks, María."

"Marina. Say it, please."

"Marina, sorry. But if you can just get me to the companionway, I think I can get down to the dock myself."

"Yes, yes, all right. Come on, sweetie." She stood up, clapping her hands like a gym instructor. "And don't worry. I can hold you up. I'm a big girl."

"I can see that."

To demonstrate her prowess, she yanked Sam upright, draped his left arm over her shoulders while locking her right arm around his waist.

"See, I've got you? Now here we go."

Side by side they started forward. Sam, without having to worry about his balance, discovered he could shuffle slowly ahead, working his rubbery limbs as he might a marionette.

"Are we there yet?"

"Don't be silly. Come on, you're doing great."

"How much farther?"

"Let me worry about that. You just hang on to Mama." Suddenly she began to giggle.

"What's so funny?"

"The way our hips are bumping, Sam, right on the beat. Don't you hear the band? They're playing a bolero. We are dancing, *mi amor*." She began to sing:

"*Bésame, bésame mucho, como si fuera esta noche la última vez . . .*"

She continued to hum the melody, then turned to compress herself against him.

"Marina?"

157

"Yes, Sam?" She licked his earlobe.

"I've got to . . . stop a moment."

Sam sagged against her as a wave of dizziness swept him. She managed to prop him up, while searching for another bench.

"Where are we?" he asked.

"I think we must cross over here, Sam." They had reached the bridge wing, and Marina pointed to the port side, where a companionway slanted down to the main deck gangway—the quickest way off the boat.

"It is just a little bit farther."

"Okay." He took a faltering step.

"Wait, I have an idea."

She deposited Sam at an angle against the steeply raked front of the pilothouse, then began alternately tugging and sliding him sideways. It was surprisingly effective, and both found it enormously funny. Then, halfway across, while he giggled at his ineptitude, Sam's knees buckled, and he clutched at Marina for support, but succeeded only in snagging her already plunging neckline and dislodging one of her breasts.

After she caught him, he stood there, studying this remarkable protuberance, which seemed to return his stare from its dark cyclopean orb.

"Sam!" Marina scolded. "I'll let you play with it later. But now please put it back where you found it, so we can go down the stairs."

"Sorry." He fumbled with the tremulous globe, then glanced up. "I think you better do it."

"I can't let go of you, or you'll fall on your face. Just stuff it inside."

It really wasn't that difficult when he applied himself. "Marina, thanks for all your help," Sam said with Jacqueline suddenly on his mind, "but I think I'd better go down those stairs myself."

"Ha! I don't think so!"

"No, really, I can do it."

He started down the companionway, then quickly realized he could not manage it alone. But Marina was quickly beside him, instructing him to grip the rail, while she encircled his waist and guided him down, step by step. Then, as sounds from below filled the companionway, he realized the party was still churning at full volume. How was he going to slip through unnoticed?

Perhaps Marina could go down first and scout out a route to the gangway.

Sam turned to suggest this—at precisely the wrong moment. Marina had just stepped down and was not where he reached. He overbalanced and began clawing air. Although he was the one in motion, her face seemed to be sailing past him, a mask of cosmetic shock with chandelier earrings aswing. When he knew he was definitely falling, and unfortunately when it was too late to do anything about it, he made an unavailing grab. As earlier, he managed only to catch the spangled fabric of Marina's flimsy dress, which came away in his hand, peeling her to the waist and toppling her in his wake. They tumbled together to the main deck.

Sam opened his eyes on a sprinkling of stars, neatly framed by the window cutouts of the enclosed main deck. But he couldn't identify the constellations. Several looked vaguely like the Big Dipper. But this was the wrong hemisphere for that, wasn't it? The Southern Cross ought to be up there somewhere, but where?

Then the sky erupted in blinding light, and Sam shut his eyes, became aware at the same instant of a good deal of pain, mostly radiating from his tailbone. But that made sense. After all, he had just fallen downstairs.

Footsteps, shouts, even laughter, began converging rapidly around him. He opened his eyes—this time not on twinkling stars, but on a ring of curious faces. Then he felt heat against his face and turned once more into blinding light. He squinted his eyes nearly shut and saw a quartz-halogen floodlight mounted above a Minicam.

Why was a TV camera pointing at him? Was a drunk falling downstairs all that newsworthy in Venezuela? And why wasn't anyone helping him up? But people were rushing forward, so there was apparently some concern. Owen Meade, for instance, was shoving aside a small individual whom Sam recognized as the minister of health. Then Owen stooped, revealing D.W. standing behind him and looking distraught. Then, pushing in front of everyone and kneeling close, was the one person Sam least wanted to see at that moment. It was Jacqueline Lee, regarding him with what seemed to be spreading horror.

"Sam!" she cried out. "Are you terribly hurt?"

"Don't think so," Sam answered in a strangely sepulchral voice. Perhaps he *was* badly injured—or disfigured or even partially paralyzed. He managed to wiggle something down there. And then all at once he remembered Marina. What had become of her?

Something large and cushiony shifted suddenly beneath him. He rolled his head to the side to see what it was and pivoted his face directly into a familiar—and very naked—breast. Instantly the video camera, which had been momentarily extinguished, bathed him again in hot light. Sam glanced over the imposing pneumatic curve at the face of Señorita Marina Estévez. She looked extremely angry, he thought.

But perhaps not as angry as Jacqueline Lee, when Sam swung back to face her. What he desperately needed then was to lose consciousness. Unfortunately, he seemed wide-awake.

24

Sam thought he was prepared for the worst when American Flight 91 touched down at New Orleans International around eight P.M. the following day. But he was wrong.

He had left Caracas seven hours earlier. And during the final hour leg from Miami, he'd been constantly on the airphone with three Proteus executives, two of them board members, then his executive assistant, Bill Tuck, and finally with Lewis Thurman, his outside counsel. With all that input, he figured he had a pretty good fix on the enemy positions and firepower. But walking down the airport concourse behind a waddling giant of a chauffeur, who had once been an LSU nose tackle, Sam glanced over at a newsrack and got a figurative arrow in the neck. He saw his media nickname plastered across a front page. He moved closer and discovered much worse.

Racked beneath the *Times-Picayune*, the two Houston dailies, the *Wall Street Journal*, and *USA Today* was a green-sheet tabloid called the *Crescent City Sun*. Its bold-type banner screamed: "Wham! Bam! Thank you, Cowboy Sam!" Immediately below was a grainy black-and-white photo showing himself, sprawling over a woman whose dress was ripped to the waist and whose face was plainly outraged. Sam, meanwhile, with tuxedo askew and mouth agape, seemed to be lost in close-range contemplation of the woman's protruding left breast. The photo was captioned:

161

"Drunken party antics of Sam Warrender, maverick chairman of New Orleans-based Proteus Industries, embarrass colleagues and may endanger Venezuelan mining project." The story, absent byline and vanishing beneath the fold, was datelined Ciudad Guayana.

Sam tossed a quarter on the counter and stuffed the rag furtively under his arm as he walked away. On the way to the limo, he unfolded it and began scanning the six-inch column. Before he finished, his initial revulsion, much of it self-directed, had become full-blown fury, directed at the anonymous character assassins behind the piece. The account was wildly speculative, although a certain humiliating truth remained beneath all the salacious goop the writer had troweled on. It described "a rum-drenched, South American yacht debauch," where "decadent party games climaxed with Louisiana's favorite corporate cowboy falling downstairs with a buxom blond TV newswoman, stripping her topless in the process and nearly landing them both in the crocodile-infested Orinoco." There was more of the same en route to a bit of terminal nastiness: "The tipsy CEO was hustled by bodyguards into a dockside limo," Sam read, "before he could wreak further damage to his company's considerable South American interests."

From the back of the stretch Lincoln, Sam phoned his executive assistant again. "Tuck, have you seen the *Crescent City Sun?*"

"It landed on my desk twenty minutes ago, Sam. I've been dreading your call."

"What's the circulation? And who the fuck is behind it? It's gotta be D.W., right? I mean, how else does a photo shot on his boat in Ciudad Guayana late last night wind up here in a scandal sheet the next day?"

"Sam, I've been making phone calls like crazy, but I don't have the answers. I can't seem to reach D.W. Owen Meade claims they knew nothing about it, but he says there was a video crew on board. Do you remember that?"

"Yeah. From Venezuelan TV."

"Then the photo was probably made from uplinked video footage. Now it gets worse, Sam. I talked to a girl on the *Sun* copydesk who says they bought the photo from Nuevomundo Features, a two-bit Latin American press syndicate out of Tampa. The Nuevomundo guy bragged to her that one of the New York

162

City tabloids also bought the photo and may run it tomorrow."

"Jesus Christ, can't we stop it?"

"I've got Rowland McCall working on it now. He's putting together a damage-control team, so you may want to talk to him. He's more worried about the weekly supermarket tabs. This is right down their gutter."

"Oh, shit! Guess I'm not making his job any easier."

"This isn't exactly going to make your fight with the board any easier, either."

"Well, what the hell. Old Sam's a character, everybody knows that. Thanks, Tuck. Keep doing what you're doing."

Sam had the chauffeur drop him at the Westin Canal Place. Proteus kept several river-view executive suites on the twenty-fifth floor, but during check-in the general manager materialized to offer Sam one of the French Quarter suites on the twenty-eighth. Well, why not? Sam figured if he was going to be holding court and calling in favors, he might as well do it in style.

This one was done in Louis something-or-other reproductions and had a far more commanding Mississippi view than did the Proteus boardroom. But Sam didn't even bother opening the outer drapes. He kicked off his shoes, hit the king-size mattress with his back, and began dialing.

Early that morning from Caracas, he had phoned Hardesty Eason to call an emergency board meeting for four o'clock the following afternoon. Hardy had harrumphed that the bylaws required at least forty-eight hours notice of special meetings and said he wasn't sure how many directors could make it on such short notice. Sam told him to go ahead anyway and start rounding them up; they could sign waivers of the notice provision at the meeting. Then, an hour ago, when Sam had called him from the air, Hardy admitted he had gotten commitments from nine of the ten directors, though two could only attend by video-conference—D.W. and one of the three outside directors. The other two outside directors would fly in from New York.

The only no-show would be Proteus's executive vice president for production, Lyman Fisher. Like D.W., Fisher was in South America, but quite unreachable. At last contact, he had been somewhere above the seventeen-thousand-foot level on the slope of Chimborazo in the Ecuadorian Andes, indulging a midlife passion for ice-climbing.

Sam had swallowed a curse. He had counted on Fisher's vote. Well, he couldn't very well wait for the intrepid ass to come down from the cold. Minus one.

"So, how bad does it look, Hardy?" Sam had asked.

"I won't bullshit you, Sam. You got big problems."

"All I'm asking is that you don't make up your mind in advance, Hardy."

"I'll listen to you, Sam. You know that."

Of course, Hardy had promised that before the *Crescent City Sun* had hit the newsracks and flung more excrement into the oscillator.

Now, supine on the king-size bed, Sam called Bill Tuck once again, asked him to pick up a quart of red beans and rice from Popeye's on Canal, then come up to the suite.

"Sam, you're sitting on top of a couple ritzy restaurants there at the Westin. Why don't you just dial down and tell 'em to whomp you up some red beans?"

"Tuck, why don't you just get your ass over here with one of them big styro cups, like I asked?"

"Yes, sir, Mr. Sam, sir."

Tuck, a compact, crew-cut ex–fighter pilot, barged in a half hour later with the takeout, a six-pack of Dixie beer, plus a suggestion that Sam make an early-morning visit to Brooks Brothers in the adjoining Canal Place Shopping Centre. Sam vetoed the idea. He'd already unwadded his gray suit from his bag and sent it out to be cleaned and pressed.

An hour later, while the two were mapping strategy, Lewis Thurman showed up, looking courtly and impeccable in one of his Savile Row suits.

"Thanks for coming, Lewie," Sam said, shaking his hand and motioning him into an armchair. "Tuck and I were just about to dope out the list of directors."

"You've been canvassing them all day, right?" Tuck asked.

"Correct."

"Well, how bad is it?"

Thurman finished polishing his bifocals, then looked up with a bleak smile. "Based on the general health of the company— its cash flow, market share, profit and sales projections, and certainly the stock performance—and on your long record and past services for the directors, Sam, I would have expected, if not strong support for you during a difficult situation, at least an inclination to give you the benefit of the doubt. Instead, except for a few instances, what I detected was a not always articulate discontent, which seems quite at odds with—"

"Hold on, *consigliere*," Sam interrupted, "I didn't call you here to pussyfoot around. If we've got a full-scale mutiny on our hands, I want to know about it."

"If I'd meant that, Sam, I would have said it. But so be it. End of preamble."

"Okay, let's go straight down the list, and I want both of you to call 'em as you see 'em."

Thurman and Tuck nodded, and they started.

First, as board chairman, Sam would obviously back himself on any resolution. One–zero.

Parry Joyce, a retired divisional CEO, a major stockholder and chairman of the executive committee, was also considered solidly on Sam's side. Parry owed Sam many past favors, not the least of which was a $200,000 annual consulting contract for doing basically nothing. Two–zero.

Hardesty Eason was a different story. The company's chief financial officer had apparently gunnysacked a great deal of resentment over the years at being overlooked in the decision-making. And Sam knew that importing D. W. Lee as president and chief operating officer had been a particularly bitter pill for Hardesty to swallow. And perversely, it seemed to have driven the big, red-faced ex-CPA to ally himself more and more closely with D.W. It was, in fact, Thurman's opinion that Hardy was actually orchestrating the pro-D.W. coup on the board.

"D.W.'s made him promises," Tuck agreed. Two–one, for Sam.

D.W., of course, would back himself. Call it two all.

John Godell, corporate counsel, was harder to handicap. Thurman, who had known Godell in law school, figured he was at that very minute taking his own straw poll and would vote whichever way the wind was blowing the strongest. "But he won't commit himself beforehand," Thurman said.

Lyman Fisher, who had enjoyed years of jeeping and tramping through Siberian wastes and Arabian deserts with Sam, would certainly vote with the chairman—if somebody could figure a way to drop a satellite phone on an Ecuadorian volcano at four o'clock tomorrow afternoon. Still two all.

All agreed that Gordon Fairfax, the thirty-two-year-old executive vice president for international sales, was securely in D.W.'s pocket. D.W. had jumped his protégé over several echelons of executives into his present job and at the last regular meeting had gotten him named to the board. Oxford-educated Fairfax looked to have unlimited upward mobility.

Which swung the vote now three–two in D.W.'s favor.

The three outside directors required more complicated analysis. Though D.W. had appointed none of them, he had recently boosted their director's fees to $50,000 a year and increased other perks, such as use of company jets and golf and ski condos. As chief executive, of course, Sam had signed off on all this largess, realizing full well what D.W. was doing. Pampering directors was axiomatic for any CEO—or would-be CEO, in D.W.'s case.

Now to specific cases. The first of the three, Elise Juergens, had been appointed by Sam five years earlier, after a short stint as ambassador to Honduras. In the interim, however, D.W. had gotten her named as token female to several other boards, each worth at least $10,000 a year. But as president of a women's liberal arts college—Woodrum in Missouri—she would be vulnerable to charges of participating in cultural and environmental exploitation of a Third World country. On the other hand, as Bill Tuck reminded them, Sam had not yet mailed his fall check to Woodrum's College Endowment—something D.W. had probably not overlooked. They decided she could go either way.

The other two outside directors were Mitchell Ross, a partner in Nunn Maltby, Proteus's principal investment bankers, and Edward Gilliland, a Wall Street lawyer. Both were apt to perceive D.W. as more of a deal-maker, and thus likelier to earn fat fees and commissions for their respective firms. And Thurman pointed out that D.W. had been throwing more of the company's antitrust litigation to Gilliland's firm, Cheval, Shay & Herriott.

"The little bastard has been awfully busy," Sam said, grinning. "I oughta vote for him myself to run the goddamned company."

The final tally was five for D.W., and only two definites for Sam—with a possible four, if Godell and Juergens both jumped aboard. Even then, Sam would have only four out of ten—unless he could sway them like Antony over bleeding Caesar. How the hell, he wondered aloud, after dozens of years of packing the board, had it gone over so quickly to D.W.? Arrogance and com-

166

placency on his part, Sam concluded, matched by D.W.'s shrewd attentiveness.

"You know, Sam, the broad support is still very much with you," Lewis Thurman countered. "If the directors vote you down tomorrow, why not take your case directly to the shareholders? This little tabloid smear"—the lawyer gestured dismissively at the green sheet on the carpet—"is utterly ephemeral. They all know what you've done for the company. And they certainly know their stock is trading at one of the highest multiples in the energy industry. Believe me, Sam, if you appeal to them, they'll listen to you."

Thurman was proposing Sam wage a proxy fight through mail and newspaper ads, advancing an alternative slate of directors and officers for the annual meeting in March.

Sam shook his head. "Five years ago I would have done it, Lewie. Maybe two or three. But right now, it's just not worth it to me. If these guys really don't want me anymore, then I'm gone."

"I don't like the sound of that, Sam," Thurman said. "I wish you'd reconsider. You know, you could raise issues that would scare hell out of the institutional investors. At least let me get Artie Glanzer to look at the idea." Glanzer was a partner in a New York law firm that specialized in proxy fights.

Sam shrugged. "Okay, Lewie, call Glanzer. Hell, maybe I'll even use a proxy fight as bluff tomorrow."

"Now you're sounding like yourself," Thurman agreed. "In the meantime, however, you might consider what sort of deal you'll cut if the board does back D.W."

"You mean, how much gold can I pack in my parachute? Not an issue, Lewie. I already fly my own plane, and I sure as hell don't need one of those ceremonial offices full of Lucite mementos."

"What about me?" Bill Tuck asked in convincingly distressed tones.

"Hey, what about you?" Sam countered dryly. "Can you ride a horse?"

Later, after both had gone, Sam reached John Godell, whom they'd considered one of the swing votes. Godell had a restored antebellum mansion in the Garden District. He sounded pretty groggy.

"Sorry, John. I didn't realize how late it was."

"It's okay, Sam. What is it?"

"For tomorrow's meeting, you know, I'm just getting all my damn ducks in a row. I wanted your opinion on how far things have gone."

"You mean has there already been a putsch?"

"Yeah, guess that's what I mean."

"The answer's no. But it's like Hardy's been saying around here, Sam. D.W.'s been doing the job you hired him to do, and now he feels like he's being interfered with. What we hear from D.W. is, all the signals are green down there, and you're the one who's suddenly putting on the brakes."

"Yeah, I understand how it looks that way. But is there anything else I should know?"

"Only in the sense that . . . well, there's a perception that for some time now, Sam, you haven't really consulted the management team or the board on major decisions. I was in Chicago when this mining thing broke, but what I heard was that you apparently breezed in and breezed out, without even asking for Hardy's or Ray's ideas, or any of the others. There's a perception that they haven't been treated with respect. You still with me?"

"I'm here, John."

"So, what happened, apparently, is that a couple of people made the suggestion to D.W. that something had to be done. Aw, hell, Sam, you know what I'm saying. That maybe this was the time for him to make a run at you."

"No names?"

"I'd rather not."

"But, anyway, D.W. looked favorably on the suggestion?"

Godell chuckled. "Yeah, you could say that."

"Okay, guess I'm guilty of most of those things. Guess I always have been. It's probably too late for a kinder, gentler Sam Warrender." Sam sighed into the mouthpiece. "Now what about this tabloid garbage, John? You seen it?"

"Unfortunately. My daughter brought a copy home. It's not a plus, Sam."

"So where do you think you stand tomorrow, John?"

"You know me, Sam. I bring a fresh yellow pad to every meeting. I'm not saying that personalities don't count, but I primarily vote the issues."

"That's all I'm asking, John. Hell, if D.W.'s right on the issues, he should win. You get back to sleep now."

No sooner had he hung up than Sam got a callback from Parry Joyce, whom he'd failed to reach earlier. Parry confirmed their handicapping right down the line, but thought that if Sam could work his old boardroom magic, everybody but D.W. and Gordon Fairfax could probably be converted—even Hardesty. "If anybody can do it, Sam, you can."

"I appreciate that, Parry. Nice to have at least one cheerleader on the field."

Sam cradled the phone, went to the window, brushed back the filmy outer curtain. On the broad river below—this would be the Mississippi, not the Orinoco—the ferry from Algiers was scattering a silver moonpath en route to the Canal Street landing. The night before battle, he thought. Napoleon before Waterloo? Or maybe Schwarzkopf before Desert Storm? But did it really matter all that much? Sam had survived more than his share of boardroom coups, won most, lost a couple, and he'd walk away from this one either way. The self-distancing that had troubled Lewie Thurman was really and truly there. Oh, Sam felt strongly about the rightness of the direction he was proposing for the company, and he intended to fight for it. But it wasn't a holy crusade. It just wasn't.

What he actually harbored now, looking out over this darkly flowing nocturne, was not the churning stomach of a battle commander, but an irreducible sense of loss—no matter how things went tomorrow. Was it loss of his company, his sense of purpose? Or something more tangible and tender?

He focused on his lamp-limned reflection hovering out there a few feet beyond the plate glass, like the night-walking ghost of Hamlet's father. A desolate figure. He tried to conjure a spectral companion, the haunting face of Jacqueline Lee beside his own. But it wouldn't come. He was truly alone out there, up here, wherever.

He turned back to the bed. Passed Xenophon on the bedside table. He hadn't cracked the book since that first night in Caracas almost a week ago. *Sorry, old warrior, I'm just too damn weary again tonight.*

Then he turned off the lamp and surrendered to sleep.

25

Sam Warrender, at one end of the black marble oval, gaveled the special session of the Proteus Board to order at precisely four o'clock. There were seven black-leather director chairs occupied, and two more directors split-screened on a thirty-six-inch color monitor at the opposite end of the marble slab. On his half of the screen, D.W. seemed very much at ease, smiling into the room from a conference center in a Puerto Ordaz office tower; Elise Juergens, on the other half, appeared stiff and self-conscious from a videoconference room at a Holiday Inn in Kansas City, twenty-five miles from her Woodrum University campus. The three limousines lined up on Lafayette Street thirty-one floors below testified to the recent arrivals: mannequin-perfect Mitchell Ross and big-bellied Ed Gilliland, both from Manhattan; and Gordon Fairfax, bright-eyed and burnished from a Palm Springs tennis week. The others—Parry Joyce, Hardesty Eason, and baby-faced John Godell—had merely ridden the elevator up from their various offices.

There were no minor housekeeping matters to get out of the way, no financials to peruse, no multimedia presentations to sit through. There was only one item on the agenda: Who was going to run the company? Sam, glancing occasionally at notes and tempering his folksiness, launched straight ahead.

"I have a brief opening statement," he said, as the auto-focus, auto-zoom camera atop the video monitor sent his voice and image, in algorithmic compressed form, over digital phone lines for decompression and display at the two remote locations. "I understand D.W. also has one. Afterward, I'll throw it open for resolutions and discussion.

"As you're all aware, my contract with the board specifies that I run this company. Unfortunately, during the last few days in Venezuela, that authority has been privately contested and, finally, openly usurped."

"I deny that charge categorically!" D.W. growled from his half of the monitor.

"You're out of order, D.W.!" Parry Joyce barked.

Seeming on the verge of further protest, D.W. clamped his jaw.

"Thank you, Parry, but I'll run the meeting." Sam splashed water into a crystal goblet from a nearby carafe. "For whatever reason, Duk-Won Lee has made decisions, in regard to the Venezuelan government and our joint mining operations, which he was not authorized to make without my consultation or approval.

"Setting aside for the moment the merits or demerits of those decisions, it was flat wrong for D.W. to have proceeded as he did. I was not incommunicado, as I believe has been suggested to certain members of this board. I spent four days at my ranch adjoining our Cerro Calvario leaseholds, waiting for a government delegation to return to Caracas. During that time, I spoke on the telephone with several people in this room, and with D.W. himself on at least three occasions.

"At no time during this period did D.W. inform me that he was conducting long-range negotiations with Venezuelan officials—I believe then in Senegal—or that he was making decisions and attempting to gain a majority backing for those decisions on this board. Furthermore, D.W. knew I'd changed my mind about resuming mining. He simply chose to ignore that, to bypass me and go directly to the board—and then, apparently getting a go-ahead from certain directors, to make commitments to the Venezuelan government.

"When I finally found out what was going on, I offered D.W. a chance to rescind his actions. He chose instead to escalate his challenge to my authority, which brings us, I'm very sad to say, to this emergency session, in which you all must now decide

171

the issue. Let me just say it again. Regardless of the merit of any decisions D.W. made or his many important contributions to Proteus Industries, I consider his recent actions to be a clear violation of the operating policy of this company, and of my trust in him."

Parry Joyce started to speak in support, but Sam cut him off and turned to the monitor.

D.W. had regained his composure. "I'm afraid that Samuel's version of events bears very little resemblance to the facts. During the time he was on his Venezuelan ranch, I tried many times to get him to confer with me directly on the situation, which was extremely volatile. I also requested that Samuel participate in meetings I was having with various executives in Puerto Ordaz. But he preferred to stay on his ranch, to go horseback riding, to take my daughter and some archaeologist on a flight over Angel Falls, and generally to act as though there were no crisis, no urgency.

"Frankly I became alarmed by his behavior, and even more alarmed when he told me suddenly, and without any explanation, that he wished to reverse our corporate position on Cerro Calvario. In other words, to walk away from the entire project! And there were other upsetting incidents. I learned from Ray Arrillaga, who came down to advise me, that Samuel had not even bothered to consult the management team before flying down.

"Of course I consulted with members of this board. As president, I am certainly not forbidden from doing so. Unlike Samuel, I do seek collegial advice whenever possible. I told several of you then about the critical nature of the negotiations, and that a breakthrough could come at any moment, but that Samuel seemed unwilling or unable to seize such an opportunity. I was then urged—by all of those whom I consulted—to seize any opportunity that might present itself. And I have done so.

"As a result, two days ago I faxed to John Godell a long-term agreement signed by the Venezuelan president and by myself on behalf of Proteus, authorizing full resumption of our joint mining venture. I have signed many such documents, by the way, as Samuel knows—with Korea and Indonesia, for instance, and Kazakhstan and several others. Work will now resume on the railroad link to Cerro Bolívar, and on construction of a workers camp. The archaeological excavations, which temporarily halted our operations, are being relocated.

"I, too, regret that a management breach has opened between Samuel and myself. We have been good friends for many years and have worked well together. I sincerely hope our friendship survives this unfortunate series of events. But I cannot base business decisions on concern for friendship. And I believe the board will agree that I have acted responsibly, and in the best interests of the company and its shareholders."

As D.W. sat back, there were grave nods from Hardesty Eason, Gordon Fairfax, and Mitchell Ross. The others, Sam thought, appeared noncommittal; and Elise seemed inscrutable on her half of the screen. But the ugly conflict was now out on the table for all to see. Before proceeding to specific resolutions, Sam called for general discussion.

To Sam's surprise, Elise Juergens responded first. "It is perfectly apparent that you have arrived at an executive impasse," she said without altering expression, "but I fail to see why it couldn't have been resolved without convening an emergency session of the entire board. Couldn't the executive committee have arbitrated this? I happen to be in the middle of important annual budget meetings at Woodrum—"

"Elise," Hardesty broke in, "I'm sure we all wish this hadn't happened. But it has, and it *is* a crisis meriting the immediate attention of the board, as I told you yesterday."

"Is there anything you want to add, Elise?" Sam asked.

"Not at this time."

"Then I'll say something." Hardy Eason whacked a pen down on a legal pad. "You know, Sam, I don't know why I got so mad when you went charging off down south without even listening to us. Because this kind of cavalier behavior on your part has happened too damn many times to be news, as I think quite a few members of this board will agree."

"Well, you're not speaking for me!" Parry Joyce snapped.

"Why don't you take a number, Parry, and wait your damn turn!" Hardy shot back.

"Now, folks," Sam said, gaveling, "I guess I forgot to mention it, but that little camera there pivots and zooms on voice actuation, so if you're all gonna talk at once, it'll just spin itself dizzy. Now go ahead and give me hell, Hardy."

"I'm just giving you straight talk, Sam. When you keep ignoring us, it makes the board and the officers feel sorta superfluous, know what I mean? And I happen to feel that's a damn perilous course for any publicly held company to be steering in this day and age. But let me back up a bit, to the part about you flying off to Venezuela, because at least I counted on you being on the same page as the rest of us in regard to getting the mining up and running.

"Then, suddenly, we hear you've changed your mind, almost like you were brainwashed or something, and are actually trying to keep D.W. from doing what he was hired to do. I'm here to tell you, Sam, Proteus needs that ore. And thanks to D.W.'s efforts, not yours, we're going to get it."

"Hardy, I'm not proposing we give up that ore. I was hoping to confine this discussion to the underlying issue of chain of command. But since you're questioning my business judgment on specifics, I'll address it briefly. That ore is not going anywhere. I'm only suggesting we hold off on going after it—until certain scientific and political conflicts are resolved—and I don't mean just swept aside with payoffs."

Hardy shook his big head. "Hold off how long, Sam? Gordon was just going over some numbers with me this morning. They don't look good—"

"The hell they don't!" Parry Joyce interrupted. "This company is paying a goddamn handsome dividend, Hardy, as we all know."

"Altogether too handsome, if you ask me," Gordon Fairfax said in clipped Oxonian tones. "We're currently paying more than twice the company's per-share earnings, around four times the industry average. This is money we drastically need for exploration and to increase reserves."

"Last time I checked, Gordon," Parry countered, "I didn't see your name on the finance committee, so I think we can do without your expertise."

"And I wasn't referring to our common stock dividend, for God's sakes," Eason resumed. "So, Parry, you can stop popping up with your damn objections every thirty seconds."

"A great man is on trial here, and I'll say what I damn feel like on his behalf."

"All right, you just said it. Now back to the troubling numbers I am referring to. In addition to depressed crude prices, we all know petrochemicals haven't done well lately. And some of our recent exploration pacts—in Sakhalin Island, another near the Caspian in Kazakhstan, and offshore drilling in the North Aleutians—have been damn disappointing. And then there's all these goddamn environmental regulations, mandating expensive refinery modifications. And now D.W. tells me our projections on what we're going to get out of our LNG platforms in the Gulf of Paria might have been too optimistic."

"Especially if some archaeologist in a submarine finds Atlantis underneath them," Fairfax quipped.

"Hardy, there's no need to belabor the obvious," Sam said. "We've all heard the quarterly gloom-and-doom report."

"Fine. We've all heard it. So what's the bottom line? We damn well need operating profits from our metal-mining division, and that means Cerro Calvario. And we need it up and running as soon as possible."

"Which would also help our bulk carriers," Fairfax said. "I understand we have two ore ships currently in Japan, doing nothing but accumulating dock fees and rust."

"Aren't we wandering rather far afield here from the main issue?" This was the first comment from the rotund Wall Street lawyer, Ed Gilliland. "These seem to be matters which require industry expertise, which I, for one, certainly do not possess."

"He's absolutely right," Parry Joyce said.

"Maybe I can bring it all back home," Sam said. "Of course, Hardy's right. We need that ore. What we don't need is a firestorm of negative publicity with it. We don't need newspaper editorials claiming we're raping some Third World country and destroying its cultural legacy. And this is exactly what will happen if we start blasting away on that mountain now—regardless of what the Venezuelan government says. The media guns are primed, believe me, just waiting for the next big-business bad guys to stumble into their sights. Exxon in Alaska, Union Carbide in Bhopal, Proteus in Venezuela. It could happen."

"That sounds awfully alarmist," Gordon Fairfax said. "I rather think that either Rowland's people, or one of our outside PR firms, could put out any such 'firestorm' on fairly short order, by emphasizing the continuing archaeological work in the area, which I understand we are underwriting, and the important contributions we'll be making to the Venezuelan economy—thousands of jobs and so forth, medical facilities, that sort of thing. That's hardly Bhopal, is it? And according to D.W., there are some rather unsavory stories regarding this archaeologist character. In addition to falsifying the locations of his discoveries, wasn't he arrested for sedition or something down there?"

"This is correct," D.W. said. "As of this moment, Dr. Laya has been removed as head of this project."

Sam lost his cool. "Goddammit, D.W., you know that's a trumped-up charge! The man falsified nothing! I was there, I know what I saw. He's being set up by one of his assistants, and a bunch of ministers, who are getting under-the-table payoffs from us, are using it to get him out of the way so mining can go forward. And it's all gonna come out. There are people down there who are not in anybody's pocket, and they're going to demand an independent investigation, and we're going to end up being reviled all over the goddamn hemisphere."

"Perhaps Sam is being an alarmist," Elise Juergens said. "I don't know. But those certainly are alarming possibilities he raises. And I, for one, certainly think all this requires more study. And again, I don't think it's an appropriate matter for a hastily called session."

"We already know how you feel about that, Elise," Hardy said.

"I'd like to add something else," Parry Joyce said. "Regardless of what happens or doesn't happen in Venezuela, I personally feel this kind of palace coup—and let's face it, that's what we're talking about here—would create a terrible impression of this company in the market."

An awkward silence descended on the table. Several eyes strayed to the monitor, but D.W. said nothing.

Then Hardesty cleared his throat. "Well, I disagree. Proteus is not a one-man operation. What we don't need is an old man Hammer or Howard Hughes label pasted on this building. That kind of thing scares hell out of investors. Which is why we've had Rollo stressing our management *team*. And Sam knows that as well as any of us. Isn't that why he brought in D.W. in the first place?"

Mitchell Ross jumped in quickly. "I have to agree. Obviously, whenever you have a situation where a successor is groomed and then repeatedly stalled, there tends to be an erosion of faith in that successor, and in the company's future. By rounding this corner decisively now, I think Proteus can definitely avoid that negative impression on the Street."

"Perhaps I can take that argument even a bit further," said Gordon Fairfax, unfolding a tabloid page. "This is today's *New York Post*, the Page Six gossip column. It contains a rather distasteful tidbit about our chairman, and a fortunately small photo inset—the same photo that graced the front page of yesterday's *Crescent City Sun*—which I believe has been faxed throughout the Proteus network. The *Post*, granted, is not the *Wall Street Journal*, but it does have a certain circulation. May I suggest—with all due respect, Sam—that an immediate closing of corporate ranks around a new leadership team might actually enhance our recently tarnished image?"

The debate bounced around the table a few more times, without turning up anything substantially new. So Sam decided to bring it to a halt. He gave himself the last word:

"Unfortunately, Parry is right when he says what this meeting is about. It's sure as hell not about orderly succession. Whether I took too long making my exit or not, the fact is D.W. didn't wait for his cue. As to the decision on mining, that's a judgment call. I happen to think D.W.'s judgment is off. But it's a clear matter of corporate governance that the call was not his to make. It was mine. Or was until this meeting. And I guess that's really all I have to say."

Parry Joyce then launched into another embarrassing encomium about Sam's manifold contributions, conjuring large blocs of stockholders to agree with him, and concluding that the company owed Sam immeasurably more than it could ever repay.

D.W. followed with his own carefully controlled praise for Sam. And when Hardy Eason began to make similar noises, Sam had had enough. It was starting to sound like a eulogy. So he gaveled an end to all discussion and called for a motion.

"Okay," he asked, surveying the faces around the black oval slab, "who's got the honors here?"

John Godell startled him by speaking first. Until that moment, the counselor had indeed been keeping his cards close to his lawyerly vest. "I guess I drew the short straw," he said with something resembling a smile.

Godell's resolution, seconded by Hardy Eason, was pretty much what Sam had expected. Sam would "move up" to chairman emeritus at his current annual salary and bonus until his mandated retirement date, while maintaining his seat on the board. D.W. would immediately assume the joint offices of chairman and chief executive and subsequently name a new president. The board, meanwhile, would announce its full support for all D.W.'s previous decisions in regard to the mining ventures in Bolívar State.

Sam listened to it with an odd feeling of detachment. Since considerable discussion had preceded the resolution, there was no opposition to his call for an immediate vote. It went slightly better than he and his advisers had figured. John Godell, having proposed the resolution, obviously voted for it, as did the investment banker, Mitchell Ross. But the remaining two outside directors, Elise Juergens and Ed Gilliland, both sided with Sam. With Parry Joyce and himself, that gave Sam four votes. Had Lyman Fisher not selected this particular time to go mountaineering, Sam realized bleakly, the vote would have been deadlocked. As it was, the resolution carried five–four.

"Well," Sam said, "that seems to be it. I accept the verdict. As the old cowboy said, 'If you ain't got a choice, be brave.' So, D.W., it looks like your end of this slab just became the head of the table. I guess you'll have to provide your own gavel."

D.W. started to speak, but Sam held up a big palm. "Hang on, I'm winding down here." He looked around, then over their heads at the big chromium wall sculpture and the New Orleans skyline gleaming through the drapes. "It's been a hell of a run. And I want you to know that I really don't harbor any bitterness toward anybody here who voted against me. If there's anybody I'm ticked off at, it's gotta be Lyman Fisher up on that damn volcano.

"I certainly don't have any resentment toward my successor. Except for the last few days, we've made a hell of a team. I wish him and all of you nothing but success. But, Duke, I'm warning you one last time, look very hard at what you're doing down there.

"Now this isn't a good-bye speech. You'll see me from time to time. But right now, I think I'll slip out the door and let you go ahead and deal with anything else you like. I would like to see your press release on this before it goes out. You can give it to Bill Tuck. Now just sit down, Parry, and hush up. We'll toast a few later. Right now these folks need your advice. Hell, they still need mine. They just don't want it at the moment. D.W., take over."

Sam stood up in his fresh-pressed gray suit and cowboy boots, felt for his formal gray Stetson, and shook hands around the table, then finally escaped. As the heavy door latched behind him, he just kept walking and smiling, right past Birdy and several others and then past the tinkling fountain under the hot atrium lights to the brass-doored elevator, then down and out across the vaulted, echoing lobby. When he hit fresh air, he breathed deeply and waved off the big uniformed chauffeur by the stretch Lincoln and started walking down Lafayette. He reached the river a few minutes too late for sunset and turned left on the Riverwalk and continued along the levee, then sat down wearily on a bench and watched a big stern-wheeler full of tourists churning upstream into evening gray, while the darkening current moved relentlessly the other way, pushing and shoving out toward the Gulf.

He felt free. Adrift, like the current. And terribly alone.

26

The big trucks rumbled through the Cerro Calvario gate, churning up red dust. There were four giant flatbeds with the Ferrominera emblem, piggybacking some of Caterpillar's finest—an earthmover, two D8 Cat bulldozers, and a motor grader with a ten-foot blade. Bringing up the rear was a dust-clad Proteus Land Cruiser, a hard-hatted Ray Arrillaga at the wheel and a Venezuelan mining engineer riding shotgun. A red-bearded flagman waved it through, scurried to close and padlock the big mesh-wire gate, then sought refuge in the Proteus gatehouse as protesters surged forward through the swirling dust, jeering and chanting.

Their ragged charge was met by a squad of baton-wielding, flak-jacketed National Guardsmen, who quickly closed ranks in front of the gate. The protesters broke and retreated before this advancing olive green wall, then reformed at a somewhat safer distance across the road, hurling taunts and waving placards and generally playing out their indignation for the benefit of nearby video cameras.

Several news crews had turned up for the event. Their microwave vans were prominent among the vehicles glinting in the midday sunshine along both sides of the two-lane access road. Even Marina Estévez was on hand in her form-fitting jungle fatigues, waiting for the dust to settle before doing her stand-up. But she counted on this being one of her last days out in the boondocks. As a result of her recent topless tabloid splash, Marina's agent was currently negotiating a news anchor position for her in Caracas—and maybe a guest shot in a *telenovela*.

The main protest contingent had flown and caravanned down that morning from Caracas. They were from Simón Bolívar University and the City University, the Natural Sciences Museum and several conservation organizations. Even so, there were less than a hundred, but by constantly milling and recirculating, they appeared far more numerous in tight camera shots. They swarmed now down the road from the gate, where a spindly man in an Oakland A's baseball cap, *liki-liki* shirt, and khaki shorts stood on the back of a pickup truck, waving a bullhorn. Dr. Arquimedeo Laya López waited for a go-ahead from an assistant, indicating the video cameras were ready, then began his prepared speech:

"My friends, five centuries ago, on his third voyage, Christopher Columbus landed on our shores and arrogantly claimed our land and all its peoples and wealth for the Spanish crown. This launched the slaughter of the Arawaks and the Caribs, our original inhabitants, a slaughter that continued under the many conquistadors who came after Columbus in search of gold.

"But ancient history, alas, is not a closed book. For what we have witnessed here today is not a new invasion, but only the latest episode in a continuing invasion by greedy foreigners—in this case a modern corporate Columbus, Proteus Industries."

Arquimedeo paused to accommodate an angry chorus of shouts and boos, then resumed:

"As you see, these latter-day conquistadors come riding bulldozers instead of horses, and in quest of iron instead of gold. But that is a minor difference. And they trample us down with the corrupt connivance of certain segments of our own government"—more denunciations burst forth—"officials who, for the right price, are apparently willing to permit the ongoing rape of our land and its history.

"My friends, these officials have run me off my own excavation and confiscated my scientific instruments and findings. But I can tell you exactly what is about to happen behind that gate on Cerro Calvario. Those bulldozers will begin cutting huge terraces around the mountain, on which to lay track for an iron-ore railway. When this is done, they will begin dynamiting the mountain to rubble, which the train will carry off to the Orinoco, exactly as has been done on Cerro Bolívar. The crushed rocks will be loaded into large ships bound for foreign ports. And among those crushed rocks, those ships will also carry away crushed artifacts from those same Arawak Indians, and from the ancestors of the Arawaks and their ancestors, prehistoric trea-sures that have lain buried for millennia.

"As some of you know, I uncovered some of these treasures before I was thrown off the mountain. I am absolutely certain that many more remain to be uncovered. But that priceless his-torical record will now be obliterated, and that process of de-struction begins now, today, here!"

This time Arquimedeo continued over their angry outburst, shouting into the bullhorn:

"The world must know what is happening here today! The world must heed . . ."

As the TV video cameras recorded Arquimedeo's impassioned speech, across the road a lone figure squinted into the eyepiece of an eight-millimeter Handycam, documenting the entire scene, including the seething circle of supporters and flanking news crews. Jacqueline Lee had positioned herself farther out by in-stinct. But realizing now that her wider focus revealed the rel-atively small turnout of protesters, she wondered if she should edit the shot out later. Then she scolded herself. She was, after all, making a documentary, not a propaganda film. The size of the crowd was a significant part of her story, and part of Arqui-medeo's struggle.

So she widened out farther, shrinking the turbulent gathering into the vast savanna horizon. Then she panned right, down the mirage-rippled ribbon of asphalt vanishing to the north, then left again to the main gate. The mountain was almost totally ob-scured now behind billowing, rust-colored clouds, through which could be heard the growling and bellowing of the diesel-powered dinosaurs, laboring with their massive burdens.

Jacqueline had been on-site since before sunrise, rolling tape to document the eviction of Dr. Laya and his shell-shocked vol-unteers by National Guardsmen after a two-day standoff. In the end, the diminutive archaeologist had had to be dragged, flailing and shouting curses, out of his tent and hustled into the back of a Guardia jeep. Three of his four female volunteers were even more shrill, and far more graphic in their obscenities. Jacqueline had gotten it all, then switched eight-millimeter cassettes an instant before a Guardia corporal spotted her and approached menacingly. She looked suitably horrified as the pockmarked soldier snatched her Handycam, ejected the blank two-and-a-half-hour cassette, and shoved it into his waistband, then handed back her camera.

"No más!" he scolded, first shaking his finger at her, then pointing forcefully toward the exit road. *"Véte, chica!"* Clearly, she was to be permitted no more footage at the camp. Jacqueline had exhibited more convincing outrage at this rude treatment, before finally retreating under his scrutiny—and managing to conceal both her sense of one-upmanship and the cassette nestled in her briefs.

Félix Rosales had not put in an appearance. He had prudently made himself scarce since the government announcement that he would be replacing Dr. Laya on the Cerro Calvario project and supervising an excavation at an alternative site at the foot of the South Hill. Simón Bolívar University had already stated its unqualified support for Dr. Laya and its repudiation of Félix Rosales and any and all allegations against Laya's scientific integrity. And in some on-the-fly reactions Jacqueline had videotaped, crew members had expressed even more loathing and contempt for Félix and his treachery than for the high-level corruption that obviously lay behind Dr. Laya's ouster. Only one volunteer had failed to curse the muscular young archaeologist—the tough little fisherman's daughter from Cumaná, Marta Mendes, who plainly had a sizable crush on him.

"Oh, come on, Marta!" Jacqueline had said, switching off the camera. She found the homely girl's blind adoration to be exasperating—and pathetic. "Félix is, is—God, I don't know— just a dirtbag with muscles. And believe me, he's already got a crush on himself."

"I suppose you think you can have anyone you want, don't you, Jacquie?"

Having delivered this schoolyard non sequitur, Marta stalked off. It was clear to Jacqueline that, if Félix intended to pursue his sham excavation while the mountain was being devoured nearby, he could count on at least one worshipful volunteer.

Now, nearing one in the afternoon, with eight hours of this unequal ordeal behind her, Jacqueline's earlier sense of triumph in smuggling out the cassette had given way to thorough exhaustion. Nor had her mood been elevated when, while tracking her camera during the main gate debacle, she had focused on the busty bottle-blonde from Ciudad Bolívar TV, the one Sam had made a drunken fool of himself over on the *Kallisto*.

It was, all in all, a considerable relief when Jacqueline realized that Arquimedeo was winding up his speech. She could use a breather. The crowd apparently felt the same way. Even before the final round of applause and cheers had died away, the protesters began dispersing down the road toward a catering van that advertised *café* and *jugos* and *cervezas*, *arepas* and *plátanos*, *hamburguesas* and *perros calientes*. And with no more heavy equipment scheduled to be rumbling through the gates that day, the media crews began quickly packing up. Jacqueline figured most of the protesters would do likewise.

She turned and hiked down the road to her own truck, conjuring its ice cooler full of diet Pepsis. Actually, in a deal hammered out during a father-daughter shouting match over her insistence on coming down here, it was an unmarked Proteus pickup, with young Bernardo along as driver and pint-size bodyguard. Even when Jacqueline was being her most mutinous, it seemed, D.W. managed to exert his control. Jacqueline could see Bernardo's spiky head silhouetted in the cab, complete with radio headphones that were probably feeding him soccer play-by-play.

But before she reached the pickup, a husky female voice accosted her from behind. "Miss Lee, may I speak to you a moment?"

Jacqueline turned to see Señorita Marina Estévez teetering toward her in high-heeled sandals. She waited for the showy newswoman to draw near, noticing with surprise how cool and collected the theatrically shadowed and lashed eyes seemed under the brim of the silly bush hat.

"Yes?"

"Miss Lee, I understand that you're here today . . ."—the newswoman was slightly out of breath—"protesting the actions of your father's company . . . and I wondered if I could induce you to do a brief interview . . . in English." Señorita Estévez's own English was quite fluent, and she gestured across the road toward the parked Noticolor TV panel truck.

"I'm sorry," Jacqueline replied curtly. "I don't do interviews. I'm here making a film actually."

"Just a few words? Really, whatever you'd like to say."

"Believe me, *señorita*, you wouldn't like what I'd like to say to you."

The blond newswoman went wide-eyed, but with just a hint of smile. "Oh? And what's that supposed to mean?"

"I'll give you one hint. After what happened on my father's boat, you actually expect me, or anyone else, to take you seriously as a *journalist?* What a joke!"

"*Bueno!* Look, honey, you may think you know what happened at that party, but you don't. So spare me the smug sarcasm. All you or anyone else saw was the end of a nasty accident—an accident that wasn't my fault. But for your information, I apologized to your father anyway."

"So, what did happen?"

"What did happen is none of your damn business."

The blonde pivoted away behind the rakish hat, but Jacqueline sidestepped quickly to confront her anew.

"Okay, so it's none of my damn business. And if I'm out of line, I apologize for the attitude. But I really want to know, okay? What happened between you and Sam?"

Señorita Estévez narrowed the Egyptiac eyes. "And why is it so important to you?"

"It just is."

"Will you agree to an interview if I tell you?"

"Yes. I mean, if it's reasonable."

"Not to worry, honey. Okay. As you may or may not know, Samuel was *muy borracho*—very, very drunk—that night, and he wanted to leave the ship."

"What were you doing together?"

Señorita Estévez smiled. "Let me tell it, okay?"

"I'm sorry."

"I was up on the deck where you keep the twin speedboats, having a drink and being propositioned by your little Boy Scout in there." The newswoman pointed a lacquered, beringed index finger at the back of the spiky head in the cab.

"Bernardo? You're joking?"

"Well, of course, *I* thought it was awfully amusing, but I suspect Bernardo was deadly serious. He had the look of a big-game hunter, if you know what I mean. Anyway, Samuel Warrender rescued me from the little sex fiend by lurching along and asking Bernardo to get his keys from his cabin and drive him to the Inter-Continental in Puerto Ordaz. Well, I made the mistake of trying to help Samuel down to the dock. He was staggering around pretty bad, and I tried to stop him, but he insisted he could make it. So, we got as far as the stairs to the main deck, when he got dizzy and started falling. I tried to grab him, but he grabbed me first"—Señorita Estévez clutched the front of her jumpsuit, miming a panicky expression—"and hung on as he fell. You know the rest of it, honey. Every fucking photographer in Ciudad Guayana was waiting for us at the bottom. We were, what's the word—celebs?"

"And that's all that happened between you?"

"Sorry to disappoint you. What'd you think, we were having a party?"

"Frankly, yes."

The blonde shrugged. "I wouldn't have minded. I happen to think he's a sexy man. No insult to Bernardo, but Samuel's more my type. Unfortunately, I don't think I'm his. Anyway, I got a lot of free publicity, and in my business almost any kind of publicity is good. So, I'm going national, maybe next week. But I heard what happened to Samuel, and I'm truly sorry. I hope you will tell him that, honey. For the record, though, I disagree with Samuel, and you, on this mining operation down here. Venezuela needs the jobs, and the foreign capital." The newswoman smiled. "Now, your turn. Can I call my guy over?"

"Sure. Thanks for telling me what happened, *señorita.*"

"Call me Marina."

"Okay, Marina. And I apologize for—well, for being a little bitch."

"Honey, if there is one thing you are not, it is little."

When the stringy-haired, Goofy-shirted cameraguy was ready, Jacqueline identified herself and stated her well-rehearsed opinions on Cerro Calvario and the irreparable damage being done to the reputation of a fine and distinguished archaeologist. When she'd finished, the technician swung his camera and tripod re-

186

flector around to get Señorita Estévez's reaction shots. The blond newswoman licked her lips, unzipped her jumpsuit top several strategic inches, and as tape began to roll, tilted her head slowly this way and that while nodding thoughtfully—and it was a wrap.

Despite all the high-gloss flimflam, Jacqueline found herself grudgingly revising her opinion of Señorita Estévez. The woman had done nothing terribly wrong—except, perhaps, to wear a gown insufficiently attached to her torso. Jacqueline was also having to revise her editorial opinions of the shipboard party, especially its scandalous denouement. She had said some nasty things to poor Sam before he was led away. Probably—she hoped—he had been in no condition to remember any of them. Then, when she had gotten word from her father yesterday about Sam's being put out to pasture by the Proteus board, she hadn't even had the decency to call or cable him her sorrow at the news. And she was sorry, dammit! And doubly furious at her father.

And even that wasn't all of it. Hadn't she been more than a bit responsible for Sam's humiliating fall in the first place? Spurting all those delicious mouthfuls of Veuve Clicquot down his throat? But, God, it had been exciting! She'd done it once, years before at a fraternity party, but with an archetypical bozo. How much naughtier and more knee-wobbling the ritual had been with Sam, with his virile, savory smell and Rodin-sculpted jaw and devilish eyebrows and hooded, gray-eagle eyes!

Not that she was entirely prepared to forgive him yet. But she was seriously thinking about it.

27

Jacqueline waited in the truck beside Bernardo, sipping her Pepsi and watching the media vans drive away and the crowd around Dr. Laya dwindle and disperse. Eventually, the archaeologist made his way wearily across the road toward her. She stepped out, offering him a cold soda.

He declined. "Thanks, I just had a beer. It's been a long morning, hasn't it?"

"Uh-huh. I just want to tell you, you were quite wonderful, Dr. Laya." She had tried for a hopeful tone, but his bitter smile made it difficult.

"How kind. And, unfortunately, how irrelevant." He sighed. "And did you capture it all for posterity?"

"Everything I could."

"I'm sure you will make an excellent film, Jacqueline, one that will, how do you say, raise consciousness? But it will be too late to save Cerro Calvario. To have any hope of that, we desperately needed CNN here today. And, well, you saw what we got. Our Minister of Mines and your father should both get down on their knees and give thanks to Señorita Jessica."

Dr. Laya was referring to Hurricane Jessica, which had laid waste the coast of Belize the day before, then swerved northwest across the Yucatán Peninsula, uprooting palms and leveling villages, leaving scores dead and thousands homeless. Jessica was now spinning capriciously over the Gulf. But by nightfall, she was expected to plow ashore again, somewhere along a five-hundred-mile arc from Tampico to Galveston. CNN bureaus and other news facilities around the Caribbean basin were all on twenty-four-hour storm watch, as wind-driven waves lashed shores and seawalls. On a slow or average news day, this political confrontation at Cerro Calvario might have elicited a couple of international camera crews. But on this day, with the eyes of the world riveted just to the north, only three Venezuelan video crews had shown up, not counting Jacqueline and her Sony Handycam.

"Dr. Laya, you're not giving up the fight?"

"No, Jacqueline. I will never do that. But I do feel a bit like the shepherd boy David seeing all his carefully aimed pebbles bounce off of Goliath's helmet, then having the giant trample him beneath his sandals and keep on going—and laughing, you see. But no, I will get up now and look for another little stone to fling."

"But so many people are rallying behind you—all the universities, the environmental groups, the anthropological society. And what about all your equipment?"

"It's all still inside. I only came out with a few boxes of personal possessions and, thank God, a complete streaming-tape backup of my hard disk."

"Well, I'm going to call my father about it. I mean, in addition to every other atrocity he's helping to commit down here, how dare he confiscate scientific equipment!"

"Thank you, Jacqueline, but I advise you to save your outrage for something of larger import. It's not the equipment I want out, it's the accursed bulldozers. Until I abandon that possibility, the generators and resistivity meters and magnetometers may as well stay where they are, as long as Félix keeps them properly protected. Heaven knows, he won't be needing them. He can make do with a case of beer and a shovel."

"The bastard!"

"I still don't know what I could have done to cause him to turn on me—other than to imagine such a visceral young man would actually share my peculiar enthusiasms."

"That's a point, Dr. Laya. You know, he really isn't very bright."

"No, Félix has a tightly circumscribed intelligence. But he came to be very handy at running an excavation and seemed to enjoy the rigors and routines of camp life, much more than I. And he had—he has—a lively sense of humor. But—as you said—he's being a bastard."

"And I can think of a few other words."

"Well, I'm very angry at him, Jacqueline. And to be honest, I'm deeply hurt."

"That's because you're sensitive. But I don't think you should take it personally, Dr. Laya. I've known guys like Félix before. You know, big hair, big muscles, tight jeans, the lazy grin, the swaggering walk. Girls fall at his feet—I almost did. It's scary. So, when conquest comes so easy, why should he work at relationships? I don't know if guys like that are incapable of forming actual emotional attachments, or if they just don't want to put out the effort. Whichever it is, trust me, Félix isn't worth one second of your concern."

"You're very perceptive. But I suspect that Félix actually feels very inadequate. His life was a long series of failures before I offered him a kind of sanctuary and a steady job. And I still can't help feeling sorry for him. I don't know what your father or the mining officials may have offered him to carry out his charade, but it won't last long. He certainly has no future in archaeology. No university would go near him after this."

"Maybe he'll marry rich."

"Hmm. Now you make me feel distinctly guilty, Jacqueline. I should have warned you about Félix. He *was* giving you a lot of attention, wasn't he?"

"Uh-huh. It lasted about two days. Pretty intense. But I survived, thank God." Mainly by getting interested in somebody else, Jacqueline thought. "But to hell with muscleboy. What are you going to do now, Dr. Laya?"

"Regroup." Dr. Laya attempted a smile, then leaned against the front fender of her pickup and stared off at the dust-wreathed mountain—his buried city, his Troy, now the exclusive precinct of lawful plunderers.

When Jacqueline had observed him several days before at the dig, the wiry little archaeologist had seemed tireless. But he slumped badly now and appeared momentarily lost. Of course, he'd been up all night, she knew, and probably most of two days before, mustering his slim resources for this showdown. And now, to all intents and purposes, he'd lost. There would be no scientific examination up on Cerro Calvario to check on the validity of Félix's charges of site falsification. With bulldozers now having the run of the mountain, and dynamite soon to follow, the evidence would quickly be destroyed—along with the archaeological record. Dr. Laya must be in profound shock.

"And you, *señorita?*" he inquired after an interval. "What will you do next? Document the destruction?"

"I guess it sounds grisly, but I may as well finish."

"No. It sounds professional and admirable. But what does your father say?"

"You mean what does he shout. We're not exactly on speaking terms at the moment. Let's see. Last night Daddy ordered me to fly home to school, and what did I call him? A thug, I think. Yes, definitely a thug. Then I hung up on him."

"Good heavens!"

Just then a mud-splattered Ford half-ton full of hay bales drove by and pulled onto the shoulder behind them. A *llanero* climbed out and started toward them. As the sun worked its way under the brim of the man's straw hat, Jacqueline and Arquimedeo recognized Sam's ranch foreman, Enrico Tosto. He tipped his hat and smiled.

"*Buenos días*, Professor Laya. Señorita Lee."

Jacqueline answered first. "*Buenos días*, Enrico. You missed all the excitement."

"I heard it. I see the dust. I smell the diesels." He turned to Arquimedeo. "And I am very sorry, Professor."

"But why should you be, *señor?* This is wonderful news for La Promesa. I predict you will sell a great many cattle."

"It is true. As a rancher, I should be happy. And as an immigrant, why should I care about buried Indian relics? But it is not right, what they are doing to you, Professor. So I am changing sides, just as Samuel did, and just as Señorita Lee has done in opposing her father." Enrico smiled with his eyes. "It is most confusing."

"Then I apologize for my sarcasm," Arquimedeo said. "And I am truly sorry about Señor Warrender. I give him much credit. And I am afraid I said many unfair things to him."

191

"Believe me, Samuel will be fine. I think he was ready for retirement. Actually, it is because of him that I am here."

"He sent you to find me?" Arquimedeo asked.

"Both of you, if possible. We didn't guess you would be together. Samuel wanted me to tell you, Dr. Laya, that he is sorry he couldn't stop what is happening. But if it will be of any assistance, he invites you to make Hato la Promesa your headquarters down here. We have several guest rooms in the *casa grande*. You also are welcome, Señorita Lee, depending on the situation with your father—"

"I jumped ship late last night," Jacqueline announced. "I was going to stay in Ciudad Bolívar tonight."

"Then I think even your father might feel better about your safety if you are with us."

"I really don't care what he thinks."

"It is an extremely generous offer," Dr. Laya said. "And I thank Señor Warrender for it. But I have many people to confer with—"

"They are welcome, too, up to a dozen or more. You are to consider it your private hotel. Call press conferences, stage protest rallies, whatever you wish. If you like, you may even camp along the perimeter of Cerro Calvario. We have tents—and plenty of good beef." Enrico grinned. "Samuel has also left his plane and will provide a pilot to fly you over the mountain, *señorita*, should you wish to photograph what is happening there."

"Well?" Jacqueline turned to Arquimedeo. "This is sounding interesting. Do you have a better offer?"

The archaeologist shook his head negatively, blinked several times, then extended his hand to Enrico's. "I accept your generous offer, *señor*. And please thank Señor Warrender for me."

"Then I accept as well," Jacqueline said.

"What about me?" called a voice just behind them. They turned to see Bernardo's head poking out of the pickup. "I'm supposed to go wherever she goes."

"You remember Bernardo," Jacqueline said.

"Yes, of course," Enrico said, turning to the youth. "You are welcome, too, Bernardo. But I must warn you of one thing."

"Warn me? About what?"

"The television at the ranch house."

"*Mierda!* Is it broken?"

"No, my friend. But if you ever try and watch the sports again when my wife and her sisters want to see their favorite *telenovelas*, they will cut out your heart and feed it to the dogs."

28

A trio of pickup trucks started up the road toward the ranch turnoff—Enrico leading in his Ford, Bernardo and Jacqueline in their unmarked Proteus Toyota, Arquimedeo trailing in his big Jimmy 4 × 4. Before leaving Cerro Calvario, the archaeologist had conferred briefly with his key university and foundation supporters, explaining to them that he would temporarily be headquartering at La Promesa and scheduling an evening conference call to discuss future strategy. But more than anything right now, he needed a few hours' sleep, and the proximity of Enrico's ranch house was wonderfully enticing.

Then, a couple kilometers north of Cerro Calvario, Arquimedeo spotted a rusty pickup ahead on the side of the road. A moment later he recognized his uncle's beat-to-shit Dodge, both halves of its two-piece hood folded back and propped open while steam geysered from its radiator. And there, standing in front, was Oscar himself, flanked by his two hired Indians, all three staring thoughtfully at the overheated block.

Arquimedeo swore. During the eviction, he had deliberately lost track of his disreputable uncle and his odd-looking deputies. The archaeologist had hoped they would all just vanish somehow. Perhaps they had tried to do so, but just hadn't gotten very far. But now Arquimedeo saw Oscar glance up and recognize the oncoming truck, then start waving enthusiastically. Damnation!

Arquimedeo bleated his horn to signal the caravan ahead, then pulled onto the dusty shoulder. Before he could shut off the engine, Uncle Oscar appeared in his side window, grinning.

"Have you a beer, my boy?" the old man said, wiping a big hand across a sweaty brow and grizzled beard.

"Have I ever failed you, Uncle? I also have a tow rope I could rig, only I'm afraid I can't take you very far."

Oscar shook his head. "No, no, just the beer—and as much water as you can spare. The old war-horse will be fine after she cools down."

Arquimedeo pulled three chilled cans of Polar from the cooler on the floor beside him, then climbed out into the oppressive heat. Oscar passed two cans to the Kamarakotas, who were now sitting on the ground beside the Dodge, in partial shade. Arquimedeo, meanwhile, yanked a jerrican of water from the back of his truck.

"Arqui," Oscar asked a moment later, while watching his nephew feed water to the sizzling radiator, "so what is your plan now?"

"Well, I don't know if you could call it a plan. But I've got to meet with various people."

"Why? What's the use of meeting and talking now? It's time for action, Arqui."

"What am I supposed to do, Uncle? Attack the Guardia Nacional? Throw rocks at the bulldozers? Or perhaps I should try to overthrow the entire government, like Colonel Chávez?"

"If I were younger, I would certainly help you do so. Did you know that Illich Ramirez Sanchez and I both studied the methodologies of revolution in Havana in the late sixties?"

"Yes, Uncle, I've heard your stories about Carlos the Jackal. I'm afraid your illustrious past helped get me fired—"

Oscar carried on enthusiastically: "Of course, Illich was a rich man's son, so he could afford to go on to London and Paris and eventually Patrice Lumumba University in Moscow and become a world-famous terrorist. But I, too, learned my craft well and practiced it with considerable success, both here in Venezuela and in Mexico—"

"Oscar, I'm *not* going to stage a coup, and I'm not going to hire you to do it for me. And now, I'm sorry to be rude, but I can't stay around listening to any more war stories."

"Arqui, I'm not suggesting a coup! I'm proposing covert action against this fascist company, Proteus Industries. After all, they're the ones who've been giving the secret orders to the Guardia storm troopers. Let me strike at them!"

"Uncle, no!"

"Why not?"

"Why?" Arquimedeo shook his head pityingly. "For argument's sake, what could that possibly gain?"

"You don't see? We'll hit their assets. Boom, boom, boom!" Oscar hammered fist into palm. "When the cost grows too high, they'll abandon Cerro Calvario. Strike hard enough, and they'll get out of Venezuela."

"Uncle Oscar, you're living in a fantasy. A dangerous fantasy. Yes, I'm very angry. Yes, I feel a desire for revenge. But have I taken leave of my senses? No, I have not. Just think a moment what you're suggesting."

"Perhaps you misunderstand, Arqui. I'm not suggesting *you* do anything. *I'm* prepared to face all the danger."

"Oscar, just stop—and listen to me. I'm sorry I have no more work for you. But I absolutely will not pay you to undertake criminal activities on my behalf. For God's sakes, you can't even drive five kilometers without your truck breaking down. How are you going to terrorize a multinational company?"

Oscar seemed to consider this. "Well, of course I'll need a bit more money. If you'd advance me, say, a mere eight thousand *bolívars*. That's a very small amount, Arqui—only what you were going to pay me anyway for the first month as security guard. But it may be enough for me and my colleagues to launch a persuasive counterfascist campaign. Perhaps we can make these bastards not only quit your excavation, but pay dearly for the damage they've done. If so, my boy, I will return your small investment a thousand times over."

A hand landed on Arquimedeo's shoulder. He whirled to find both Kamarakotas grinning at extreme close range and holding empty beer cans upside down in their brown fists. Arquimedeo took the hint, retreating quickly to his truck and returning with his last three cans of Polar.

If this motley trio only had the means, he decided, they'd all be dead drunk before sundown. And, Arquimedeo decided on a bit more reflection, that might not be altogether a bad thing.

"Look, Oscar," he said when his uncle punctuated a long swallow with a loud lip-smack, "I'll say this one last time. I can't help you. And I order you to forget all your wild and violent ideas. You'll only end up in jail, or dead, you and your 'colleagues,' as you call them. And your poor widow will scream at my mother, who will scream at me.

"Now, for the sake of family peace, I'd like to help you get your truck to Ciudad Bolívar, or wherever you need to go. But I don't have eight thousand Bs to give away. And if you'll remember, I already gave you two thousand when I hired you." He pulled out his wallet, extracted six "orchids," the five-hundred *bolívar* notes nicknamed for the national flower engraved on the reverse. "Here's another three thousand. It's all I can spare."

Oscar wet his thumb and counted the bills twice, then stuffed them into his greasy work pants. "Many thanks, Arqui, my boy. I'll defer to your wishes." Oscar glanced up then and focused on the two trucks of Arquimedeo's caravan, now parked along the shoulder ahead. "I mustn't keep you. Your friends are waiting."

"Yes, they are. Ciao, Uncle."

"Where are you going, by the way? Isn't that the foreman of Hato la Promesa in the Ford Ranger?"

"Uncle, don't worry about it, okay? Just go home."

A moment later, after a final rearview mirror glimpse of his uncle gesturing violently at the two Indians, Arquimedeo swung his pickup back onto Route 16. God willing, the Dodge's junkyard motor would have cooled down enough to get them all to the next *cantina*. Or maybe the Kamarakotas would pull their knives and relieve Oscar of his newfound *bolívars* on the spot. One way or another, Arquimedeo hoped he'd never again have to set eyes on the old family bandit.

As night descended on the savanna, the dilapidated Dodge pickup was again parked alongside Route 16 north of Cerro Calvario. But this time it was farther off the blacktop and screened behind scrub trees. Inside, the floorboards were strewn with greasy food wrappings and empty beer cans, while the recent peripatetic diners—Oscar Azarias Rivilla and the two Kamarakotas, Chucho and Angel—had moved quickly across the road, three dark shapes slipping easily, one after the other, through three-strand barbed wire into Hato la Promesa rangeland.

Once inside, Oscar led off in a crouching walk, away from the road and paralleling the much more formidable barrier between the cattle ranch and the Cerro Calvario federal property—eight vertical feet of tightly woven steel mesh, topped by razor-edged concertina wire.

Oscar was excited to be back in covert action again, taking his first steps in an ambitious, if somewhat amorphous, scheme. And thus far, circumstances seemed to be playing right into his hands, to the extent of providing a thick cloud layer to blot out a full moon. Somewhere off to his north, the direction from which a breeze brought the steady stench of concentrated cow-flop, was the ranch house where Arquimedeo was obviously in hiding. And along with him, Oscar was quite sure, was Jacqueline Lee, indulging her youthful rebellion and filmmaking fantasies, both at her rich father's expense. She made a most tempting target—but one for another night.

Now, if Oscar could just locate the padlocked gate to Cerro Calvario, the one he'd watched Sam Warrender unlock on his ride with Señorita Lee several days earlier. Just when Oscar was convinced he'd missed the concealed gate in the darkness, his flashlight beam strayed upon the padlocked hasp.

He motioned to Angel, and the larger of the brothers stepped up with big bolt-cutters and sheared off the lock's steel clasp. At the first push, the gate hinges let out a rusty protest, giving Oscar a quick scare. He hadn't remembered hearing *that* when Sam had opened it. Anyone within a couple hundred meters would have heard the metal shriek. But Oscar was counting on Proteus *not* maintaining tight perimeter security. The company would hardly consider a bunch of irate archaeologists and academics a serious threat to their operations. As proof of this, while waiting beside his overheated truck that afternoon, Oscar had watched the fully loaded Guardia Nacional troop transport pull out of Cerro Calvario's gate and head north.

With the gate now open enough for them to squeeze through, Oscar turned to the smaller Chucho and explained, one last time, the route the brothers should follow to reach the Proteus construction shed unobserved, and exactly what they should look for once inside. Chucho nodded rapidly; Angel would do whatever his brother told him.

"*Buena suerte,*" Oscar concluded, "and be quick, for God's

sake." Then he hunkered down, his back against the gatepost, as the brothers departed on their stealthy mission. He marveled at how silently and quickly they melted into darkness. Oscar decided the pair might work out after all.

A moment later his nose was twisted painfully.

"Wake up, old man!"

Oscar opened his eyes to find a monstrous blob towering above him. Then Chucho was kneeling close and grinning. Then Oscar caught the hovering gleam of teeth and eyes—the blob was Angel.

Oscar turned to Chucho. "What happened?" he whispered urgently.

"No problem, Oscar. We got it."

Oscar now saw a sack dangling in front of his face, then suddenly being swung around his head.

"Angel, are you crazy!" he gasped. "You want to blow us into bloody bits!"

"But Oscar, you said this stuff was stable," Chucho said.

"*Imbécil!* I said it depends on what kind you got!"

"We must have got the right kind because it didn't go off when Angel dropped it on the way back."

"*Hijo de la chingada!* Angel, just set the bag down—gently! —and let me see."

Oscar, now completely wide-awake, directed his flashlight beam into the bag. Inside were three kilo-size bricks of what looked like Composition C-4 in fiberboard wrappings, intended obviously for ore blasting. Oscar breathed a profound sigh of relief. Though one of the most powerful explosives on earth, C-4 was also extremely stable.

"We did good, boss?"

"Very good, Chucho. Except you forgot the fucking detonators."

Chucho gestured back into the bag.

Oscar lifted a brick, revealing copper-sheathed electric blasting caps and coiled wire. All they'd need now were six-volt batteries and a windup clock.

Oscar scrambled to his feet. "Let's get the hell out of here."

Angel shut the gate, and Chucho fastened a new padlock on the hasp. Then the trio headed back along the fence toward the road.

29

The Cessna came in from the east with the midmorning sun behind it, chasing and finally catching its own shadow as it settled into a perfect three-point landing. The little twin-prop plane ran the length of the ranch strip, then taxied to the pathway leading to the ranch house, off-loading Jacqueline Lee and Enrico Tosto. Then the pilot—a retired Venezuelan air force captain—continued on to the tie-down area near the stables. At Sam's suggestion, Enrico had located a qualified flier through the international Cessna Pilots Association. Up until yesterday, the former officer had been managing his Tropiburger franchise in a city in northeast Venezuela, and he had jumped at the chance to escape his smoky grill for a few days.

Enrico offered to shoulder the camera bag on the brief hike to the ranch house, but Jacqueline waved him off. She was used to lugging it on shoots. They had been aloft an hour, first watching the dozers and graders chewing at the flanks of Cerro Calvario; then moving north where more graders were pushing a railroad corridor across La Promesa property, while relays of trucks dumped loads of gravel and burned clay for the track bed; and finally surveying the adjacent area across Route 16 where the mine workers' encampment was being laid out. The pilot had made several low-flying passes at each location, to give Jacqueline the best camera angles.

The sights had not been pretty, but for his part, Enrico had enjoyed watching Jacqueline doing her thing. Her lustrous hair had whipped in the wind blast as she poked the compact Handycam through a gap in the side window. Frequently she had twisted around to share some intense reaction to what she had just seen below. At such times, Enrico would listen and nod in understanding, but he tended to pay more attention to her artful gestures and compelling facial expressions than to her jet-propelled commentary over the headset.

Why was it—as he had wondered many times in regard to his sisters-in-law—that so many young ladies spoke with such bewildering rapidity? Were their brains that much more skillfully linked to their tongues, so that sentences and paragraphs were delivered in machine-gun bursts, while poorly wired male brains had to search haltingly for each next word? Whatever the reason, this particular young lady was certainly pleasant to listen to, even if one missed an excited word or phrase here and there.

He glanced over at her now as she suddenly pirouetted once around, scanning the savanna and the sky-domed horizon, before resuming her lanky forward stride.

"I can see why you love it out here, Enrico, and Sam, too. Have you ever been to his Oklahoma ranch?"

"A few times."

"Is it anything like this?"

"In many ways the land is very similar. Of course, the Lazy S is at least four times bigger than La Promesa. Samuel has around twenty-two thousand acres up there. And his *casa grande* is truly grand—and most impressive. But if you ask me, the house is too big for him."

"Why do you say that?"

"Why? Because he has no one to share it with."

She laughed. "Sam told me you were always trying to get him married. To one of your sisters-in-law, wasn't it?"

"There was some truth to that, but no more. I have told Romalda to forget this." Enrico fingered a cigarette out of his shirt-pocket pack and lit it, after determining that Jacqueline was upwind.

"Ah? I take it you've finally decided he's a hopeless bachelor?"

"No, *señorita*, I don't think so. If you ask me, I think Samuel is ready to be saddled."

"You do?"

"Most certainly I do."

"Why are you looking at me that way?"

Enrico smiled and shrugged elaborately. Jacqueline stopped in her tracks.

"You think *I'm* the one who should saddle your *jefe?* Did Sam talk to you about me?"

"He said nothing in words. But I know him very well, *señorita.* I watched the way he looked at you. And I saw him when he came home after riding with you. It had been many years since I had heard him whistle. I didn't know the tune. Also the next day, at my cousin's wedding, Samuel acted like a happy young *llanero* who just got paid. All night he drank and danced with everybody."

"Well, the drinking part I was aware of."

"Yes, I am truly sorry for that. But you know, Jacqueline"—she had suggested he call her Jake, but he preferred the more formal and feminine name—"the thing that happened with Samuel and the woman—*la rubia oxigenada*—how do you say, blonde from a bottle?"

"Peroxide blonde?"

"Peroxide, yes. This was nothing. Nothing!"

"I believe that now, Enrico. In fact, according to your little theory, I suppose it was my fault. First I made him whistle, then get drunk, then fall downstairs. Isn't that what you're saying, all this peculiar behavior of Sam's, you attribute to *my* influence?"

"Well, I'm not sure. But I think yes. Perhaps."

They resumed their progress toward the rear courtyard in silence. Then, after a moment, Enrico cleared his throat and tentatively launched a different approach:

"You know, *señorita,* men of a certain age, they do not necessarily lose their power. On the contrary. When it comes to matters of love—"

"Oh, for heaven's sake, Enrico! I can't believe we're having this conversation!"

"I am sorry, Jacqueline, if I speak improperly."

"No, no, you're absolutely proper. In fact, you sound almost Victorian—except that part about saddling Sam like a horse.

Look, I'm very flattered, Enrico. In fact, I think I'm probably blushing. But, if you don't mind, I'd rather we just drop it, okay?"

"As you wish."

Enrico stepped on his cigarette, held open the back door, then saluted nonchalantly as she entered the air-conditioned ranch house. He, meanwhile, had livestock and *llaneros* to look after.

Along the tiled corridor, Jacqueline passed the den and smiled in at Romalda, who was curled on the leather couch, and her sister Anacleta, standing behind an ironing board, both watching television. Bernardo had been banished from daytime TV and was out on horseback somewhere being a tenderfoot *llanero*. The young man apparently loved it.

She found Dr. Laya behind a big mission-style writing table in his guest bedroom, wearing his Oakland A's baseball cap and speaking Spanish on the telephone. The cap, she had learned, concealed a bald spot no larger than a quarter—or a two-*bolívar* coin. He waved at her, then pointed to the handset and mimed the word *interview*. Jacqueline sat on the corner of the bed and leafed through a catalogue of pre-Columbian art.

After a few minutes, Arquimedeo hung up. "I was speaking to a reporter for one of the Caracas dailies, *El Nacional*."

"Really? That sounds good."

"Right now, it is very hard to be hopeful—"

"Wait, Dr. Laya. Is it all right if I shoot while we chat?"

Arquimedeo nodded. Jacqueline had earlier prevailed on him to let her film his candid reactions from time to time, for edited inclusion in her final documentary. Despite his dubious assent and initial self-consciousness, the archaeologist seemed gradually to be relaxing into the process. She dug into her bag, quickly mounted and positioned the Handycam atop a tabletop tripod, and let it roll.

"Now. You were saying it's hard to be hopeful."

"Yes, I was. And I say that, having just received—less than an hour ago—some fantastic news from the university. The bone flute fragment—the one Félix stole—returned a radiocarbon date of seven thousand B.C., plus or minus a century. Nine thousand years old. That makes it one of the earliest artifacts ever discovered in the Orinoco region."

"But that's wonderful! Won't that help your case?"

"I doubt it, Jacqueline. My allies in the cabinet have already done all they could. I understand several left-wing factions staged a street demonstration supposedly on my behalf yesterday, but mostly, I suspect, to condemn the influence of Proteus and all other multinationals in Venezuela. Unfortunately, that sort of thing probably hurts me at the moment."

"Was the demonstration on TV?"

Dr. Laya nodded. "One of my colleagues videotaped it, so I can probably arrange to get you a copy. Is that why you ask?"

Jacqueline nodded. "I still don't see how the government can ignore such scientific evidence. They can't possibly believe Félix."

"Of course not. It is truly maddening. And, you know, Jacqueline, the irony is that our government is actually doing many good things to preserve primitive cultures. For instance, deep in the rain forest, we are finally working to preserve the Yanomami and other indigenous tribes from contamination by our culture. We have set aside a jungle biosphere of forty thousand acres and are doing everything possible to stop illegal prospectors, who use mercury to extract gold, then poison the streams and rivers with the residue.

"So, you see, even the Yanomami have a lobby. But the Arawaks who carved this flute are long vanished. Who cares about them anymore? And the government's mathematics are simple. My work generates no money, no jobs. In Caracas, they weigh thousands of private-sector jobs against a dozen dedicated volunteers, and a mountain of iron ore against a scrap of old bird bone. Who do you think wins?

"No, I'm afraid that flute is the last relic we'll get from Cerro Calvario. I, too, can't believe it. I look out that window and I see that reddish hump on the horizon, and I think about what is happening so close. If only I could have had another six months. Or even a month." He sighed. "So, what did you see going on over there? I haven't heard any blasting yet."

"I've got it all on tape, if you'd like to see."

"Your description will suffice."

"Well, it looks like they're just grading around the base so far. And they've moved most of the equipment tents below the South Hill."

"Did you see my erstwhile colleague there? But perhaps you didn't fly that low?"

"He's there. When we flew over, a bare-chested man came out of one of the tents and looked up. He probably had Marta Mendes in there."

"They haven't touched my summit trenches yet?"

"Not yet, Dr. Laya. It looks like there's a lot of preparatory work they need to do—cutting the terraces, laying the track, stuff like that. So maybe there's still hope. Tell me about your morning. Did you line up any other interviews? What about from other countries?"

"Well, I'm told there's an ITN crew filming the mop-up in Yucatán from Hurricane Jessica, and the chairman of our anthropology department knows the producer, and he's trying to lure them down here afterward to do an interview with me. I understand their footage sometimes gets picked up by CNN."

"That would be wonderful."

Jacqueline had just managed to mask an instinctive reaction of professional jealousy. She had come to regard Dr. Laya and his cause as her exclusive documentary domain. But there had been no such agreement between them. The archaeologist was perfectly free to invite in ITN or CNN or anyone else he wanted to. And if anything could now put pressure on Caracas to change its policy, it would be high-profile media exposure. Her film project, on the other hand, would require weeks or months of postproduction even after she concluded taping, and frankly, it was more likely to further her ambitions than Dr. Laya's.

It took Jacqueline a few seconds to hack her way through this thicket of self-interest. And she emerged with the consoling thought that even if somebody else's interview with Dr. Laya was broadcast all around the globe, it would probably be highly edited and quickly forgotten. Even so, it might whet the appetite for her film, which would eventually emerge in hour or half-hour documentary form and have far more impact.

She switched off the video camera and smiled over at Dr. Laya. "You know, you're an awfully good sport, Doctor."

"I have many fine qualities."

Arquimedeo smiled and blinked back at her. His chin was up, and clearly he was putting on his staunchest face. Yet he reminded her suddenly of a forlorn child in his baseball cap, with his scrawny arms and legs and delicate features behind the wire spectacles. Jacqueline felt an impulse to go to him and comfort him in her arms—an impulse she wisely checked.

She had enough complications with men already.

30

"Get off—now!"

"Make me!"

"I'm serious. I'll throw you off."

"Bet you can't!"

Félix Rosales was flat on his back and held in pubic clench by Marta Mendes, who knelt astride his hips, rocking and bouncing his backside relentlessly against the ground under the sleeping bag. To make good on his threat, Félix gritted his teeth, contracted his abdominals, and jackknifed his upper body, bringing him suddenly face to face and torso to torso with the sweat-slick young woman.

"Now, come on!" he commanded.

Her eyes remained half-hooded and lust-glazed, as her head shook defiantly. When he reached to force her, her strong arms flew around him first. Félix fought free, seized her upper arms, and shoved her sideways. Marta yelped as they came uncoupled, then toppled onto her side. But she rolled up giggling, flailing her muscular legs—and nearly flattening his tumescence with one playful heel-kick at his exposed inner thigh.

"Damn you, Marta! Stop it—and listen!"

Outside, a truck motor could be heard laboring on the rugged South Hill perimeter track.

"A mining truck, so what?"

But this one sounded different—and closer—to Félix. He crawled over Marta, peeled back the tent flap, and saw a dust cloud part to reveal one of the Proteus Land Cruisers. It swung around and pulled to a stop a few feet from the control pit, which had lain untouched in the three weeks since Arquimedeo and Félix had completed its stratigraphic profile. Félix ducked inside.

"Get your clothes on! They're from Proteus!"

"So? You don't work for them."

"Well, you work for *me*, dammit, and I'm telling you to get your damn clothes on!"

Félix kicked his legs into his khaki shorts, zippered up gingerly over his bulge, stuck his feet into huaraches, wrestled into a muscle shirt, pawed at his lank forelock. He turned to find the Portuguese fisherman's daughter still sprawled bare-ass on the sleeping bag, and still eyeing him hungrily.

"Don't be long, lover."

"Do what I say, Marta, or the party's over." Félix spoke in a muted growl, having heard two doors open and shut outside. "Those guys just might poke their heads in here." Finally she rolled her eyes theatrically and reached indolently for the cotton briefs that hung from a nearby tentpole, and Félix crawled through the flap into the sun.

Two men were out of the truck. Félix knew them both. The big sandy-haired man in the golf shirt was Owen Meade, the local mining honcho, and the smaller and older Hispanic guy with steel glasses was Meade's boss, Ray Arrillaga, whom Félix had met on D. W. Lee's ship, the *Kallisto*.

They greeted him and shook hands, both speaking Spanish. "Ray asked to have a look at your operation," Owen explained, shading his eyes with a clipboard and squinting down into the five-foot-deep control pit. "Kind of quiet here."

Félix nodded. "We just got the last of the equipment and tents moved over yesterday, with the help of some of your guys. We're still sorting things out."

"You say 'we,' " Ray said. "Where's the rest of your crew?"

"Actually, I haven't had a chance to get a new digging crew. I thought you knew. Most of them walked out with Dr. Laya."

Ray nodded. "Right. Academic solidarity and all that. But can't you recruit volunteers from other campuses?"

Félix ran a hand through his sweat-soaked hair. "I'm not optimistic about that. Dr. Laya is well connected with most of the university departments. I was thinking of contacting one of the archaeological societies. They cater to amateurs and novices, some of whom like to volunteer on excavations."

"Sounds like a good idea," Owen said.

"I'd say jump on it." Ray Arrillaga glanced back after his own inspection of the abandoned trench. "Looks like you're going to need some help to get in gear down here."

"Oh, absolutely. No doubt about it."

Just then the tent opened and Marta Mendes stepped out. She was barefoot, wearing an unfocused smile, skimpy cutoffs, and an oversize white soccer shirt with a big 69 in red numerals. Despite her tomboyish figure, she looked, Félix thought, exactly like a girl who had been banging her brains out. He introduced her to both men.

"Marta is one Bolívar University volunteer who decided to remain. So at least I've got a start."

"I'm sure Félix is grateful for your loyalty, señorita," Owen said. "Pretty hard work out here, though, isn't it?"

"I like hard work," Marta said. "I bet I could operate one of those big bulldozers you got up there, as good as anyone."

"I bet you could," Owen said. "If we have any openings, we'll keep you in mind."

Ray Arrillaga had already swung his attention back to Félix. "Owen and I have invited some media people down here, escorted by our local PR director, to take a look at your activities. They'll want to take some shots, ask some general questions."

"Uh, when might that be, Señor Arrillaga?"

"We were hoping sometime tomorrow. It would be nice if there was a little more going on—whatever it is you do on a dig. Shoveling, sifting, looking at artifacts through microscopes, that sort of thing."

"I understand."

"Maybe we could help Félix round up some temporary volunteers," Owen suggested to his boss. "Maybe borrow a labor crew from the railroad grading."

"I'm afraid that wouldn't work," Félix said. "It's not a matter of shoveling earth. We're talking about careful scraping and sifting, along with constant note-taking, sketching, and photographing. And you have to know what you're looking for—or you'll miss it. Even with constant supervision, day laborers would be more destructive than helpful."

Owen grinned sheepishly. "Another one of my bad ideas. Well, you and Señorita Mendes do what you can. By the way, I guess you heard that bone flute you delivered to the university turned out to be pretty old. You must be excited."

"I haven't had a chance to unpack the radio. How old?"

"Eight thousand years, wasn't it, Ray?"

"Nine, I think."

Félix whistled. "That makes it early Holocene. About what Dr. Laya and I estimated."

"And there should be more artifacts where that came from, correct?" Arrillaga asked.

"I hope so," Félix said.

"Well, frankly, from a somewhat selfish point of view, Félix, that's what we'd really like to see. If you could come up with some more major finds here, it would take a lot of political heat off us. And also, obviously, tend to confirm your serious allegations that Dr. Laya falsified the location of artifacts." Arrillaga went again to the lip of the trench and peered down. "Where exactly was it found, the flute?"

"Down at that end," Félix answered, trying to recall what documentation he'd invented for the artifact pouch. The figure of three meters flashed in his mind. But he desperately hoped he hadn't written that, since the pit was barely two meters deep. "We found it right down there at the bottom."

"Where the water has collected?"

"Yes. That's just from this morning's rain."

"Don't you usually cover excavations when it rains?"

"Normally, yes. But in the confusion of moving and unpacking, it apparently got neglected."

Marta stood close beside Félix, keeping silent. But her hand stole behind him and pinched his left buttock cheek—hard. She was obviously enjoying this.

After all the other volunteers had denounced Félix, Marta had slipped into his tent to announce she was taking his side. Félix hadn't known how to react. Everybody in camp knew the flute had been uncovered exactly where Arquimedeo said. Then Marta had peeled off her shorts and crawled into Félix's sleeping bag—and made clear exactly what she expected in return for her loyalty.

"Well," Owen Meade said, "we'll clear out and leave you two to your labors."

Arrillaga nodded to them both, his eyes, behind the steel-rimmed spectacles, laser sharp. Félix found himself perspiring even more than warranted by the morning savanna sun.

"Um, before you go," Félix said, "there's one thing I wanted to ask about."

The two Proteus men stopped. "What is it?" Owen Meade asked.

"About my funding. With the university support being cut off in protest, I understood that Proteus would be filling in."

Owen slapped the clipboard against his thigh. "I believe that was already arranged with you on the ship."

"Short term, yes. I was wondering about a longer-range basis."

Arrillaga spoke up: "When we come back tomorrow to inspect your work, why don't you submit a budget and we'll take a look at it."

A moment later Félix stood watching angrily as the Land Cruiser vanished behind a billowing dust plume. *"Lameculos!"*

Beside him Marta cackled. "Why are you calling *them* ass-kissers? You're the one puckering up."

He whirled on her. *"Cállate la boca!*—shut up! Look, if we're going to get any money out of those bastards, we have to make this whole area look like an actual dig site. So listen up. I need you to help me lay out a baseline alongside the pit, then drive stakes and extend string lines at two-meter intervals."

Marta snorted. "What's the point of laying out a grid? There's nothing down there to excavate."

"No me chingues! Don't fuck with me!"

"Tsk, tsk, don't be such a nasty boy."

He seized her arm, but she pulled away. "I'm kidding, Félix. I'll help you. *After* you finish what you started." Catlike, she brushed up against him.

"Jesus, how many times do you want it?"

They'd been at it, with a few stuporous time-outs, since the previous sundown. Somewhere along the way Félix had stopped counting his climaxes. Whatever the number, it had been sufficient to exhaust him, yet leave him in a state of painfully protracted engorgement—a condition Marta obviously found irresistible.

"Please, Félix, just give me one more good ride, and I'll work my butt off for you, I promise."

"*Mierda!*" Félix growled, and turned back toward the compact tent. "But this isn't going to be any marathon."

"Whatever you say, *felicidad*, sweetie."

None of this was working out the way he'd intended. The trouble was, he'd never had an actual plan—just a series of violent reactions when Jacqueline Lee, after two days of nonstop flirtation, had ignored him, then dumped him altogether—for a wrinkly old buzzard who happened to have a zillion bucks.

But it wasn't just jealous rage that had sent Félix into his tailspin. Watching his dream girl ride out of his life was like having all the doors of opportunity slam shut at once, plunging him back into the recurrent failure of his life. And the most tempting revenge—waiting for her to come back from her ride, then luring her off somewhere and taking her by force—would have been suicidal. One word from Jacqueline to her father, or to Sam, and Félix figured he'd be hunted down and shot like a dog.

So instead, he had come up with his wild scheme to betray Arqui, hoping for a sizable payoff from Jake's father. And it had all worked, or seemed to—stealing the bone flute, switching the location tag, delivering it to that fantastic yacht along with the story about Arqui's radical political connections. All the little Asian bastard had to do was open his fat wallet and count out some real money. With even a few thousand dollars, Félix could open a little bodybuilding gym somewhere. And he could have aerobics classes to bring in the ladies—not sweaty jock types like Marta with her flat pecs and knobby shoulders, but jiggling, giggling *chicas* right off the beach in their string bikinis.

But Félix had walked away from his shipboard meeting with less than five thousand *bolívars* in pocket and airy promises of further, much more substantial funding. Except for Félix to qualify for any future rewards, Señor Lee and his Proteus pals had required him to return here and carry on this sham South Hill excavation. Of course, they had all acted as if it would be a real excavation, as if everything on Cerro Calvario was exactly as Félix had told them.

And now they wanted to put him on display, like a trained monkey, in front of invited media. How long did they think they could jerk him around, and just how dumb did they think he was? Did they think he would really fall for that crap about submitting a budget, which they would "take a look at"? Assholes! They'd better open their wallets tomorrow, or he was blasting out of here in his truck and never coming back.

Just outside the tent Félix nearly tripped over a spade propped against a wheelbarrow. In a flare of anger, he booted the hickory handle—forgetting he was wearing rawhide sandals. Pain seared upward from his big toe, and he screamed, grabbing his right foot and nearly toppling sideways into the tent.

Marta, a step behind, wrapped her arms around him and held him up. She was strong enough to ease him down and help him into the tent. As he cursed and writhed on the sleeping bag, she kept hold of him, murmuring comforts. Then, as the pain relented slightly, Félix realized Marta was digging inside his waistband and working on him again.

"Hey, not now, Marta. Give me time to recover."

"That's what *you* say. But Marta just found another little Félix down here who's ready for big action. Matter of fact, this little Félix ain't so little."

It was difficult, under the circumstances, to argue. And for the moment, Félix was too tired to protest further and too crippled to escape. So he lay there in the sweltering nylon cave while she peeled them both naked, then grappled him like a well-oiled wrestler.

The first night Señorita Mendes had invaded his sleeping bag with her fiercely whispered promises and ultimatums, Félix had managed to replace her in his mind with erotic images of Jake, imagining what it would be like to have *her* naked against him, instead of this sinewy and inexhaustible little athlete. Now, however, he was unable to summon his imagination, or anything else. Oh, well, he thought, let her do the fucking work, if she wanted it so bad.

Abruptly, he felt himself tilted and rolled onto his back. Then, after a disapproving cluck, Marta set about methodically restoring his nodding erection till it suited her needs. A moment later she had settled herself comfortably and begun her rhythmic ride.

31

Sam Warrender crossed the New Mexico–Texas border fifty miles northeast of Tucumcari on U.S. 54, angling back up toward the Oklahoma Panhandle and the Lazy S. For cross-country driving, he usually opted for the Seville or the Sovereign. But because of his daughter's insistence on keeping his identity in the closet, on this Albuquerque trip, as on previous ones, he had taken one of the ranch pickups.

And again as on previous visits, there had been an initial awkwardness between Teresa and himself, almost like two actors still feeling out their characters early in a run. Which was, of course, understandable, considering the rarity of his visits. Teresa had been only six when María had left the ranch for good. In the eighteen years since, Sam had been reduced to a cometary orbit in and out of his daughter's life—unfortunately more out than in. As a result, their relationship had been pieced together cross-sectionally out of birthdays and graduations, phone calls and letters, weekend and holiday outings—and presents that, by maternal fiat, could never be as frequent or expensive as Sam had wanted to give. Yet, despite all the absences and handicaps, Sam had been determined not to lose his daughter, as he had his son, Tony, on the far side of an unbridgeable gulf. And unlike Caroline—thank God!—María had never attempted to freeze Sam out of their child's life.

214

Pursuit into Darkness

By the end of their brief visit, Sam thought, most of the wariness was gone from Teresa's glance. But he still sensed a certain unstated limit on the degree of his involvement in her life, and a subtle withholding on her part even at the moment of embrace, or when she called him "Dad" and his heart leaped. Perhaps, though, he was expecting too much.

She lived in an adobe-and-stucco complex two blocks from the University of New Mexico campus, in a one-bedroom, patio apartment that reflected her magpie delight in festive and artistic clutter. Basketry and ceramics and sculpture thronged tabletops and shelves. Gallery posters and weavings and acrylic abstracts turned all available wallspace into a wraparound collage. Even an ugly-textured plaster ceiling had been put into play, festooned with a bright armada of oriental paper kites shaped like butterflies and birds.

Only Teresa herself escaped adornment. She came to the door wearing a paint-spattered sweatshirt over baggy jeans and tennis shoes, her dark hair ponytailed, her pretty face sans makeup. Sam couldn't help recognizing her mother in the welcoming smile that bunched her olive cheeks, and in the quick brown eyes behind the oversize round frames—which were tortoiseshell, just like the phantom feline who dashed past his shins as the door opened. Of himself, fortunately, Sam detected traces mostly in his daughter's height, which was midway between his own and María's.

"Come on in, Dad," she said, stepping back from a hug. "I was just decorating some sun-dried pottery for a class I'm teaching tomorrow." She displayed fingers liberally splotched with poster paints. "But I've got a stew going. Kind of a kindergarten version of mom's posole."

She produced two cold Coronas, and they settled at right angles on a Navaho-blanketed sectional. "Did you see Mom yet?"

"I stopped off for lunch on the way in. She told me I looked like the Man of La Mancha. I think she meant gaunt and haggard, but, God knows, I've been tilting at windmills lately."

"I want to hear the whole sordid story."

"Maybe later, if I drink enough of these. But I'm afraid after your mother got through stuffing me, there may not be any room for your posole."

"No way! You'll eat every pinto bean. We Cárdenas women know how to feed our menfolk. Doesn't she look great?"

Sam nodded. "She told me she's got a new steady. A cop."

"Hector. He's got kids and grandkids already, from another marriage. But he's fun. Did you meet him?"

"María thought he might drop in. I waited around a while. Maybe I'll meet him at the wedding. What do you think?"

"*Quién sabe?* So, where are you staying?"

"A TraveLodge on old Sixty-six. I figure it goes with the Dodge Dakota and the hardscrabble-rancher disguise."

"It's not fair to you, Dad, I know it isn't. But I'm making progress on my identity crisis, I really am. Just give me a little more time, okay?"

"Excuse the squawk. Whatever you want, Teresa, you know I'll go along with. So, can I assume I'll be seeing Wally later on?"

Wally Torres, an assistant basketball coach at UNM, was Teresa's current guy. In recent years Teresa had hinted that once she was married—and Wally seemed to be a likely candidate—she wouldn't feel the compulsion to hide Sam's real identity anymore. But until that happened, she didn't want her circle of friends or any prospective boyfriend being influenced, one way or the other, by knowing her father was this big-rich oilman.

"The team's got a late practice. He'll try and stop by for dessert."

Over dinner on her tile-topped kitchen table, she'd asked about Venezuela.

Sam had tried to get by with a sardonic once-over-lightly. But Teresa wasn't having any. As a devotee of Native American arts and crafts, her sympathies were aroused at the mention of primitive artifacts, and her anger inflamed at the thought of their being willfully destroyed. She'd kept asking questions, until finally Sam began to recount the story in more detail.

When he got to the part about the ancient bone flute, he'd tried to sketch its delicate shape for her on a nearby scrap of newspaper—a recipe she'd torn from the *Albuquerque Journal*. He told her how he'd imagined it lying in buried silence through the millennia. When he'd glanced up from his crude drawing, he was startled to see his hesitant feelings reflected and magnified in his daughter's dark eyes.

"That's so neat, Dad! I'm really proud of you!" She got up

from her place and came around to kiss his cheek—easily the high point of his visit. Sam couldn't remember eliciting that kind of spontaneous reaction, and that special look, from Teresa before, not after any birthday gift, and certainly not for any of his blockbuster business conquests, most of which she'd never expressed much interest in. Apparently it took being canned from his job on a matter of quixotic principle to make his little girl proud of him. Maybe it was worth it after all.

"You have to realize, Teresa, your old dad didn't save anything. He lost right down the line." He went on to describe a little of the corporate slugout. She was appropriately sympathetic, but clearly less engaged. Yet she picked up immediately on his passing mention of D.W.'s being opposed by his own daughter.

"She sounds a lot like me. So you and she must have been allies, which must have driven D.W. crazy. Tell me about her."

Sam did the verbal equivalent of his quick sketch of the flute, being careful not to betray any of his personal feelings for Jacqueline, or hers for him. Yet somehow Teresa's suspicions were alerted. "Dad, you never described her. Is she short, tall, fat, skinny, or what? God, I hope she doesn't look like D.W. in drag."

Sam chuckled, then began haltingly to describe Jacqueline, realizing it was a tricky assignment. And so it proved. After a few fumbling sentences, Teresa was on to him.

"I knew it!" she said, clapping her hands once in delight.

"You knew what?"

"You're smitten, Dad! Obviously something happened to you down there, okay? Some kind of epiphany. Only it wasn't a buried artifact that did it to you, it was a girl! Dad, that's fantastic!"

"Teresa, I'm afraid you're jumping to conclusions here—"

"Okay, okay. I promise I won't tease you, and I promise I won't tell Mom. But please, I want you to tell me all about Jacqueline. Or do you call her Jacquie?"

"Actually her nickname is Jake."

"*Much* better. So, did you kiss her?"

"Good Lord, Teresa!"

"I do believe you're blushing!"

He stonewalled her as best as he could, but there really was no escape from her avidity. So, after dinner, while they washed and dried and put away, Sam began the terribly difficult task of sharing with his daughter his nascent feelings for a girl two years younger than herself. Teresa had promised not to interrupt, at least not every other sentence. But when he began to explain that whatever had happened between them was now over, she cut in angrily:

"How do you know that?"

"Well, let's just say it ended messy. Anyway, it should be over. Hell, it shouldn't have happened in the first place. It was damn-fool behavior on my part."

"I'd say your being alone all these years is damn-fool behavior. You *need* someone, Dad. Mom and I talk about it all the time."

"Thanks, I'll take it under advisement. The question is, who the hell would want to put up with an ornery old critter like me—unless for the money?"

"Now you're starting to sound like me. Okay, you said it ended with Jake. But did she actually say it was over?"

"Something like that."

Sam was spared further painful revelations by the bustling arrival of Wally Torres. He pumped hands and greeted Sam as "Mr. Warren" before settling into first names. Teresa had asked Sam to adopt the slightly altered surname around her friends, although she thought it extremely unlikely that any of them, Wally included, read the business periodicals that occasionally featured Sam's name and face. It turned out Wally hadn't eaten yet, so Teresa heated up the posole, pork and corn-husk stew, and they joined him around the kitchen table.

Wally was a good-natured and swarthy young man with a booming laugh whom Teresa had once described as "your basic teddy bear." Thanks to a narrative gift and an uncanny ear for ghetto jive, Wally kept them in stitches recounting the antics of his players, most of whom were black and all of whom he obviously regarded with great affection. In between anecdotes, the boyish assistant coach asked Sam about his cattle ranch—it having been established, at their two previous meetings, that Sam was in that business over in Oklahoma. Sam responded by complaining, candidly enough, about feed prices, the ongoing drought, and—with a wary eye at his daughter—increasing attacks by environmentalists on the whole damn livestock industry. Wally was sympathetic, and Teresa kept still.

But it was obvious to Sam that his daughter was, in her phrase, very much "smitten" with her young man, and he with her. Sam observed them touching frequently and constantly in eye contact. And there seemed a fair reciprocity of interest. Teresa asked good questions about the Lobos' upcoming game with BYU, concerning matchups and strategy, and Wally offered appreciative comments about her current ceramic project, then gave Sam an enthusiastic account of a visit they'd made to the San Ildefonso Pueblo north of Santa Fe, famous for its black matte pottery. This was one jock-type apparently willing to have his horizons widened beyond the sports page, Sam decided. At the same time, he seemed the sort of basic guy who wasn't likely to lose his bearings if he found out that Teresa's father's ranch was a whole helluva lot bigger than he'd been led to believe. But that was Teresa's call.

After dessert and coffee and more talk, it was late enough that Sam figured he'd better go. And though nobody had said anything, it was obvious that Wally wasn't going anywhere. So Sam levered to his feet and ambled to the door for handshakes and good-byes and as wholehearted a daughterly embrace as he could remember getting in years and years.

"Night, Dad," she said as he stepped out into the surprising starlight of the high plateau. "Now you call me. I want more details."

Wally stood close beside her, an arm around her waist, the other waving. Even after all these years, Sam discovered it could feel strange to be the one leaving while another man exercised a claim of primacy over his little girl. Sam waved back, then started down the dark pathway toward a distant lamppost and his pickup.

Driving back to his motel, he passed a flashing neon sign advertising topless dancers. On an erratic, lonely impulse, he went back and parked in a back lot beside a lot of souped-up metal. Inside, music thudded and men whooped and hollered while a big-breasted girl in floppy sombrero, G-string, and boots pranced down a perimeter-lighted runway. Sam settled in a dark corner, had a long-neck beer, and looked around. There seemed to be a lot of raucous regulars, who shouted out the names of the dancers and bikini-clad barmaids. Except for a couple of sad-looking senior citizens ogling the vital young merchandise from ringside, Sam figured he was the oldest guy in the place.

A chunky Latina waitress came by with a high-kilowatt smile and improved his mood slightly with a few flirtatious comebacks. Sam declined a second beer, but tipped her lavishly, then walked back out into the star-studded night, feeling old and foolish and just a little sorry for himself.

Shortly after dawn he was booming east on the interstate, pointing the Dakota's blue Plexiglas bug shield back toward Oklahoma and the ranch—and wondering what to do with the rest of his life.

32

Sam reached the Lazy S turnoff just as the postal truck was pulling away. So he maneuvered the pickup alongside the big galvanized box and fished out his mail before turning into the long paved drive to the ranch house. He left the Dakota in front of the garages for Bert Hooper, the foreman's stepson, to wash down, then headed up the flagstone walk, flipping through circulars, magazines, catalogues, solicitations, bills, and more bills. Not a damn letter in the lot.

Then a long envelope slid out of an Orvis catalogue. It bore a Miami postmark and the return address of an international remail outfit Enrico occasionally used for forwarding business correspondence, rather than rely on the vagaries of Venezuela's "Expreso Internacional." Offhand, Sam couldn't think of any documents that might call for his immediate attention.

Hearing the muted roar of the housekeeper's vacuum cleaner behind the big hand-hewed doors, and realizing his boots and jeans were probably layered with the dust of three states, he bypassed the entranceway and took the outside stairway directly up to his second-story office. Inside, he sank into his leather swivel, propped his bootheels on the corner of his desk, and glanced through his phone messages. There were several from Hardesty Eason, God only knew why. Sam tossed them aside, then sliced open the remail.

Inside was an airweight envelope plastered with blue stamps bearing Bolívar's familiar visage. Why would Enrico put stamps on a remail? Then Sam focused on the unfamiliar handwriting, backslanted with numerous tails and flourishes. The return address was "J. N. Lee, c/o Tosto, Hato la Promesa, Edo. Bolívar, Venezuela."

Jake.

He sliced it open and unfolded four closely written pages in the same stylized hand, on salmon-colored stationery with the embossed letterhead of the Mt. Irvine Bay Hotel, Scarborough, Tobago, West Indies. It was dated three days before.

> My dearest Sam,
>
> Excuse the fancy stolen stationery. As you see, I've succumbed to your generous offer to stay at Hato la Promesa, and so has Dr. Laya López, or Arqui as he now permits me to call him. I've also been up in your Cessna, videotaping government-sanctioned, corporate criminality—sights so totally unlike the flight into Shangri-la I took that wonderful morning with you (and a certain nameless Neanderthal).
>
> By the way, Enrico is a perfect host and a real mensch—or should I say hombre? And already a dear friend. And of course our favorite topic of conversation is El Jefe, aka Señor Sam. So before I go any farther, I want you to know that you are very much with me here, and that I think about you constantly.
>
> And let me get something else off my heart, Sam. I'm truly sorry—for everything. Selfishly, more than anything, for what happened to us. But sorrier than I can say for what happened to you, and to Arqui. Of course, his academic colleagues have rallied wonderfully to his support, while the Proteus gang has apparently acted more à la Félix. I would never have believed that Daddy would turn on you as he did. But then, Arqui never thought Félix would stab him in the back either. So much for loyalty. But more on that later.
>
> Mea culpa continued: I guess you figured out (if you cared) that I thought you'd dumped me for Señorita Blond Bombshell after I left you at Daddy's party. I hope you don't remember the horrid things I said—once I discovered you had survived your terrible fall! I got a measure of comeuppance several days later when Marina Estévez (her name, in case you forgot) ran into me outside

Cerro Calvario and told me what really happened that night—how she was only trying to help you off the ship. And at least for her, the disaster turned out to be a stroke of luck. As a result of her "exposure" (sorry about that!), Marina got promoted to an anchorette slot in Caracas.

But levity aside, I realize now I was at least partly responsible for what happened to you. Obviously, the last thing you needed when you were trying to clear your head was a giddy girl with a bottle of bubbly. Sam, I am so sorry. And I feel even more guilt when I think of what happened later with the Proteus Board—knowing they must have used what happened on the *Kallisto* against you. I still can't believe those people could join my father in his sordid little putsch against you, after all you've done to build that company. In my eyes, and I'm sure in yours, my dad is now very much an assassin. *Et tu*, D.W.? I've never been so ashamed.

Sam, is there anything I can do to make you forgive me? If there is, I swear I'll do it. It occurred to me that you might even think I was somehow in league with Daddy and deliberately set you up for some kind of shipboard fiasco by getting you drunk. Oh, God, I hope you don't think that! Believe me, Sam, I will never forgive Daddy for what he did—and I have told him so.

Of course, *he* thinks it will all blow over. I've played the prodigal daughter so many times, always coming back in a state of impecunious contrition—for the paternal handout, or whatever. But I have a little money of my own. Enough to buy Handycam cassettes and other necessities—though Enrico refuses to accept a single *bolívar* from me. Meanwhile, Daddy keeps ordering me to end my little mutiny and return to the ship. He wants to sail away and let Ray and Owen handle the atrocity from here on. I hung up on him.

So basically I guess I am doing what I wanted to do with my life, using my fledgling cinematic talents to document what is going on here, trying to further a cause I believe in—a cause that, in some sense, unites me with you. And while I ply my craft, part of me thinks about you, and about us. And about what Enrico told me.

He's worried about you, Sam. He says when you left, and when he talked to you on the phone later, you looked and sounded defeated for the first time he can remember. He says he's seen you knocked down, but that you always got up fighting. He doesn't see that now. He's afraid you've gone back to your ranch to grow old.

If he's right, Sam, then make him wrong. You mustn't let that happen, my darling. Yes, I do still think of you that way, and I dare to say it, after all these paragraphs of building my nerve. I feel like hysterical Scarlett, begging her Rhett not to go off to Charleston and sit on a rocker, sipping whiskey the rest of his days, begging him to still give a damn!

Sam, there is a part of me that wants so much to fly north and rent a car and put on a picture hat and drive down this long dusty road to your ranch, like the one in *Giant*. That's how I kind of visualize the Lazy S, only not with that horrid Charles Addams house. I can just imagine those snowy eyebrows of yours lifting in surprise—and maybe in other miscellaneous emotions.

But I'm not coming yet. I've hardly ever finished a project, so I've decided to darn well finish what I've started here, Lost Cause though it may be. Then I thought of phoning you, but there was too much to say, and I got cold feet, or cold fingers. So finally, like a Jane Austen heroine, I turned to the post to convey my fugitive emotions. I hope this gets to you quickly, Sam. I'm putting all kinds of stamps on it, but when Enrico comes back from wherever he's gone, I'm going to ask if there's some faster way of getting it to you—like Fed Ex or something. (Yes, I'll admit corporate America does have its uses.)

I see I've got room to squeeze in a final paragraph, and my vagrant thoughts turn naturally toward naughtiness. Sam, though I apologized for hyping your blood-alcohol level that night on the sun deck and said I feel guilty, the truth is, when I think about what went on between us, what I really feel is excitement. I mean, I start horripilating and everything. (Look it up, my darling!) And then I start thinking of other things we could do together. Like . . . and like . . . Sorry! This was supposed to be a contrite letter, a letter of resignation and ineffable sadness, like Bogey saying good-bye to Bergman in the fog. Instead, it's becoming incendiary. At least for me, and I hope a wee bit for you, too. And you know, the more I think about it, Big Sam, the more I'm convinced we really do belong together. In all ways. And believe me, that's . . .

Pursuit into Darkness

Not the last you'll hear from
Jake—the Jungle Girl

Sam put it aside halfway through the third read and stared out the window, which commanded a view of the long drive. He visualized her arriving as she said, in a convertible, black hair whipping in the wind under a big sun hat. What else could he visualize, after she got here? Jacqueline in the big bedroom next door, padding around or stretched out sleek and splendid. Hell, yes. Jacqueline long-striding out to the stables in tailored riding habit, then cantering out to the four corners. No problem.

Jacqueline living here, as mistress of the ranch? Jacqueline, an Oklahoma matron, Eurasian pillar of the charity league and the garden club? Not really. She'd eventually go crazy cooped up here. Oftener and oftener, she'd be wanting to fly off to somewhere smart and sophisticated—New York, London, Geneva, Paris—anywhere but Tulsa or OK City. And why not? Jacqueline Lee was an exotic jewel that belonged in those settings. Sam would traipse along, becoming over the years an increasingly decrepit companion, squinting at the bills. It would be a hell of a revenge on D.W. though. He had to grin at that.

But she still wanted him, desired him. What an unlikely revelation—and every bit as incendiary as she hoped. Of course, Jacqueline was obviously affected by his apparent idealism, just as Teresa had been. What would happen when Jacqueline realized his antimining posture was more of an aberration than a conversion? Without having seen that prehistoric flute, to be honest, Sam would still be solidly with D.W. Because, dammit, Venezuela *did* need the jobs, and Proteus *did* need the ore.

He sighed. Recrossed his ankles. Held a one-man board meeting. Well, there was no future in it, him and Jake, that was clear. But it couldn't hurt to imagine the two of them, try it on for size, think about it. And remember the way it had been between them—on the ride, and under the stars that night. In the bookshelf behind him was a dictionary. Sam spun the chair, tipped it out, and thumbed through. Pretty much as he figured, *horripilate* meant to get goose bumps, though the causes enumerated ran to fear, disease, and cold, not erotic excitement.

He reached for the letter again, reread a few favorite parts,

looked at the envelope, speculated about the *N* in J. N. Lee.
Natalie? Nancy? Or something Korean? Of course, he could dial
La Promesa and ask her direct. Hell, he could go down there.
And do what? Help her film? Carry her camera bag? New job
description: chairman emeritus slash gofer. But who cared, if it
would work out? But how long before her cinematically inspired
emotions evaporated, and she discovered he wasn't Gable or
Bogart? How many Félixes would start circling then, and how
would Sam deal with that? Christ, whom was he kidding?

He swung his boots off the desk, decided to shower and change,
grab a sandwich, and go out and check the herd. He was, after
all, just Sam "Warren" now, small-time cattleman and big-time
coupon clipper. Was that being whipped, as Enrico said? Maybe
so. One good tilt with a windmill could do that to a man. But
there'd been a nice long string of victories before he'd been sum-
marily unhorsed. And now, well, there just didn't seem any more
reason to go out jousting.

He was out on the north end with Chick Hooper in the Wrangler. They'd spotted a pair of buzzards exiting a ravine, so they'd
parked to check it out. Found a cow carcass down on the rocks,
picked clean. Probably a stray, ran over the edge trying to escape
being rounded up. As they climbed back into the Jeep, the cellular phone rang.

Chick answered, handed it to Sam.

It was Hardesty Eason.

"The damnedest thing, Sam. Somebody's blowing up our
equipment down there."

"Aw, shit, Hardy. What happened?"

"I've been trying to reach you since dawn. Didn't you get the
messages? Somebody burned out three dozers last night, plus a
gas truck and a water truck and one of our motor graders. Plus
they blew up a huge section of track, most of it stored right on
your ranch property. We think they used our own dynamite,
stole it from a construction shed on the mountain. We figure
it's that archaeologist's Commie uncle, and maybe the archaeologist himself."

"Dr. Laya's plenty pissed off, but he's no bomb thrower, believe
me."

"Whoever did it, Sam, dropped a bunch of revolutionary fliers, demanding Proteus get the hell out of Venezuela. The usual Marxist crap."

"Was anybody injured?"

"Not so far. But I gather D.W.'s daughter is still down in the area—"

"She's on my ranch. Jesus, is she okay?"

"Yeah, she called in, but D.W.'s pretty crazed about her being down there with terrorists operating—her being the boss's daughter and all. He wants her out of there fast."

"Yeah, I agree absolutely. Tell D.W. I'll cooperate in any way I can. I'll call my foreman down there right now, tell him the same thing, make sure she's got good protection."

"Thanks, Sam."

"Is there anything else you want me to do, or are you just keeping me informed as a courtesy?"

"Aw, hell, Sam. You're still on the board, so you got to know what's going on. And you'll always be part of Proteus."

"Let's not get too sentimental here, Hardy. I tend to cry easy, and I don't really figure D.W.'s looking for my input."

"You're right about that, Sam. But it occurred to me and Parry that maybe that wouldn't be such a bad idea—getting your input. We got to remembering how you negotiated with those Colombian guerrillas back in the early seventies, remember, the ones threatening to blow up our pipeline?"

"I bought 'em off is basically what I did, Hardy."

"Right. Well, suppose things get out of hand down there and Caracas can't handle it. Maybe we should think about that."

"Maybe so. But D.W. surely knows how to make a payoff. Unless you want me to be your back-channel negotiator."

"I'm just trying to keep you plugged into the war room, Sam."

"And I appreciate that, Hardy. Keep me posted."

Sam cradled the phone. Chick Hooper glanced over. They were bumping along over the brush, heading for the perimeter track. Sam gave him a shorthand summary of Hardy's news.

"You thinking about heading back down there, Sam?"

He thought about it, then shook his head and reached for the phone again. "No, Chick. Got to make some phone calls is all. Then you can go back to teaching me the cattle business."

33

Jacqueline Lee had been able to document some of the sabotage from the air that morning, but on the Cessna's second low pass over Cerro Calvario, National Guardsmen had appeared, waving assault rifles. Under the circumstances, Jacqueline agreed with the ex-air-force jockey that further overflights were not a good idea.

So that afternoon she and Dr. Laya squeezed in beside Enrico in his Ford pickup and jounced out to see what damage, if any, had been done to the railway-grading equipment along the ranch's eastern perimeter. They had heard detonations during the night and smelled smoke and hydrocarbon stink. A trace of acrid stench remained in the air as they approached the long mesh-wire barrier that marked the rail corridor, and Jacqueline leaned out the truck window with her Handycam.

She didn't have long to wait before the first casualty appeared. An enormous earthmover had been turned into a fire-blackened hulk and its one-ton tires into steel-belted sludge. At Jacqueline's request, Enrico stopped so she could jump out and poke the videocam's eye through the woven fence. She zoomed close on the carbonized chassis, then up to the swivel-console cab, reduced now to a mangled metal cage. Panning beyond the wreckage, she came upon several uniformed guards patrolling the opposite fence alongside Route 16. An instant later, one of the men swung around, pointing his rifle directly at her.

She scampered back to the Ford, and they accelerated away along the barrier. Less than a minute later they came upon the charred remains of a giant Caterpillar rock loader. But as they slowed and Jacqueline steadied her Handycam, three Guardia men stepped suddenly from behind the ruin. The two flanking soldiers had their auto rifles unslung and trained forward, while between them an officer unholstered his sidearm and gestured for them to come forward.

As Enrico killed the motor and opened his door, Jacqueline slid the videocam under the bench seat. Then she and Dr. Laya followed Enrico toward the fence and the waiting officer—a *te-niente*, first lieutenant, by the twin stars on his kepi and shoulder flaps. It was the second time in several days Jacqueline had been under the guns of the Guardia, and she found herself, incredibly, almost getting used to it. Her immediate fear was that they would confiscate her Handycam and the day's footage.

Enrico, meanwhile, was his usual insouciant self, chatting with the scraggly-mustached lieutenant as one man of the world to another. The ranch foreman swept his arm back, first to include Jacqueline and Dr. Laya as his guests, then encompassing the entire La Promesa rangeland. The lieutenant returned a minimal nod and turned to squint at Dr. Laya—who was much too fidgety, Jacqueline thought—and then at Jacqueline. She acknowledged the lieutenant's inspection with an amiable smile and maintained it even when his gaze slid down the front of her sweat-stained denim shirt and snug jeans. She damn well wasn't going to react. She'd been peripherally aware that the rifle-toting soldiers had been conducting a similar surveillance. At least they'd untargeted their lethal toys.

She turned back to see Enrico push a soft pack of cigarettes through the mesh wire. The lieutenant shook one out and passed the pack back to his men. After savoring a few lungfuls, the lieutenant made a quick, dismissive gesture. Enrico nodded, mumbled something, then swung lazily toward the pickup, motioning Arquimedeo and Jacqueline to precede him. A moment later all three were bouncing around on the bench seat as the Ford angled off into the brush.

"Enrico, you were fantastic!" she said.

He shrugged, then explained what he had learned: "They don't want us driving along here now, even to pick up strays. It's for our own safety, he says. They're looking for terrorists, at least four or five people. In addition to what we saw burned out, someone blew up a big pile of steel rail—the explosions we heard last night."

"Well, I can understand their calling out the National Guard for something like that," Jacqueline said. "But not to drag archaeologists out of their tents and herd them off a mountain."

"Ah, but you see, Jacqueline, our Guardia is a most flexible force." Arquimedeo was visibly delighted by her sarcasm. "The Armed Forces of Cooperation they call themselves—Fuerzas Armadas de Cooperación. Which means, in practice, they do anything they wish, and the rest of us must cooperate."

Enrico chuckled. "They do have many functions. And among these are protecting natural resources, such as mines and oil fields—whether from terrorists or archaeologists, it seems."

"Equally dangerous, in their eyes," Dr. Laya said.

Enrico glanced over at him. "The lieutenant tells me they're expecting some help from the Ministry of Interior. The DISIP are being sent down to investigate."

"What's that?" Jacqueline asked.

"Dirección de Seguridad e Inteligencia Policial," Enrico explained. "The Directorate of Security and Police Intelligence."

"Political police," Dr. Laya added. "Descendants of the old, hated Seguridad Nacional, or SN. I expect they'll want to interrogate me about my political sympathies, and how to locate dear old Uncle Oscar."

"But Enrico just said they're looking for a gang—four or five terrorists. Your uncle and those two Indians couldn't possibly have done all that sabotage by themselves—could they?"

Dr. Laya shrugged his small shoulders. "It would seem unlikely. Personally, I've always considered Uncle Oscar to be an incompetent old windbag. But who knows? Perhaps he is good at something after all."

The National Guard lieutenant had been correct in predicting the imminent arrival of federal security investigators. By the time they got back to the *casa grande,* a plain-gray Buick sedan was parked in the courtyard, and two shirtsleeved, sweat-drenched men were smoking in the shade of the big araguanay tree. Enrico pulled up behind the sedan, biting off a one-word comment: *"Federales."*

And so they proved, flashing credentials from the Interior Ministry, specifically the DISIP. The spokesman was a bronzed man with a gray pompadour and a long, puckered scar down one cheek. He introduced himself, in a bass rumble, as Capitán Marco-Aurelio Siso. And he showed little interest in either Enrico or Jacqueline, turning his attention immediately toward Dr. Laya. He asked, in Spanish too rapid for Jacqueline to follow, how long the professor had been staying at the ranch.

Enrico quickly interposed. "Captain, I can assure you, Dr. Laya was here with us at the ranch house last night when the sabotage was committed."

"Thank you for that, Enrico," Arquimedeo said, also in Spanish. "Now, assuming that is sufficient to allay your suspicions about me, Captain, I have some work inside I'd like to attend to."

Siso grinned. Jacqueline had fleetingly considered whipping out her Handycam—hoping that, by so doing, she might head off any rough handling of Dr. Laya, or even possible violations of his civil rights. But one look at the captain's grin, and the way it twisted his scar, changed her thinking.

The security man unleashed another guttural burst of Spanish, and Arquimedeo turned to interpret: "It is precisely what I was just telling you, Jacqueline. He has come here to ask—I should say to demand—my help in locating Uncle Oscar and his 'pals.' "

The archaeologist swung back to the plainclothesman, maintaining that he had absolutely no knowledge of his uncle's whereabouts for the past several days—and had, moreover, absolutely no intention of ever seeing the old man again.

Though unable to fathom Dr. Laya's rejoinder, Jacqueline could certainly detect its pompous and pedantic tone and thought it unlikely to satisfy the DISIP cop. Her intuition was quickly confirmed as Captain Siso growled back forcefully. She appealed to Enrico, who obliged with a running translation:

The *federales* weren't just investigating sabotage, she learned now, but threats of further terrorism. In response, Dr. Laya was offering to cooperate fully, suggesting, with Enrico's immediate acquiescence, that they all go inside to continue the interview. But Captain Siso was shaking his pompadoured head, requesting instead that the archaeologist return with them to their offices in Puerto Ordaz.

At this juncture Jacqueline whirled on Siso:

"But why take him away for interrogation? He's being candid with you right here. And anyway, Dr. Laya's uncle and those two Indians couldn't possibly have set all those explosions and fires—at least not according to the Guardia lieutenant who spoke to us out there. He told us you're looking for a gang of four or five terrorists, not an old man and a couple of innocent natives. When is this official harassment of Dr. Laya ever going to end? He's an archaeologist, a scientist, not a common criminal!" She turned to Enrico. "Please, tell him what I said!"

"That is no necessary, *señorita*," Siso replied, looking faintly amused. "Believe me, I understand very good."

The dark-sunglassed agent behind Siso, meanwhile, looked eager to end the parley and to simply toss Dr. Laya into the back of their Buick. Jacqueline was particularly unnerved by the way this man was resting his big palm on the checkered butt of his belt-holstered revolver. Captain Siso, however, persisted in his calm rumble, switching to English for her benefit:

"Let me say that we are making the investigation here, Señorita Lee, not a 'harassment.' Who you are speaking to in Guardia Nacional is no my business, but I telling you that no one can say how many terrorists are doing these thing. So we are looking at everything and everybody. As for Oscar Azarias Rivilla"—he glanced down at some notes—"on one of the big machines somebody is writing"—he mimed a moving spray can—" 'Bandera Roja.' It signifies Red Flag. This is a group of *guerrilleros urbanos*, how you say?"

"Urban guerrillas?" Jacqueline suggested.

"*Bueno!* Urban guerrillas. Bandera Roja is a group that Oscar Azarias is joining many years ago, after he is leaving a Mexico City prison for robbing banks, and before he is working for Carlos Lehder. You know this name, *señorita?*"

She shook her head.

"A very famous man." He turned and snickered to his deputy.

Enrico provided an explanatory aside: "Lehder was a big Colombian coca smuggler, now in prison in the U.S."

"Captain, you don't have to recite Uncle Oscar's criminal record," Arquimedeo protested. "I am aware of it and properly ashamed of it. And, as I keep telling you, I have every intention of cooperating with your investigation."

"Yes, I know. I am explaining this now for Señorita Lee, okay, Professor? There are other things written, *señorita*." Again Siso pantomimed the spray can. Then he paused, scratched his scar, and reverted to Spanish, which Enrico quickly interpreted into English:

"The captain is saying there were revolutionary slogans painted on one of the bulldozers which wasn't set on fire: 'Proteus out of Venezuela!' 'Death to *Yanqui* Fascists.' Things like this. He says they aren't ruling out other likely groups, but *his* job is to investigate Dr. Laya's uncle and all his activities while he was down here."

"Okay! But why do they have to take him to Puerto Ordaz?"

Captain Siso heard and obviously understood her question, but was unequal to an English reply. Once more, Enrico provided the translation: "He says it is unfortunately necessary. For instance, he says, they may wish to attach Dr. Laya to a polygraph machine, which he does not have in his car."

"And if Dr. Laya refuses to go or to take the test?"

"Jacqueline!" Arquimedeo cried out. "I appreciate your concern, but please, don't get me in any more difficulty than I am already!"

Captain Siso grinned, mopping his forehead. The sky was thickening with thunderheads, the humidity becoming more and more oppressive. He spoke in English: "If the professor refuses, we must to insist."

Jacqueline looked at Arquimedeo. "Do you have an attorney?"

"Well, there is a law professor, a colleague at the university."

"Why don't you call him?"

Laya glanced apprehensively at the captain, who gestured acquiescence. "By all means, Professor, call your lawyer. And you may call him again from our office in Puerto Ordaz. Believe me, you will no be incommunicado."

So Enrico accompanied Dr. Laya inside to the telephone, and Jacqueline, suddenly uncomfortable alone with the two government cops, turned quickly to follow. But halfway to the entrance, she heard the thumping approach of a vehicle on the ranch road.

233

She looked back to see the midnight-blue Proteus Land Cruiser run under the big crossbeam gateway into the courtyard. She stood motionless as it slowed and crunched over the gravel, then slid under the araguanay's leafy shade, close enough for her to make out the front-seat faces. Owen Meade was behind the wheel, Ray Arrillaga beside him.

Jacqueline had the absolute and instantaneous conviction that they, too, had come here to take someone into protective custody—namely herself, and obviously on her father's orders. Well, she decided on the spot, they would both go back empty-handed!

As the two men from Proteus climbed out, she wheeled back toward the ranch house, hurrying around the brightly tiled fountain. Then, a third door slid open behind her and slammed shut, and a voice boomed out:

"Jacqueline!"

She froze. It was her father.

34

She ignored the greetings of Ray and Owen, glaring past them at the smaller man in the mirrored sunglasses, pink golf shirt, and twill slacks. D.W. looked, in fact, exactly as he did stalking a fairway after maiming a tee shot, his face every bit as grim. Jacqueline spoke first, without a greeting:

"What are you doing here?"

D.W. shook his head gravely—obviously ruling out the very question.

"Dammit, D.W.," she said, knowing her use of his initials would wound him, "what right have you to come here? This is Sam's ranch."

"I have the right to protect my daughter."

"Well, your daughter doesn't want to be protected—by you."

D.W. did not flinch. "You have a very strong will, Jacqueline. Many times, even when you were very tiny, your will was stronger than mine, and you got your way. Besides, what father wants to say no to his child? But this, this is not a contest of wills you can win. You will come back with me. I am prepared to discuss it with you, but the issue is already decided."

She shook her head. "Look around. Does this look like the Proteus boardroom? Your word is not law here, Chairman Dad. I'll do as I damn well please. And I damn well please to stay here."

"You can hurt me, I accept that, Jacqueline. But I will not let

235

you hurt yourself or endanger yourself. And I will not let you bring anxiety to your mother."

"Dammit, did you call her and scare her? You'd better not have."

"No, she knows nothing of the danger you are in. But if she did know—as is her right—and if she knew that I permitted it, she would condemn me as a terrible father, and she would be right. Do you hear me, Jacqueline? You are in danger here, and I will not permit it."

"I feel perfectly safe with Enrico."

"You are not his responsibility. You are going back with me, Jacqueline, so please gather your things and say your farewells. You may curse me all you like, but you will go. The *Kallisto* is sailing in the morning."

"Not with me aboard."

D.W.'s mouth tightened below the sunglasses. He uttered one word: "Ray."

Jacqueline tensed, ready to flee as Ray Arrillaga took several steps forward. But when the mining executive merely cleared his throat to speak, she swung her attention angrily back to her father:

"Do you really imagine I'm going to listen to Ray or Owen or any of your other flunkies?"

"Jacqueline," Ray cut in, "you can go ahead and hate my guts, along with your dad's, for whatever you think we did to Dr. Laya or Sam—"

"Thank you, Ray. I'll do that."

"But please, just listen to one thing. You can't stay on this ranch. Hell, you can't even stay in this country now. Maybe you have some idealized sympathies for these terrorists, or for whatever you imagine they're protesting, I don't know. You may even think they're your comrades—"

"Oh, for God's sakes, Ray! You don't know anything about me or my sympathies. I'm not Patty Hearst. I don't condone bombing, any more than I condone backstabbing a lifelong friend or bulldozing historic artifacts."

"Okay, so I'm way off base there. But you could be Patty Hearst, and you know what I'm talking about. The fact is, as D.W.'s daughter, you're a prime target now—for political terrorists, or just plain criminals. You know damn well your father worries about this all the time and has ever since you went off to nursery school. And I can tell you, we've all been especially aware of it from the instant we heard you were going with him to Latin America. We've taken many steps to safeguard you, Jacqueline. A lot of them you're not even aware of. And now, with what's happened down here last night . . ." Ray shook his head at the enormity of the situation.

"I mean, we're talking about highly skilled terrorists, eluding our perimeter security, stealing high explosives out of our own construction shed, then infiltrating several work sites and blowing up heavy equipment, setting petrol fires, spraying terrorist graffiti around—"

"I'm well aware of what was done, Ray. I've been photographing it."

"Then for God's sakes, Jacqueline, let's not suggest we're any of us overreacting here. Your dad and Owen and I, we'd be criminally negligent if we didn't take immediate and drastic steps to protect you—and ourselves, and everyone in the Proteus family."

Jacqueline realized that, during Ray's speech, Owen Meade had drifted closer on her other side. An over-the-shoulder glance showed her the two federal cops leaning on their Buick thirty feet away, smoking and looking bored. She began to back away from the Proteus triumvirate.

"Don't you dare!" she warned them all.

"Jacqueline," D.W. growled, "no one's doing anything to you."

But she took another backward step and glance—and was relieved to see the *casa grande*'s front door open. Enrico stepped out, settling his ranch hat on his head, followed closely by Arquimedeo. She turned and began walking toward them.

"Enrico!"

He paused, waiting for her. She heard her father and his men moving behind her on the gravel, but she didn't turn around.

"Enrico, it seems we have more company. My dear papa has come to take me away. The problem is, I don't want to go. He says I have no say in the matter. I'm to be taken into custody, just like Dr. Laya. So now, as your guest, and as Sam's guest, I ask you a personal favor, Enrico. Please don't let him do this."

But the ranch foreman could not sustain her imploring gaze. He looked uncomfortably beyond her—at her father.

"Enrico, please! I have work to do here!"

D.W.'s now-hear-this voice boomed behind her. "Señor Tosto, I believe you have received a telephone call from your employer in the past few hours. Is this so?"

Jacqueline saw Enrico nod slowly. She whirled on her father. "Sam called here?"

"I had Hardesty Eason notify him this morning of the terrorist attack, and Sam promised he would telephone Señor Tosto and ask him to ensure your safety until you could be evacuated from the area. He also promised to tell Señor Tosto to cooperate fully with me."

"Enrico, is this true?"

Once again he nodded. "Samuel called while we were out. He spoke to Romalda. It is just as your father says."

"Well, damn him then, and damn you! All of you!" Jacqueline tried to back away again, but found herself encircled by enemies, all of the masculine persuasion. She was livid, and when she felt a touch on her arm, she wrenched it free—then swung around to find that it was Arquimedeo who had dared to approach her.

"Jacqueline," the archaeologist said, blinking owlishly behind his lenses, "you must not blame Enrico. Whoever these Bandera Roja people are—Oscar and his Indians, or others—and whatever they are seeking, this is not a place for you to be now. In this respect, you must listen to your father."

"Oh, well, thank you for that! How wonderful and protective everyone is! Let's all go off into protective custody and let other people run the world."

"But I did not intend an insult."

"Well, I'm insulted. Sorry, Arqui. You can go trotting off like a good boy with your *federales*, if you like, but I'm not going to be dragged away without bitching to high heaven." She turned on Enrico: "Arqui's right, I mustn't blame you, Enrico. But you can tell your *jefe* in Oklahoma that I won't be patronized. Now, if you'll all excuse me, I'm going to pack."

Inside, in the corridor leading to her guest room, she came upon Bernardo, looking vaguely furtive. "We're going to Puerto Ordaz, Nardo. I'm not sure if I'm being kidnapped or kicked out. Amounts to the same thing. You better pack your bag."

"I was watching." He put something into her hand. She looked down at a thirty-six-exposure roll of Kodachrome 64.

"What's this?"

"I took pictures—through the window—of those men in the Buick talking to you, and then of your father and Señor Meade and Señor Arrillaga." In his other hand she now saw the little Olympus auto zoom she'd let him use. "You always say, 'Shoot everything, edit later,' right?"

She stared at the roll, then at his ardent expression, and threw her arms around him. "Thank you, Nardo. You've got the instincts of a real photojournalist. And right now, you're about the only dude around here I can trust."

She turned at footsteps behind her. Enrico was standing near. "I am sorry for what has happened, Jacqueline. But after what we saw this afternoon, I was afraid for you. I am glad they came for you, truly."

"It's okay, Enrico." She went to him and hugged him. "You've been wonderful, and I had no right to let my anger at my dad and Sam spill over onto you. Can you forgive me?"

"It is for *you* to forgive me. Romalda and I want you to come back, as soon as all these crazy people are put in prison, and stay as long as you like. You will always be welcome at La Promesa."

"I accept. Now, dare I ask one last favor?"

A moment later she handed him a plastic bag containing a dozen eight-millimeter cassettes, two and a half hours each— all her Venezuelan footage—plus Bernardo's little roll of Kodachrome. "Enrico, will you keep these hidden until I telephone you where to send them? Right now, I can't trust my father or any of his employees."

He nodded solemnly.

Ten minutes later, after emotional good-byes to Enrico's wife and several of her sisters, Jacqueline found herself bouncing down the ranch road by herself in the back of the Proteus Land Cruiser. Owen Meade was driving, with D.W. on his right. They also had a couple of shotguns up there, she'd noticed. Just ahead, Ray Arrillaga was driving the unmarked Toyota pickup with Bernardo. As they swung out onto the north-south road toward Puerto Ordaz, she glanced back through the back window and caught a last glimpse of Cerro Calvario receding under threatening skies.

35

A few kilometers north of the ranch turnoff, the Proteus convoy passed a Venezuelan phone truck off on the shoulder, with a lineman halfway up a power pole. Before the vehicles were out of sight, the lineman began descending the pole with his safety belt and climbing irons, unharnessing to drop the last meter to the ground.

Then, giving a tug to his baggy coveralls and adjusting an oversize hard hat, the elfin-faced lineman approached the service truck, where the passenger window was already winding down. A mournful, gray-bearded face appeared. Like the lineman, the seated man wore coveralls with a CANTV logo, but neither was an employee of the Compañía Anónima Nacional Teléfonos de Venezuela.

"Boss," the undersized lineman said, "you saw the rich girl?"

"No. She must have been in the back of the rear truck. Chucho, get your brother and let's get out of here."

As Oscar Azarias scooted over behind the wheel, Chucho unbuckled the climbing irons and slung them into the truck. Then he hiked a short distance into the brush, where his younger and larger half brother, Angel, knelt beside a freshly turned mound of earth. Angel was still brooding. The brothers exchanged some words and gestures, then Chucho returned to the CANTV truck.

"So where's Angel?" Oscar asked.

"He prays still for the spirit of the telephone man. Angel is not happy about leaving this man in the earth."

"What the hell does he want us to do with him?"

"It is a matter of tradition, Boss. Angel wishes to burn the body, then grind the bones and collect the ashes in a small gourd. When the time is right, he will mix these ashes with some fruit paste and eat it."

"Chucho, tell your brother he gets his ass in the truck, or we leave without him. He can come back later and take care of etiquette."

Chucho scurried off again. Oscar started the engine and revved up, hoping the urgent noise would shock the big Indian out of his mystic funk.

It turned out that the scary-looking Kamarakota, who had boasted of having been an enforcer for the Medellín cartel, had never killed a man before this morning. The victim was a CANTV serviceman they'd ambushed on a side road. Angel had snuck up from behind and clubbed him on the hard hat with his huge fist. The CANTV man had dropped like a rock, head lolling, a cervical vertebra obviously snapped. Angel had slumped beside the body, inconsolable and mostly useless from that point on. Oscar and Chucho, meanwhile, had busied themselves stripping off boots and coveralls, then locating a second uniform in the truck.

Only when Oscar had finally resorted to bullying had Angel helped them stuff the dead lineman into the back of the panel truck. While Angel attended to burial rites nearby, they'd spent hours parked beside various power poles near the La Promesa turnoff. The stakeout had allowed them to monitor all traffic entering or leaving the ranch, and incidentally to admire some of their previous night's sabotage. Two burned-out earthmovers were quite visible from the road.

Both Chucho and Angel had performed remarkably on that assignment, Oscar thought. Incendiary and demolition work was tricky enough, but to do it well, while also avoiding detection, especially exfiltrating security areas with pyrotechnics in progress, required rare skills. And the brothers seemed especially proficient in night operations. Frankly, Oscar had no business complaining about the big Kamarakota's funerary superstitions.

And Chucho had proved surprisingly adept today with the

pole-climbing apparatus, even with boots and coveralls several
sizes too large. But as Chucho had modestly explained, Kamarakotas and other forest tribes had long fashioned their own
climbing slings of ropes and palmwood, with which they shin-
nied up tall plantain trees or scaled the smooth-boled moriche
and the thorny trunk of the *pijigua*.

Finally, as Oscar gunned the engine for the tenth or dozenth
time, Chucho appeared with his large and morose brother in
tow. When both had squeezed inside, Oscar let out the clutch
and pulled the phone truck onto the road. The little convoy from
the cattle ranch was long gone, of course, and the afternoon
darkening under dense rain clouds. But there was no need for
undue haste. From his snooping at the Cerro Calvario camp and
chatting with the volunteers, Oscar knew exactly where father
and daughter must have gone. And after last night's successful
rehearsal, he felt his little team was ready to tackle something
truly big.

Félix Rosales had filled the short bed of his Mazda pickup with
electronic gear and other valuable items left behind by Arquimedeo and the rest of the crew. There were several microscopes,
a canister vacuum, a metal detector, the single-sideband radio,
two Polaroid cameras, TV, VCR, the Tandy laptop Félix had
inherited when Arqui got his Toshiba, two camp stoves, binoculars, even a compact refrigerator and small Honda generator.

The decision to clear out had been made in the middle of the
night. Félix had been jolted out of postcoital stupor by a distant
concussion, a rumble that shook the earth under his tent. He
told himself it was only a Venezuelan air force F-16 or Mirage
jet streaking low over the savanna. Then he smelled smoke. He'd
had to shake Marta awake, then practically shove her out of the
sleeping bag to escape her clutches. Finally he'd grabbed up his
twelve-gauge over-under and hustled out. Immediately he'd
heard a roaring, climbed a rock, and seen a bulldozer a half mile
away in fireball silhouette, canopied by oily smoke. That was
altogether enough night reconnoitering for Félix. He sat up till
dawn in a camp chair outside the tent, the shotgun in his lap.

In the morning he'd gone prowling again, very carefully. He'd
encountered two incinerated Caterpillar hulks, an untorched

242

flatbed sprayed with Bandera Roja graffiti—then walked right into the assault-rifle sights of a National Guardsman. Félix had dropped his shotgun, thrown up his hands, and shouted his innocence. Fortunately, old Jaime, one of the Proteus guards, had been just a step behind the Guardia man and quickly vouched for Félix.

Jaime also had a message to deliver—one Félix had already figured out for himself. The Proteus folks had phoned the guardhouse to say they wouldn't be arriving today to inspect archaeological trenches or artifacts. The company obviously had more pressing problems. The real import of the message, for Félix, was that there would be no more Proteus money trickling his way. The bogus excavation, like the real one, was now history. It was finally time to pack up and get the hell off this godforsaken piece of rock.

Félix was furious—yet secretly relieved. On the way down to his tent, he booted over a wet-sieving barrel, then grabbed a shovel and, whirling like a hammer thrower, flung it far out into the brush.

"*A la chingada!*" he cried, then listened to the flat echo off the rocks: "*A la chingada . . .*"

Marta Mendes was quickly beside him, eyes blinking in concern. "Félix, what's happening? What did you find out?"

He told her tersely.

"So what are you going to do now?"

"Get the fuck out of here, *chica*, that's what I'm going to do now."

She didn't ask her next question, but he read it in her eyes: *What about me?*

He struck his tent, inventoried his pitiful possessions at a glance. Rage and relief gave way now to well-worn despair. He was walking away with nothing to show for his whole archaeological career. Which put him right back where he'd been after the collapse of his bodybuilding career, before he'd first gone to work as a digger for Arquimedeo.

Another futile episode in the life of Félix Rosales. Only this time he'd run out of relatives to bail him out. In fact, thanks to Arqui's academic contacts, it was likely Félix would never again be hired by any university archaeology department. And there was worse to contemplate. He'd already spent the entire crummy advance he'd gotten from Jacqueline's father and still owed six payments on his beat-up truck.

Damn, he had to make out *some* way! One answer, of course, had been staring him in the face for days, not fifty paces off— two work tents crammed with equipment that had been trucked down from Cerro Calvario by Proteus crews. Most of it belonged to Arquimedeo or Simón Bolívar University—or in some cases, to the foundations that had loaned it. If it was missing, there'd be no particular mystery about who'd run off with it.

But supposing he left all the hefty, specialized stuff—the soil-resistivity meters and photon magnetometers—and just swiped consumer items? He could head for the nearest city, sell the stuff piece by piece, then vanish. He could even fix up a new identity. Félix was a silly-ass name anyway, more suited to some mincing *maricón*—a fag. While this plan was taking shape in his mind, and he was mulling over aliases, Marta finally made her approach:

"I was thinking, Félix."

"What about?"

"That you and me could go back to Cumaná together. I know my brothers would give you a job."

He stared at her, momentarily at a loss for a sufficiently scathing comeback. Did she actually think he'd agree to haul slimy nets and take orders from her stinking brothers—all for the privilege of sticking it to her at night? Or was she even more delusional? Did she imagine he'd want to marry her and learn to fish and talk Portuguese? Was that the pathetic dream that seemed to shine now out of her homely face?

But then he thought, *why not!* Why not take off to Cumaná with Señorita Mendes? That was one sure way to keep her from ratting to the authorities. Once there, he could lie low, even do a short stint on one of the damn boats, till he was sure nobody was looking for him anymore. He'd sell stuff, stash the cash. When he was ready, he'd just take off, head for some other beach city—and better-looking chicks.

He pretended to study her thoughtfully. "Do you really think they'd give me a job, Marta?"

She leaned against him, hugged him tight. "Of course!"

"Then let's go."

In her jubilation, she squeezed most of the air out of his solar plexus. When Félix regained his voice, he explained there was a lot of work to do before they could actually leave. They spent the next several hours combing through equipment, sorting and selecting and packing. Félix didn't explain what he intended to do with it all exactly, only that it was too valuable to leave on the mountain with terrorist crazies running around.

Now, late in the afternoon, there was just enough space left in the back of the Mazda to wedge in their own backpacks and sleeping bags. And they were finishing just in time. As Marta helped him spread a tarpaulin over the bed and tuck it in, the rain clouds seemed ready at any moment to open their bellies. Marta suggested punching grommets along the edges of the tarp and lashing it down to make it watertight—the way her brothers had taught her. Félix only laughed and told her to get her little buns in the truck.

"We're not expecting storm waves out here, Marta, just a good hard rain. Mostly, I'm worried about covering everything so at the gate Jaime can't see what the hell we got back there."

He started the engine, then the wipers, as the first fat drops began splashing the windshield and drumming across the roof. Then they were off, thumping along the rough track for the last time. But just this side of the Proteus gatehouse, Félix braked and turned to Marta.

"When we reach the gate, maybe you could kind of lean forward and smile, put on a little show for the guard?"

"No problem."

She shrugged off a tank top strap, tugged downward on the scooped neckline, and grimaced toothily. At least, it looked like a grimace to Félix, though apparently it was intended as a seductive smile. And Marta certainly didn't have much in the way of *chi-chis*, but there was a nice little pectoral groove from all her hours of iron-pumping.

"How's that, *felicidad?*"

"It'll have to do."

The rain was falling steadily as Félix pulled up to the gate and cranked down the window. An unfamiliar soldier sat beside Jaime in the guardhouse. Félix shouted into the downpour: "Any more messages from Proteus?"

Jaime shook his head, not coming out. The *Guardia* man,

meanwhile, was staring right past Félix. Whatever Marta was doing over there was working. Then Jaime waved them through.

Adiós, Cerro Calvario!

Moments later they were on solid asphalt, pointing north on Route 16, which would take them all the way to Barcelona on the Caribbean, where they'd hang a right, ninety klicks more to Cumaná. Make it sometime tomorrow. No point in pushing too hard. Stop at a *hostería* somewhere along the way. Give the horny little tomboy a night to remember.

Félix's mild euphoria persisted even in the teeth of the worsening storm. Dark skies, driving rain, and battering winds were all magically transmuted by his phantasmic brain into sunshine and a long, sugary beach beside turquoise and emerald water. He had tuned in again to his old *telenovela* daydream—with Marta Mendes, of course, not part of the picture. In fact, he was still visualizing Jacqueline. But the loot in back would certainly help him cast a new and spectacular leading lady.

Without warning, then, the bright blue water in his mind turned into bright blue canvas flapping in his rearview mirror. He whirled and confirmed the worst: a gust of wind had gotten under an edge of the tarp. It billowed up again as he watched, then tore loose on all four sides and went sailing off into the back draft.

Marta screamed, and Félix snapped his head forward, fighting the wheel. Christ, he'd nearly steered them into a ditch! But even staring straight ahead, it was hard to see the road. The rain was exploding against the windshield, exactly like the storm waves he'd joked about.

"Marta, can you see what's happening back there?"

"Everything's getting drenched!" she yelled. "You should have lashed it down!"

Félix nearly slugged her for that little comment. He was afraid to turn around again, and the mirror view was a total white-out. But he could picture the disaster back there in vivid detail. The stuff they'd spent all day selecting and packing—computers, cameras, VCR—was rapidly being converted to floating scrap metal.

He skidded to a stop, shouting at Marta to get out and help.

Outside, they were soaked through instantly, barely able to see one another or hear anything above the roaring onslaught.

He bent close to her and yelled, "Did you pack another tarp?"

She shook her head hopelessly, her face streaming.

Mierda! Why hadn't he at least taken along one of the big tents? But what about his sleeping bag? Maybe he could unzip it, spread it flat. But how much could it cover, and how could he anchor it? The rain was coming down like Angel Falls, the water on the asphalt swirling around his ankles. It was already too late to save anything. And why the hell was he standing in the middle of the highway, where somebody was going to come barreling along out of the rain at any instant?

Marta was still staring at him, desperate to help.

He shouted at her, "Get back inside!"

They both sprinted for the cab, dived in, and slammed the doors. Félix shoved it in gear, peering forward as some maniac in the sky kept heaving buckets of water on the windshield. Nice timing up there, God. Thanks for another big break. What a totally helpless, fucked-up feeling!

Marta touched his forearm. Félix nearly swung at her, but settled for a quick, mean glare.

"What is it now?" he growled.

If she dared to mention again anything about the tarp, he'd knock her right out the fucking door and leave her on the highway.

Instead she smiled tentatively. "I'm so sorry, Félix. But it'll be okay. You'll like my brothers, and I know everyone will like you. You'll see, baby."

Félix looked away in disgust. Outside, the storm battered the roof, shook the cab—and continued to convert the cargo bed into a big bathtub on wheels.

And beside him, trying her best to combat his ugly mood, the fisherman's daughter laced her hands around his thick right arm and snuggled closer.

36

Jacqueline Lee lingered on the *Kallisto*'s tiny sun deck, sipping chardonnay and watching a fiery Orinoco sunset fade to pallid pastels. She was aware of standing on the spot of her attempted seduction of Sam Warrender—how long ago? Counting back, she realized the shipboard party had been fully eight nights before. So much upheaval had occurred in the meantime that Sam's tipsy pratfall, which had seemed so apocalyptic that night, was now all but occluded in memory. What stood forth, instead, were the multiple betrayals, the Proteus boardroom massacre, the *Guardia* troops rousting fossil hunters out of their tents like so many criminals. And it had all ended today in a morning of ashes, after a night of fires and explosions.

And the results of all this upheaval?

Sam was now in exile—literally put out to pasture on his ranch. Dr. Laya López was under detention, whatever euphemism was being officially employed, while security forces combed the countryside for his crazy, anarchic uncle. As for Conan the Archaeologist, who—other than perhaps poor Marta Mendes—knew or cared about his inconsequential fate?

Then, of course, there was dear old Dad. For the past several hours Generalissimo Lee had been closeted below with his lieutenants—or should that be Colonel Arrillaga and Major Meade?—no doubt placing endless squawkbox calls to Caracas

248

and Puerto Ordaz and New Orleans, updating contingency plans and keeping his exploitative options open.

And what about herself—once more immured in her gilded, filial cage? Well, if she had any real guts, she'd march off the boat this minute—or get Bernardo to drive her away in a company car, since the macho little guy was basically up for anything. Then she'd hunt up some of Dr. Laya's academic allies and volunteer to join—and document—their ongoing struggle.

But she obviously wasn't acting on any such stalwart impulses. The inescapable verdict was cowardice, though her reluctance wasn't hard to rationalize. With Arquimedeo in custody, and Enrico and Sam having withdrawn their protection, she lacked either guide or chaperon. And she couldn't recruit Bernardo without jeopardizing his job as Proteus's local factotum. The ultimate rationalization, of course, had to do with her father. If she dared stage another mutiny at this late date, D.W. would go absolutely berserk, no question about it. And he would not be stopped by anything short of a small cannon.

So, nominally, she would obey. Sail away in the morning, maybe fly home from Trinidad the day after next, as D.W. had wanted her to do originally, instead of coming down to Venezuela with him. True, she could fly directly from here. But even under the strained circumstances, she was looking forward to another day or so of winding through tropical greenery on the Orinoco. One way or another, she'd get back to her TriBeCa loft and NYU. Then she'd phone Enrico to air-express all her eight-millimeter cassettes, chain herself to a video-edit controller, and see if she had the makings of a film—a film whose dismal ending was still being played out.

And then, finally, there was the man from Oklahoma to think about. Or not think about. However she justified it, he had certainly been subjected to some wildly erratic mood swings on her part over the past couple weeks—alternately enticed and disdained, forgiven and unforgiven. Even more fantastical, she now realized it was possible that her "My dearest Sam" letter of two days ago, and her "Damn him!" comments relayed to Enrico just this afternoon, might reach Sam at about the same time. What could he possibly think of her? One thing was sure, he had to be thoroughly fed up with her. The kindest thing she could do for him now, obviously, was just leave the poor man alone.

The trouble was, she'd never ceased talking to Sam in her head. She had, in other words, already started mentally composing another long letter to him, full of her usual unsolicited revelations and blatherings. What a hopeless tangle! And beneath all her conflicting feelings and convoluted thoughts lay the simple truth—she wanted desperately to see him again.

Not now, of course. He deserved a respite from her, and she had work to do. But when this was all over, and her film was in the can . . . In fact, she might phrase it exactly that way in the final paragraph of her letter or embed it perhaps in a tender postscript. Of course, she'd try to be more careful with her endearments. . . .

On the broad river, meanwhile, the silvery reflections were quickly tarnishing as the equatorial night flooded across the sky. All along the quiet San Félix waterfront, lights began taking effect. Around a corner, then, and moving slowly along the adjacent passenger wharf, came a panel truck, without its headlights. Jacqueline squinted and made out the acronym of the Venezuelan phone company—CANTV—which, D.W. had told her, like other notoriously mismanaged government enterprises, had recently been sold to a private consortium. The phone truck glided past the *Kallisto* and continued on beside the ore-crushing plant, where it parked in deep shadow. She watched a moment, but no one emerged.

Some repairman taking a snooze, probably, while waiting for his next assignment. After the god-awful day she'd been through, the thought of unconsciousness seemed wonderfully seductive. Anticipating the starched embrace of linen sheets, she picked up her empty wineglass and turned to go below. Perhaps she'd fall asleep reading a few pages of *Green Mansions*, a well-worn copy of which she'd picked up in Puerto Ordaz. The poetic novel took place in and around the Orinoco and featured an impossibly exotic jungle girl who talked to animals and birds and seemed to be falling in love with an older man. Unfortunately, at least as far as Jake had penetrated its narrative thickets, the couple didn't look much like having a happy-ever-afterlife.

Inside the CANTV panel truck, Oscar Azarias Rivilla was losing patience. It was time to give final instructions to Angel and Chucho—and to make some last-minute operational changes.

Pursuit into Darkness

The ore ship berthed not far from Señor Lee's luxury yacht presented them with an unexpected and spectacular target—if they could adjust and accelerate their plans. Though by the name and home port on its counter, it was obviously not a Proteus ship, to Oscar that was almost an irrelevance. A capitalist was a capitalist was a capitalist.

But Oscar's urgings had small effect on the brothers. Angel merely shrugged and went on rummaging through his woven-palm bag, which contained a machete, blowgun, darts, a gourd, and other colorful items. Chucho, meanwhile, said they were willing to attack any number of ships—one, two, or even more than two (Kamarakotas had a fairly rudimentary numbering system). But, Chucho explained, no self-respecting warrior would do battle without first summoning the forest spirits, or *hekurá*. And this could be done only through the ritual magic of *yopo*. Oscar pleaded in vain that there was no time for rituals. And when he resorted to outright bullying, the brothers' faces turned stony. Wisely, Oscar had backed off.

Now, trying his best to temper his growing impatience with curiosity, he slumped in the front seat, smoking a cigarette and eyeing their mumbo jumbo through the rearview mirror.

First, from his bag, Angel took a half-meter bamboo tube, then a sealed plastic bag full of black powder—presumably their stash of *yopo*. "Black cocaine" was the first thought Oscar had. But Chucho had explained earlier that *yopo* was made from the fruit of a certain acacia, compounded with various barks and jungle vines. Oscar vaguely remembered hearing "black powder from the Amazon" discussed by a jailhouse *brujo*, or sorcerer, in Mexico City back in the late seventies. According to this well-traveled critic, the stuff was a vegetable alkaloid with hallucinogenic effects similar spiritually to those derived from the Mexican peyote cactus and sacred mushroom.

The brothers now hunkered down in the narrow aisle between racks of telephone gear and took turns blowing pinches of the dark dust through the bamboo directly into each other's nostrils. Back and forth the tube was passed—once, twice, and more than twice—and the *yopo* inhaled explosively as their eyes closed and their heads shot back. Finally the tube was laid down reverently.

In a few minutes, Oscar saw first one brother, then the other, begin to sway. Next, heads and shoulders and arms began to jerk

251

spasmodically. Totally absorbed now, Oscar swiveled in his seat and confirmed what he'd just glimpsed in the murky mirror. Both men were drooling heavily.

Oscar's impatience yielded to disgust and a certain trepidation. A deranged and bloodthirsty denouement conjured itself in his imagination. But even if the hallucinating Indians proved harmless, they would be completely useless for several hours. After their prebattle ritual, the *yopo* warriors would be stoned out of their skulls, unable to walk a straight line, let alone carry out a terrorist operation. So, what should he do? He couldn't stay parked here all night. Somebody at CANTV was eventually going to miss that lineman or his truck and alert the police.

Suddenly Chucho was tapping him, offering him the bamboo tube. Oscar declined. But Chucho persisted, and behind him, Angel began nodding his head violently. Oscar stared into their enlarged irises and discerned that this wasn't exactly a polite invitation. Refusal to participate in their psychedelic ritual would be taken as an insult, and perhaps as sacrilege. His glance strayed next to the machete protruding from Angel's kit bag. Of course, the huge-fisted Kamarakota hardly needed an edged weapon to kill a man, as he had demonstrated on the telephone man this morning.

So Oscar accepted the tube and inserted it into his left nostril. Chucho placed a pinch of dust and the other end of the bamboo to his lips, shut his eyes, and then distended his cheeks, as if preparing to propel a dart high into a forest canopy at some appetizing monkey. Finally, with a plosive grunt, the Indian shot the potent particles through the tube, straight up Oscar's nose and into his brain.

At first, Oscar detected nothing out of the ordinary. At Chucho's prompting, he transferred the tube to his right nostril for a second infusion. Again, his perceptions seemed perfectly normal afterward. It was only very gradually that Oscar realized he was no longer confined to his body. He could, if he wished, slip out of it to one side or the other or hover above and slightly behind his own head, like an ethereal, tethered balloon. Yet this didn't seem in any way hallucinatory, just a natural state of affairs. And although the truck interior had grown quite dim, illumined only by ambient leakage from a warehouse bulb, Oscar was somehow able to see Chucho and Angel quite clearly, and

252

both were steadily grinning at him. He grinned back. And why not? It was an amusing thing, floating around one's body.

And something else he'd never noticed before. With every heartbeat he went blind, and the world went out of existence. Just for an instant, but it happened every time. Oscar studied this phenomenon carefully, struggling to comprehend. And then he felt it, felt the blood actually pulse into his optic nerve and black out his vision for a split second. Suddenly, then, he was seeing differently—a world pieced together out of strobed images, exactly like a projected movie. Or perhaps the world actually did go out of existence during those dark interstices, its atoms and molecules dispersing and then recoalescing. What an incredible discovery! And, this being so, "Oscar Azarias" was not solid flesh, but only the most porous illusion.

Angel began cackling, and Chucho joined in with a giggle. Oscar remembered being told by the *brujo* that the Mexican Indians mixed their forest potions and induced their trance states in order to pursue their "spirit animals" through some mystic forest. But Oscar had the distinct feeling that these two Venezuelan aboriginals, squatting in this boxy, vehicular cave, were each aware of his thoughts on a sophisticated level and were tracking his metaphysical wanderings. So perhaps they, too, were seeing through the grand illusion of matter and laughing at the absurd joke of selfhood.

Whatever the source of their amusement, it was highly infectious. Oscar found himself now crawling back to join the brothers and partake in their laughter. It went on and on, a giddy hysteria culminating in a convulsive crescendo. At this point Oscar felt himself drawn up into a kind of spirit dance with the Kamarakotas. He became suddenly one of three intoxicated warriors whirling over three squatting forms. When the mad caracole stopped, would they each be able to squeeze back into the proper body? Or did that even matter?

The dance did end, and apparently each did claim his rightful flesh, for Oscar found himself, sometime later, curled fetally, while Chucho shook him roughly and poked at him. It felt as if he were being jabbed with the bamboo tube. Oscar whined and gestured in the negative. Any more black dust and he'd leave the planet.

"No, boss, is not *yopo*."

Chucho switched on a flashlight, played its beam over one of the tubular-molded chunks of C-4 Oscar had prepared earlier. Wired to the explosive were copper-sheathed electric blasting caps, six-volt batteries, and a small windup clock. Chucho grinned and pointed outside. Obviously he still wanted to do the operation.

Oscar glanced beyond Chucho. Angel was slumped heavily against the truck's rear double doors, eyes staring blankly, while saliva slid from a corner of his large mouth. Scratch one mystic warrior from the strike team. But Chucho seemed at his keenest, just as he had the previous night on Cerro Calvario. The smaller Kamarakota had been quiveringly excited by all the petrol fires and explosions. Oscar had finally had to drag him away from setting another blaze, so they could make good their escape.

Oscar tried to weigh the decision to go ahead, but his brain refused the problem. Danger, for instance, was an elusive concept, as was death itself. Both specters definitely hovered in the air, nearly palpable. But Oscar also had a sense of his own invulnerability—thanks to the magic of *yopo*. Chucho obviously shared this spiritual confidence, and the far-ranging powers that accompanied it. For instance, to facilitate carrying out his mission, why couldn't Chucho simply render himself invisible or walk through walls, disassembling his atoms on one side and reassembling them on the other? And many other such techniques seemed suddenly and eminently plausible.

Even so, Chucho would need his guidance. So Oscar modified his plan to include a visitation to the ore ship. Then he went over it several times, while the small Kamarakota nodded eagerly.

"I understand," Chucho said. "No problem, boss."

"You will have exactly one hour," Oscar said as he began setting the alarm timer both to arm the device and provide the requisite delay. It was a tricky manipulation, especially considering that Oscar's hands seemed somehow to have been switched—the right where the left should be, and vice versa. And of course the slightest slip of the fingers would close the firing circuit and change them all, in an incandescent instant, into permanently disembodied warriors.

But there was no apocalyptic slip. Oscar completed his meticulous work, while Chucho stripped off his coveralls and covered his face and naked body with flat-black camouflage cream, then tugged a black watch cap over his dark, shiny hair. Finally, Chucho stuffed the completed bomb into his black nylon daypack along with a coiled line and shrugged his small arms into the straps.

"Okay, boss," he said, thumbs up and grinning.

Together they managed to topple the stuporous Angel and roll him away from the door. Then they opened it a crack, just enough for the small black figure to slip out into the darkness.

37

A dozen years before, as a young Kamarakota warrior initiated into the ritual of *yopo*, Chucho had discovered the name of his kindred spirit-animal—the jaguar. And it was this soft-footed stalker of the forest that he became now, as he glided soundlessly through the layered darkness beside the ore-crushing plant. He was accustomed to hunting under the influence of the black powder's secondary phase. After the drug's initial visionary effects passed, a magical wellspring of energy was released, and sense perceptions, especially night vision, were heightened. Another name for *yopo*, in fact, was "hunting powder."

Chucho was very much aware of tapping these magical powers now. Off to his right, berthed portside, was the ore-oil carrier that had excited Oscar. The forecastle and the much larger aftercastle surrounding the funnel were washed by docklights, but the long well deck in between escaped illumination. Behind it, perhaps two hundred meters back against the old San Félix docks, was the sleek white stem of the *Kallisto*.

Chucho scuttled on beside the cargo ship, past a too-exposed accommodation ladder amidships, till he drew even with the break of the forecastle. A half dozen ropes fanned out fore and aft from the ship's steel flanks. After surveying these mooring lines, Chucho selected the one in deepest shadow—a forward

breast rope, angling slightly aft from foredeck to dock and helping to hold the ship close alongside.

It was toward the bollarded end of this rope that he now stole,
in a crouching run that exposed him to view for perhaps two
seconds—far too long a time, to be sure, if anyone on the aftercastle bridge was watching the dockside approaches. But no Klax-
ons sounded, no searchlights blazed. The Kamarakota-jaguar
waited motionless a full minute, hugging his knees beside the
anvil-sized bollard, catching his breath but unable to slow his
heartbeat. Then he slithered out along the thick manila and wire
rope, twining around it with arms and ankles and suspending
himself upside down.

With grave slowness, then, he began to work his way outward,
hand over hand, then bunching and straightening his legs like a
monkey or a creeping caterpillar—no longer a jaguar. In order
to spot him, the officer of the watch would have to lean outboard
from the port bridge wing—and then look very closely at the
exact right spot for a span of several seconds. For Chucho's progress remained furtive, and nearly undetectable to himself. Yet
he did move incrementally up the rope and, eventually, nearing
the ship's side, touched his watch cap against a circular tin shield
designed to deny shipboard entry to wharf rats.

The shield, however, was to Chucho no more than a momen-
tary impedance. He doubled his knees to his chest, clamping the
rope securely between ankles and shins. Then he let go both
hands, letting his trunk dangle straight down. The tricky part
came next—contracting his stomach muscles and whipping his
head, shoulders, and torso back up again on the far side of the
rat guard while grabbing upward for the rope.

On the first attempt he barely missed it and swung down so
violently he nearly lost his foothold and splashed into the oily
black channel between ship and dock. *That* would certainly have
startled awake any less-than-vigilant officers or deckhands
above. Still dangling upside down, Chucho took a moment to
catch his breath and relax his strained abdominals, before
launching himself into a second attempt. This time his right
hand snagged the rope, and an instant later his left hand clamped
beside it. He was then able to release his leg grip and hang
vertically by his hands.

Uncomfortably exposed now and swaying slightly, he began to work himself hand over hand toward the ship. When he was far enough beyond the tin shield, he swung back up and scissored his feet and ankles around the rope, then resumed his slothlike upward progress.

Finally he bumped his head against steel plate. A glance over his shoulder showed the thick mooring rope passing through a fairlead opening in the foredeck bulwarks. A rat could squeeze through the scuppers, but not a man—not even a very compact jaguar-man such as Chucho. But he was able to lift and wedge one bare foot in the fairlead, then reach and swing an arm over the bulwarks. An instant later he landed silently in the grooved waterway at the edge of the foredeck. He crouched here, catching his breath, assessing his safety and his next moves.

A hundred meters aft, the ship's principal superstructure loomed up, sparsely lighted at the funnel and on the ladder between bridge decks. The bridge wings appeared deserted, but Chucho knew danger lurked on the navigating bridge itself. It was from behind those dark windows that any unauthorized movement on deck—among the night-shadowed thicket of ventilators and derricks, king posts and catwalks—would be detected.

He checked his digital watch, a present from Oscar, who had bought it off a Caracas pickpocket. A full twenty-seven minutes had elapsed, nearly half Chucho's allotted time. The effort thus far had sheened him with sweat; thought of the looming deadline now increased the slick coating that smeared his camouflage. It was the jaguar's fault! The fiendishly patient predator had no sense of passing time.

Chucho eyed the nearest ventilator hood, perhaps two meters away. This, as Oscar had explained, probably served the forwardmost cargo bay immediately below. Next he slipped off his small backpack, carefully extracted the armed device, checked and recoiled the attached line. Then, cradling the bomb in his hands, he crawled forward on his belly—a jaguar again, approaching his prey through the savanna grass—inching toward the ventilator. In a moment, he could touch its base. Another moment, and he extended the bundled explosive upward and dropped it into the ventilator cowl, letting the line uncoil through his other hand. He lowered the small weight gently into the number one hold, until he felt the line slacken. Then he tossed the rest of the rope in after it and began worming backward toward the ship's side.

With the lethal countdown proceeding below him, Chucho could no longer afford long motionless intervals. No sooner had he gained the bulwarks than he slid over them and began shinnying down the breast rope. A few heart-pounding, sweat-soaked minutes later he was crawling over the cold iron bollard and onto the wharf. Then, without pausing for breath, he scuttled straight across the dock and into the welcome shadows of the ore-crushing plant.

By Oscar's watch, less than six minutes remained until detonation when the CANTV truck's back door squeaked open and Chucho scrambled inside. Oscar flicked on the interior light and swiveled from the driver's seat to see the Indian's grinning thumbs-up.

Oscar started the motor. "We're too fucking close," he explained. "We could get blown to shit here."

He relocated the truck around a dark corner, where it would be shielded from any blast by the corrugated metal sides of a transit shed. Three minutes to go.

Then he climbed quickly back beside the two brothers—not out of any desire for camaraderie, but to be as far as possible from the windshield. As a further safeguard, he instructed Chucho to get himself and Angel underneath a tarpaulin, then had them all lie flat on the floor close behind the front bench seat.

They waited like this in the darkness for what seemed an eternity. When Oscar checked his watch by flashlight, only five minutes had passed—but two minutes beyond the alarm detonation time he'd set.

His eyes met Chucho's and exchanged mutual apprehension.

"Is no good, boss?" Chucho whispered. "Clock broken maybe?"

"Give it a couple minutes." Oscar feigned a calmness he did not feel, switched off the flashlight. He began counting silently—to sixty, then a hundred. Then a hundred twenty—two more fucking minutes. Maybe the damn clock was no good. Or Chucho had botched the job somehow. Or the bomb had been discovered and disarmed. The secret police or Guardia Nacional would be surrounding the truck even now, guns trained. Or they were on their way.

Mierda! He couldn't lie here and wait to be arrested or turned into a hunk of bleeding meat. The operation was fucked up. It was time to run.

Just as he decided this, the world erupted in a monstrous, shuddering roar. The windshield burst inward, the seatback slammed on top of them, and the back doors were blown from their hinges and flung off into the night. At the same time, the entire truck was being shoved backward and sideways, battered by sheets of corrugated metal, skidding on its tires, yet somehow staying upright.

A moment later, as Oscar huddled under the tarp, blast debris began to clatter down on the truck roof. Oscar clasped his head, his ears still ringing. Then came a second blast, of lesser ferocity; the bomb must have caught the ship's fuel tanks. Oscar tried desperately to recall what he was supposed to do next, and to summon the will to do it, but the *yopo* had messed up his mind. It was Chucho who reacted first, groping around in the truck's glass-strewn interior, finally locating the flashlight and switching it on.

The beam skewered Oscar as he peeked from under the tarp and managed a hopeful grin. It wouldn't do to let the Indians know he'd nearly fouled his pants; that was hardly the appropriate reaction from a veteran demolitions man. Chucho's black-camouflaged face, meanwhile, was creased with concern as he peeled back the tarpaulin. Finally, his flashlight revealed a big mounded shape that shifted and stirred and groaned.

"Angel!" Chucho cried out, continuing in the Pemón language. "Please, Angel, say something!"

A moment later Angel's melon-sized head rolled into view. But his eyes were focused, and his teeth bared in a fearsome grin. It had apparently taken the double concussions to rouse him from his *yopo*-induced trance. The big Kamarakota proceeded to wag his shaggy head like a bear emerging from hibernation, then turned his grin upon his half brother.

"Hey, Chucho," he asked, "did I miss something?"

The half kilo of C-4 detonated in the number one hold of the ore carrier had drastic consequences. They seemed all to occur in one shattering simultaneity, but were actually linked in an intricate chain of destructive events. The lateral force of the explosion, with a velocity of more than twenty-six thousand feet per second, ruptured the ship's forward collision bulkhead and totally obliterated the cargo-bay walls and the watertight bulkhead aft. The downward blast, meanwhile, blew out the double bottom plates, as well as the fore peak ballast tanks and the bottom skin.

The entire forward portion of the ship—from the number two hold to the bow—was thus severed and sent scudding along the wharf a considerable distance before settling to the river bottom. But there was no one left alive in the forecastle to experience this brief, bizarre ride. The two men sleeping in the crew quarters there had been killed by the concussive blast—a hellish instant before being pulped by flying steel.

Fortunately, the bulk carrier had not yet taken on its tons of crushed iron ore, for anything in the number one hold would have been turned into volcanic ammunition to rain down on the surrounding harborside. Still, there was no shortage of deadly shrapnel. Steel decking, metal fittings, mast stays, pipes, shattered derrick posts, iron match battens, shredded hatch covers, all were snatched up by the exploding gases and sent flying.

In one lethal instance, an iron cleat traveling at high velocity decapitated the already stunned third officer on the bridge, a ghastly price for his having failed to detect Chucho's stealthy incursion. Likewise the radio officer, fleeing the wireless room on the lower bridge, was whipsawed by a detached funnel stay, then struck by the collapsing funnel itself and flung overboard.

But the more spectacular effects were proceeding below. After buckling the plates and strongbacks that supported the decks and bulkheads, the fiery blast had expanded until it ignited the fuel oil bunkers amidships, which sent a second explosion ripping through the hull. This thunderous boom was punctuated by a massive geyser shooting hundreds of feet into the Orinoco night, then cascading down onto hissing deck plates. Wearily, then, the entire gutted after-portion of the ship rolled onto its beam ends and subsided in flames, consigning three more crewmen to watery graves.

Even without iron ore erupting skyward, the shower of destruction from the ship was considerable. The air blast had already stripped galvanized sheeting from nearby buildings, torn off rooftiles, twisted gantries, ripped up huge sections of wharf, and smashed every window in sight—and some far beyond. Now the following rain of fiery debris set blazes all along the docks and adjacent offices and sheds—and on the nearest ship.

Which happened to be the *Kallisto*, two hundred meters astern.

38

Jacqueline Lee had a childhood habit of sleeping with her face sandwiched between pillows. And on this night it proved a very fortunate habit. Though the top pillow did nothing to muffle the thunderclap from the exploding ore ship, it did shield her face from flying glass when the shock wave shattered her stateroom window—and every other window in the luxury yacht.

Without knowing quite how, she found herself on her feet in her darkened cabin. The first thing she saw after she found the wall switch was a blank panel where her closet mirror had been. Next she noticed the carpet and bedspread and writing desk were all strewn with broken glass—and she was standing barefoot on more glass shards, her left big toe covered in blood. Her stateroom window was now an empty rectangle with jagged edges and shredded drapes. Then a second deafening detonation shook the *Kallisto*—and pitched her into a corner.

She scrambled up, verifying, at a single glance, that she was now bleeding from her left elbow and calf—and probably several other places she couldn't see. But obviously graver dangers were at hand.

Night before last, in her room at Hato la Promesa, she'd heard more distant detonations—on Cerro Calvario—yet hadn't felt personally endangered. But these terrifying blasts confirmed all her father's warnings: the terrorists would not stop with destroying Proteus's corporate property; D.W. and his family were prime targets. Late last night, when he told her he'd arranged for National Guardsmen to patrol the docks, and for two Venezuelan security men to spend the night on board and travel with them all the way into the Caribbean, Jacqueline had thought her father a bit melodramatic. Now she was profoundly grateful for his foresight and only prayed the terrorists would be driven away from the ship.

But she couldn't stand here waiting like a helpless ditz.

She belted a white terry robe around her nakedness, scraped bloody glass dust from her bare feet, scuffed into her down booties, and slipped outside—banishing a wild impulse to snatch her Handycam and document whatever was going on.

The lower-deck alleyway, dimly lighted by art deco sconces, was deserted. In fact, nothing was out of place there, with the exception of a cock-eyed Erté print. As she hurried forward past the guest cabins, the door to the master stateroom opened inward and D.W. burst out. There was a wild look in his eyes and a blued-steel .45 automatic in his fist. Blood trickled down one side of his face and patterned his blue, quilted-satin robe.

He turned the pistol aside and seized her shoulders. "Jacqueline, thank God! Are you hurt?"

"Daddy, I'm okay! But you're not! Let me see."

"Not now. Listen, you must stay inside your room! Don't go outside for anything! Understand?"

"Did you call the police?"

"Yes, yes. But we cannot wait for them. Go inside!" His scowl, and the vein pulsing at his temple, brooked no opposition. With his free hand, he dug into a pocket and pulled out a snub-nosed, nickel-plated revolver—a lady's handbag gun she'd practiced with before. "Five shots, all chambers loaded," he growled at her, "double action, plus a grip safety here, remember? Just point and shoot."

He slapped the rounded rosewood grip in her palm and rushed off down the alleyway. As she watched his stumpy legs pounding up and around the curving stairs, she suddenly realized two very frightening things—she was smelling smoke now and hearing an ominous crackling from somewhere close by.

"Daddy, wait!"

But he was gone. She stuffed the gun in her robe and hurried after him. Above, illumined by muted wall fixtures, the salon was in shambles. All the wraparound windows and etched-glass panels were blown out, and the same chaos prevailed in the enclosed afterdeck. The shelves here behind the wet bar were swept of stock; the smashed bottles had emptied their contents on the mauve carpeting. Tables, lamps, and art objects had likewise been hurled onto the carpet, which glittered from wall to wall with crystalline debris and crunched wherever she stepped.

But all this was incidental. What seized Jacqueline's attention was the salon's utter emptiness. Her father had rushed elsewhere. But where were the five crew members, or the two tough security types? Then she noticed the starboard door gaping open and smoke curling in over the coaming.

She had moved in that direction when a popping and spitting noise behind made her turn. The white vinyl-upholstered benches around the fantail were on fire. Before she could react, one of the young crewman—freckle-faced Denis with the Cajun accent—appeared with a Halon cylinder, directing a stream of liquefied gas on the flaming cushions. An instant later, the fire had leaped to his pantlegs. The youth screamed and went right over the side in a flat dive, still holding the extinguisher.

Jacqueline ducked out the starboard door, looked forward—and gasped. All along the waterfront, lurid flames danced against the night sky. And two hundred yards away, the last flaming wreckage of the ore carrier cast skittery orange reflections across the dark water toward the *Kallisto*.

But the fire was already on board, and spreading all around her. She felt its heat strongly out here, saw and heard it attacking the teakwood decks and paneling. Then came a shout from forward. She stared into thick smoke on the tapering foredeck in time to see her father backing out, shouting again at someone and gesturing wildly upward. The boat deck above obstructed Jacqueline's view, but she feared the pilothouse was in flames. Or perhaps the entire upperworks were engulfed—just as panic was engulfing her now. But how could the steel-hulled *Kallisto* burn like this—like so much cordwood? And hadn't her father boasted of the automatic Halon suppression system in the engine room? A lot of good that was doing now!

She cried out to him—"Daddy!"—and raced forward.

D.W. had seen her, but yelled and motioned her back violently.

Then she saw why. Flames were eating along the varnished teak rails between them and lashing out through the shattered window frames of the dining salon. Still, she would have dashed through, defying D.W.'s orders out of her need for him, but with each step now she felt the blistering heat of the decking through her ridiculous down booties, as the tar boiled up between the teakwood planks. She cursed herself for not taking an extra few seconds below to put on real shoes.

Thank God, her father was braving the flames and rushing toward her. But when he was halfway to her, a yard-square hunk of upper deck tore loose and crashed between them in a thudding shower of smoking ash and sparks. Jacqueline's backward leap saved her life, for immediately afterward a smoldering section of the radar mast slammed down on the rail and toppled partway overboard. Jacqueline escaped with only minor cuts from the trailing tangle of guywires.

Across this impassable, burning-metal barrier, she and her father stared helplessly at one another. D.W. was yelling—she could not hear his words over the flames—and motioning for her to jump overboard. But the smoking debris of the mast effectively blocked the entire section of railing before her and sizzled in the swirling current below. Worse, a panicky glance to her right showed a fresh hemorrhage of flames cutting off her path astern. She was trapped there—with the soles of her feet starting to fry.

There was one way out. She bolted back through the salon, zigzagging to avoid pockets of flame. She trampled through broken glass and banged out the opposite door onto the covered port deck. Large portions of dockside were ablaze here, too. She scanned swiftly fore and aft, hoping that her father had circled to meet her. But the only person she saw was a Venezuelan security guy, leaping overboard from the flaming fantail, still cradling his submachine gun.

Perhaps her father had also jumped ship. God, please!

Then she grabbed the heat-blistered rail and swung her legs over. She dangled a moment, scorching her palms and the back of her thighs through the cotton robe as flames licked upward from the lower-deck windows. But she was afraid to drop into the gap of oily black water, where hissing, red-hot debris continued to splash down. Instead, she leaped outward for the smoldering edge of the wharf.

She landed on a plank that nearly crumbled to charcoal beneath her, scrambled up, and sprinted blindly through smoke, scanning ahead to find uncharred footing. Then she felt searing heat on her legs, glanced down, and saw the entire bottom of her robe in flames. She ripped the garment off and ran on naked, doubling back toward the *Kallisto*'s burning bow, hoping to find her father. Through swirling smoke now, she saw several other figures, silhouetted against the flames and running in different directions on the wharf. A soldier thumped right by her in his boots, rifle in hand, then vanished into acrid vapors. But there was no sign of her father, though she shouted his name continuously now.

Then someone touched her arm. Jacqueline whirled to find an Indian padding along beside her. Except for a black stocking cap, the top of which barely reached her chin, the man was naked like herself—actually running barefoot on the smoking dockboards—and smeared all over with some kind of black grease. He was smiling at her and seemed totally unconcerned. Strangest of all, Jacqueline knew she'd seen him before, but couldn't recall where.

"You looking for father?" the Indian asked.

"My father? Where is he? You've seen him?"

"*Sí, sí.* Father is okay." A grin accompanied this assurance. "We take you to him."

"*We?*"

Jacqueline turned to see whom the Indian meant. A much larger Indian, wearing telephone company coveralls, was now right behind her. She recognized him, too. Were they the natives who sold her the blowgun and darts at Canaima Camp? She wasn't sure. But this giant scooped her up in his arms as though she were weightless, swung around, and began thumping along through the smoke, away from the *Kallisto* toward what looked like a warehouse—one still untouched by fire. The smaller Indian tagged along beside them.

And suddenly Jacqueline remembered where she'd seen them. On Cerro Calvario. Hanging out with Arquimedeo's funny old uncle. Uncle Oscar.

The terrorist!

She screamed, then kicked and clawed at her big captor, but the man seemed impervious. And wrapped in his arms, she was unable to make use of her tae kwon do combat techniques. Even when she managed to slash his cheek and draw blood, his grin only broadened. So, he found her fury amusing, did he? She went for his eyes next, but the smaller Indian clamped his hands around her wrists.

Now they were loping down a smoky alley between embedded rail tracks, as flickering firelight threw their demonic shadows ahead. She spied the phone truck parked beside a loading dock. She knew she was going to be put inside it and driven away. Kidnapped. A moment later she was dumped over the doorless tailgate. The Indians followed, the small one warning her idiotically to watch out for broken glass.

Inside this black hole, she lashed out with a side kick and slammed her heel painfully against a metal wheel well. Then the engine coughed and sputtered to life, and she saw someone in the front seat, etched against the dashlights and blown-out windshield. The dark head turned, and in the faint light she knew it was Oscar Azarias. The police were right all along about him being the Bandera Roja terrorist.

"Please, Señorita Lee," he said with a certain gravelly unction, "don't fight us. No harm will come to you."

"Then let me go, you bastard!" she spat back. "I'm Arquimedeo's friend—yes, I know who you are, and the police know *exactly* who you are. And they've put Arqui in jail just because he helped you! Damn you, let me out of here!"

Perhaps it was not the most persuasive tack. In any case, the old man didn't even bother to respond. He simply barked something in Spanish to his men and turned back to the wheel, releasing the hand brake and driving off, without lights.

Jacqueline felt this would be her last chance to escape. Later, no matter how much money her father paid in ransom—if he was even alive!—they'd rape her, kill her, or both. Wasting not a breath on screaming, she struggled once more to get free, at least to reach the door handle. Then, when they swarmed on top of her, she raked her hands blindly at them. The large Indian grunted beside her, a massive arm pinned both of hers. Another hand slapped a wet cloth over her mouth and nose.

Pursuit into Darkness

Jacqueline tried to bite the fingers, but she felt a dry, burning sensation on her lips, and her head was reeling from cloying fumes. *Chloroform*, came the instant thought. But she couldn't give up! Then, as the hand clamped tighter, she suddenly remembered the little revolver she'd stuffed in her robe. Dear God, please let it still be there!

Fighting blackout, she groped for the weapon, slapping feebly at her thigh, then pawing at her lap. But there was no gun. And no robe. She'd thrown it away, and the revolver with it.

She was totally helpless now—and even if she had a pistol in her hand, far too weak even to pull the trigger. Her boiling rage, her bitter anguish, amounted finally to no more than a muffled cough behind the chloroformed handkerchief. Then she went limp in the Kamarakota's arms.

39

The southeastern-facing rooms of the Inter-Continental Guayana are all advertised as *con vista del río*, "with a view of the river." But this is gross understatement. Certainly the penthouse suites on this favored side boast one of the hotel world's truly spectacular panoramas. From the fifth-floor windows, one can see the lush greenery of three parks and two waterfalls. Eddying and flowing between these cataracts is a considerable sweep of Venezuela's second great river, the Caroní, nearing the finish of its 500-mile journey north from the Guayana Highlands to the Orinoco.

On the morning after the San Félix waterfront bombing, the tenant of one of these luxury suites stood before this grand vista, but without the slightest interest in what he was seeing. In fact, Duk-Won Lee saw very little, and that swimmingly. He had gone to the window wall only to put his back to the room and hide his welling tears from the half dozen men who had come there to offer him their comfort and counsel.

A gauze pad was taped to his right forearm over a second-degree burn, and his left temple and cheek were bandaged where they'd been lacerated by flying glass. But the gravest injury could be seen as D.W. wiped his face and turned back to the others. His eyes, though dry now, remained inflamed and haunted by despair. They obviously did not wish to focus on any of these associates and functionaries arrayed so conscientiously before him. They were the eyes of a man who wanted to see one thing only in all the world—his daughter, safely returned.

Part of the hellish night D.W. had passed at the hospital. He'd been treated and released very early that morning. En route to the hotel, he had prevailed on his security escort to stop by the docks. There, in the sudden tropical dawn, he'd viewed the charred remains of his $2-million motor yacht. The *Kallisto* was still afloat, and tethered with fresh ropes, but was little more than a mangled and eviscerated hulk.

D.W. gave it barely a passing glance. Among the investigators prowling the stretch of blackened wharfside, he had spotted Captain Marco-Aurelio Siso of the DISIP. The security policeman had clearly had a long night of it himself. His pompadour had collapsed into a grizzled nest, and his scarified cheeks were dark-stubbled and sunken.

Divers had so far recovered four corpses from the submerged halves of the ore ship, Siso had confirmed, and grisly parts of at least three more victims. Another body had washed up a kilometer downstream and been identified as the ore ship's radio operator. All five of the *Kallisto*'s crew, meanwhile, were safely ashore and accounted for, plus the two security men D.W. had hired.

Which left Jacqueline.

Siso now had two pieces of evidence—one physical, one verbal. Both indicated that D.W.'s daughter had also escaped the fiery ship—only to be carried off by persons unknown, presumably the terrorists who had planted the explosives.

The first they'd found wedged between charred dock timbers. It was an incinerated clump of fabric. Wrapped inside was a fire-blackened and badly mangled Smith & Wesson Lady Smith .38 special revolver. The wooden grips were burnt out, the top strap ripped open, the two-inch barrel cracked. But make, model, and identification numbers were all still readable. The round in line with the barrel had fired. The other four rounds had ignited in their chambers, primer and powder, bursting their cartridge cases and splitting the cylinder.

Captain Siso recounted this information from his notebook.

271

When he found his voice, D.W. explained that he'd given his daughter the pistol right after hearing the explosions. He also confirmed that she'd been wearing a white terry robe.

The second piece of evidence came from a National Guardsman, who'd seen a naked girl being carried away from the waterfront by a large man, and a smaller, black man running beside them. All three had vanished into the pall of smoke. Because of the blasts and spreading fires, the Guardia man had naturally assumed he was witnessing a rescue and had not thought to pursue them.

Upon receipt of this devastating information, D.W. had been bundled off to this hastily commandeered penthouse, where his security detail felt far more comfortable. D.W.'s agony, however, was unabated and seemed to worsen by the minute. Only reluctantly had he accepted a small dose of Valium to help him cope, after the hotel physician assured him it would not sedate him. Still, he had not slept.

Among the many things that tortured him now was the fact that it had all been utterly preventable, and therefore entirely his fault. That damning truth had been driven home to him again a few minutes earlier, when he'd telephoned his ex-wife's attorney in Boston.

The dockside explosions and fires had, of course, been bannered in local headlines and newscasts. And now, despite official denials, the terrorist-Proteus connection and Jacqueline Lee's disappearance had also been discovered, with early details set to move on world wire services. D.W. couldn't have Jacqueline's mother hearing this nightmarish news secondhand. The attorney was now contacting her physician and would phone back. Then D.W. would have to make that dreaded call. Julienne would blame him, of course. And this time she'd be right.

Back in the Caribbean, when first notified of the work stoppage on Cerro Calvario, D.W. had ordered Jacqueline to fly home. Predictably, she had defied him, and just as predictably, she had won the contest of wills. Now, in stark hindsight, D.W. saw the terrible escalation, not of his daughter's rebellion, but of his negligence as a father. He did not blame himself so much for permitting her to play anticapitalist filmmaker. But he would never forgive himself for allowing her to camp out on that mountain among radical rabble, where the chief security guard now turned out to have been a notorious terrorist and drug smuggler! It was a miracle she hadn't been snatched earlier.

But the self-indictment didn't end there. For, finally, he had had Jacqueline safely back in his custody, only to lose her a second time—and perhaps irrevocably. The extra Guardia Nacional harbor patrols he'd arranged had proved ludicrously inadequate, and the two private security guards had succeeded only in saving themselves. He should have hired a small army to protect the *Kallisto*—or far better, flown out last night or even sailed downriver immediately, instead of waiting for first light to oblige his captain.

If only he could have any of those choices back again . . .

But the worst, the very worst for him was reliving those last critical minutes and reviewing all his culpable mistakes: rushing topside after the two explosions to assess the damage to the fucking ship—and abandoning his daughter! Fighting fires, directing crewmen—and leaving her unprotected!

And then came the ultimate moment, when he and Jacqueline had stared at each other through the boiling wreckage of the radar mast. Had he to do it over again, how gladly he would hurl himself over that burning barrier to reach her. Instead, he'd retreated all the way around the blazing bow and back to the portside deck—and she was gone. D.W.'s terror had spread like the flames then, as he tried to fight his way below to the cabins, screaming her name, until an impenetrable wall of smoke had forced him back. . . .

"D.W." Ray Arrillaga separated himself from an executive conference on the black leather sectional and crossed the plush penthouse carpeting. "You'd better get some rest. I promise I'll wake you the moment we hear anything."

"Why the hell is everybody just waiting around to hear something, Ray? Why the hell can't somebody find these bastards?"

D.W.'s anguished growl reverberated across the big room, where the black-bearded, red-bereted Colonel Higueras of the Special Intervention Brigade, Venezuela's crack antiterrorist unit, was conferring with Captain Siso, who had restored his pompadoured look of the suave Mafia don. These two men were working together on the case by presidential order and would continue to do so around the clock till it was resolved. Both men now turned toward D.W., but neither showed a reaction. Certainly they understood his anguish. In any case, they'd briefed him last within the quarter hour and had nothing more to report.

Since learning of the sabotage on Cerro Calvario two days before, teams of investigators had been running down the sordid back trail of Oscar Azarias Rivilla. With the cooperation of Dr. Laya and DISIP's computerized records, they'd already talked to scores of relatives and acquaintances and jailmates, very few of whom had anything good to say about the man. More investigators, along with National Guardsmen, had prowled the barrios of Caracas, San Félix, Barquisimeto, and several other cities where Oscar had landed between prison terms. But they had failed to uncover any leads to his whereabouts, or to the identities of the two Indians who had been seen on Cerro Calvario with him.

With the apparent kidnapping of Jacqueline Lee, of course, that search had taken on a terrible new urgency. Unfortunately, as the security men had explained to D.W., Oscar's trail ran cold in Maracaibo, where he'd apparently lived after getting out of Sabaneta National Prison in 1992. Captain Siso had pointedly not told D.W. that Azarias had been released with three years left on his drug-smuggling sentence, as quid pro quo for informing on several Colombian associates. By rights, the old bastard should still be doing hard time.

Of course, if Oscar doubled back anywhere on his past, they'd have him. Unfortunately, that left most of Venezuela wide open. He could, in fact, have gone to ground right under their noses in Ciudad Guayana, exactly as Brigate Rosse and Hezbollah kidnappers liked to keep their captives in nondescript apartments in Rome or Beirut, or moving frequently from one to another.

But there was no point in rehearsing these dismal facts again and again. And they'd already given D.W. the most encouraging news. This was a consensus among Siso and his colleagues that, despite the revolutionary graffiti on the bombed and burnt-out bulldozers, Oscar Azarias had for many years been nothing more than a straightforward criminal. In which case, this was not likely a long-term hostage-taking for some political goal, but a short-term snatch strictly for ransom. Eventually, if the old man didn't blunder into their nets, he'd have to surface to name his price and method of payment. They'd get him then. And Colonel Higueras and his hostage-rescue team would be in the vanguard, keeping Jacqueline out of harm's way.

Ray Arrillaga, meanwhile, had led D.W. out of the living-room command post and into the master bedroom, where he veiled the world-class view behind heavy drapes.

"It's no use, Ray," D.W. protested. "I can't sleep. If I close my eyes, I hear her calling me."

"At least lie down, D.W., and take your shoes off. Listen to me now. If you don't get some kind of rest, you won't be in any condition to help her."

Eventually D.W. agreed to take another Valium and give sleep a try. Ray was right, of course. Jacqueline's safety might depend on D.W.'s ability to function effectively and decisively in the unfolding crisis. He must remain strong for her and not allow this gut-churning torment to master him.

But the instant he lay down and shut his eyes, he heard her, exactly as he had told Ray. She was crying out to him childishly. And to think that only yesterday he had cared more about the future of an iron mine or corporate quarterly earnings or his executive image. What incredible blindness! All those things were no more than plastic counters in a global board game for grown-ups, and he had allowed them to obscure the real treasure of his life.

And there was nothing, absolutely nothing, D.W. could do to bring her back. She was beyond his reach—exactly as she had been in that final glimpse aboard the *Kallisto*, through a barrier of fire. He could not know where she was, nor what was being done to her, nor even if she was still alive. And in this dark void of unknowing, nightmares were endlessly spawned and all his parental fears unleashed. He replayed her voice, torturing himself with it, while trying vainly to ward off the hideous visions that swarmed in his mind.

Finally, he got off the bed and knelt beside it. Then, after a desolate moment on the emotional brink, he began to weep bitter tears. He found himself repeating prayers he had learned forty years before as a six-year-old orphan in a Methodist missionary school in Pusan. He petitioned as well Confucius and Lord Buddha, two adopted spiritual fathers of the Korean people. He received only the most fleeting comfort. But at some point, he did sleep.

Owen Meade was shaking him gently.

"What is it?" D.W. mumbled. Then, as memory flooded back, he sprang up, seizing Owen's shoulder. "What's happened?"

"They didn't find her yet, D.W. Sorry. But they think they've found the truck she was kidnapped in."

D.W. hurried down the hall to the living room, barefoot and buttoning his shirt. Siso was waiting there to brief him, with an interpreter at his side.

They had located a Venezuelan telephone truck, one reported missing early the day before south of Cerro Bolívar—and slightly north of Cerro Calvario. In fact, Siso recalled having spotted a CANTV truck parked alongside Route 16 when he and his partner left the cattle ranch with Dr. Laya. The phone company driver had not yet been located and was feared—

"The hell with him!" D.W. cut in on the laborious translator. "Where did they find this truck?"

"Ah, yes. That would be near Espinero. Which is on the margin of Guri Lake, the western side, about a hundred kilometers south of Ciudad Guayana."

"And there was no sign of Jacqueline?"

"Alas, no."

Captain Siso continued in quick bursts, but D.W. had to force himself to await the translator's long, convoluted renderings. The truck had been run off the road into the forest, he was finally told, perhaps a half kilometer back from the lake—

D.W. momentarily abandoned his struggle for patience: "I don't understand! Why do you think my daughter was in this truck?"

"Señor Lee, I am apologize," Siso said in his own Spanish-inflected English. "But you only must to listen and I think will be soon clear."

And it was. The truck roof was scorched and pockmarked, D.W. learned next, presumably from blast debris. The rear doors were gone, and the windshield had been blown out—or rather inward, for the interior was strewn with glass fragments. The obvious conclusion was that the panel truck had been parked in the blast vicinity, then driven south—before roadblocks had been thrown up—and abandoned. While DISIP investigators searched the nearby lakeside, lab techs were combing the truck interior, gathering and bagging trace evidence for later analysis. For comparison purposes—since the *Kallisto* had burned to the waterline—Siso had sent a technician to the La Promesa ranch to try to obtain samples of Jacqueline's hair.

"Okay," D.W. said, "this narrows the search, right? I want to tell you, Captain, if you see the slightest problem in financing a massive search, I will pay whatever is necessary."

D.W. was surprised by the slowly translated response. It seemed he had not properly understood the implications. Oscar Azarias might simply have had one of his Indians drive the truck south and abandon it. If so, Jacqueline and the kidnappers might still be holed up somewhere in San Félix or Puerto Ordaz. The search radius, in other words, was now vastly widened, not narrowed. In addition to the metropolitan area of Ciudad Guayana, with its airport, roads, and great river, their investigatory net must now spread to include all the five thousand square kilometers of the Guri Lake basin, along with its two great tributary rivers—the Paragua and the Caroní—as well as lesser feeder streams.

To illustrate, Siso unfolded a large map of Bolívar State on the black marble coffee table. From geological survey maps and a recent flyover with Venezuelan mining officials, D.W. was fairly familiar with the local topography. But he watched closely as the federal cop traced the ragged lakeshore with a hovering finger. On the map Guri Lake looked as if it had been outlined by a badly palsied hand. Those tortuously indented banks would provide almost unlimited hiding places, D.W. realized.

Not exactly the optimum terrain for Colonel Higueras and his boys, with their body armor and stun grenades, Browning Hi-Powers and Heckler & Koch submachine guns. Their specialty was storming airliners or urban strongholds, not tracking Indian guides through rivers and jungles. As if in confirmation of this, when D.W. glanced across the room, he saw the Special Intervention Brigade's bearded commander talking to someone on the phone and shaking his head emphatically.

Blindsided again by despair, D.W. stumbled away from the table. He managed several steps toward the hall before his face crumpled. Siso and the other security men looked respectfully elsewhere. But Ray Arrillaga sprang up from the sofa, waving off Owen Meade, who was vectoring in from the bar. A moment later the mining executive had steered his boss back to the master bedroom and onto a leather settee. Then, as D.W. fought and shuddered helplessly against his grief, Ray held him in his arms.

"They're doing everything they can," he said. "We'll get her back, goddammit, I swear we will."

D.W. turned a ruined face to his friend, his tears streaming, wanting to believe, trying to nod, but looking utterly without hope.

40

Sam was out after breakfast, behind the wheel, bouncing over the stubbled range, checking the herd and stopping periodically to fork bales of winter hay out of the back of his Dakota pickup. He was heading in for a second load when the cellular phone chirped, and he found himself talking to Ray Arrillaga in Puerto Ordaz.

"What's going on, Ray?"

There was the usual overseas delay as digitized signals caromed off a satellite and pulsed through land links. Then:

"A terrible thing has happened down here, Sam."

In a dry voice, Ray began relaying the stark facts of the terrorist attack on the waterfront and Jacqueline's kidnapping. After the first indelible sentence, Sam reached out and killed the dash radio, silencing a rabid sportscaster in midhyperbole. Like D.W., Sam was already cursing himself for negligence. The prairie morning, sullen for starters, had turned exceedingly grim. Sam's chest felt hollow.

"Ray, what's being done? Who's in charge?"

Arrillaga filled in the names and agencies, then capsulized recent developments. "I don't know, Sam. They all seem to feel fairly optimistic about finding this guy and rescuing Jacqueline. But I'm afraid neither D.W. nor I share their confidence."

"I don't blame you. Have they given you their no-negotiating-with-terrorists line?"

"Yeah, you got that right. The word just came down—apparently from the presidential palace."

"And how's D.W. reacting to it?"

"Jesus, what do you think, Sam? He's been screaming at a whole roomful of suits here, and not making a fucking dent. Actually, that's one of the reasons we called. If you don't mind, I'm going to put him on. He's kind of shaky, okay?"

"I understand. Put him on, Ray."

D.W.'s voice came through a moment later, without its usual command authority:

"Sam, Ray told you?"

"I'm still in shock. Duke, if there's anything I can do, you name it."

"That's just it, Sam. I don't know what to do. And I don't think the police know what the hell they're doing. I've never been so scared in my life, Sam."

"I understand that."

"There's this antiterrorist colonel here, he wears a red beret. Sam, I can tell this asshole wants to charge in with his commandos firing Uzis at the first opportunity. And he looks crazy enough to do it, even if it were his own daughter at risk."

"You gotta understand, D.W., these hostage-rescue guys, they all act like that. If you need 'em, and they do it right, they're goddamn heroes. But from what Ray told me, except for finding this bombed-out truck by Lake Guri, nobody's heard from the kidnapper, who we assume is this Oscar character—Dr. Laya's crazy uncle, right?"

"Right. Nothing."

"So I'd say it's a tad early to be talking about commando raids."

"That's what I told them, Sam. I pointed to this colonel and I said, 'This is the last thing we're going to do here. We try everything else first.' "

"Exactly. The thing is, D.W., even if these guys are final-option, they've got to be on standby and ready to move fast, starting now."

"Dammit, Sam, it doesn't ever have to come to that. They say this Oscar Azarias guy—"

"Wait a minute, Duke. Who exactly is 'they'?"

"A captain from the security police, Señor Siso, and also his boss, who just showed up, another colonel. They're all in the next room."

"Got the picture. So what are they saying about Oscar?"

"That all this anti-Proteus bullshit is just a smoke screen. That whatever he used to be in the sixties or seventies, he's nothing now but a low-life criminal—dope dealer, thief, and now, apparently, a kidnapper. But strictly for money."

"Okay, I buy that."

"Me, too. So I say, fine. Whatever this bastard wants, absolutely I will pay it. Not Proteus. *I* will pay. No questions asked. And absolutely no police, no red berets. Put me on television now—today, tonight. Let's not wait around here for him to contact us. I'm dying here every second, and God only knows what it's like for Jacqueline! I'll put out the word, offer the old bastard whatever he wants—money, or even money plus a straight hostage trade, me for Jacqueline."

"I bet that went over well."

"You know, Sam, they looked at me like I was the criminal! Then somebody calls Caracas. Then they tell me the president of Venezuela says no. No TV, no negotiation. He's a tough guy, they tell me. I say, call him back, let me talk to him. He knows me. Absolutely not. *El jefe* guy can't talk to me now. The son of a bitch! Tough guy my ass. It's not his daughter out there!"

"D.W., hold on now. What you've got to do here—"

"Sam, don't you see? I'm going crazy. First they tell me this old bastard is not a terrorist, just out for ransom. Okay, so it's not a political issue, let's pay the fucking ransom and get Jacqueline out of there. Then go in after the bastard. But they say no. If he's *pretending* to be a political terrorist, and *acting* like a political terrorist, he must be *treated* like a terrorist! And Caracas doesn't negotiate with terrorists or give in to their demands! Goddammit, Sam! Those goddamn high-and-mighty sons of bitches!"

It sounded like a distant bomb had gone off in Sam's earpiece. Then Ray Arrillaga's calmer voice came on:

"Sam, D.W. stepped away from the phone a second. He's, uh,

281

he's had a pretty rough night of it, as you can imagine. Just give him a minute."

"Of course. Jesus, Ray, it's got to be the worst thing in the world. I mean, hell, we've both got daughters. I'd be a basket case. I may be already."

"That pretty much describes me, Sam. We're both looking for some kind of guidance here, I guess you can tell. And I figure you've dealt with about as much of this kind of South American craziness as anybody, starting back in the fifties, right?"

"I'm afraid so, Ray. In Colombia there for a while, it got to be kind of a cottage industry, kidnapping multinational executives for ransom. But Jacqueline—Christ Almighty! We should never have let her go down there."

"Obviously, in hindsight, I agree. D.W. blames himself, of course, but we were all negligent to some extent. Still, the way it went down, Sam, on the ship with bodyguards around her, even the Guardia Nacional staked out on the dock, how can you figure that? The way I look at it—hold on, Sam. Here's D.W. again."

"Sam, are you still there?"

"I sure am."

"Sam, I need help." The guttural voice thickened with raw emotion. "Not that I have any right to ask—"

"Oh, for chrissake, D.W.! That's pretty damn irrelevant."

"Yeah, I guess so. I appreciate your saying so."

"Look, I don't know how much help I can be over the phone, three thousand miles away. You want me to come down there?"

There was a pause, then: "Would you, Sam?"

"Hell, yes."

"Okay. I'd appreciate it, Sam."

"I'm on my way. I'll call you back when I'm in the air."

"Sam?"

"Yeah?"

"You're not going to fly that little Cessna down?"

"Don't worry, it's still parked at La Promesa. I'll hitch a ride on the first and fastest damn thing out of here—private, military, commercial." Sam debated, then added: "You hang in there, Dukie, you hear? We're going to get your little girl back."

When D.W. choked on his answer, Sam said good-bye fast and

hung up. The ranch house was coming into view ahead, and he had a lot to do.

The fastest nearby transport turned out to be a Cessna Citation V business jet belonging to a Fort Worth law firm that handled a lot of Proteus litigation. Sam arranged to be picked up in Amarillo that afternoon and was in the air by four with the plush cabin all to himself. Given the CV's long-range cruising speed of 350 knots, Sam figured to be on the ground in Puerto Ordaz in seven and a half hours, or about one-thirty in the morning local time.

The Citation allowed Sam to stretch out and attempt sleep, which he did immediately after telephoning Ray Arrillaga at the Inter-Continental Guayana and arranging for Bernardo to meet him at the airport in Puerto Ordaz. But before sleep could come, Sam had finally to deal with the turbulent emotions he'd kept bottled up ever since that morning phone call.

Here, with the day's hectic logistics behind him, and the westering sun burnishing the bizjet's starboard wing and cloud canyons below, there was no more escaping Jacqueline Lee. A terrible, paralyzing dread had fastened itself upon him, shadowing every heartbeat. His anguish for her safety could scarce be mentioned in the same breath as her father's, Sam knew, but he felt it all the same. And he thought, *I would have come down here whether D.W. had asked me or not. I couldn't have stayed away.*

And then he thought, *Because I love her.*

That was a lightning strike to the heart. How many days and nights had he tiptoed around that little revelation, only to have it seared into his mind, three miles in the sky, with the force of holy writ?

When it was too late.

No, not too late, pray God! This time Sam was flying south with a mission he wouldn't fuck up, as he had Cerro Calvario. And that was only because he'd changed his mind on the ground. But this he could pull off, if anyone could.

Let DISIP hew to its official intransigence regarding hostage takers. Sam understood and accepted all the political and PR justifications for that hard-line policy. But what he intended to get—either at the ministerial level or even from the resident of the Miraflores Palace if he had to—was permission to *pretend* to play the kidnapper's game. Crazy old Oscar had to be contacted or lured out of his hidey-hole, had to be convinced there really was big money there for him—but there only if Jacqueline's safety was absolutely assured. And that Sam could, and would, accomplish.

And in one moment of pure cinematic fantasy, he went considerably farther. He saw himself participating in the actual rescue, charging into some jungle clearing alongside that red-bereted colonel and his men, and being the one to pick the palm-thatched hut containing the raven-haired princess, and of course the one to scoop her into his arms and deliver her from her living nightmare.

Not very probable, Samuel, he thought, tightening his jaw into something like a smile. And, as D.W. had said, it would be a whole helluva lot better if those hostage-rescue boys could stay safely on the sidelines, checking out their deadly weapons. But one way or another, Jake was going to be free, and Sam was going to do his damnedest to bring it about. And for what it was worth, he wasn't doing it for D.W., or even Jacqueline now, but for himself. Of such tarnished motives, apparently, were older heroes compounded.

There was a certain detached comfort in these gallant resolves, Sam realized. As long as he indulged them and envisioned variously desirable outcomes for this droning journey, he could keep at bay those other images, those nightmarish companions of his fears that he'd fled all day long. But finally, as a dark tide swept the Caribbean and still sleep would not come, those terrible imaginings had to be faced. For they, too, were intimate links with *her.*

Where is she now? he wondered, staring past his Plexiglas reflection at a blue-black sky. *What is she feeling, what is happening to her at this very instant?*

41

Jacqueline Lee tried to assemble her shattered senses. For a long time now, sound had been reduced to a lone vibrato growl. It was the exact noise signature of an apple-green riding mower in Grandpa and Grandma Langlois's huge backyard in the Berkshires, where she'd spent her grade-school summers. Grandpa Jack liked to cut his own grass and sit her in his lap while they went back and forth in the sun and then under the shade of the big maples and around and around the trunks, with a Red Sox game buzzing all the while.

But those were warm memories, and she was shivering now, as a chill wind and hard handfuls of water stung her face. Beyond her eyelids, which she dared not open, the world was dark, wet, and cold. Underneath these perceptions was a layer of constant, shifting pain. Turn or scrunch how she might, an unyielding surface abraded her shoulders and hipbones, and there were all these odd-shaped places on her hands and feet and legs that wouldn't stop throbbing.

Nor would fear let her go. It was a spreading wake teeming with monstrous events and grotesque images. Some were only imagined, others were real, and you couldn't be sure which was which. That was because of the drug they gave you—the black powder they blew up your nose, even when you fought and shut your nostrils. They pinned your arms and poked your face with a bamboo tube, just like a giant coke tooter. Jacqueline had had one cocaine experience as an undergrad at Berkeley—two hits of pure China white that launched her heartbeat on a terrifying gallop, like a spooked horse she couldn't ride or rein. She'd never tried it again. But as scary as that had been, the black dust was far worse. Her head began to expand and grow hotter and hotter, till her skull felt ready to burst. She remembered screaming, seeing fire shoot out of her mouth and liquid pour from every other orifice. Then the earth dissolved beneath her feet and she was sucked down a bottomless black hole like Alice, with hands grabbing at her but unable to stop or slow her down. . . .

And now she was here, wherever this was, lying in the dark close to the endless lawn-mower sound. But where had she been all those jumbled hours before? She remembered only popping in and out of different nightmares, like wandering through a giant cineplex with a dozen screens and never finding the movie that was her own life. . . .

In one dark theater she sat on Grandpa Jack's lap, but when she looked up into his face, he turned into a huge Indian staring down at her—the same Indian who'd been tracking her for days and who held her arms while the little Indian blew the black dust up her nose. And she remembered being completely naked, fighting arms like tree trunks—then seeing sparkling glass everywhere and realizing that the big Indian was really protecting her. . . .

Later she'd awakened on her back, still naked, in a forest in steaming sun with ants crawling over her and the big Indian crouching over her. He was doing something to her—smearing her legs with sticky brown paste. Her palms were also covered with this strange goo and smelled like river mud and resin and crushed leaves. The little Indian was nearby, watching this curious ritual. And she thought, *The big one's rubbing the sticky stuff where the pain was.* Then she remembered the ship and the fire and screamed for her father, but a huge muddy hand was clapped over her mouth and she vanished. . . .

Or did they blow her away with more black smoke? And among all the partly recalled horrors, had she occluded rape? Yet she had this strange sense of *intactness*, and that the big Indian was protecting her from that, too. But from whom? The little Indian? Or were they simply saving her for later? She had read somewhere of remote Amazonian tribes, after many defective births, raiding neighboring tribes—and even missions and towns and trading posts—for new wives. Maybe she was being carried off into the jungle to replenish badly inbred genetic stock. She shivered with fresh horror, visualizing a life of Stone Age servitude—hunkering on the ground, cooking monkeys, eating grubs, obeying men with clubs . . .

Another spray of water hit her face and opened her eyes, shattering the long, drug-induced reverie. She was on a lake on a starry, moonless night, her aching tailbone pressed into the waterlogged bottom of a narrow wooden boat. Thank God, she was wearing something, a baggy jumpsuit of some kind. The lawn-mower sound was an outboard motor puttering behind her as the water rushed swiftly past them. In front of her were the dark shapes of two men and the tapering prow of a dugout canoe, the kind burned and hollowed out of a single log. She caught a blow-back of tobacco smoke on the wet wind. Between the men and her was a jumble of gear.

Those must be the two Indians. And they wouldn't know she was awake. There might be an advantage to that. But then who was steering? She twisted around. Against the faint smear of constellations and the dark, converging riverbanks, she saw the squat-bodied silhouette of the small Indian manning the outboard tiller. She twisted forward again. A point of light flared orange, etching a bearded face, and Jacqueline's whole scarified memory slammed back into place.

Arquimedeo's crazy uncle. Oscar, the ex-convict and terrorist. These were *his* Indians. *He* had firebombed Daddy's ship, then kidnapped her.

And she thought, *I have to escape! I have to do something!*

But what? Try to overpower them? Scream for help? Who would hear her? Jump overboard and swim? Where? She couldn't even see the shore. And what if they were on Guri Lake, really just a huge, dammed-up reservoir of the Caroní, a jungle river? The water could be infested with snakes and piranha and alligatorlike caimans.

In the pulsing cigarette glow, she caught the gleam of teeth. The bastard was smiling! "*Buenas noches*, Señorita Lee," he said. "You have a good sleep?"

"Fuck you!"

Then Jacqueline recalled an even filthier Spanish equivalent she'd learned from one of Dr. Laya's volunteers on Cerro Calvario:

"Chinga tu madre!"

Oscar had chuckled at Señorita Lee's little outburst. He had been anticipating the moment that she regained her senses, relishing the interview that would ensue. And at least to that point, he had not been disappointed.

How deliciously aristocratic the girl was, even in her attempt at cross-cultural vulgarity. But then, how else was a rich American bitch to rebuke a man immeasurably her social inferior, an ignorant *campesino* qualified only to carry her bags or hand her a towel at the country club swimming pool? Next, perhaps, she would demand her immediate return to her papa's yacht—unless, of course, she chanced to remember the unpleasant little detail that papa's yacht had been in flames when she'd fled it. But Oscar would not be at all surprised to discover that successive doses of chloroform and *yopo* administered over the last twenty-four hours had temporarily scrambled significant chunks of her memory.

Whatever she recalled of the kidnapping, and however she might choose to denounce him for it, Oscar knew the interview would end happily for him and badly for her, as she was made to realize the extent of her helplessness and of his ascendancy.

But he was wrong.

Their conversation was brief and ended badly for both of them. Only a few minutes afterward, in fact, it would have been difficult to say which of them was the more miserable. Both were then soaked to their skins and shivering. For his part, Oscar could not even light a cigarette. He'd just unbuttoned his shirt pocket to find his last pack a soggy ruin, while she suffered the further indignity of a noose around her slim neck, the other end of the rope tied to the thwart on which she sat.

Oscar was still stunned by what had happened.

After cursing him out, Señorita Lee had continued imperiously, demanding to be set free, then to know exactly where she was being taken—and by what right! One arrogant demand followed another. Oscar had laughed his most contemptuous laugh.

But Angel, who was seated in the prow to watch for snags and

288

rocks and other nasty obstacles, had also heard her and was instantly solicitous. Naturally. The big Kamarakota had appointed himself her primitive champion from the first, protecting her in the truck from broken glass, then slathering her burns at the lakeside with some native slime he'd made from leaves, bark, sap, and gobs of wet clay. Worst of all, Angel had then stripped off his coveralls to clothe the unconscious girl—surely a crime in itself, not only diminishing her vulnerability, but depriving them all of an endlessly stimulating vision. And now he wanted to pass her a bottle of Chinotto soda and the remains of his salty white cheese! Oscar told the lovesick simpleton to shut up and keep his lookout.

The girl was not as easy to silence. When screamed at, she screamed right back. Ultimately, Oscar had threatened to drug her again, and that had worked. Or so he thought.

Then he heard a hollow clunk behind and felt the canoe tip slightly. Oscar turned. Her silhouette was suddenly tall and black against the night. Was she going to strike him? *Mierda!* Had she found their machete? Oscar raised his hands to ward off the deadly blow. Instead, the dugout rocked violently, followed by a girl-sized splash.

She'd jumped overboard!

In the middle of Guri Lake, in pitch black! Questions exploded in Oscar's brain: Was it suicide? Madness? The *yopo* kicking in? Or was she willing to die trying to escape?

Whatever her impulse, Oscar's was only an instant delayed. He launched himself over the side after her. If the bitch heiress was lost, so was everything else! She represented his last hope of riches and revenge against a lifetime of failure. He thrashed blindly, gulping air and water. And when miraculously he bumped against her in the cold current, he grabbed with both arms to prevent her getting away. The ensuing struggle nearly drowned them both.

Only the swift work of the Kamarakotas prevented it, in fact. Chucho slammed the outboard into reverse idle, letting the canoe glide backward with the current and steering toward the churning commotion. As they drew abreast, Angel slipped his huge bulk over the side, keeping a hand on the gunnel while the other clawed for bodies.

Oscar's scraggly jaw was the first thing he felt—and shoved

aside. An instant after, the Indian's splayed fingers raked through tendrils of hair underwater. He made a fist and yanked hard. There was a throttled scream as the long hair jerked tight. Angel yanked again and felt her coming to him. In an instant he had an arm and used it to reel in the rest of her. Then she burst upward and against him, gasping for breath. For a split second, the Indian stared close up into terrified eyes under streaming hair. Then he submerged, using both hands and all his strength to boost her bodily out of the water and into Chucho's waiting arms.

Angel was less gentle with Oscar, hauling him in, then rolling him headfirst over the side. Finally, taking care not to overbalance the narrow wooden craft, Angel dragged himself inboard straight over the prow.

Now, in the shivering aftermath, Oscar fought to regain some measure of mastery over the entire out-of-control operation. And it didn't help that he could hear her behind him, chomping the cheese and slurping the soda Angel had insisted on providing her.

At least Chucho wasn't in sullen rebellion or smitten with their capitalist captive. Then again, the elfin Indian was less quick to obey orders than he had been. For instance, when Señorita Lee was beginning to emerge from her chloroform haze, and Oscar had suggested she be put back under with *yopo*, Chucho had dared to refuse. Apparently the hallucinogenic powder wasn't an approved ritual for females. Only after the most laborious persuasion had he gone along with the program. And Oscar thought he had detected a similar hesitancy on Chucho's part just now in tethering Señorita Lee's neck to the thwart— an obvious precaution against further suicidal plunges.

Despite these rankling shortcomings, Oscar had to admit that so far the brothers had performed better than he had any right to expect. On Cerro Calvario they'd shown themselves first-rate saboteurs. And on the San Félix docks, Chucho had not only carried out an assignment Oscar secretly considered to be kamikaze—planting the bomb on the ore ship—but actually escaped undetected. Then, just a few hours ago as darkness descended on Guri Lake, the Kamarakotas had ventured out to steal a boat and come back with an authentic curiara—an Indian dugout canoe—with a thirty-horsepower tiller-steer outboard on its transom and enough fuel drums stowed forward to take them hundreds of kilometers upstream on the Caroní. True, Oscar might have wished for something more comfortable; but according to Chucho, the curiara was ideally shaped for the Sabana's lesser tributaries.

Considering all these accomplishments, it was ironic to think that Oscar had hired them under false pretenses. For almost certainly, they'd fabricated their criminal past that night in the San Félix *cantina*—or at least embroidered it. Oh, undoubtedly they'd done time for brawling or public drunkenness or something trivial. And their account of teenage escapades that turned them into tribal renegades seemed authentic. But their responses to some of Oscar's queries in the last few days had convinced him that neither had worked for any Colombian cartel—not even as lowly mules. And when Angel had plunged into daylong grief after accidentally killing the CANTV man, it was clear he'd never been an enforcer for the Ochoa brothers or anyone else. Oscar figured they must have been desperate for any kind of work and simply repeated jailhouse stories to impress him.

Which made them, in a way, exactly like himself—outcasts. Oscar, too, had been banished from his past, had failed to acculturate into the present—and had no discernible future. Having outlived his fanatic youth, he'd become more or less a middle-aged brigand, bereft of revolutionary justification. Even in prison, with all his impressive credentials, the young *pistoleros* there had treated him with open contempt, or at best, the sort of supercilious tolerance he had regularly endured from his smart-assed little nephew. So perhaps, after all, Oscar and the Kamarakota brothers were a well-matched team.

Unfortunately that had all changed with the addition of their willful hostage. From the moment she'd arrived—like an exiled princess in the back of the phone truck, cradled in Angel's arms—the dynamics among the three of them had been thrown way the hell off. It was made instantly clear, for instance, that Oscar was to be denied intimate access to his lovely captive— and thus denied a reward that was properly any kidnapper's, and certainly one of the more anticipated facets of the whole scheme.

He had not, after all, scouted and pursued this privileged creature simply for her ransom value, though he might have done so, had she been plain. No, he had coveted Señorita Lee from that first afternoon glimpse through binoculars on Cerro Calvario, watching—with the seasoned avidity of the connoisseur —her bouncing, denim-stretching bottom as she rode out beside Sam Warrender. But here, when the girl was wholly delivered to him, he dared hardly glance at her with strong intent. And only by killing both Angel and Chucho—now his indispensable bush guides—would he be able to lay a single hand on her!

To make matters worse, she was obviously aware of all this. Right now, as he sat shivering, listening to the outboard snarl and the wooden boat's whispery cleavage through the enveloping void of lake and sky, he could feel the hostility radiating from her back there. And there was nothing to prevent her from mocking him, so long as she was under Angel's watchful protectorate.

Indeed, Oscar had a sudden and irrevocable sense that from here on, everything would go wrong, and that there wasn't one damn thing he could do to alter it. And now, because of his unscheduled midnight swim, he couldn't even enjoy a good smoke!

To hell with her ransom value. He should have let the bitch drown!

42

"To understand why Caracas is taking such a hard-ass line," Sam was saying to D.W., "you just have to look at 1976, when an American executive got himself kidnapped down here by some terrorist faction. One of the demands was for the company—it was Owens-Illinois—to publish an indictment of itself and of the Venezuelan government in the foreign press. President Pérez—that was his first term—had already refused to negotiate. But the company caved in and ran the rhetoric anyway. Pérez responded by expropriating all its Venezuelan property."

"I'd make that deal in a second to get Jacqueline free!" D.W. shot back. "I'd repeat any damn garbage they want. Let Caracas take our assets, let the Proteus board fire me later."

"Hey, you'll get no argument from me. I'm just trying to show you how they look at it—and how most governments look at it. And they're in total charge on this. So any dealing we do with this bastard Azarias, assuming it's him, it's got to be strictly between him and us, not through the media. And you have to understand that Captain Siso and that red-beret colonel are going to be breathing down our neck all the way."

It was early afternoon of the second day after the kidnapping, with no word from Jacqueline or her captors. And except for the abandoned truck, there were still no leads to their whereabouts.

In consequence, the search radius had not diminished. And D.W. was having an increasingly hard time holding together, Sam thought, and just getting through each minute of each agonizing hour. Sam, who had managed precious little sleep himself in the Citation jet coming down, and none at all during the morning briefings, figured he probably didn't look much better.

They were one floor below D.W.'s penthouse in the Inter-Continental Guayana, in Sam's smaller, wrong-side suite with a treetop and roof-tile view of Puerto Ordaz and the Río Caroní. Owen Meade was out arranging with Proteus's local bank for a hefty withdrawal of U.S. dollars and *bolívars*, in anticipation of a ransom demand. After considerable arm-twisting on Sam's part, Captain Marco-Aurelio Siso of the Seguridad Policial had finally agreed to this, but with several provisos.

First, if a ransom demand was privately received and seemed authentic, and the media were kept out of the loop, D.W. could pretend to go along, no matter how outrageous the demands—financially, politically, or whatever. But once he'd gotten instructions for ransom delivery and received proof of his daughter's current safety, the federal cops would take over—the DISIP agents lying in wait to entrap the kidnapper, and the Special Intervention Brigade ready to rescue Jacqueline.

Siso had also suggested they might electronically "tag" the money, by concealing miniaturized transmitters in the packets. His agents could then home in on the signal and apprehend the fleeing kidnapper. Sam and D.W. strongly objected to the idea of double-crossing a wily old bastard such as Oscar, a man who might have dealt with large currency payoffs and similar dirty tricks during his years in the cocaine trade with Carlos Lehder. But they decided to let the matter pass. The immediate priority was to get the cash in hand.

Meanwhile, news of the presumed terrorist kidnapping and photos of the American industrialist's exotic daughter were all over the newspapers and TV. As a result, police and Guardia stations throughout Venezuela were receiving calls from people either claiming to be the Bandera Roja kidnappers or to have seen them or the missing heiress. Investigators were busy running down all these blind alleys, thus far verifying none of the sightings, but managing to phone-trace and detain several unbalanced individuals. Captain Siso and his boss, a Colonel

Acosta, had not judged any of the claimants worth being put in negotiating contact with Señor Lee. Should that occur, however, technicians from DISIP and CANTV were also in place in the penthouse to monitor and trace the calls.

Augmenting the police search, since dawn Venezuelan air force planes and helicopters had been flying low-level patrols over the vastness of Guri Lake, tracing its ragged margins and following out the many roads and rivers radiating from it. U.S. satellite reconnaissance photos of the area had also been officially requested. Jacqueline Lee's presence in that abandoned CANTV truck had now been confirmed, as forensic scientists had matched hairs recovered from its interior with others found on an armchair in the guest room she'd occupied at La Promesa ranch.

Against this background of hectic and so far fruitless activity, there seemed little for Sam or D.W. to do. Or so both men had reluctantly concluded after a brief conference in Sam's suite. Wearily now, D.W. turned to go back upstairs to the penthouse command post. But at the door he hesitated.

"Sam, there's something else I came down here to say."

"I figured there was."

"I screwed you, Sam. We both know it, but I have to say it."

"Why doesn't that sound exactly like an apology, Duke?"

"I didn't say I was sorry. You jerked me around a lot of years, Sam, after promising me your job. So when I saw my chance with the board to get even, I did it."

"Well, I guess that sets the record about straight. Looks like we've been a couple of poisonous old Gila monsters, circling in the noon sun, snapping and hissing. And you're right, Duke. I did jerk you around a couple years longer there than I should have. Hell, I'll go farther than that. Booting me out was maybe the only damn way you were ever gonna get rid of me. Make you feel any better for what you did?"

D.W. grunted. "I admit I was wrong."

"How's that again?"

"Sam, everything I did was wrong, from the moment I sailed up the Orinoco. And now I'm paying for it, and so is Jacqueline."

"Don't do that, D.W. Maybe you screwed up some as an executive, but not as a dad. She's a hell of a girl, and a lot of what makes her great is directly a result of you. Your strength, your determination, your—" Sam broke off, seeing a tremoring around D.W.'s mouth. But he couldn't leave it there. "That strength is gonna get her through this, D.W. And believe me, we're gonna get her back."

D.W. nodded meekly, but looked completely lost.

Sam went on, changing the subject, "You know, Duke, there's someone else you shafted pretty good down here, besides me."

"Dr. Laya?"

"That's right. But what I want to know is, did you help that muscle-bound assistant of his cook up that story about Dr. Laya falsifying the location of his findings?"

"No. Rosales came to me with it. Naturally Ray and I wanted to believe it. And for a while we did. But later it was clear the man was just a, you know, a . . ."

"A hustler?"

"Exactly. A two-bit hustler." D.W. managed a weak smile. "Not ready for the prime time—like you and me, partner."

"So what about Dr. Laya? Does he rate an apology from you?"

D.W. shrugged. "I thought about it. But when I saw him, I couldn't do it. How can I forgive him for letting that madman get anywhere near Jacqueline? He exposed her!"

"Wait a minute, D.W. When did you see Dr. Laya? I thought he was still in police custody."

"I don't know his legal status. But he was upstairs a few minutes ago. They brought him in to work with a police artist, drawing a sketch of the two Indians that Oscar had with him on Cerro Calvario. They've got prison photographs of the old man, but nothing on the Indians."

Sam was intrigued. "Think he's still up there?"

"Perhaps. Captain Siso was waiting to talk to him."

"I'm going back up with you. I'd like a word with the professor."

Arquimedeo kept apologizing to the police artist that he'd not really paid much attention to his uncle's native sidekicks. Despite this, the composite image built gradually on the computer screen, until two quite distinct faces had emerged in laser printout for duplication and distribution. Both men were wide mouthed and blunt nosed under basin-cropped bangs. But one was boyishly delicate, with large eyes, elfin ears, and a pointed chin; while the other was coarser of feature, with jutting brow and jaw, flaring nostrils, and a snarling curve to his lips.

Finally, having declared himself satisfied and insisting he had nothing further to offer Captain Siso, the archaeologist turned to leave—and ran into Sam Warrender. They shook hands.

"They're letting you go?" Sam said.

"Yes, I'm apparently off the prime-suspect list. I think the captain is beginning to realize that nothing would give me greater satisfaction than finding Uncle Oscar myself and putting a bullet into his vicious little brain."

"You definitely think it's him?"

"He's much worse than I ever realized, Sam. They told me about crimes he committed in Mexico City in the late seventies, and for Carlos Lehder in the Caribbean in the early eighties. Bank robberies where guards were shot, execution-style killings on Lehder's island. I swear I never knew this. I knew my uncle was bad; I just never knew he was evil. Still, that's no excuse for what I did. Even given the little I did know, I should never have let him anywhere around the dig—or Jacqueline. That was criminal."

"There seems to be a lot of guilt going around just now, Professor. I guess you're welcome to your share of it. I take it you have no idea where your uncle would hole up?"

"In the bush somewhere, I imagine. That's what I told Captain Siso."

"But he's got to come out, doesn't he? I mean, if he wants to profit from this?"

"I would think so. Oscar is quite shrewd. He's a lifelong criminal failure on an incredible success streak—industrial sabotage, terrorist bombings, a headline kidnapping. But of one thing I'm certain. He's not in any sense an idealist. He wants money out of this—a lot of it, I imagine. I just pray he's smart enough to know that if he harms Jacqueline in any way, he hasn't a chance in hell of collecting a *bolívar*."

"Amen to that."

Arquimedeo gave a deprecatory shrug. "Now I've got to drive down to Cerro Calvario. They're allowing me access to make a list of all the equipment my erstwhile associate made off with, and to estimate how much seismic damage those explosions did to the excavation and site substructures. By the way, Sam, I thanked Enrico for his hospitality at La Promesa, but I never had the opportunity to thank you personally. It meant a great deal and obviously came at a time when I needed allies."

"You've still got one in me, Professor. I'm gonna make you a promise. When this insanity is over, we're gonna get those bull-dozers the hell off that iron mountain and get you back to work."

"We? You mean you and Señor Lee? After what he did, I'm surprised you two are on speaking terms. He and I certainly aren't, as you can imagine."

"Well, we all share an awfully overriding goal here—don't we?—getting Jacqueline back safe, as quick as we can. Believe me, when that happens—and it will, dammit—D.W. will go along with whatever she wants."

"Whether or not I ever get back my excavation, I certainly hope your promise comes true, Sam."

But, in the archaeologist's departing glance, Sam did not see any such hope reflected.

43

Afterward, Sam went down to his suite, slid the blinds across his wrong-way view, and embarked on much-needed sleep.

At some point thereafter, he found himself windmilling his arms and convulsing his legs in a frantic race across Canaima Lagoon. Unfortunately he was losing, and one sideways glance showed him why. His opponent was a fifteen-foot caiman, the South American alligator. It was cruising along, its broad, black snout arrowing the surface.

Suddenly Sam grasped the full horror of the situation. The point was not just to see which was the faster swimmer, man or beast, but which would reach the girl treading water and crying for help out there. And that girl, Sam realized, was Jacqueline. As usual, she'd wandered off without informing anybody.

In desperation, Sam lunged sideways and managed to grasp the beast's tail, then hung on blindly as it thrashed the water, lacerating him with bony-scaled armor and gnashing at him with fang-filled jaws. But at some point in their struggle, Sam's adversary metamorphosed into Félix Rosales, not as muscular and vicious as the caiman, but just as threatening to Jacqueline. Sam fought on . . .

A persistent knocking suspended the battle, leaving the outcome undetermined.

Sam swam upward, rolled off the mattress, and shuffled toward the door without having reached consciousness. He felt like somebody yanked out of open-heart surgery. He threw back the bolt, realized he was stark naked, left the chain attached, and peeked around the crack. Bernardo was out there, sucking in a just-burst bubble-gum bubble.

"Señor Sam, can I talk to you a minute?"

"I'm taking a nap, Nardo. Can't it wait?"

"Hey, I'm real sorry about Jake."

Not counting her father, Sam thought, that made at least three guys she'd given permission to use her pet name—Félix, himself, now Bernardo.

"We all are, Bernardo. Was there something else you wanted to tell me?"

"Yeah, I got a couple more things."

"Okay, come on in." Sam unhooked the chain, turned, and staggered back to bed. Bernardo, meanwhile, dropped into a chair and balanced his unlaced high-tops on the marble coffee table.

"Here's the deal, Señor Sam. I want to come work for you."

"Nardo, if you're going to speak American, skip the *señor,* okay?"

"You got it, Sam."

"Okay. Now what does Owen say about this? He didn't fire you?"

"No. The thing is, Sam, some days he uses me, some days no. Now he wants me to call him every morning. And he doesn't want me to take the Cruiser home."

"That bad, huh? So what makes you think I have any work for you? As soon as we get Jacqueline back safe, I'm flying out of here."

"I mean at your ranch. Enrico said I did a good job down there for him."

"Let me get this straight. You want to be a *llanero?* Can you ride?"

"Can José Canseco hit dingers? You bet. Enrico and one of his *caballeros* taught me good. Plus I can do all kinds of other stuff."

"Like watch the satellite TV?"

Bernardo looked suddenly hurt, even stopped chewing his gum.

"Sorry, Nardo, forget that. I get cranky when I miss too much

300

sleep. From what I hear, you're a heck of a worker. The thing is, Enrico's in charge down there, not me. Why don't you give him a call, see what he says? If Owen can't give you the hours, I say go where you can get 'em."

"Can I use the phone here?"

Sam heaved a sigh. "Yeah, sure. Will that do it for you, Nardo?"

"I got something else."

"Shoot."

"I was talking to Señor Owen upstairs, and I saw those pictures."

"What pictures?"

"Those Indian dudes who hung out with Dr. Laya's uncle—on Cerro Calvario."

"Shit, I forgot! You were down there, too!"

"You sent me, remember? To be her chaperon." Bernardo pronounced it with a hard *ch*.

"And you recognized the sketches? They're pretty accurate?"

"They're okay. But why don't they just use the video?"

"What video?"

"Jake's video, man. She shot everybody on Cerro Calvario—me, Dr. Laya, all the diggers, those brothers. She liked their faces."

"Nardo, did you tell them about this upstairs?"

"No. I just thought of it on my way down to see you."

Sam rubbed his sandpapery jaw. "So, where's the stuff she shot? Shit, I bet it all burned on the *Kallisto*."

"No way, man! She left all her tapes with Enrico."

"Why would she do that?"

"So Señor Lee wouldn't get 'em. She was going to phone Enrico later and tell him where to send 'em. I was there!"

Sam reached for the bedside phone. "I'm calling Enrico now. And Nardo. You just got yourself a goddamn job."

Ten minutes later, sleep once more banished, Sam was riding south on Route 19 with Bernardo behind the wheel of a Proteus Land Cruiser. Sam had decided to check out Jake's video cassettes personally before notifying Captain Siso. Other than Enrico, they'd told no one of their departure, not even D.W.

They covered the ninety-some miles in an hour and twenty minutes, while silver and gray thunderheads reared high in the

301

western sky. They were rolling into La Promesa's graveled courtyard as the first raindrops fell, and hurried inside.

Enrico had the stack of eight-millimeter cassettes waiting in
the den, beside Jacqueline's Handycam in its small Halliburton
case. The bad news, Enrico said, was that the tapes didn't fit his
VHS videocassette recorder. Sam cursed silently. Why hadn't he
thought to check that before driving down? Whom could he call
for help? Or should he just hand the damn tapes over to the
police?

Then Bernardo came to the rescue. "No problem, Sam. You
don't need the VCR, just the camera and TV. Jake showed me
how to do it."

The spiky-haired youth was already on his knees, pulling ca-
bles out of the Handycam case. He explained what he was doing
as he went along, but Sam understood little of it.

"You plug this end into the camera's S-Video output plug. The
other goes into the S-Video input—here, on the back of the set.
There's another way to do it, but S-Video gives better resolution.
Now this one's for stereo sound. Two plugs, red and white, output here, input back here. See, now you don't need the VCR.
The Handycam has all the buttons—fast-forward, rewind, play,
pause-still, everything. Okay, where's the remote? You got to
switch the TV to 'external input' first."

Bernardo turned on the TV and popped a cassette into the Sony
camcorder. The screen hissed with high-contrast fuzz, then resolved into the postcard panorama of Hacha Falls across Canaima
Lagoon. An instant later a bare-chested Félix Rosales popped
into the frame, mugging for the camera and bulging his biceps.
What a preening asshole! Sam thought. Then suddenly he recalled his interrupted nightmare—Jacqueline far out in the
water, Sam racing and wrestling the caiman, who became Félix.
If Bernardo hadn't awakened him, who would have won?

"Wrong cassette," Sam told Bernardo. "She must have some
kind of dates or numbering system."

Sam took a look at the cassette boxes. There were a dozen,
each two and a half hours. The labeling was on the spine, in her
neat printing. Some kind of alphanumeric code. Date and location? At least a half dozen included the letters *CC*. Cerro
Calvario?

Sam picked one at random. He had Bernardo fast-forward all

302

the way through it, a queasy-making visual ordeal—and one that made him feel slightly voyeuristic. This was, after all, raw footage, for her eyes only. Sorry, Jake. There was a lot of speeded-up, Chaplinesque movement. Close-ups of red earth. Talking heads. Conan the Archaeologist digging a trench, muscles rippling. Scurrying people spreading a tarp over a trench. The camera peeking out through a tent flap at a downpour. Félix again. The jerk was obviously following her around. Then Sam was seeing the fossil flute in its plastic pouch, held up to lamplight by a beaming Arquimedeo. Sam experienced a shiver of excitement. Then the flute and his feelings vanished, and two sweaty, scraggly-looking girls were struggling like Sisyphus to lug heavy electronic surveying gear up a slope.

Enrico brought beers, and the evening rain spattered the windows. They were into the third cassette when Sam recognized Oscar Azarias, walking away in filthy pants, obviously not eager to be filmed. Sam was about to tell Bernardo to back up when suddenly there were the two Indians. Bernardo had seen them, too, and quickly switched from fast forward to playback mode.

The brothers stood side by side now, smiling stiffly. The height differential was comical. The little one wore a *liki-liki* shirt and Day-Glo shorts, the big one camouflage pants and a faded T-shirt featuring Las Tortugas Ninjas—the Ninja Turtles. The camera came in close as they chattered back and forth in some Indian dialect. A moment later they began to box playfully. The frame pulled back to capture the big one taking an obvious dive, as the little guy threw a wild roundhouse right. Sam told Bernardo to reverse to the full-face shots, then hit PAUSE/STILL. When the brothers were frozen on-screen in midgrin, Sam turned to Enrico.

"Do you still have that Polaroid camera around here, *amigo?*"

Enrico nodded and hurried out of the den.

Five minutes later they had several pretty good Polaroid likenesses. They got the best screen resolution shooting in PLAY, not PAUSE/STILL.

Enrico thought of something else. "You know, Sam, I recognized some of those words when they were talking. It's definitely Pemón." This was the common language of the indigenous tribes of the Sabana—Arekunas, Kamarakotas, Taurepanes.

"How do you know?"

"From Roberto I bet," Bernardo said. "He's half-Indian."

"Who's Roberto?" Sam asked.

"One of my *llaneros*," Enrico said. "He and I taught Bernardo to ride."

"Well, why don't you get him in here?"

Roberto was ushered into the den a few minutes later, hat in hand and looking distinctly uncomfortable. He was still in his *llanero* outfit—unbuttoned work shirt, cowhide half-chaps over threadbare jeans, bare feet. He was also dripping wet; the rainstorm was still having its way outside. Enrico gestured to a space on the sofa, but Roberto smiled and squatted cross-ankled on the carpet in front of the TV monitor. Bernardo replayed the entire scene with the two brothers talking and clowning.

"Well?" Enrico prompted when it was over.

Roberto looked eager to oblige. "*Jefe,* what do you want to know?"

"Do you recognize them?"

"No. I never see these guys before. They're Kamarakotas."

"From the Kamarata Valley?" Sam asked.

"*Sí,* I think from the mission."

Jesus! Sam thought. *We could be very close to something here.* What if they were taking Jacqueline back to their valley, to some hideout nearby? He should notify Captain Siso immediately. But then what? Sam could visualize big choppers landing in the midst of the Indian village, rotor blasts stripping the palm thatch off the huts, red-beret paratroopers swarming out with submachine guns. If Oscar and the Indians were anywhere in the vicinity, they'd be scared off—and harder to find than ever. Which would put Jacqueline at greater risk. And with the Seguridad Policial and the Special Intervention Brigade down here running the show, any chance for a clean ransom payoff would be gone forever.

And what if it was just a blind alley? Just because the Indians were Kamarakotas didn't mean they'd be heading home. The plain fact was, they could be taking her anywhere or still be holed up in San Félix.

The prudent thing to do was check it out himself early tomorrow morning. Show the Polaroids around the mission, find out whatever he could about the brothers. Then decide.

While working through these musings, Sam stood quickly to

304

thank Roberto for his help. Then, as Enrico exited the room with his *llanero*, Sam swung to Bernardo. "Still want to work for me?"

"Yeah."

"How about driving back to Puerto Ordaz in the rain?"

"No sweat. What for?"

"I left without telling D.W. anything, and I promised I'd keep him informed."

"Why don't you just call his penthouse?"

"Hey, why didn't I think of that, Nardo? Look, D.W. is surrounded up there. They're tracing calls, probably recording everything in and out. It's probably nothing, this Kamarakota stuff, but I don't want the *federales* barging down here just yet. Okay?"

"I got it. You want me to take some of the Polaroids?"

"No, don't take anything. Just be cool, you know? Walk up to him and make small talk, till you can get him alone. Then tell him we saw the Indians on the tape, where they're from, and that I'll be flying down to the Kamarata Valley tomorrow to check it out. Tell him I should be back by noon, and I'll call him. Got all that?"

After Bernardo drove off, Sam apologetically declined Romalda's offer of dinner in favor of a hot shower and bed. He cut it pretty close—he had just enough energy left to peel back the sheets and crawl in. He succumbed to sleep without struggle or thought.

It seemed another century—not nearly long enough—when he felt himself being shaken awake. Gray light filled an unfamiliar room, and D.W. was staring down at him. Sam couldn't put the pieces together.

"Where am I?"

"At your ranch. La Promesa."

"What—what are you doing here?"

"Bernardo drove me down."

"Wait a minute. This isn't making sense."

"You're flying down to Kamarata this morning to look for those Indians. I'm coming with you."

"No, you're not." Sam managed to scoot halfway up against the headboard. "Jesus, Duke, you're supposed to stay by the phone, in case Oscar calls. Does what's his name, Siso, know you're down here?"

"No. I just walked out of the hotel two hours ago. I called

305

from a gas station, told one of his deputies I'd stay in touch. I don't trust those bastards, Sam. If Oscar did call, I don't think they'd tell me."

"D.W., you know they're gonna go apeshit up there."

"*I'm* going apeshit. I have to do something, Sam. Please!"

Sam swung his feet onto the floor, found himself staring at a blue Avensa zippered carryon. "What's in the bag, D.W.?"

"A million dollars."

44

A flash of lightning reversed the world into photo negative—white sky and river against gray-etched, black-slashed jungle. An after-flash strobed three shapes huddled under a tarp along the riverbank, watching rain lash the raging current and pound the upturned bottom of their thirty-foot dugout canoe, which now sheltered their supplies and outboard motor. An instant later came the eruption of double thunder—not a mere crackling boom, but a doomsday sound like the sky's entire fabric being ripped apart, horizon to horizon.

Oscar Azarias, one of the three huddled figures, had witnessed countless tropical thunderstorms over his fifty-plus years. But somehow being pinned down out here on the edge of the Sabana, lacking even a cave in which to hide from the elemental fury, made this storm particularly disturbing. These nuclear white flashes and rending crashes, and the unceasing roar of falling water, nearly overwhelmed all his other anxieties with undiluted fear.

Yet he dared not neglect his other urgent concerns. This river, for instance—the Kukurital, just east of its joining the Caroní —was it rising too rapidly? Should they be dragging themselves and their boat even now to higher ground? But if so, then surely Angel, who knew these parts intimately, would be initiating the panic, not squatting stoically beside Oscar, chin on knees.

Another prime concern, of course, was poor Chucho, out in
this wild night on yet another critical mission. Fortunately, the
smaller Kamarakota had vetoed Oscar's plan to have the ransom
demand delivered overland all the way to Canaima on the Río
Carrao. Fortunately, since Oscar's plan would have entailed several hours' night hiking across the intervening savanna. And after
an evening of light rain and nearly a half hour's unremitting
downpour, that savanna trail had probably become impassable
swamp. Wisely instead, Chucho had elected to carry Oscar's
carefully printed ultimatum only a short distance from where
they'd beached their dugout, to Puerto Kukurital. This riverside
outpost of palm-thatched shelters was linked northward to Canaima Camp by a rough track, only an hour-and-a-half drive by
Jeep or Land Cruiser. Chucho had assured Oscar that a ransom
note posted there tonight would be discovered early in the morning by Indian employees of Canaima Camp and communicated
quickly to camp headquarters—and thereafter to the Guardia
Nacional and the girl's father. The success or failure of the entire
scheme now hinged on Chucho's being correct in these as-
surances—and being able to deliver the note as promised. By
Oscar's watch, the Indian had been out in the storm twenty
minutes already.

And if this were not sufficient worry, there remained the third
figure huddled under the rain-bludgeoned tarpaulin. Oscar had
availed himself of the last blue-white lightning flash to check
out their hostage and had been startled by what he saw. Señorita
Lee was not cowering in girlish fear. On the contrary, her profile
was the equal of Angel's in stolid endurance. And other resem-
blances between her and the Indians struck Oscar in that blinding instant. There was a subtle similarity in facial contouring—
an upper eyelid curve, a prominence of cheekbone, a slight frontal flatness—and of course in straight black hair of glossy thick-
ness. The ethnic link, he realized, came through the Asian half
of her heritage, since the prehistoric ancestors of the Kamarakotas, like all the native tribes of the Americas, had supposedly
migrated here from Asia via an ancient land bridge.

Like Angel, Jacqueline Lee squatted on her haunches, resting
her forearms and chin on her knees, staring into the storm. Her
neck was freed of its noose, but a short rope now hobbled her
ankles. If she was shivering under her cotton coveralls, she did

not betray it. Her bearing, in that lightning-etched tableau, was too much like that of some caged pantheress, he thought, enduring the temporary ignominy of capture, only awaiting the moment to reassert her supremacy. If Oscar could get the glossy creature alone, he could crush that arrogant spirit, he knew. But not so long as Angel sat nearby.

In any case, her humbling could wait. Far more urgent problems confronted Oscar now, with no earthly way of avoiding them. He and the Kamarakotas had committed themselves to running a deadly, one-way gauntlet, with the entire Venezuelan security forces arrayed against them, and a pot of gold waiting at the gauntlet's unseen end—if, that is, Oscar contrived to have the gold deposited there. Only by snatching that prize and fleeing the country under an altered identity, Oscar knew, would he again be free. The Indians, however, were unlikely to avail themselves of such a course, being reluctant to leave their tribal lands. And once their identities were known to the authorities, there would be no escape for them.

But so far, amazingly, all had gone well. By Chucho's estimation, since leaving Espinero on Lake Guri two evenings ago, they had covered more than two hundred kilometers on the Caroní—all under cover of darkness and against the current, averaging around fifteen to twenty kilometers per hour from the two-stroke Mariner outboard. At dawn yesterday they'd slipped past the mouth of the Río Paragua, beaching and concealing their curiara just beyond the confluence, in sight of the village of San Pedro de las Bocas.

All that long day, as planes had droned suspiciously overhead, tracing both rivers, they'd remained in their overgrown riverbank lair. There was no shortage of tinned food, and water was only a long scoop away. The Caroní, which appeared blood-red along its pink-sand shallows, when captured in a tin cup had nearly the color and clarity of champagne. During the forenoon, while Señorita Lee watched in some fascination, the Indian brothers had extracted some special tree sap, mixed it with palm oil, and painted their bodies black. It made an effective night camouflage, Oscar had to admit, especially since Chucho had used up the only tube of black camo cream. The long, torrid afternoon found all four cocooned in tree-slung hammocks under mosquito netting. But Oscar had devoted several of those oppressive hours to the careful composition of a ransom note, and—because he was prevented from using physical coercion—to begging Señorita Lee for just one little bit of authenticating information, information that would, after all, only let her father know she was safe and facilitate her deliverance. Finally, after being cursed and reviled and actually spat upon—all under the vigilant glare of the big Kamarakota—Oscar had come away with her mother's maiden name, Julienne Langlois, and pet name. So, their arrogant bitch was really an exotic mongrel, part slant-eyes, part French!

Again at first darkness, they were pushing off in a heavy drizzle, using their heart-shaped paddles periodically to bail the fast-filling bottom. Despite the gradually worsening rain, they'd made steady progress, reaching the Carrao around eleven. By midnight, as lightning began to pulse all around the sky, they'd gained another fifteen kilometers to the fork of the smaller Kukurital, where Chucho swung them sharply left. Moments later, they were dragging the dugout onto the Kukurital's shelving bank as the heavens opened and the deluge began in earnest.

But the night was still far from over, Oscar thought, and there were fifty more kilometers to make upstream before sunrise. If only Chucho would get back and report success, and if only the accursed rainstorm would ease off to something less than waterfall strength, they could get under way again.

A quick squishing sound told him somebody was now beside him in the dark.

"Chucho?"

"Who else, boss?"

This reply was punctuated by far-off lightning, which showed Chucho's grinning, dripping, sap-blackened face. *The little guy really enjoys this stuff*, Oscar thought.

"So, you did it? Left the note in a good spot?"

"Sure, boss. I can swim good, huh?"

Jacqueline Lee was terribly frightened and terribly cold, yet determined not to show either. She had decided she was going to survive this ordeal, no matter what. She'd kept telling herself that, through two shivering nights with a rope around her neck, securing her to the bench of the dugout canoe. She'd renewed her resolve again and again during the long, sweat-drenched, insect-ridden day they'd lain in hiding beside the river. And when her secret litany had become so many meaningless syllables, and she felt herself sinking into a sea of helplessness, she'd resorted to little mind games.

She'd pretend herself elsewhere. To combat cold, she conjured herself into a Palm Springs patio, complete with the scent of sunblock and random boing of diving board. Several times she'd re-created all the little tactical moves with which she'd maneuvered Sam Warrender into that first kamikaze kiss—and nearly knocked him out of his saddle! And to survive the all-day agony of being hammocked in a jungle steam bath with her ankles tied together, she'd visualized Arquimedeo in his khaki shorts and baseball cap, squatting for hours in a trench, patiently scraping away at some tiny outcrop of history. And for the last trembling half hour here beside Oscar and Angel, while the sky exploded over their heads and threatened to reduce her to a whimpering child, she had simply prayed to God to keep her safe.

And perhaps her plea had been heard, for shortly after little Chucho had returned from wherever he'd gone to leave the ransom note, the overhead fury quite suddenly ceased—even the rain stopped falling. Immediately Chucho and Angel scrambled out to turn the canoe rightside up and mount the outboard on the rough-hewn transom. A moment later, Angel loomed out of the darkness, apologetically slipping the noose around her neck and lifting her into the narrow, wobbly craft.

Jacqueline suffered this disgrace without outward protest, believing the big Kamarakota had taken this onerous task upon himself only to protect her from rougher handling. Chucho remained a smiling enigma, but she did not wish to think about the kinds of things Oscar might do to her if Angel ever once left her side. She only hoped that the Indian's obvious feelings for her could somehow tip the balance in her favor in any coming crisis, or—pray God!—when the moment came for her to escape or be rescued.

But for now, they were back in the water, strung out in their customary positions in the narrow dugout—Angel in the prow, Oscar next, Jacqueline tied to the thwart abaft the fuel drums, and Chucho silhouetted in the stern with his left arm guiding the outboard tiller. All she knew was that they were heading up some smaller tributary now into a featureless abyss, accompanied as always by that monotonous lawn-mower sound that, even when they stopped, continued to growl in her subconscious.

After they were a half hour under way, stars began to glitter here and there as the storm clouds rolled and shredded off to the east. This afforded Chucho incremental light to steer by and made it easier for him to see Angel's arm signals. About when he expected it, the immense black brow of Auyán Tepui reared up on his left, crowned with constellations. For the next forty or fifty kilometers, the Río Kukurital would scallop the western base of this great table mountain, all the way south to the Kamarata Valley, where it fanned out into the broad savanna in a maze of subtributaries and feeder streams.

At that point, Chucho had proposed to Oscar they abandon the curiara and follow on foot another small river, the Kavak, back through many twists and turns and traversing several waterfalls, into a deeply recessed canyon at the southern tip of Auyán Tepui known as La Cueva—the Cave. Here they could safely hide until it was time to recover the ransom—and go their separate ways.

If the weather and their amazing luck held, Chucho hoped to be off the little Kukurital and climbing up into Kavak Canyon before first light. But already the Kamarakota's keen eyes caught the first patch of shallow, tricky water ahead—a low-angled rapids frothing in the starlight.

Angel had seen it, too, and was shouting back. Chucho cut off the motor and dropped instantly over the side into the frigid current. His bare soles slithered over the riverbed boulders, but he never lost his footing. As infants, Kamarakotas were taught how to slide along on river rocks till the foot stopped and gripped of its own accord, then to take the next sliding step. While Angel did his grunting and pulling alongside the prow, Chucho steered and shoved the curiara's transom upward against the fierce current. Then, realizing they still had two passengers, the little Indian screamed at Oscar:

"Boss, get out and push! Five, ten minutes only, then we go again full power!"

Or perhaps, Chucho thought, with less current and a little more depth ahead, they might try running the motor at low speed, while Angel squatted in the bow with the long paddle to push them off submerged rocks. But for the moment, they clearly needed all three men grunting in the rapids, while the lovely *señorita* rode amidships like a princess. Besides, it was amusing to see old Oscar slipping and stumbling over the moss-slick boulders and screeching like a macaw every time he went under.

45

It was a first for Sam, flying so close to Auyán Tepui without venturing in for a glimpse of Angel Falls. Yet so imperative was the business at hand that this thought scarcely crossed his mind. The sheer-sided "lost world" plateau this morning was no more to him than a gigantic guidepost, allowing him to follow the Río Kukurital along the *tepui*'s western base. He need only keep his six-place Cessna chasing that quicksilver thread down there through the broccoli-topped greenery, and eventually he'd come to the Kamarata Valley. Then he'd hang a sharp left and head for the Capuchin Mission airstrip.

The three cabin passengers were equally subdued, with the twin 260-horsepower engines providing an ominous, double-bass accompaniment to their separate preoccupations. D.W., beside Sam, showed a grim-visaged profile, his mirrored lenses catching the sun-fire that, moments ago, had cleared the rim of Auyán Tepui off to their left. In the two seats behind, Enrico Tosto studied last night's box scores from Venezuela's winter baseball league; while Bernardo had his nose mashed against Plexiglas, as he saw, for the first time in his young life, his country's ancient island mesas rising out of oceanic jungles and grasslands.

Sam could guess at one added component to D.W.'s anguish. Besides agonizing over his daughter, the man must now be endlessly second-guessing himself. Should he have remained captive in his command-post penthouse, the pawn of the security guys, waiting for that phone call and relying on their hardball tactics to save Jacqueline? Was he crazy to be going off on this wild-goose flight with a man whose erratic behavior and corporate irresponsibility he'd just denounced to the Proteus board? So long as Jacqueline's fate remained unknown, Sam knew, D.W. would find no correct answers to his questions. And if the outcome proved tragic, his guilt would be unending.

Before taking off from the ranch at sunrise, D.W. had phoned his hotel and been yelled at, apparently, by no less than Colonel Acosta, Siso's superior in the security police. D.W. told Sam afterward that he'd refused to divulge his whereabouts, but since the connection had lasted for at least a minute, it was possible the call had been traced to the ranch.

Sam agreed. And he decided not to mention that his flight plan had been filed with the civil aeronautics agency in Ciudad Bolívar. Failure to do so could cause big problems for Enrico and the ranch, as well as himself. But obviously, if the *federales* made a few phone calls and deductions, they'd know where D.W. was, and where he was likely to be going.

The purpose for D.W.'s call, of course, had not been to antagonize the security chief. He'd called to learn of any overnight developments. But there had been no overnight developments, or so Colonel Acosta had flatly informed him. And when D.W. had requested an itemized progress report, Acosta had replied that if D.W. wanted to stay informed on the investigation, he should get his ass back to the hotel. D.W. then repeated his request for information, upping the volume and adding career threats. In the end, all he got for his efforts was the vaguest sort of rundown.

An expanded search area was being worked from the air by planes and helicopters, on the ground by boats and cars, even by foot patrol around parts of Guri Lake. Law-enforcement agencies nationwide, meanwhile, were still beating the urban bushes to locate Oscar Azarias Rivilla, but so far had gathered only more sordid details for his criminal résumé.

In short, D.W. learned little that he and Sam and Enrico hadn't already gotten from the early A.M. Venevisión and CNN news roundups at the ranch. Again and again, they had seen Oscar's hangdog mugshot, dealt out beside smiling photos of the "beautiful American heiress" and her "industrialist father," followed by graphic lists of Proteus's extensive holdings superimposed over a map of Venezuela. And there were references to the two notorious Carloses in Oscar's criminal past—the Jackal and Lehder, the legendary terrorist and the ex–Medellín drug kingpin serving life plus 135 years in a U.S. federal pen. There were frequent appeals for information and, finally, with facts hard to come by, a lot of dire speculation. Obviously mercy was not to be expected from such a hardened criminal. But authorities so far were refusing to comment on what, if any, demands had been made. . . .

Sam had walked into the den after filing his flight plan and found D.W. transfixed by one of these ghastly bulletins. So Sam had switched off the set and started hustling him and the others out to the Cessna.

Better to do anything, even if it proved fruitless, than wallow in impotence. An hour flight down, maybe a couple of hours there, then an hour back, Sam figured. Afterward he and D.W. could sit down and weigh the options remaining. Meanwhile, with almost no hope of its being needed, D.W. was taking along the Avensa zipper bag bloated with so-far-unsolicited ransom— close to a million dollars in U.S. hundreds and Venezuelan "orchids," five-hundred-*bolívar* notes. As long as he was going, he might as well go prepared to buy his daughter back.

For D.W.'s sake and his own, Sam tried continually to turn off his own feelings. He could function tolerably with the situation as a steady, abstracted heartache. But the instant he let himself think personally about Jake—out there somewhere, in the hands of that predatory old man—it was like getting a paralyzing injection of rage and despair.

At the moment, for instance, Sam had just recalled his single encounter with the kidnapper. It was that afternoon on Cerro Calvario, when he and Jacqueline had gone riding, and he'd flushed Oscar from behind the rocks. The old man had been spying on them through his binoculars. And as Sam now knew, not just spying, but stalking his future prey. If only Sam had had his Winchester Model 70 scabbarded alongside the saddle horn that afternoon. Just shoulder the butt, center the bastard's head in the cross hairs, and squeeze the fucking trigger. *Adiós*, scumbag! A life sentence in a Venezuelan jail would be a sweet price to pay.

While savoring this impossible vengeance-in-hindsight, Sam was unaware that all the lines of his long face had drawn tight. Nor did he realize that the verdant panorama into which he flew was for the moment veiled behind a red mist.

They came in from the southwest, watching the Kamarata Valley floor conform with their gradual descent into grasslands, gallery forests, and a lacework of verdure-fringed tributaries radiating from a medial river, the Río Akanan. The distant, flat-topped peaks studding the horizon ahead and to their right remained in lavender remoteness. But on their left, the striated walls of Auyán Tepui, a long, irregular march of majestically eroded battlements, lifted high above them now into the day's early brilliance.

Farther on, a clearing appeared suddenly on the left bank of the Akanan. A moment later they saw the runway—a slender, asphalted scar in the savanna—and a scattering of palm-thatched structures that made up the Kamarata Mission and adjacent native village. Then, with a negligible bounce, they were down, and D.W. could let go of that fractional anxiety about his own safety. The controlling dread, having to do with his lost child, remained intact.

A moment later they were rolling off the pocked asphalt and bouncing along a dirt taxiway toward several bronze-skinned, barefoot young men in shorts and bright bathing suits, standing beside a rusty wheelbarrow. One of the delegation, D.W. saw, was shaking an admonitory finger at them. Sam responded by spinning the Cessna's nose and, when the finger widened to a flat palm, coming to an abrupt stop.

The welcoming committee seemed perplexed when D.W. declined to deposit his flight bag in their wheelbarrow. Enrico and Bernardo, next off and each shouldering only a light daypack, also bypassed the luggage service. Once the propellers had spun down and everything inside was switched off, Sam came down the retractable steps, handing the nearest man the chocks. He spoke briefly to the other Indians in Spanish, pointing at the cockpit, then at his watch, and D.W. saw their expressions brighten, their faith in humanity apparently restored.

D.W. was relieved to be on the ground, even though the hard-packed clay was already scorching through the soles of his chukka boots. But his spirits were not lifted by the encircling grandeur or the dazzling-hot clarity of the morning sky. On the contrary, as the four visitors fell in behind the Kamarakotas trundling their empty wheelbarrow on a well-worn path toward a nearby cluster of huts, D.W. found himself again thinking of last night's thunderstorm. He tried not to envision Jacqueline's having been out in it, exposed to its full fury, but such images insinuated themselves again and again into his embattled mind.

Continuing this self-flagellation, D.W. kept pace with the others, toting his blue bag and striding purposefully, while feeling completely powerless in this maximum crisis of his life. It was to Samuel now that he must look for leadership—just to keep himself plodding on, step after step, through this sun-blasted valley.

The path from the airstrip widened out into the main street of the Kamarakota settlement, which was being patrolled by several roosters and a tan, shifty-looking dog. Spaced out along this and radial avenues of sun-baked earth were traditional Indian *churuatas* of adobe brick painted white or ocher with palm-thatched roofs. Variety was served in floor plan—round, oval, rectangular—and roof design—conical, peaked, curbed, even mansard-hipped. In the village center was what Sam took to be either a communal dwelling or meetinghouse, a large circular structure topped by thirty-foot-tall conical thatching.

Sam followed Enrico toward its deep-shadowed doorway now, pausing under the shaded overhang to inspect an ocelot curled up in a small chicken-wire cage. Then they went inside, adjusting their vision to the obscurity. A plump girl got up from a bench and waddled forward, a baby straddling her hip. Enrico asked directions to the Kamarata Mission school, while Sam scanned the earth-floored, unpartitioned interior. He estimated its diameter to be at least fifty feet. A noose of daylight sliced through a gap above the mud-brick walls and palm-thatched eaves. Furled hammocks hung between poles. At long wooden tables a half dozen women and girls worked, braiding fibers, stringing beads, weaving baskets. But the girl was already leading Enrico back outside. In the sudden sun, her exoticism was strik-

318

ing. Sam thought she looked like a Spanish-mulatto-Indian blend. She was pointing down the road toward a distant, elongated adobe structure shaded by moriche palms.

"*Escuela es allí*," she was saying.

They thanked her and started toward it. Midway there, the rough track skirted a hardpan *campo de fútbol* with painted goalposts and a game in spirited progress. The mission school was apparently in recess, since the players were mostly small boys, with one or two larger players. It could have been a soccer game in any Caracas barrio, Sam judged. The boys wore shorts or cutoff jeans, and several had T-shirts blazoned with imported pop-culture icons. Among the sideline onlookers Sam saw pirated shirt-likenesses of such mythic heroes as Bart Simpson, Tortugas Ninjas, Michael Jordan, and the ubiquitous Mickey. Several boys, with broad brown feet that could scale trees or walk all day over jungle trails, plainly coveted Bernardo's psychedelic high-tops, which looked to Sam only slightly less cumbersome than ski boots.

"Where's your padre?" Enrico was asking one of the sideliners.

"Over there."

The boy pointed midfield at a thin, spectacled man in maroon shorts, who was apparently refereeing the game. But when the ball bounded near, the man angled quickly after it, stopped it with his foot, then nudged it frantically along ahead of him. A pursuing chorus screamed "Padre!" and "Uribe!" The man eluded several defenders before tripping and tumbling on the hardpan. By the time he scrambled back up, the ball had been kicked diagonally far across the field.

Enrico called out and motioned to him. A moment later, he had walked over to them, a bony, middle-aged man with thinning, fair hair. He was still out of breath, perspiring heavily and wiping his glasses with a corner of soggy T-shirt. Beneath baggy maroon shorts, his knobby knees were scraped raw. But the most noticeable thing about this Father Uribe was a gold-inlaid smile that knotted his cheeks, squinched his blue eyes inside a mask of wrinkles, and somehow transformed his homely features into unaffected radiance.

But Enrico hesitated to shake his hand, and the Capuchin friar was puzzled—till he glanced down and discovered his right palm, like his kneecaps, was abraded and bleeding from his spill. His smile turned sheepish then, and he wiped the wounded hand on his shorts.

Sam left the introductions to Enrico. The moment it was explained that D.W. understood almost no Spanish, Father Uribe switched to English:

"I hope my English will be good enough to answer your questions then. I do try to keep my hand in, as they say, rereading all my Hornblower novels, and of course listening to the Beeb and Fats Waller records. I'm very 'up' on old nautical terms and Harlem slang. Now, gentlemen, if you don't mind, I'm afraid the rectory is being rethatched this morning. But perhaps this will serve."

Only a few strides from the playing field, he led them into the shade of a "caney," a crude shelter made of four corner poles supporting a palm-woven roof. Uribe chased a large rooster outside the shaded perimeter, then gestured at a long bench. It was surprisingly cool inside, and cooler yet when a Kamarakota boy trotted in with an ice tub studded with cans of Polar and Coke. When they all grabbed beers, even Bernardo, Father Uribe decided to do likewise.

After a long swallow, Sam launched into their morning's business. The priest was appropriately distressed. He had no television, but had heard a bulletin about the kidnapping on the radio. Enrico unzipped his daypack and passed out the Polaroids of Chucho and Angel. Uribe didn't recognize the faces.

"But I wouldn't, don't you see? I was only transferred to this mission last year. But Padre Tomás would know them, if they're from here."

A few minutes later, they were joined by two older men—a squat, leathery, baseball-capped Kamarakota with a soft handshake; and Padre Tomás, a wizened, white-bearded man in brown Capuchin robes and sandals, who pumped hands vigorously all around. Uribe summarized the reason for the strangers' visit, as Enrico handed them the Polaroids. Both men reacted instantly to the faces, chattering together in the Pemón language—plus a little Spanish and a lot of gesturing. All this eventually got digested and translated, first into Spanish by Tomás, then into English by Uribe.

There had been a bit of scandal five years earlier. The big one—Angel was his mission name—had lain with a forbidden woman, a fifteen-year-old girl who also happened to be his "unlawful cousin," the daughter of his father's brother. Father Uribe explained that, among many indigenous tribes, the children of two brothers, or of two sisters, were not permitted to mate. A traditional duel with *nabruxi* clubs had ensued. Angel had hit his opponent on the skull and fled into the bush, thinking he had killed him. Angel's half brother, Chucho—the smaller one —had run after him.

The brothers had apparently hidden up in the Kavak caves, but a week later were discovered lower down in the canyon. They fled again, this time by curiara down the Río Kukurital all the way to Canaima Camp. The last the old Kamarakota had heard of the brothers, they'd joined the indigenous community there, but had run away again after more trouble with the Canaima authorities.

"Could they tell us more about these caves?" Sam asked.

Kavak Canyon, they learned, had been carved out of the southern tip of Auyán Tepui by the Kavak River, which was tributary to both the Akanan and Kukurital. Its canyon narrowed finally to a long, constricted passage between towering rock walls, then opened into a cul-de-sac grotto—La Cueva, the Cave. This grotto was also the basin for a spectacular waterfall—one of the Río Kavak's long leaps from the heights of Auyán Tepui.

According to legend, a great Kamarakota chief, fleeing a massacre by a rival tribe, had sought refuge in the grotto. His enemies had failed to find the way in, and the chief was spared. His deliverance was attributed to divine intervention, and ever since La Cueva had been considered sacred to the Kamarakota.

The old Indian squinted expectantly from under his cap, but there were no further questions. After they'd thanked him and Padre Tomás for their help, D.W. turned to Uribe to ask another favor. Was there any way he could contact the Hotel Inter-Continental Guayana and check in with the police? The gangly priest assured him that could be accomplished with the mission's radio and led off toward the schoolhouse. Perhaps, he said, they could already see the sapling-mounted antenna behind the thatched structure. The wire connected to a hundred-watt base station transceiver in an alcove beside the school's kitchen.

While D.W. was being patched through, Sam waited outside with Enrico and Bernardo in the shade of the overhang. He listened to the wind rustling the loose thatch of the eaves. Aside from that, a humming silence prevailed, as the gathering heat slowed activity. Even the *fútbol* field had fallen quiet now. Westward across the valley, the quartzite-slabbed ramparts of Auyán Tepui seemed to sparkle and vibrate with reflected light.

Was she over there, Sam wondered, up in Kavak or some other hiding place? Or was she a hundred, even five hundred miles away? Unfortunately, aside from the interesting background information they'd just uncovered on the Indian brothers, there was no reason to suppose Jacqueline might be near. And though Sam tuned himself now to the vast silence, he received no mystic message either. Perhaps Father Uribe could consult with the tribal shaman for such auguries.

"Sam, look."

Enrico pointed with his cigarette. Hustling up the path came Padre Tomás, holding his cassock skirts, followed by the old Indian in the baseball cap.

The Capuchin priest hurried up to them, obviously full of news, but shorter of breath. In fact, he just stood speechless, mouth agape and frail chest heaving, and the old Kamarakota began to deliver the information himself, augmenting his Spanish with pantomime and occasional lapses into Pemón. By the time he'd finished, Father Tomás had recovered enough to clarify details.

Just moments ago, it seemed—right after the pair had identified the photographs and explained the legend of Kavak—they'd come upon a young man returning from that canyon, which was a favorite place for gathering orchids. Tracing the watercourse down from the canyon mouth, the Indian had discovered a curiara with an outboard motor concealed on a sandbank, under a heap of macheted shrubbery. The man had come back to ask what should be done about it.

"Does that stream connect to the Caroní?" Sam wanted to know.

Enrico thought it did, and this was confirmed by the old priest and the Kamarakota. Indeed, the dugout could have traveled all the way from Guri Lake, either straight up the Caroní to the Kukurital, or by switching to the Carrao at Canaima and following it upstream around Auyán Tepui's eastern flank to the Río Akanan.

322

Sam felt an adrenaline rush. This could be it, he thought, the break they'd been needing. Those bastards could be right across the valley! Enrico's eyes flashed the same thought.

Sam turned to get D.W., but the man was suddenly there, having emerged from the schoolhouse and looking around.

"D.W.—" Sam started, then broke off. His old associate looked stunned. "What is it, Duke? Did the police hear something?"

"A ransom note was found this morning in Canaima—from the Bandera Roja."

"What does it say?"

"They have Jacqueline. They want five million dollars."

46

Sam fired off several questions, but D.W. just stared back—not at Sam, but with his focus inward. He seemed almost to be smiling. Then he leaned heavily against the doorframe.

"Duke, are you all right?"

"Father, could you help me here?" D.W. managed to focus briefly on Sam. "The note was in Spanish. They read it to us that way first. Father Uribe took notes."

The Capuchin priest had appeared behind D.W. "Perhaps you'll give me a moment to excuse my pupils for another recess? They won't object, I assure you. Then we can all come inside."

They heard Uribe make the announcement within. Then came a flurry of feet on hard clay, and the doorway began hemorrhaging brown-skinned children. It was impossible to tally the blur, but after they'd dispersed, rejoicing, in all directions, there seemed to have been at least two dozen. In the quiet aftermath, the four visitors filed inside the oblong structure and took seats along the front bench. Father Uribe stood facing them, studying his notes.

On two sides of the schoolroom a series of embrasures admitted more than enough sunlight for students to read their lessons on the slate chalkboard, and the cursive alphabetic models bannered above. The whitewashed walls were decorated with maps and faded calendar scenes of Angel Falls and other

Venezuelan vistas—including the Andes and Caribbean coasts. Above a rough-hewn corner desk were portraits of Jesus and Mary, the pope, Saint Francis of Assisi, and Simón Bolívar.

Father Uribe went to a large wall map of the Gran Sabana. "The ransom note was discovered early this morning here in Puerto Kukurital. That's not even a village, as I recall, just some shelters built by the Indians who run a dugout ferry across the Caroní between Taraipa and Canaima Camp. But there's enough daily traffic that the kidnappers could be sure the note would be discovered.

"It was printed on the back of a label from a can of Spam. It was signed Bandera Roja—Red Flag. It mentioned—this is a quote—'bombing the capitalist iron mine on Cerro Calvario and capitalist ships docked in the port of San Félix.'" The priest cleared his throat. "And it goes on to mention 'taking hostage the daughter of a capitalist'—well, the word used was *tirano*, which means 'tyrant.'"

"Padre," Sam said, "as D.W. knows, the police have gotten quite a few notes and phone calls from people pretending to be the kidnappers. Why do they think this one is legitimate?"

Uribe glanced over at D.W. "I believe the note correctly identifies the, um, *apellido de soltera*, the unmarried name—"

"*Maiden* name," Enrico contributed.

"Yes, the maiden name of Señor Lee's wife, is it not so? Julienne Langlois?"

"Ex-wife," D.W. corrected. His arms were folded, his eyes cast down at the earthen floor.

"D.W., that isn't exactly privileged information," Sam said. "You've been profiled in a lot of business publications, in a lot of countries."

"They also know my pet name for her—Chewy. That's how she said I used to pronounce *Julie*. Besides Julienne and me, only Jacqueline knew that."

"Okay. Go ahead, Padre."

"What have I mentioned? Ah, yes. To obtain her release, this Red Flag demands a sum of five million dollars, which is to be left at a designated place in the Gran Sabana. I will show you this place on the map. It is only fifty kilometers from here. Let's see, the money must be left on Sunday night, that is three nights from now."

"Or?"

"If the Red Flag messenger does not return safely with the money, or if he is followed, the note says Señorita Lee will not be released. There is a further, um, unspecified threat."

"Unspecified?" D.W. shouted.

"What the note actually threatens is"—Uribe glanced down again—"to, quote, do unto yours what you have done unto us, unquote, and to, quote, seek retribution equal to the rape and destruction of Venezuela by Proteus and other foreign exploiters, unquote."

"And if the ransom *is* delivered?" Sam asked.

"They promise only that Señorita Lee will be released, but not where or when. We must trust them, they say."

"How do they want the five million?"

"In dollars, *bolívars*, diamonds, gold. The proportions aren't specified."

Enrico got up and walked to the map of the Sabana. "Padre, you said you could show us where they want the ransom left?"

"Yes," Uribe said as the others joined them. "Here is the Sabana Road. It runs from El Dorado all the way south to Brazil, three hundred kilometers. But here at kilometer one hundred forty, this side road leads west sixty kilometers to our mission at Kavanayén, then another twenty kilometers beyond to the Karuay River. The road ends at the river, and a trail leads through forest to Karuay Falls." Uribe consulted his notes again. "The ransom is to be left at midnight, in a waterproof sack, under a thatched shelter beside the trail head. The money will be collected before sunrise on Monday morning."

"You know this place?" Sam asked Enrico.

Enrico nodded. "I've been there."

"Okay. Padre, thank you very much," Sam said. "We apologize for disrupting your morning here."

"Please, I'm at your service."

"Then perhaps you could stay with us a while longer? I have some more questions." Sam turned to D.W. "Duke, Enrico and I just found out something else—while you were on the radio to Puerto Ordaz. It may fit in with all this."

"What is it?"

"Maybe we have an idea where Oscar and his buddies have

326

gone to ground." Sam told about the Indian finding the concealed dugout outside Kavak Canyon. He pointed to the map.

"Here's Canaima, where the ransom note was found. Or actually by the Kukurital River. Now, as Father Uribe just showed us, here's where they want the money dropped three nights later. Judging by this legend, it's got to be at least a hundred kilometers. Assuming they're in a dugout, how would they do it? Padre?"

"The long way—by the Río Carrao—goes right through Canaima Camp and requires portages around waterfalls and rapids. They would almost certainly be seen. The shorter way is to come right up the Kukurital to our valley, then take the Río Kavak to reach the Akanan.

"From here, the ransom drop location is only about fifty kilometers by various tributaries across the savanna to the southeast. In fact, there were plans to continue the road from the mission there to our mission here in Kamarata. Fortunately, the government created Canaima National Park, and the plan was canceled."

"So, basically, Padre, here in Kamarata—or in Kavak, just across the valley—we're halfway along the most direct route between where the ransom note was found and where the money is supposed to be picked up."

"That is correct."

D.W. stared at the map, then placed a stubby forefinger on the tiny, indented canyon of Kavak at the southern tip of arrowhead-shaped Auyán Tepui. "Sam, you actually think they're here now . . . the kidnappers . . . and Jacqueline?"

"It's worth checking, D.W.," Sam said. "They need a place to hide out during the day—maybe longer, if Oscar sends his Indians to fetch the ransom. If not, where the hell did that outboard canoe come from, and why is it being hidden there?"

D.W. swung toward the priest. "Father Uribe, how far is that canyon from here?"

"Fifteen kilometers. An hour by motorized dugout."

After an interval of silence in which anxious glances were exchanged, Sam spoke: "Padre, perhaps if you could leave us a moment? I think we need to decide some things in private."

The Capuchin left, taking, at Enrico's suggestion, a reluctant Bernardo with him. Sam resumed:

"Obviously, it's your call, D.W. But maybe I should go over the options as I see 'em.

"One, we get back on the padre's radio and call in the troops. Tell them everything we know. They'll be down here fast—hell, there's gotta be a planeload on the way already. They can send a hostage-rescue team to explore Kavak.

"Two. We radio Acosta and Siso, tell them we found out who the Indians are. Tell 'em everything except about Kavak. Then, because that's the only way they'll play it, we let them arrange a phony, electronically tagged money drop or set up a high-powered ambush, or whatever.

"Three. We go and check out this Kavak Canyon ourselves. Today. Right now, before anybody else shows up. Get a Kamarakota guide to take us to the entrance. If we find Oscar and his pals, we try and convince him to deal with us instead of the feds. Make him see it's in his best interest. Trade him Jacqueline for the money you've brought. If he demands a guarantee of safe conduct out of the area, hell, he can take me along as a hostage.

"Anyway, those are the three options I see. You guys see any others?"

The *llanero* leaned against the wall, smoking a cigarette. He shook his head. D.W.'s response was not to Sam's question:

"You definitely think security forces are on their way here?"

"They sure as hell know where your radio call originated. And they know you're holding out on 'em. I'd say we have two hours at the most before the first government plane hits the mission runway."

D.W. regarded both men in turn, then spoke brusquely:

"I can't ask either of you to risk your life. If I choose Sam's third option, I'll go in alone."

"No, D.W., that's a *fourth* option, and it's no good. We all go in together, and you call the shots. Agree or disagree, Enrico?"

"Agree. Señorita Jacqueline is also my friend."

"I'm in no shape to argue." D.W. finger-combed his thinning hair. "So I won't. I'll just say that I'm grateful, deeply grateful. I won't forget it, whatever happens. But here's another question for you. I've been carrying around my .45 auto ever since the fire aboard the *Kallisto*. Did either of you happen to bring anything along?"

"No gun," Sam said.

"I have a lever-action thirty-thirty," Enrico said, slapping his daypack. "It's a take-down gun, in four pieces. In the States what you'd call a deer rifle. It goes back together in thirty seconds. From a hundred meters I can put five bullets into that old bastard's head—if he stands still."

D.W. nodded thoughtfully. "Excellent. But please leave it disassembled, understand, Enrico?"

"Yes, absolutely, I agree with you, *señor*. We must do nothing to endanger your daughter. I think that is why you do not wish to send in the *federales* with their machine guns."

"That's exactly right."

"So," Sam asked, "we go in?"

D.W. hefted the zipper bag. "We go in."

47

Bernardo had talked himself into the expedition only to be dismissed on the threshold of adventure—left behind with their dugout canoe outside the entrance to Kavak Canyon. But the youth's dejection was visibly relieved as Enrico emphasized the importance of his assignment. He must not only stand watch over their canoe, but also keep an eye out for Oscar and the Indians—since the kidnappers' canoe, assuming it was the one discovered earlier by their Kamarakota guide, lay concealed right around an upstream bend of the river. Most importantly, if Oscar and the Indians did appear—with or without Señorita Jacqueline—Bernardo was to stay out of sight and radio immediately for help. The spike-haired youth was given a hand-held transceiver preset to a frequency being monitored both by Enrico, with an identical two-way, and by Father Uribe at the Kamarata Mission base radio.

Having motored and pushed their curiara as far as possible up the Kavak's boulder-strewn main channel before beaching it in Bernardo's charge, the others now continued on foot. Their guide, a barrel-chested, bowlegged young Kamarakota named Julio, led off barefoot beside the churning river. His faded T-shirt advertised an unlikely Hollywood connection: ARACHNOPHOBIA CREW 1989—ON LOCATION, VENEZUELA. He was closely followed by D.W., squinting beneath a golf cap and carrying his airline bag.

330

Then came Sam, bare headed and unencumbered; and finally Enrico with his ranch hat, daypack, and belt-attached radio. Though wearing their own shoes, all three men now sported shapeless, faded walking shorts courtesy of Father Uribe. Apparently they could expect a lot of wading ahead.

Once past the other dugout in its brushy concealment, Julio began to crouch periodically and peer closely at the riverbank path they were following. After many such inspections, he announced that several people had passed that way since last night's rain. Two Indians, a man wearing shoes.

And a woman? Enrico prompted. Julio shrugged.

Directly ahead of them now reared the massif of Auyán Tepui, a brooding presence in the noon savanna sun, with shredded cumulus wreathing its purple-streaked brow. But here, at its southern apex, the great plateau had crumbled in places into projecting spurs and forested foothills. It was through these fallen ramparts that the Río Kavak first emerged, slicing a knife-edged gorge; then, in a series of headlong plunges and lazy serpentines, carving out a canyon that gradually widened into a broad, alluvial wedge, fanning far out onto the valley floor.

As they headed up this twisting, tumbling watercourse, the stocky Kamarakota occasionally pointed things out to them. Here and there in the embankment thickets, lavender orchids could be glimpsed. A morpho butterfly jinked across their path, flaunting iridescent blue forewings and brown hindwings. Julio also indicated that the Kavak was running higher than usual, owing to the previous night's thundershowers.

But the rest of his party was plainly not interested in tropic scenery, flora, or fauna. All were internally preoccupied and, as far as externals, attuned only to danger, not beauty. And after their hour-long dugout voyage, the first few minutes of midday hiking up the winding riverpath had them mopping sweat-stung eyes and laboring for breath. Even Enrico moved without his usual nonchalance. Only their guide remained unaffected by the wilting heat.

Had Sam Warrender and Duk-Won Lee compared their besetting fears, they would have found them horribly parallel. Naturally, both men were afraid of what they might find ahead. What if Jacqueline was already dead, having been carried in as a corpse—thus leaving no footprints? What if her precious life

331

was being snuffed out this very instant, while they wheezed and plodded up this path, amateur cavalry late to the rescue? Or what if she was in no immediate danger, but their clumsy arrival caused her death? Were they, in fact, endangering her simply to assuage their sense of helplessness? Should they have relied on that roomful of professionals?

And both men feared what they might *not* find up-canyon. Nothing at all, or perhaps an innocent party of adventure trekkers. Such futility would crush whatever feeble hope each was harboring. It would be like losing Jacqueline a second time.

Sam and D.W., of course, had argued these points together in rationalizing their present course of action. It seemed clear, for instance, that the security police's primary concern was that this terrorist kidnapping not engender others. Which meant that Jacqueline's safety could only be a secondary objective. Which explained why the police were rejecting all demands in advance, refusing to negotiate and instead readying their shoot-to-kill commandos. Under these circumstances, it was too easy to visualize Colonel Higueras and his red berets rappelling out of choppers or charging up this canyon path, intent only on taking out the bad guys, even if it imperiled their hostage, and unleashing a full-auto barrage the instant they were fired upon. On the contrary, D.W. and Sam had agreed to put Jacqueline's safety above their own. And in a discussion that had not included Enrico, each had expressed a willingness to offer himself as hostage, if it would avail her release.

But suppose they were wrong in all this? Or suppose they were right, yet their best efforts still proved fatal to Jacqueline?

Such unanswerable anxieties exacted a far greater physical toll on them than did the heat or humidity. Fear clutched the throat, coiled in the chest and stomach. A sharp sound in the bordering underbrush could lift the hairs along the back of the neck and forearm. The eye swept ahead for danger, while the mind perversely withdrew, observing this march into the unknown and wondering under what irrevocably resolved circumstances they would pass this way again . . . or if they would pass this way again.

The Kamarakota crouched again as the footpath narrowed, encroached upon by foliage. He was pointing at the light green underside of fresh-slashed leaves. Machete work. They saw similar blade wounds ahead, as the trail traced the brink of an undercut embankment; and even more as it turned away from the rushing water, tunneling through a solid tangle of exposed roots, screening undergrowth, and hanging vines and lianas. Their guide was moving much more slowly and cautiously now, watching and listening at almost every step—especially when the path looped down to rejoin the river, depositing them on an exposed rock ledge. His aural and visual acuity had been demonstrated during the journey by curiara, when he had heard an aero engine over the savanna and pointed to the sky—long seconds before the others could detect its presence.

As they followed him now along another curve of the canyon, they heard a sound ahead like polite applause. A moment later, at the end of a steep-sided, green-bordered glade, they stared at a sunlit, white-water staircase. From a forested verge at least a hundred meters above them, the Kavak in its full width cascaded down a theatrically faceted, horizontally striated cliff. It was like coming upon the overgrown ruins of an ancient jungle pyramid, so stair-stepped was the exfoliated face. But closer inspection showed the rugged stone laminations to be geologically formed, with projecting ledges polished by water and carpeted with moss. An intricate fringe of rivulets laced together with the main cataract to spill finally into a boulder-formed pool that sparkled with the tint of sherry wine.

"La Cueva?" Sam asked.

The Indian shook his head and held up three fingers.

"The Kavak, it has three waterfalls. This one we call *ducha*, the shower. You climb up and stand in this. The next one, it is the *piscina*, you swim in it. The last one, it is La Cueva. Most beautiful place."

"Can't we move faster?" D.W. barked.

No sooner had he said this than he lost his footing, flailing one arm as he held up his Avensa bag with the other. Julio was quickly beside him, bracing his elbow. With no further protest then, the quartet proceeded single file, crossing the foaming river on a bridge of boulders and fallen trees and continuing on the other bank.

D.W. felt a pounding pulse in his head now. Stress had mastered him days ago, but inaction was the most unbearable torture of all. It had seemed better, then, to be in motion, bringing near the fearful resolution—an end to the agony of unknowing. But the deeper they had penetrated this overgrown maze, the more he had doubted the convoluted, Sherlockian deductions that had led them here, and the less he sensed his child's presence in this wild landscape.

They should turn around and go back—at once.

D.W. should arrange to leave the $5 million when and where the terrorist bastards wanted it and just keep Siso and Higueras and all the rest of the gun-toting bureaucrats the hell out of it. That was probably his only chance to get his daughter back alive. They were wasting precious time, all because an Indian had found a canoe under some bushes and now saw some machete marks!

The column halted as Julio squatted to inspect a muddy patch of trail. In the rear, D.W. dropped his zipper bag and sat down heavily. A few inches from his eyes spiderweb strands drifted in the breeze. But something seemed odd. He focused. It wasn't really webbing. More like black threads snagged on a low, projecting branch.

He tugged one loose. It wasn't a thread at all. It was a human hair, black and coarse and easily two feet long. Much longer than any of the Kamarakota men he'd seen wore their hair. And the women artisans in that communal hut this morning, and the schoolgirls, they all had close-cropped hairdos. The tom-tom pulse in D.W.'s head grew stronger. Could Jacqueline have yanked it out and left it as a telltale? But who would see it down there? Unless she, too, had rested here, seizing upon an unobserved opportunity, with nothing else handy to indicate she'd passed that way. Perhaps she had also scratched a sign in the mud nearby with a twig or a fingertip. But there was no such mark.

D.W. called out. Julio scrambled over, examined the hair, sniffed it, regarded D.W. with sudden respect, obviously impressed that a *blanco* had seen something he'd missed.

"Is no Kamarakota," he said, meaning the hair. Sam and Enrico were also bending over now, staring at the strand and its mates floating on the twig.

"What do you think?" D.W. asked.

"Perhaps," Enrico said.

Sam nodded.

Pursuit into Darkness

She's alive! D.W. thought. His heart began an erratic gallop. *Sweet Jesus, Mary, Mother of God, Lord Buddha, keep her safe!*

They'd been all night fighting their way up that river. Again and again, all three men had spilled out, leaving her noosed to her bench—ensuring her death by drowning if they capsized. But she'd reached a state of apathy and exhaustion where she simply accepted that. She'd hear them splashing and bellowing around her in the darkness, trying to coordinate their efforts as they manhandled the log boat up yet another stretch of unseen rapids. Then, exhausted and freezing, they'd tumble back in, Angel would restart the outboard, and they'd be off again at full snarl.

Just before dawn they'd turned the corner on a broad valley, silver in the anticipatory light. After a blank moment, Jacqueline had suddenly recognized it from having flown over it two weeks before with Sam. This was the veldlike Kamarata, so the dark, overshadowing colossus on their left must be Auyán Tepui. Over the horizon, then, lay all the Gran Sabana, its sweeping grasslands unpeopled clear to Brazil, except for a scattering of missions and native settlements. Again, it was not as if any real hope of escape or rescue had been quenched by this bleak realization. Jacqueline simply took it in.

In short order they had veered off their diminishing stream and pushed up another tributary, until its rock-studded shallows were no longer navigable. Then they'd beached and hidden the boat, apportioned the supplies among the three men, and started up this long, winding canyon climb. The point of it—at least all Oscar would tell her—was that the ransom note had been safely delivered by Chucho. Now they were going into their hiding and waiting place.

It was some consolation to realize that the crazy old man was as exhausted as she, and the Indians only a little less so. During the hike they had stopped frequently, finding it harder each time to push on. At one point, Oscar stumbled about the path like a zombie and dropped his pack. Some of it had to be abandoned, the rest divided between Chucho and Angel.

Jacqueline found the numbing fatigue actually helped blunt the ache from the burns on her feet. Otherwise, she knew, every step would be unbearable, despite repeated applications of Angel's forest salve. And for all the cushioning she got from the

335

charred remnants of her down booties, she might as well be barefoot. But when she foundered, which happened frequently, Angel was always there to steady her, and to lift her entirely over the more difficult stretches.

At such times, she would nearly lapse into unconsciousness, eyes shut, hearing sluggish footfalls and ragged breathing, and the random wet hiss of Chucho's machete lopping off leaves and vines and meddlesome branches. Then she'd open her eyes on a scene of transcendent beauty—such as that first incredible cascade, a baroque, angel-haired fountain; and farther on, a series of pellucid, slab-sculpted pools, linked by plashing cataracts, each deliciously inviting. But they had staggered on, toward God only knew what destination.

Eventually, with the sun above the treetops and beating relentlessly down, they'd all gotten their cooling bath. A collapsed portion of embankment detoured them onto the Kavak's eddying margins. They moved first along a stone-scalloped apron, then, as this sloped into the river, waded thigh deep through the onrushing current. Jacqueline slipped and plunged several times on green-slimed rocks, but declined to be carried. The liquid embrace was too wonderful, and she mourned its loss keenly when the time came to rejoin the trail. The instant she emerged, she felt the hot imprint of rock on the bottom of her foot and realized she'd lost one of her booties in the river.

Well, good! she thought. That would make a better clue than near-invisible strands of her hair. But still, who would ever see it underwater?

Aside from the remote chance of rescue or ransom then, her only hope remained to stay close to Angel at all times and pray that his devotion was indeed genuine, and that he would be equal to the task of protecting her from Oscar, when her fate hung in the balance.

In order to keep flogging himself forward, Oscar tried to reconstruct the intricate elements of his plan. But again and again, it would all fold up on him, and he'd be ready simply to drop in his tracks and abandon everything. Why was he doing any of this? Why this bone-wearying climb after that freezing, all-night battle with that fucking dugout canoe?

Five million dollars.

Ah, yes! Finally, that chimerical, fantastical number took flight and hovered in the air, like one of those dancing blue butterflies, and Oscar staggered up the trail after it. Five million dollars. Just follow the plan.

Oh, sure, there were pitfalls, but look how far they'd come already. It could work. When they finally reached the end of this accursed canyon, they'd sleep one whole day and a half. That would also be Oscar's last chance at his hostage, something that didn't bear thinking about. Of course, his original plan was simpler and far more satisfying. They'd have their fun with her, leave her body up here, and take off together in the canoe for the ransom pickup. Now, because of Angel's pathetic attachment, Oscar and Chucho would slip out tomorrow night, leaving the girl with Angel another day or so.

If the big Kamarakota spent that time treating her like a princess instead of his slave girl, he was even dumber than he looked. But—alas!—that wasn't Oscar's problem. Everything would be okay, so long as Angel showed up at their rendezvous on time, and the bitch didn't find her way out of the canyon until the three of them were far south on the Río Karuay with all the money, en route to Brazil.

Suddenly Chucho was calling a halt. Oscar, who had been carefully planting his squishy tennis shoes on the stony path, looked up at a preposterous sight. Just ahead was a calmly rippling pond, maybe fifty meters across, entirely surrounded by steep, vine-draped rock walls. Apparently, the canyon and the river both ended abruptly right here, in a forested cul-de-sac. Where the hell did the Río Kavak come from then, some underground spring?

He shuffled up to Chucho, who was already squatting and rummaging into his daypack for canned edibles. Likewise, Angel had slung down his woven bag containing blowgun, machete, and other Kamarakota essentials, while behind him Señorita Lee, a limp figure in her tattered coveralls, stood gaping at the small body of water exactly as Oscar had.

"La Cueva?" Oscar asked, gesturing all around.

"No, boss," Chucho said. "The cave is around the corner. But now we stay here." He tossed Oscar a can of peaches.

Oscar couldn't see any corner for a cave to be around. But he was far too weary to argue the point and was already savoring the siesta to come. He backed away into canyon shade, lowered his bony rear onto a flat rock, punctured the can with his pocket knife, and sucked out the syrupy contents. When he glanced up, Angel and Chucho were cross-legged and face-to-face in the full sun, taking turns poking their bamboo stick in each other's nostrils and shooting up with their black magic powder.

Just look at 'em, Oscar thought. *A pair of fucking* yopo *addicts!*

He watched, fascinated, as the hallucinogen kicked in. Their tongues protruded, saliva pearled and drooled from their slack jaws. Eyelids fluttered, eyes rolled up. Persimmon skin, already slick with perspiration, now seemed to be streaming sweat. In a moment, Oscar realized, both men would be senseless.

But it took an instant for the significance of this to hit him.

When it did, he glanced slyly around—and directly into the dark, suddenly frightened eyes of their captive, who was slumped against a boulder less than five meters away. Obviously, she, too, had realized the possible ramifications of this quaint Kamarakota ritual. Her guardian "angel" had temporarily checked out of this world and into another. Until he returned, she was without her protector.

Oscar winked at her.

48

But the girl didn't react properly. She simply stared back at him. And the look Oscar had read as simple fear seemed subtly compounded now with other emotions. Wariness, perhaps. Even cunning. And then it struck Oscar, as it must have her: with the Kamarakotas in psychedelic stupor, not only had Señorita Lee lost her protector, but Oscar had lost his backup. The instant Oscar succumbed to sleep, there would be no one watching her. She was obviously waiting for that to happen. And then what? Would she try to escape down the canyon? Or come at him with the machete?

Lagarta! Lizard-bitch!

It was about time Oscar taught her a real lesson. Unfortunately, that long-overdue resolve and the gratifying images it conjured lasted hardly a moment. She might appear bedraggled, but the level look in her eyes told him she was far from defeated. She'd fight back like a she-cat and scream her lungs out to rouse her unconscious champion. And Oscar didn't much feel like wrestling a just-awakened, drug-crazed monster. The bitch definitely wasn't worth that kind of risk.

Of course, he could outwait her, stay vigilant till she collapsed. But the sweetly insidious tide of sleep was already tugging at him. He had to act while some strength remained. He shuffled over to the packs, pulled out the things he needed. Both brothers had now toppled over, Angel emitting an intermittent growl not unlike that of their outboard motor.

"Please do not scream, *señorita*," Oscar said as he approached her. "I am not going to touch you—if you cooperate. But I have to take a siesta, and I have to make sure you will be here when I awaken."

She eyed the ropes dangling from his left hand and replied in disgust, "Where am I going to go? I can barely walk."

"Please, it is not a discussion, *señorita*. Here."

In his right hand he proffered an open can of peaches and a plastic jug of water.

"Just put them down. I'll have them later."

"You will have them now, *señorita*. Or you must wait hours from now, if you're lucky."

He squatted near, trying to keep his eyelids open while she gulped down the contents of both containers—angrily but greedily enough. When she was finished, he instructed her how to hobble herself, tying knotted loops around each ankle with a short rope. Next he had her make a knot around one wrist, then stretch both hands behind her.

"It's too damn tight," she complained, even before he'd finished securing her wrists. "You're cutting off the circulation. I can't sleep like this."

Oscar loosened his knot slightly. "Is that satisfactory, Your Highness? And may I suggest that you lie on your side?"

She flashed a look of pure malevolence as he stepped back. Then she did, indeed, roll onto her side away from him—an awkward maneuver with her arms pulled behind. The reclining posture also accentuated the plump swell of her hips as the river-damp coveralls traced her curves. Though barely sensate now, Oscar felt the stab of desire. But even without the risk, he was too far gone. He parked his butt back on his rock, positioned a canvas pack in what he figured was just the right spot, then fell backward and asleep before his head hit the improvised pillow.

Jacqueline, however, did not sleep. While repelling wave after wave of fatigue, she was already trying to kick loose her ankle bonds and was feeling around for sharp stones to cut through her wrist ropes. But all the rocks and pebbles she fingered were river-smoothed, and her wrists seemed awfully secure, even though Oscar had pretended to loosen the knot after her complaint. Her best bet, she decided, was to concentrate on her legs. She had tied those hobbles herself and had managed a slipshod job, despite his watching. If only she were a contortionist, she'd jackknife down and open the knots with her teeth. But in order to accomplish anything, she had to stay awake.

It was just after one o'clock when they came to the chain of spillways and rock-rimmed pools. Sam and Enrico, their shirts and shorts saturated with salty perspiration, exchanged a quick glance. Then, after removing a few nonimmersibles such as wallets and Enrico's belt radio, the pair climbed down to the nearest pool and slid in fully dressed. Moments later they were joined in the pink-tinted, crystalline water by D.W. Those portions of his round face not masked by golf cap and mirrored sunglasses were seriously sunburned; sunblock had not been on their morning checklist. After a welcome cool-off, which, under other circumstances, would have been wonderfully refreshing, all three hauled themselves out, allowing their guide his own brief dip.

Shortly after they'd gotten under way again, wading through shallows upstream from the pools, Enrico reached down and brought up what looked to Sam like a soggy red scuba bootie or leather-bottomed mukluk. But D.W. grunted as if stomach-punched, then took the dripping article in his hands.

The quilted-nylon uppers were badly torn up, most of the goose-down stuffing gone. He turned the booty over, staring at the suede bottom, and in particular at several burn-scalloped holes. Again, D.W.'s distress was partly concealed by his sunglasses, but the bitter set of his lower lip revealed much. It wasn't necessary for the others to know that D.W. had seen his daughter wearing this slipper that night on the burning ship, or that he'd ordered it from her favorite outdoor catalogue.

There was no question now that they were on the right trail, and that they were very close. But what did its abandonment mean? Had she dropped it on purpose, as she'd wound those glistening black telltales on that low branch? Or had the booties simply come loose in the stream somewhere above and been carried down?

D.W. slipped the waterlogged bootie into Enrico's pack. Then they continued quietly, all four men eyeing not only both embankments now, but also the swirling current for any other objects.

Chucho, who had been roving the forested hills in his jaguar spirit-body, returned suddenly to his *yopo*-tranced form and shook himself awake. There had been a sound—not the constant lullaby of the river or the afternoon windsong in the trees, and not an animal cry or birdcall. No, he had heard the heavy, lifeless tread of *civilizados*. People were coming. He sat up, ears and eyes tracking, nostrils dilating.

Yet everything seemed normal. Beside him, Angel was sprawled on his back, limbs thrown out, head thrown back, mouth agape and snarling with each inhalation. A dozen paces away, old Oscar also slept on his back, fingers curled around the handle of Chucho's machete. And beyond Oscar, turned away, with her wrists secured behind, was their captive. She stirred restlessly now in her sleep.

But Chucho had heard something.

He reached for his blowgun and darts, moved past the sleepers and over the rocky slope bordering the pond and headed back downstream, keeping within the trees. Again, he heard the noises—rocks dislodged, shoe thuds, labored breathing. He crept to the edge of the trees, peering through screening undergrowth. Thirty meters down the riverpath, there were four men—coming to shoot them, Chucho decided, or else take them back to filthy prison cells.

Two of the men Chucho did not know—the tall, white-haired one and the thin, dark one in the straw hat. But the one carrying the blue bag was Señor Lee coming to steal back his daughter. Oscar had shown Chucho magazine pictures of the hard-faced millionaire before they attacked his ship in San Félix.

And the fourth man was from their old village—Julio, once a thief, and now a traitor, leading even more outsiders to the sacred cave of the Kamarakota.

Chucho raised his blowpipe. He wished for his old two-meter *cerbatana*, not this half-size toy for *turistas*. He selected a *mamocori*—a curare-tipped, fire-hardened palmwood dart with a band of jungle cotton on its tail—slid it down into the mouthpiece. Then, as the four men moved up into range, he slowly hyperventilated, sighting down the wooden shaft.

Then, with lungs and abdominals at full distention, he erupted air through the blowpipe.

Whoough!

Chucho watched Julio slap his neck and scream like a woman, then fling himself into the brush. The other three looked on in puzzlement. But Chucho had already fingered his next dart, twirling it down the tube and swinging to the next man, targeting his white hair. Then, as he sucked in his air, he saw the man in the straw hat reach into his shoulder pack. A rifle barrel flashed in the sun.

Chucho adjusted his aim, exploded his cheeks, sending the dart flying. Then, having been shot at by a Guardia soldier once in his life, and knowing also that a single curare dart would only temporarily disable a man, Chucho whirled and fled back into the brush.

49

In frightening succession, Sam heard the men on both sides of him cry out in pain. On his right, Julio went sprawling on the trail, then slithered forward behind a rock; while on his left, Enrico, reaching for his rifle, glanced down in puzzlement at the wooden spine suddenly protruding from a reddening ring just above his shirt pocket. Then both men locked eyes and made a dive for the shelter already occupied by their Indian guide. In the scramble, Sam lost track of D.W., who had been right behind them.

"Curare," Julio gasped, examining the brown-smeared tip of an eight-inch dart. His other hand was pressed to the side of his neck, with blood trickling through his fingers. "It is from Chucho or Angel. You shoot up there." He gestured up into the flanking trees.

Peering fearfully over the top of their rocky barricade, Sam quick-scanned the hillside and caught a flash of someone moving up there, brown skin with black-daubed stripes rippling through the greenery, then vanishing and reappearing higher up. An Indian—fleeing, he sure as hell hoped!

Then, only a few yards away, a head appeared above the embankment on the other side of the path, and Sam ducked down. When he dared a second look, D.W. had struggled up from wherever he'd been hiding and was hurrying up the trail, toting his zipper bag.

Sam shouted after him, "D.W., get back here!"

But D.W. wasn't listening. His commanding bass-baritone boomed across the valley:

"Chucho, Angel! This is Señor Lee! Don't shoot! I bring money! One million dollars! Do you hear me! Chucho, Angel! One million dollars! Let my daughter go!"

He can't help himself, Sam thought, *and at least he's doing something.* Sam himself felt a paralysis of will in the face of these simultaneous crises. He forced himself to focus his immediate anxiety back on Enrico and Julio. At the Indian's urging, Sam pulled the sharpened spine out of his friend's chest, causing an outwelling of blood. Still, the wound didn't seem grievous; it was the poison that terrified Sam. He had to get both men med-evaced somehow, and fast. Until that was arranged, he dared not go rushing off mindlessly after D.W. or even think about Jacqueline.

But Enrico, though looking pale and frightened, was way ahead of Sam, grabbing his belt radio and barking into it, "Kavak Dos, Kavak Dos, *cambio*. Kavak Uno, Kavak Tres, *adelante*. Kavak Two, calling Kavak One and Kavak Three, over. Go ahead, Kavak One. We have an emergency . . ."

As Enrico continued, Sam turned quickly to Julio. "Padre Uribe will radio the authorities for help. There could even be a military helicopter in the area to pull you guys out of here. But, Julio, what can I do right now?"

Julio shook his head. "It take four, five darts to kill a little monkey. If no more curare, I think we okay, just long sleep."

"You're sure?"

Enrico glanced over from his radio. "It's not really a poison, Sam. It's a son-of-a-bitching muscle relaxer, which I can already feel. They even use it in surgery now. But get enough of it, and your diaphragm stops working, and you stop breathing. As long as that *cabrón* up there doesn't come back for more target practice, I think we'll be okay."

"Did you reach Uribe?"

"Yes. We're in luck. A chopper full of those red-beret guys

already landed at the mission. Uribe just ran outside to find them. I'm waiting for him to get back."

"Okay. Then I'll stay here to man the radio and talk 'em down."

Enrico shook his head, his voice already alarmingly weaker. "I know you want to go after her, Sam, so do it. Take my rifle."

"Rico, you can hardly talk. How the hell is the pilot gonna find you?"

"I told Uribe where we are—above those pools. And Bernardo knows. They'll find us. Go on, *caballero*. And watch your ass." Enrico made a feeble gesture of dismissal, then got back on frequency. "Kavak One, *adelante* . . ."

"You go," Julio said, trying to smile. "Me and your friend, we just having a little siesta."

"Son of a bitch!" Sam snarled—more at his irresolution than anything else. Then he snatched up Enrico's pack with the rifle barrel still protruding and sprinted up the path after D.W.

Jacqueline had quickly rubbed her ankles raw against the ropes, but persisted through the pain, using it to fight off sleep, while she strained and flexed her legs. When she saw the blood on her feet, she simply shut her eyes, gritted her teeth, and kept going. Finally she felt the knot give way. It was a moment of pure exhilaration, though her wrists remained bound behind, and her shoulders ached from the prolonged backward stretch.

But this was only a tiny victory. She rolled onto her back and swung her head over to check out her captors. Oscar still slept a few paces away. Farther down the pebbled slope, she saw Angel splayed out, still venting those ferocious snores she'd heard, still clutching the bamboo tube. But on his other side, where Chucho had collapsed after snorting the powder, there was no one. The little Indian was not in sight.

Dammit! Where had he gone?

Still, she had to take the chance. She wasn't likely to get another one. Maddeningly, it took another minute on her back of thrashing and kicking before she loosened the ankle knot enough to free one foot and leg.

Thank God! Now to get out of here!

But she discovered that, with her hands tied behind her, it was no easy matter to stand up. In junior-high gymnastics, she'd been able to kip off a mat and onto her feet. But she wasn't going to pull that stunt on this rocky slope, with rope still looped around one ankle. She did manage a sit-up, though, putting her legs straight in front of her. Halfway there. Then she tried curling them underneath her—and immediately toppled over. Shit!

She rolled again onto her back, did another sit-up. *Don't panic. There has to be a way to do this.* She tried bracing herself with a forearm while drawing her legs up, ignoring the grinding pain on the point of her elbow—and still couldn't maintain her balance. Down again, sit up again. How could standing up be this hard? *Think, dammit!*

Jacqueline spotted a boulder several feet behind her and scooted back to it. By jamming her elbow even more painfully against this, she was able at least to lever her butt off the ground. But it wasn't until she wedged one bleeding foot against another rock—*screw the pain!*—that she was able to get her legs underneath her, elbow herself upward, and balance her shifting weight all in a single teetering motion—

And it was done! She was actually on her feet! Her coveralls were soaked with sweat now and blotched with blood, but that only enhanced her sense of triumph.

Now, to get the hell out of here.

The next instant the rocky canyon walls resounded with shouts:

"Chucho, Angel! This is Señor Lee! Don't shoot! I bring money! One million dollars! Do you hear me! Chucho, Angel! One million dollars! Let my daughter go!"

Her father! *Don't yell back! Just run!*

But it was already too late. Oscar had leaped to his feet, machete in hand, scanning the circling hills for the source of the shouting. It took him a dizzy second to discover her, then another moment of blinking shock as he caught up to the reality of his trussed-up captive standing and staring at him, her legs unbound.

Then she saw the next realization hit him, as it just had her: he'd awakened just in time to block her escape.

Now she shouted back to her father:

"Daddy, I'm here! But watch out! He's got a machete!" She refocused on Oscar. "Didn't you hear him? He's got the ransom. Just take it and let me go!"

Oscar's face betrayed panicky calculations. Then he made up his mind and was moving purposefully toward her. Her father was calling her name, too far away to help. And backed into an angle of rock, there was nowhere for Jacqueline to flee. Instead, she pivoted a quarter-turn and crouched into her tae kwon do stance, readying a side kick. The old man growled:

"Try it, and I cut you open. Stand still, and you live."

Oscar emphasized his threat by slicing the air with the broad steel blade. Jacqueline felt the wind of its whistling passage and her courage drained away. She stood in perfect, nauseating passivity as he moved behind her and grabbed a fistful of her coveralls. Then he pressed the blade point into the small of her back and marched her down the slope and into plain sight.

Her father, red faced and gasping, was staggering up the trail toward them, yet still about fifty yards away. He was carrying a blue airline bag.

"Stop," Oscar bellowed, "or I cut off her head!"

Jacqueline saw her father cry out, stop dead, then throw out his arms. "Take the money! Take my life, *señor*! But please don't touch her!"

"Daddy!" she screamed back, and now felt the flat of the blade—scorching hot from the sun—against her jugular.

Then—alas, too late!—behind her father, Sam Warrender suddenly appeared in a ragged run. He was holding a rifle in two pieces—barrel and receiver; buttstock and lever action—and trying to jam it together. D.W. whirled on him:

"Drop it, Sam—or he'll kill her!"

Sam took in Jake's peril at a glance, let go the rifle sections, and halted in his tracks.

"Thank you," Oscar called out, keeping his tight grip on her coveralls, the blade against her neck. "No move! Now, Señor Lee, tell me. Where are the *federales*? They are waiting down there?"

"No! They don't know you're here. We came alone—with an Indian guide."

Oscar vented a vile laugh. "This is not the truth."

"Yes, it is! The *federales* don't know anything. Let her go, Señor Azarias! I brought a million dollars! I'll show you."

"No, please don't open the bag, *papacito*. And, you know, the figure was *five* millions."

"I raised the money before the note was found."

"Okay, you found the note! But how you find us?"

"Through the Indians," Sam spoke up. "Señorita Lee took videos on Cerro Calvario. An Indian recognized their tribe—Kamarakota. We flew to their village today. Another Indian mentioned this canyon—the brothers used it once before. And our guide found your boat. So we took a chance. But we never told the *federales*. We don't trust them either."

"It's true!" D.W. said. "They have too many guns. We just want her free. Please, we don't care about you. You can tie us up, anything. Just take the money and go."

Oscar's foul breath was against Jacqueline's cheek now, and she sensed his fear and indecision. Meanwhile, Sam had taken up the appeal again:

"Look, Oscar, if you think it's a trap, take the money and march us ahead of you as hostages. But let the girl go. She's suffered enough."

"*Capitalistas sin cojones*," Oscar muttered under his breath. Then he spoke in full voice: "Okay, *amigos*, you can all be my hostages. You go first. But the little girl, I want her right next to me all the time."

Hearing that malevolent mumble in her ear—and not even understanding the slang—Jacqueline got a sudden psychic fix on Oscar Azarias Rivilla. The old man was not, obviously, a calculate-the-odds criminal, just out for a big score. Nor, obviously, was he a revolutionary idealist. He was a dangerous outcast, a predatory one, who had seduced two other outcasts, innocents by comparison. And the main purpose of this whole deranged enterprise was not to succeed—like most terrorist objectives, it had been doomed from the start—but to create maximum havoc along the way. It didn't matter if he failed, so long as he took a lot of people down with him.

And that reckoning had just come due, Jake thought. Oscar must know his dangerous game was over, that he'd never get away from this canyon or the savanna or Venezuela, no matter how many hostages he paraded ahead of him. What he was obviously savoring now was bloody revenge on her father and Sam—in exchange for his lifetime of failure. Whatever happened, Oscar would make sure at least one of them died. And she couldn't let that happen.

50

Now, she thought, *you've got one chance, so do it right!*

She scythed her right leg out and around, kicking viciously back at Oscar's right leg. At the instant of contact, calf to calf, she ducked under the machete blade and spun behind him, tearing free of his grip.

Oscar yelped and stumbled, dropping the machete. On the point of running away, Jacqueline stopped to grab for the weapon. It was a mistake. Oscar reached it first and swiped viciously at her ankles. She screamed and dodged away—and in so doing, allowed him to scramble up and again block her escape.

Behind him now she saw her father and Sam rushing forward—but still precious seconds away. Oscar, meanwhile, seeming more eager to kill her now than regain her as a hostage, closed in with the machete, backing her down toward the pond.

There was only one way for her to go. She dashed down the rocky incline and—because her hands were still tied behind—overbalanced and nearly pitched face forward. Oscar's crunching footfalls were right behind her. And just ahead, the big Kamarakota rolled in his stupor and opened one bleary eye. Then she had raced past, plunging at full stride into the cool, reddish-hued water.

* * *

351

Angel, returning slowly from the first stage of his mystic journey, heard a piercing scream and sensed immediate danger. With his soul still far away, he opened an eye and watched the girl, her arms bound, flee past his sleeping body and into the pond. Then the old man clumped after her, brandishing Chucho's machete. Angel blinked. Farther away, two other men were also running toward him.

A dream? Or was Oscar going to kill the adored one?

Even if it was only a dream, still Angel must enter it—and save her spirit-form. He dare not even wait for his soul's orderly return. With a shout, Angel ripped open the cloying cocoon of sleep. Then he leaped up and charged into the water, using his powerful arms to shove it out of his path, churning his strong legs over the pond's slick-paved, shelving bottom.

He glimpsed her sleek black head out where her feet would no longer touch bottom, and Oscar right behind her. He watched them slide, one after the other, from sunlit surface into cliff shadow. He could imagine her kicking frantically, trying to stay afloat and move herself forward without the use of her arms. Didn't she see she was heading into the dead end of the far canyon wall? And bobbing along on the surface not far behind her was the oily-silver head of Oscar Azarias, clawing the surface one-handed, while the other certainly grasped the unseen machete.

She must flee into La Cueva! Angel thought. As he bulled forward through the water, he called out to the ancient Kamarakota chief: *Open your cave to her, let her find its entrance, and she will be saved. I will slay her enemy.*

Jacqueline had planned only to flee into the small pond. She had not considered that the water might be over her head; or that, if it was, she might have difficulty, without the use of her arms, keeping her head above the surface. But both those unfortunate circumstances proved true. And though she considered herself a strong swimmer, it took all her panicky reserves, and a constant scissoring of her coveralled legs, just to keep from drowning.

Great! she thought. *Who needs Oscar? I've just engineered my own death.*

352

Pursuit into Darkness

Except for a rocky shelf on the far side, the pond was hemmed in by vine-draped cliffs, so there was nowhere to swim to. Instead, Jacqueline thrashed around, trying to kick back into the shallows—just as Oscar's grizzled face came out of the water a yard away. He spat water, grimaced with effort, then lifted the dripping machete blade into the air and brought it down, cleaving the surface inches from her shoulder.

Jacqueline gasped, swallowed water, and sank. Why was he still coming after her? She flail-kicked away at an underwater angle, then kicked hard again, arrowing upward—but failing to reach the surface. She managed one last frantic kick—and burst into blessed air.

She also saw something she'd missed before. The back end of the pond curved around to her left, following an indentation in the cliff wall. The river flowed gently out of what looked like a dark, vertical fissure. She didn't think she could make it that far. But she could hear Oscar splashing close behind her. She had to try! Her head slid under, and she kicked out—but the result was pathetic. Again she tried, and again, and knew she was sinking, losing her horizontal attitude.

An instant later her feet touched bottom, and her head came up—and out of the water! She gulped oxygen.

Then, as Oscar surfaced right behind her, Jacqueline whirled toward what she prayed was an opening in the monolith.

Sam whacked the pond surface in a flat dive, while D.W. high-stepped in beside him, clawing water as soon as he was deep enough. Both men were spent from an all-out sprint—and obviously dead last in a desperate race. After Jake had tripped Oscar and sent him sprawling, they were hardly surprised to see him go after her, waving his fucking machete. But her second pursuer, the giant Kamarakota, had risen up out of nowhere, a pure nightmare figure. Then an eternity had passed, it seemed, before they reached the water and fought their way out toward the cliff-shadowed depths.

Sam led the way, D.W. dog-paddling after, but moments later both were treading water side by side in terrible confusion. Jake and her pursuers had vanished, apparently into sheer walls. It took them a further anguished moment, scanning around the

shimmering circumference, before they spotted, in steeply furrowed rock shadows, what looked like a deep crevice. They
swam closer.

It was barely a meter wide, a tapered opening to a winding
passage through jaggedly opposing, fantastically sculpted escarpments. As they entered the sunless gap, the bottom shelved
up, allowing them to wade in shoulder deep and single file. Surg-
ing ahead, Sam glimpsed a shadowy movement down the cavernous zigzag. Behind him, D.W. was shouting. Sam leaped
forward and stepped into a pit, submerging completely. He recovered, windmilling forward till he found solid footing again.
But the distant figure was gone now. There was only the quiet
channel snaking between moss-encrusted, steep-buttressed towers, vaulting hundreds of meters over their heads toward an aloof,
sky blue thread.

They plowed this gauntlet in tandem, their lungs aching, sliding and plunging repeatedly on moss-slimed rocks, but floundering on. They dared neither think nor feel now, only go forward
against hope—and perhaps toward their own deaths, as well as
Jacqueline's.

Sam, still in the lead, was first to glimpse the bright stripe of
water at tunnel's end, but both men had heard the crescendoing
roar—not polite applause this time, like the first Kavak cascade,
but a full ovation. Just ahead now, the canyon walls widened
out into a ragged proscenium, framing another sun-lacquered,
sherry-tinted pool. Then, still groping for handholds against
treacherous riverbed footing, they emerged into the full sunshine
and reverberant thunder of an enclosed waterfall grotto—what
their Indian guide had called the "most beautiful place."

But they gave hardly a glance at the encircling precipice, or
the radiant explosions of water from high overhead. Instead their
eyes raked anxiously along the wet-varnished rocks and recessed
shadows of the rough-quarried basin, and into the fuming caldron
at the base of the falls, simultaneously seeking and fearing
discovery.

Suddenly, almost lost in the crashing foam, there was Jacqueline's seal-black hair, her face unseen. And closing in on her
from either side were two men, one with a blade that gleamed
in the sunlight.

* * *

354

Pursuit into Darkness

Alternately swimming and wading, Jake had burst through the gap several yards ahead of her pursuer. And her flash impression of La Cueva, as she went floundering out into its funneled sunshine, was that it was a trap—a deadly one. The feeling was sharpened moments later as she glanced over her shoulder. Oscar Azarias had staggered out of the dark tunnelway, stood sagging against a projecting rock, jaw hanging, glancing vacantly around—scanning for her.

In vain Jacqueline searched for a hiding place. It was too late anyway. He'd seen her now.

So she retreated, following the right-hand grotto wall. She kept to the pebbled shallows, avoiding the treacherously polished slabs, especially green-carpeted ones. And as she hurried on, she was pelted constantly from above by cascading droplets, plummeting from the grotto's circling rim like long, glistening strands of diamonds.

She could no longer hear Oscar over the barrage of falling water. But she knew he was back there, so she hurried on, unable to stop the nightmare. Still, it couldn't go on much longer. She was ready to drop and, in fact, fell frequently now. One pantleg was ripped open, exposing a bloody knee. The next instant the ball of her foot slithered on moss and she lost her balance again. Unable to catch herself with her pinioned arms, Jacqueline twisted violently, hoping by falling backward at least to protect her face. She landed hard against the grotto-side, bruising her forearms, wrists, and left hip, then slid down and banged her tailbone on a submerged ledge.

Get up! demanded a merciless inner voice. *Damn you, get up!*

Somehow she obeyed and discovered as she did so that the abrading rock had severed her wrist ropes. Her arms were finally free! In a burst of euphoric energy, Jacqueline plunged straight out toward the churning, sunlit center of the grotto. Only she wasn't wriggling along like an armless tadpole now, but really *swimming*—thrusting her long legs, overhand-stroking both arms, digging and pulling against the turbulent current.

Dear God, maybe she could simply outswim the old bastard! Stay out here like a seal till he gave up! That would give her father and Sam a chance to ambush him as he came out of the passageway—or better, for Sam to blow Oscar's fucking head off with that rifle she'd seen.

355

But the nearer she got to the spilling thunder, the harder it was to make headway. She was only a dozen strong strokes from the edge of the maelstrom now. Yet suddenly, not only wasn't she gaining, she was being shoved steadily back by the outward surge.

One rearward glance crushed her brief euphoria. The annular current was sweeping her directly toward Oscar! Jacqueline gasped, gulping water. Then she kicked and clawed, trying to sidestroke out of the millrace. But her arms and legs were lifeless and leaden. She had expended too much precious energy battling in toward the waterfall.

Oscar, just beyond the full tidal force, now lunged forward on a perfectly timed intercept course. In seconds he was within reach of her. Jacqueline saw the machete blade lift clear of the water, gilt-edged and lustrous in the high sunlight. Her scream was lost in the cascading roar.

Then, as the blade reached the top of its arc, a huge form reared out of the water behind Oscar and wrapped him in muscular arms. Jacqueline, who had closed her eyes on her life, opened them again to see Angel and the old man wrestling in the foam at her feet.

The big Kamarakota had saved her! But danger remained. Suddenly the Indian came up for air and found himself momentarily blinded by clinging strands of his own thick hair. As he swiped at his eyes, Oscar, too, surfaced, having somehow held on to the machete. He seized the instant to deliver a murderous, two-handed slice across Angel's midsection.

Jacqueline, still backing away, gasped at the gaping red wound, and the hideous, intestinal spillage. Angel, too, his vision cleared now, could only look down in bewilderment at the yawning incision and the bright red cataract of his blood splashing down into the tannin-stained pool.

There was nothing Jacqueline could do now. Oscar closed in for another deadly stroke, mercifully blocking her view of the gore. She shut her eyes anyway, then opened them in time to see the Indian stagger, yet stay somehow on his feet. Then, impossibly, he lurched forward, reaching to grapple his executioner. Oscar swung again. Still Angel did not go down, but came on.

It must have occurred to Oscar then that the Kamarakota

might be killed, yet not stopped. For the old man began now to back away in terror from this butchered giant. And Angel followed him, kicking through the bloodied water, arms extended. Oscar whirled, dropping his useless blade at his feet.

Despite their best efforts, Sam and D.W. had arrived in the thundering grotto in time only to witness the denouement. They, too, saw Angel rise up and—miraculously and inexplicably to them—rescue Jacqueline from the madman's blow. The two tardy rescuers rushed forward, horror giving way to uncomprehending shock at the ensuing struggle between murderous accomplices. As Jacqueline shrank back from the thrashing figures, Sam and D.W. veered toward her. But like her, they were riveted by the appalling battle, with its swift, grisly reversal.

They saw Oscar, on the verge of extinction, stagger up and deliver uncontested slashes to the Indian's stomach, one after another. Then, stupefied, they watched as the gutted Kamarakota refused to acknowledge his death and continued in tottering pursuit. And finally, dripping his entrails, they saw him pin a terrified Oscar against a slab of the grotto wall. The finale played out in grotesque pantomime, to the incessant barrage of water. Angel fastened a death grip around his victim's neck, then collapsed fully on top of him, taking both under.

Neither man surfaced from that embrace. But, to the astonishment of both Sam and D.W., Jacqueline—apparently still unaware of their presence—waded back toward the suddenly motionless, entangled corpses. D.W.'s frantic shouts to her were blown away by the blasting water. They could only hurry forward, falling and scrambling up again, while she stooped in the shallows, reaching down to take the Indian's head tenderly in her hands.

They saw her turn his bloodless face upward and stare down a long moment. Finally, then, she heard their close-echoing shouts and looked up. Even then, as anguished relief flooded over her, she took a moment to gently put down the head of the Kamarakota warrior.

Now that Jacqueline was safe, Sam let D.W. surge past him. While watching their fierce embrace, he began to feel slightly dizzy, as though the cylindrical cavern, with its top fringe of jungle foliage, was wheeling slowly around him. He put out a hand, touched unmoving rock, held it there.

When he glanced back, father and daughter still crushed one another jealously. The sight lifted a heavy burden from Sam's heart. It had been a hell of a few days. Then Jake gave a characteristic whip-toss of her dripping mane, uncovering her face over D.W.'s shoulder. She was looking directly at Sam now. And suddenly his heart felt even lighter.

Several times, to renew the miracle of her deliverance, D.W. held his daughter off at arm's length, then embraced her anew. At some point he began to cry shamelessly. But perhaps she couldn't tell because chains of droplets were spilling steadily from above, diademed in the sunlight when he squinted up. It was the most utterly ecstatic moment of his life.

Finally, nearly overcome with his joy and relief, he let her go. Blinking back tears, he watched her slosh through the rippling, crystalline current toward Sam, who stood in a shadowy niche —looking, D.W. thought, completely worn-out and haggard. What happened next, however, came as a complete shock. Jacqueline waded straight into Sam's opening arms—actually throwing her arms around him. Then, as Sam's large, bony hands spread across her back, she kissed him full on the lips!

At that moment, for D.W., the full volume of the waterfall cut off to eerie silence. Had he gotten his beautiful daughter back only to lose her—and to the last man on earth he would have suspected?

Was this, at last, Samuel's revenge?

Chucho had watched the proceedings from high on the canyon wall. He had seen the two bodies being brought out of La Cueva in rubber rafts, fitted into slings, then winched up into the low-hovering military helicopter. The first had been Oscar's, the second one Angel's, and Chucho had followed every bit of its fitful ascent into the belly of the orange-and-white machine, whose rotors whipped the pond surface into a swirling fury.

Then the others followed, swaying up in harnesses. The *millonario*, then his daughter, the *norteamericana* princess, then the white-haired man, and finally a uniformed crewman. A moment later the cabin door banged shut—on the living and the dead—and the helicopter dipped its nose and went thrashing away down the canyon toward the savanna. Chucho had watched it take almost the exact same line earlier, when it came to pick up the two curare sleepers. He followed it now till it was only a tiny glint of gold in the late-afternoon sun. Then it vanished, and the valley was quiet again.

It was all a mistake. Chucho's mistake. Angel had not wished to go with Oscar that night in the *cantina*. But Chucho, knowing it was in his power to do so, had convinced him.

Where else can we go? he had said when the old man went to fetch fresh bottles. *We have no home. We cannot go back to Canaima Camp. And we are too proud to go back to Kamarata. Perhaps you miss the penitentiary of Tocuyito. But I, for one, do not wish to sling my hammock again in that filthy cell in Sabaneta.*

Chucho could always talk, and Angel could only listen and nod. Yet Angel had been right.

Now he resumed the long climb to the top of the great plateau of Auyán Tepui, Devil Mountain. He didn't know where he would come down, or where he would go when he did, or what he would do if the *federales* found him. But those were not important matters now. Chucho used to think that he had lost his tribe long ago, but truly, that was not so. He had only lost his tribe today, when he lost his brother.

So now he simply climbed and grieved with every upward step. Except for his black body paint and leather breechcloth, he was naked. And he carried only the little woven basket with foodstuffs and blowpipe over one shoulder, and dangling heavily from his left hand the blue Avensa bag.

Epilogue

▂▂▂

Unlike many of his business friends, Sam had never boasted of hating New York, nor of having any particular love affair with it. Manhattan was simply a necessary venue for high-powered meetings, a movie-set backdrop for hit-and-run forays out of the corporate apartment at the Mayfair Regent. He tended to fly away from these cometary visits with a hangover-hazed memory of conference rooms, astronomically priced eateries, and some brassy Broadway show whose tunes he could never recall.

But this trip was different. For one thing, he was on his own, not staying at the Proteus apartment—though his current contract gave him that privilege. He was at the Plaza, on a whim, and woke to find the city dusted by an early-December snow and Christmas beckoning from every window display.

He prowled Fifth Avenue in ranch hat, shearling coat, jeans, and boots. Pedestrians hustled past him on their random urgencies, bundled against winds that knifed down the geometric canyons, while tires plowed back and forth through the street slush, making surf sounds. After a fast-food lunch and a brief hotel nap, still not having found exactly the right item, Sam grabbed a cab south to a recommended boutique, which turned out to be within easy walking distance of her TriBeCa loft.

On the appointed hour of six, he walked up to the correctly

numbered warehouse and pressed the button Dymo-tagged J. N. LEE. Then he stood in the recessed chill, holding his red-ribboned box and feeling not very different from how he had on antediluvian high-school dates. He had, after all, been anticipating this precise moment all day long. Longer. And he had a respectable stomach squadron of honest-to-God butterflies. Suddenly her remembered voice buzzed through the intercom:

"Sam?"

"Jake?"

"Don't move! I'll be right down."

He heard a long, muffled grind within, followed by double sliding bangs. A moment later the steel door beside him swung back and she was standing there. She wore a paint-stained NYU sweatshirt, faded jeans, and had her hair pulled back into some kind of sumo topknot. Sam experienced a moment of total vulnerability—and didn't give a damn.

Jacqueline came to him, reaching around the gift box and his bulky coat. But before their lips could meet, she stepped back, unzipped his long coat, and stepped inside it, snaking her arms all the way around his back. In the time away from her, Sam had often inventoried their previous kisses—that first one on horseback, the champagne exchange on the *Kallisto*, the climactic embrace in Kavak Canyon. This one was sweeter, less demanding, more of a "Remember?" kiss. Yet quite enough to make a man giddy, if he was inclined that way. Then she pulled back a few inches.

"Sam, I'm sorry to be such a complete mess, especially with you looking like the cover of *GQ*. But I've been squirreled away for days now, just wearing my grubs and trying to make sense of all the tape I shot."

"Hush up. I know gorgeous when I see it."

"Excuse me, what was that deranged compliment? Never mind. Come on up."

She led him into a tiny lobby and onto the elevator, which was elaborately graffitied and smelled of ammoniated cleaner. As the tight metal box went lurching up, Jacqueline leaned against him. "Sam, it's wonderful to see you. I can't believe you're really here."

"I told you I'd track you down."

362

"Yes, you did. Is that for me?" She pointed innocently to the cubical, red-ribboned package.

"Ah, you noticed. It's not a bowling ball, by the way. Tell me, what does the *N* stand for?"

"Nicoletta. After mother's mother. She came from Genoa—a Genovese. I'm part Eye-talian. Does it show?"

"I don't know, but whatever you are, they should patent the recipe."

She kicked at him playfully. "You're going to be awfully good for my ego, Sam. But a girl can only take so much flattery."

"Just how much would that be?"

"I'll let you know if you get anywhere close, okay?"

"So, how have you been, Jake?"

"I still get the sweats sometimes, or something will bring it all back—even the sound of the shower—and I'll get pretty shaky. Working helps. Helps a lot, actually."

The platform shuddered to a stop on four, opened onto a Sheetrock-paneled hall with two steel doors. "Winston Tolliver has most of the floor. Have you heard of him?" Sam shook his head. "He does these mammoth blue-green acrylics that look like underwaterscapes. I have the space left over."

Jacqueline's "leftovers" were pretty extensive, Sam thought, considering the probable price per square foot in lower Manhattan. High ceilings with whitewashed beams, gallery partitions, oak floors with area rugs that looked Central Asian. He could provide Teresa this kind of loft-studio, Sam thought, if only she'd let him.

Sam paused near the entry to admire several watercolors of English floral gardens. He could read the signature: Julienne Langlois.

"Mother wins prizes every year from some watercolor society or another," Jacqueline explained. "She's really good, isn't she?"

Sam agreed, then pointed at a long, swirling turquoise abstract on the panel opposite. "Say, that looks like a Tolliver."

"Sam, you are *so* hip. One of his miniatures, actually, and strictly a neighborly gesture on my part. But it's starting to make me just a bit queasy."

They passed through an open kitchen with a lot of stainless steel, acquiring a Dos Equis each, then continued through her tall-windowed living and dining space, on into an office and workroom. A long editing table held rewinds, racked film cans, moviola, and film bin, with strips of film hanging from hooks. At a right angle was portable video equipment—videotape recorder, monitor, and mixing console.

"You do the whole editing process here?"

She shook her head. "Nope. I do the actual editing on computerized equipment at school. Mostly I've just been looking at everything I shot, storyboarding, and making a zillion notes. A few minutes ago I was on the light table over there checking some slides Bernardo took at your ranch. They show me and Dr. Laya being interrogated by Captain Siso. Good stuff—if I were making an indictment of Proteus and the Venezuelan government. Trouble is, with Daddy suddenly changing his mind on Cerro Calvario and Caracas going along, I've lost my political edge."

"Maybe you could leave out the happy ending. Just fade out on the bulldozers coming through the gates."

"Honest, Sam, I am having a hard time figuring out what viewpoint to take. Objectivity seems so boring! Anyway, I can't really decide yet. Not when I've got more stuff to shoot."

"What's left?"

"Didn't you get your invitation? From Dr. Laya?"

"I've been on the road a few days."

"One of his colleagues reconstructed that prehistoric bone flute and arranged some Indian melodies for it. They're going to have a recital in a couple weeks—at Simón Bolívar University —with proceeds going to support the archaeological work on Cerro Calvario. I was thinking of documenting the recital, maybe even ending with it, and using the music as a film score. Anyway, I need footage of Dr. Laya back at the dig."

Jacqueline paused, looked wistfully out the window. "The trouble is, I don't have a date for the recital."

"Well, golly, missy, I'd be right pleased to take you."

She batted her eyelashes. "You would?"

"Yes'm, I would. It just so happens that I would dearly love to hear that flute." Sam dropped the aw-shucks drawl. "I'd especially love to hear it with you."

364

"You know, I kind of hinted to Daddy I might be going down there with you."

"I bet D.W. loved hearing that."

"He grunted his blessing. He doesn't detonate anymore, you know. I really ought to arrange to be kidnapped from time to time, just to keep him tractable."

"Well, it's just a good thing your father already killed our friendship. It sure as hell wouldn't have survived this."

"Oh, Daddy'll come around, you'll see. Anyway, I really do want to go back to Venezuela, Sam. I think it'll be—what's the word I'm looking for? *Purgative?*"

"*Cathartic* maybe?"

"Maybe both." She grinned and hooked his arm, steering him back to the dining room table, where he'd left the gift. "I can't wait any longer."

"I was rather hoping you wouldn't."

She tore open the box, but lifted the contents out slowly. It was a palm-straw ranch hat, with rolled brim, black grosgrain hatband and chin strap, and a frontal spray of striped feathers.

"Sam, it's perfect! You know, of all the stuff I lost in the *Kallisto* fire, the hat you bought me was what I missed most."

"Unfortunately, I couldn't find one with feathers from the Venezuelan sparrow hawk. So you'll have to settle for pheasant quills and hackles. Unless you want to trade it in for one with a snakeskin band and a rattlesnake skull."

"Ugh, no, thanks. Where did you find it?"

"Well, I started with Saks and Bergdorf's and about every place else Midtown this morning. But I wound up at a little western store just north of here, on Prince Street."

"Mmm, I've window-shopped it." Jacqueline unwound her topknot, shook out her glossy mane, and slid the ranch hat back onto her head, tying the chin strap in a bow. Then her dark eyes altered suddenly, swimming out of focus, while her eyelids grew heavy, lashes pressing together. The effect on Sam was mesmeric—an irresistible commandment to be kissed. He obeyed, placing his big palms on the satin-smooth cheeks of his urban cowgirl and his captive heart into the meeting of their lips.

It was almost a solemn kiss, full of withheld delight. Then, by gradual mutual consent, they eased out of it, leaving the promise wonderfully unfulfilled. While Sam stabilized his vital signs, Jacqueline heaved her shoulders and adjusted the tilt of her hat.

"You know, if it wasn't so darn cold out, we could go riding tomorrow in Central Park and I could wear my hat."

"Do they still do that?"

"Of course, they do, silly. Strictly English saddles, though. Or maybe we could go ice-skating at Rockefeller Center. Are you going to be—I mean, do you have business tomorrow?"

"I sure do."

"What is it?"

"You."

"Hmm. I like the sound of that. Where are you staying?"

"The Plaza."

"Well, maybe you are and maybe you aren't. We may not let you go back there."

She said it flippantly, but its effect on Sam was considerable —enough that he swallowed his reply.

"Now," she went on, "I know I promised on the phone to awe you with my homemade mostaccioli. But I've been cooped up all day, and I kind of told some friends we'd meet them at Arturo's for a pizza around six-thirty. Would you mind?"

"Hell, no! Arturo's? Gotta be my kind of place."

"It'll give me a chance to show you off. All I ask is, don't be too judgmental."

"Me, judgmental?" Sam grinned. "Well, now and then perhaps. Let me put it this way, Jake, if this makes any sense. I didn't come up here to make judgments, or with any set of expectations. Except one—to see you. Period."

"We'll just have to play it by ear then, won't we, darling Sam?"

"I guess that sounds about right."

He helped her into a fuzzy magenta wool coat. And they went thumping back down the elevator and out onto the wintry street, arm in arm in their matching ranch hats.

Félix Rosales had violated one of the cardinal rules of the mariner: *Never vomit to windward.* Now thoroughly befouled, he was helped by two of the Mendes brothers around the prow of the forty-foot, steel-hulled fishing boat. And because the little *Vasco da Gama* was lifting and spanking heavily in the quartering Caribbean swell, the two brothers steadied him at the lee rail until he was done retching.

But when Félix slowly straightened up, gray faced and groaning, they were still close by, both looking solicitous. Matteo and Felando—like their sister Marta—were compact and wiry, swarthy and hard-faced. Unlike her, they could be truly frightening.

"Feeling better now, brother-in-law?"

Félix nodded, then coughed, tasting bile. His entire musculature ached—and not from the vomiting. The brothers had just taken him below and given him the beating of his life.

"Then let me explain something," Matteo continued in a tone of utmost calm. "Marta does not know about our little talk this morning. She does not know you screwed that prostitute on the beach yesterday. But for some reason, our foolish Marta loves you.

"So here is the way it will be. No more *putas* for you, Félix. None, you understand me? No more stealing things, as you did from the archaeologist. Now, here is what you will do. You will treat our little sister like the queen of Portugal. You will kiss her tiny feet, if she wishes. If we ever hear that you have made her unhappy, Felando and I will not be so gentle with you as today.

"And if you run away, believe me, brother-in-law, we will hunt you down and bring you back. Or perhaps we will just cut off your *huevos* and bring *them* back to Marta, with our condolences. But, believe me, you will not be as hard to find as you may think, muscleboy." Matteo gave Félix's biceps a brutal squeeze with his fisherman's grip. "The Mendes brothers have many, many friends—in Venezuela, Colombia, Brazil, and all through the Caribbean.

"Now, please clean yourself and prepare to use all those pretty muscles to do a real man's work. We have many *langosta* pots to raise this morning."

With this, Matteo and Felando strolled aft toward the helm, where another brother, Juan, was holding a course parallel to the cliffs of Cachimena west of Cumaná.

Félix, who had let go of the rail during Matteo's discourse, now regripped it and bent forward. He had been watching the gray, wave-peaked horizon slowly rising and falling and was about to be horribly sick again. This time he didn't know if it was caused by the beating or the threats or the endlessly heaving sea. And for the moment, he didn't care.